PENGUIN BOOKS

THE WHITE PEACOCK

David Herbert Lawrence was born at Eastwood, Nottinghamshire, in 1885, fourth of the five children of a miner and his middle-class wife. He attended Nottingham High School and Nottingham University College. His first novel, *The White Peacock,* was published in 1911, just a few weeks after the death of his mother to whom he had been abnormally close. At this time he finally ended his relationship with Jessie Chambers (the Miriam of *Sons and Lovers*) and became engaged to Louie Burrows. His career as a schoolteacher was ended in 1911 by the illness which was ultimately diagnosed as tuberculosis.

In 1912 Lawrence eloped to Germany with Frieda Weekley, the German wife of his former modern languages tutor. They were married on their return to England in 1914. Lawrence was now living, precariously, by his writing. His greatest novels, *The Rainbow* and *Women in Love*, were completed in 1915 and 1916. The former was suppressed, and he could not find a publisher for the latter.

After the war Lawrence began his 'savage pilgrimage' in search of a more fulfilling mode of life than industrial Western civilization could offer. This took him to Sicily, Ceylon, Australia and, finally, New Mexico. The Lawrences returned to Europe in 1926. Lawrence's last novel, *Lady Chatterley's Lover*, was banned in 1928, and his paintings confiscated in 1929. He died in Vence in 1930 at the age of 44.

Lawrence spent most of his short life living. Nevertheless he produced an amazing quantity of work – novels, stories, poems, plays, essays, travel books, translations, letters . . . After his death Frieda wrote: 'What he had seen and felt and known he gave in his writing to his fellow men, the splendour of living, the hope of more and more life . . . a heroic and immeasurable gift.'

D. H. LAWRENCE

The White Peacock

WITH AN INTRODUCTION BY
RICHARD ALDINGTON

PENGUIN BOOKS
IN ASSOCIATION WITH
WILLIAM HEINEMANN LTD

Penguin Books Ltd, Harmondsworth, Middlesex, England
Penguin Books, 625 Madison Avenue, New York, New York 10022, U.S.A.
Penguin Books Australia Ltd, Ringwood, Victoria, Australia
Penguin Books Canada Ltd, 2801 John Street, Markham, Ontario, Canada L3R 1B4
Penguin Books (N.Z.) Ltd, 182–190 Wairau Road, Auckland 10, New Zealand

—

First published by William Heinemann Ltd, 1911
Published in Penguin Books 1950
Reprinted 1954, 1961, 1966, 1968, 1971, 1973, 1974,
1976, 1977, 1979, 1981

—

—

Made and printed in Great Britain by
Hazell Watson & Viney Ltd,
Aylesbury, Bucks
Set in Linotype Granjon

CONTENTS

Introduction by Richard Aldington   7

PART ONE

1 The People of Nethermere   13
2 Dangling the Apple   23
3 A Vendor of Visions   34
4 The Father   46
5 The Scent of Blood   59
6 The Education of George   73
7 Lettie Pulls Down the Small Gold Grapes   92
8 The Riot of Christmas   111
9 Lettie Comes of Age   124

PART TWO

1 Strange Blossoms and Strange New Budding   149
2 A Shadow in Spring   172
3 The Irony of Inspired Moments   186
4 Kiss When She's Ripe For Tears   206
5 An Arrow from the Impatient God   221
6 The Courting   229
7 The Fascination of the Forbidden Apple   237
8 A Poem of Friendship   252
9 Pastorals and Peonies   260

PART THREE

1 A New Start in Life   273
2 Puffs of Wind in the Sail   287
3 The First Pages of Several Romances   296
4 Domestic Life at the Ram   307
5 The Dominant Motif of Suffering   318
6 Pisgah   330
7 The Scarp Slope   346
8 A Prospect Among the Marshes of Lethe   356

INTRODUCTION

BY RICHARD ALDINGTON

There is a special interest in the first books of world-famous men. Few readers can be so unimaginative as not to think of the time when such a book was being written by its then unknown author, the hopes and fears put into it, the disappointments at its first reception, its seeming lapse into oblivion, and slow revival as its author gradually fought his way through prejudices and indifference to fame.

D. H. Lawrence was very young and very obscure when he began the first draft of this book in the autumn of 1906. He was then at Nottingham University doing a two years' course preparatory to taking his certificate as an elementary-school teacher. He had reached the University by his own efforts, for his father, a coal-miner with five children, could not possibly have afforded to send him there unaided. Lawrence was an exceptionally clever lad at school. When he sat for the open King's Scholarship he amazed his friends by coming out in the First Division of the First Class, and but for the breakdown in his health he could have had a distinguished academic career.

The White Peacock, written and re-written three or four times during the leisure hours and holidays of three years, grew from his experiences of life in the Midlands. From the very beginning of his literary career he showed his originality and disregard for literary fashion, which at that time was all for 'form' in the novel with corresponding emptiness of matter. To Lawrence the writing of a novel was neither the artistic presentation of an invented story nor a mere piece of exciting entertainment – it was an 'adventure of the mind'; above all it aimed at putting the reader in touch with life. He abhorred any kind of 'formula' writing, and his faults are due mostly to this passionate determination to be true to life as he experienced it. For the same reason his books usually end quietly, almost indeterminately – for the slick or dramatic ending must nearly always be false to life.

Bearing this in mind the reader will be prepared for the fact that *The White Peacock* is no artfully constructed work of fiction. It is a portion of Lawrence's youth imaginatively reconstructed, though it is not an autobiographical novel, like *Sons and Lovers*. These are the places and people among whom he grew up. If the book has a serious fault, it is due to the author's shyness and self-mistrust which led him to take working-class characters and give them a middle-class veneer. The best scenes are those when the young man forgets his pseudo-gentility, and gives us the life at Strelley Mill farm and the Ram Inn without any attempt to make it middle-class.

What was he trying to do in this oddly mis-named *White Peacock* which has nothing to do with peacocks, white or blue-green, and everything to do with English people of the soil and of the mine of half a century ago? Lawrence was a very complex and self-contradictory person, in whom two hostile selves seemed always struggling for mastery. He was remote from the artificial 'consistency' of the political or literary careerist. Thus he loved his Derbyshire ('my own Midlands', as he used to say proudly), yet feared and fled from what to him was 'the blight' of industrialism creeping over it, the repudiation of the old 'organic' life of England for the new 'mechanical' life, 'stinking of money pleasures'. In *The White Peacock* – which dated back to the days when the motor-car was a novelty – this passionate division in him was only beginning. It is the book of his youth, and full of tender love and wistful regret for youth's passing.

A few facts will show how closely Lawrence is identified with this book. Cyril (horrid name!) is a stilted portrait of himself in his naïf youth, with much of his fun and all his malice and bossiness left out. 'Lettice' was one of the unused names of his favourite sister. 'Beardsall' was his mother's maiden name. Everyone knows the saga of Lawrence's intense love for his mother and dislike for his father; so it is significant that the father in this novel dies of drink, and 'Cyril' settles down happily with his mother and sister. The dream of Lawrence's youth was to possess a cottage and thirty shillings a week, and live for ever with his mother, painting, and helping with the housework.

Drink! The most striking character in the book is George, the handsome uneducated young farmer who loves Lettie, is played with by her and jilted for Leslie, and who in pique marries the soft sensual Meg of The Ram, and in disillusion ends up a drunkard. Lawrence's mother was a ruthless teetotaler and brought up her children to despise their father for spending his time and *their* money at the public house. Lawrence grew up believing that the family had been kept in poverty because his father drank. Hence the picture of George's downfall. How much this first novel was written for his mother's approval may be judged from this Band of Hope portrait of George and from the fact that Heinemann had a single advance copy of the book printed and bound for Lawrence to give his mother just before she died.

Passage after poetic passage in this book already show what an eloquent and beautiful natural writer Lawrence was. Look at the paragraphs beginning 'The long-drawn booming of the wind' (Chap. 2); 'Some wooden horses careered' (Chap. 4); 'After a while we went out also' (Chap. 5); 'I was born in September' (Chap. 6); 'At last however winter began' (Part 2, Chap. 1); 'So we went along' (same chapter); almost the whole of 'A Shadow in Spring'; and many others. Do not miss the description of the pigs at the opening of 'The Courting' – a piece of ironical humour and perfect observation. At the first attempt he equalled – some think he surpassed – his master, Thomas Hardy, in just such passages where Hardy was thought to be inimitable. Lawrence knew the life of the mining-town, for he was brought up in one; he knew the countryside, the names of every flower and plant and bird; and the life of a farm, for he worked on one. Only with his people is he here uncertain. Yet in them there is essential truth, even to the flippant vulgarity of his students.

Lawrence was to soar far beyond the achievement of *The White Peacock*, but when it was first published in January 1911, a great new personality came into English literature almost unperceived, for few critics noticed the book and only one or two at most understood it.

PART ONE

CHAPTER I

The People of Nethermere

I STOOD watching the shadowy fish slide through the gloom of the mill-pond. They were grey, descendants of the silvery things that had darted away from the monks, in the young days when the valley was lusty. The whole place was gathered in the musing of old age. The thick-piled trees on the far shore were too dark and sober to dally with the sun; the weeds stood crowded and motionless. Not even a little wind flickered the willows of the islets. The water lay softly, intensely still. Only the thin stream falling through the millrace murmured to itself of the tumult of life which had once quickened the valley.

I was almost startled into the water from my perch on the alder roots by a voice saying:

'Well, what is there to look at?' My friend was a young farmer, stoutly built, brown eyed, with a naturally fair skin burned dark and freckled in patches. He laughed, seeing me start, and looked down at me with lazy curiosity.

'I was thinking the place seemed old, brooding over its past.'

He looked at me with a lazy indulgent smile, and lay down on his back on the bank, saying:

'It's all right for a doss – here.'

'Your life is nothing else but a doss. I shall laugh when somebody jerks you awake,' I replied.

He smiled comfortably and put his hands over his eyes because of the light.

'Why shall you laugh?' he drawled.

'Because you'll be amusing,' said I.

We were silent for a long time, when he rolled over and began to poke with his finger in the bank.

'I thought,' he said in his leisurely fashion, 'there was some cause for all this buzzing.'

I looked, and saw that he had poked out an old, papery nest

of those pretty field bees which seem to have dipped their tails into bright amber dust. Some agitated insects ran round the cluster of eggs, most of which were empty now, the crowns gone; a few young bees staggered about in uncertain flight before they could gather power to wing away in a strong course. He watched the little ones that ran in and out among the shadows of the grass hither and thither in consternation.

'Come here – come here!' he said, imprisoning one poor little bee under a grass stalk, while with another stalk he loosened the folded blue wings.

'Don't tease the little beggar,' I said.

'It doesn't hurt him – I wanted to see if it was because he couldn't spread his wings that he couldn't fly. There he goes – no, he doesn't. Let's try another.'

'Leave them alone,' said I. 'Let them run in the sun. They're only just out of the shells. Don't torment them into flight.'

He persisted, however, and broke the wing of the next.

'Oh, dear – pity!' said he, and crushed the little thing between his fingers. Then he examined the eggs, and pulled out some silk from round the dead larva, and investigated it all in a desultory manner, asking of me all I knew about the insects. When he had finished he flung the clustered eggs into the water and rose, pulling out his watch from the depth of his breeches' pocket.

'I thought it was about dinner-time,' said he, smiling at me. 'I always know when it's about twelve. Are you coming in?'

'I'm coming down at any rate,' said I as we passed along the pond bank, and over the plank-bridge that crossed the brow of the falling sluice. The bankside where the grey orchard twisted its trees was a steep declivity, long and sharp, dropping down to the garden.

The stones of the large house were burdened with ivy and honey-suckle, and the great lilac-bush that had once guarded the porch now almost blocked the doorway. We passed out of the front garden into the farm-yard, and walked along the brick path to the back door.

'Shut the gate, will you?' he said to me over his shoulder, as he passed on first.

We went through the large scullery into the kitchen. The servant-girl was just hurriedly snatching the table-cloth out of the table drawer, and his mother, a quaint little woman with big, brown eyes, was hovering round the wide fire-place with a fork.

'Dinner not ready?' said he with a shade of resentment.

'No, George,' replied his mother apologetically, 'it isn't. The fire wouldn't burn a bit. You shall have it in a few minutes, though.'

He dropped on the sofa and began to read a novel. I wanted to go, but his mother insisted on my staying.

'Don't go,' she pleaded. 'Emily will be so glad if you stay, – and father will, I'm sure. Sit down, now.'

I sat down on a rush chair by the long window that looked out into the yard. As he was reading, and as it took all his mother's powers to watch the potatoes boil and the meat roast, I was left to my thoughts. George, indifferent to all claims, continued to read. It was very annoying to watch him pulling his brown moustache, and reading indolently while the dog rubbed against his leggings and against the knee of his old riding breeches. He would not even be at the trouble to play with Trip's ears, he was so content with his novel and his moustache. Round and round twirled his thick fingers, and the muscles of his bare arm moved slightly under the red-brown skin. The little square window above him filtered a green light from the foliage of the great horse-chestnut outside and the glimmer fell on his dark hair, and trembled across the plates which Annie was reaching down from the rack, and across the face of the tall clock. The kitchen was very big; the table looked lonely, and the chairs mourned darkly for the lost companionship of the sofa; the chimney was a black cavern away at the back, and the inglenook seats shut in another little compartment ruddy with fire-light, where the mother hovered. It was rather a desolate kitchen, such a bare expanse of uneven grey flagstones, such far-away dark corners and sober furniture. The only gay things were the chintz coverings of the sofa and the arm-chair cushions, bright red in the bare sombre room; some might smile at the old clock, adorned as it was with remarkable and vivid poultry; in me it only provoked wonder and contemplation.

In a little while we heard the scraping of heavy boots outside, and the father entered. He was a big burly farmer, with his half-bald head sprinkled with crisp little curls.

'Hullo, Cyril,' he said cheerfully. 'You've not forsaken us then,' and turning to his son:

'Have you many more rows in the coppice close?'

'Finished!' replied George, continuing to read.

'That's all right – you've got on with 'em. The rabbits has bitten them turnips down, mother.'

'I expect so,' replied his wife, whose soul was in the sauce-pans. At last she deemed the potatoes cooked and went out with the steaming pan.

The dinner was set on the table and the father began to carve. George looked over his book to survey the fare, then read until his plate was handed him. The maid sat at her little table near the window, and we began the meal. There came the treading of four feet along the brick path, and a little girl entered, followed by her grown-up sister. The child's long brown hair was tossed wildly back beneath her sailor hat. She flung aside this article of her attire and sat down to dinner, talking endlessly to her mother. The elder sister, a girl of about twenty-one, gave me a smile and a bright look from her brown eyes, and went to wash her hands. Then she came and sat down, and looked discon-solately at the underdone beef on her plate.

'I do hate this raw meat,' she said.

'Good for you,' replied her brother, who was eating indus-triously. 'Give you some muscle to wallop the nippers.'

She pushed it aside, and began to eat the vegetables. Her brother re-charged his plate and continued to eat.

'Well, our George, I do think you might pass a body that gravy,' said Mollie, the younger sister, in injured tones.

'Certainly,' he replied. 'Won't you have the joint as well?'

'No!' retorted the young lady of twelve, 'I don't expect you've done with it yet.'

'Clever!' he exclaimed across a mouthful.

'Do you think so?' said the elder sister Emily, sarcastically.

'Yes,' he replied complacently, 'you've made her as sharp as yourself, I see, since you've had her in Standard Six. I'll try a potato, mother, if you can find one that's done.'

'Well, George, they seem mixed. I'm sure that was done that I tried. There – they are mixed – look at this one, it's soft enough. I'm sure they were boiling long enough.'

'Don't explain and apologize to him,' said Emily irritably.

'Perhaps the kids were too much for her this morning,' he said calmly, to nobody in particular.

'No,' chimed in Mollie, 'she knocked a lad across his nose and made it bleed.'

'Little wretch,' said Emily, swallowing with difficulty. 'I'm glad I did! Some of my lads belong to – to –'

'To the devil,' suggested George, but she would not accept it from him.

Her father sat laughing; her mother with distress in her eyes, looked at her daughter, who hung her head and made patterns on the table-cloth with her finger.

'Are they worse than the last lot?' asked the mother, softly, fearfully.

'No – nothing extra,' was the curt answer.

'She merely felt like bashing 'em,' said George, calling, as he looked at the sugar bowl and at his pudding:

'Fetch some more sugar, Annie.'

The maid rose from her little table in the corner, and the mother also hurried to the cupboard. Emily trifled with her dinner and said bitterly to him:

'I only wish you had a taste of teaching, it would cure your self-satisfaction.'

'Pf!' he replied contemptuously, 'I could easily bleed the noses of a handful of kids.'

'You wouldn't sit there bleating like a fatted calf,' she continued.

This speech so tickled Mollie that she went off into a burst of laughter, much to the terror of her mother, who stood up in trembling apprehension lest she should choke.

'You made a joke, Emily,' he said, looking at his younger sister's contortions.

Emily was too impatient to speak to him further, and left the table. Soon the two men went back to the fallow to the turnips, and I walked along the path with the girls as they were going to school.

'He irritates me in everything he does and says,' burst out Emily with much heat.

'He's a pig sometimes,' said I.

'He is!' she insisted. 'He irritates me past bearing, with his grand know-all way, and his heavy smartness – I can't bear it. And the way mother humbles herself to him –!'

'It makes you wild,' said I.

'Wild!' she echoed, her voice, vibrating with nervous passion. We walked on in silence, till she asked:

'Have you brought me those verses of yours?'

'No – I'm so sorry – I've forgotten them again. As a matter of fact, I've sent them away.'

'But you promised me.'

'You know what my promises are. I'm as irresponsible as a puff of wind.'

She frowned with impatience and her disappointment was greater than necessary. When I left her at the corner of the lane I felt a sting of her deep reproach in my mind. I always felt the reproach when she had gone.

I ran over the little bright brook that came from the weedy, bottom pond. The stepping-stones were white in the sun, and the water slid sleepily among them. One or two butterflies, indistinguishable against the blue sky, trifled from flower to flower and led me up the hill, across the field where the hot sunshine stood as in a bowl, and I was entering the caverns of the wood, where the oaks bowed over and saved us a grateful shade. Within, everything was so still and cool that my steps hung heavily along the path. The bracken held out arms to me, and the bosom of the wood was full of sweetness, but I journeyed on, spurred by the attacks of an army of flies which kept up a guerrilla warfare round my head till I had passed the black rhododendron bushes in the garden, where they left me, scenting, no doubt, Rebecca's pots of vinegar and sugar.

The low red house, with its roof discoloured and sunken, dozed in sunlight, and slept profoundly in the shade thrown by the massive maples encroaching from the wood.

There was no one in the dining-room, but I could hear the whirr of a sewing-machine coming from the little study, a sound as of some great, vindictive insect buzzing about, now louder, now softer, now settling. Then came a jingling of four or five keys at the bottom of the keyboard of the drawing-room piano, continuing till the whole range had been covered in little leaps, as if some very fat frog had jumped from end to end.

'That must be mother dusting the drawing-room,' I thought. The unaccustomed sound of the old piano startled me. The vocal chords behind the green silk bosom – you only discovered it was not a bronze silk bosom by poking a fold aside – had become as thin and tuneless as a dried old woman's. Age had yellowed the teeth of my mother's little piano, and shrunken its spindle legs. Poor old thing, it could but screech in answer to Lettie's fingers flying across it in scorn, so the prim, brown lips were always closed save to admit the duster.

Now, however, the little old-maidish piano began to sing a tinkling Victorian melody, and I fancied it must be some demure little woman with curls like bunches of hops on either side of her face, who was touching it. The coy little tune teased me with old sensations, but my memory would give me no assistance. As I stood trying to fix my vague feelings Rebecca came in to remove the cloth from the table.

'Who is playing, Beck?' I asked.

'Your mother, Cyril.'

'But she never plays. I thought she couldn't.'

'Ah,' replied Rebecca, 'you forget when you was a little thing sitting playing against her frock with the prayer-book, and she singing to you. You can't remember her when her curls was long like a piece of brown silk. You can't remember her when she used to play and sing, before Lettie came and your father was –'

Rebecca turned and left the room. I went and peeped in the drawing-room. Mother sat before the little brown piano, with her plump, rather stiff fingers moving across the keys, a faint smile on her lips. At that moment Lettie came flying past me, and flung her arms round mother's neck, kissing her and saying:

'Oh, my Dear, fancy my Dear playing the piano! Oh, Little Woman, we never knew you could!'

'Nor can I,' replied mother laughing, disengaging herself. 'I only wondered if I could just strum out this old tune; I learned it when I was quite a girl, on this piano. It was a cracked one then; the only one I had.'

'But play again, dearie, do play again. It was like the clinking of lustre glasses, and you look so quaint at the piano. Do play, my dear!' pleaded Lettie.

'Nay,' said my mother, 'the touch of the old keys on my fingers is making me sentimental – you wouldn't like to see me reduced to the tears of old age?'

'Old age!' scolded Lettie, kissing her again. 'You are young enough to play little romances. Tell us about it, mother.'

'About what, child?'

'When you used to play.'

'Before my fingers were stiff with fifty odd years? Where have you been, Cyril, that you weren't in to dinner?'

'Only down to Strelley Mill,' said I.

'Of course,' said mother coldly.

'Why "of course"?' I asked.

'And you came away as soon as Em went to school?' said Lettie.

'I did,' said I.

They were cross with me, these two women. After I had swallowed my little resentment I said:

'They would have me stay to dinner.'

My mother vouchsafed no reply.

'And has the great George found a girl yet?' asked Lettie.

'No,' I replied, 'he never will at this rate. Nobody will ever be good enough for him.'

'I'm sure I don't know what you can find in any of them to take you there so much,' said my mother.

'Don't be so mean, Mater,' I answered, nettled. 'You know I like them.'

'I know you like *her*,' said my mother sarcastically. 'As for him – he's an unlicked cub. What can you expect when his mother has spoiled him as she has. But I wonder you are so interested in licking him.' My mother sniffed contemptuously.

'He is rather good looking,' said Lettie with a smile.

'*You* could make a man of him, I am sure,' I said, bowing satirically to her.

'*I* am not interested,' she replied, also satirical.

Then she tossed her head, and all the fine hairs that were free from bonds made a mist of yellow light in the sun.

'What frock shall I wear, Mater?' she asked.

'Nay, don't ask me,' replied her mother.

'I think I'll wear the heliotrope – though this sun will fade it,' she said pensively. She was tall, nearly six feet in height, but slenderly formed. Her hair was yellow, tending towards a dun brown. She had beautiful eyes and brows, but not a nice nose. Her hands were very beautiful.

'Where are you going?' I asked.

She did not answer me.

'To Tempest's!' I said. She did not reply.

'Well I don't know what you can see in *him*,' I continued.

'Indeed!' said she. 'He's as good as most folk –' then we both began to laugh.

'Not,' she continued blushing, 'that I think anything about him. I'm merely going for a game of tennis. Are you coming?'

'What shall you say if I agree?' I asked.

'Oh!' she tossed her head. 'We shall all be very pleased, I'm sure.'

'Ooray!' said I with fine irony.

She laughed at me, blushed, and ran upstairs.

Half an hour afterwards she popped her head in the study to bid me good-bye, wishing to see if I appreciated her. She was so charming in her fresh linen frock and flowered hat, that I could not but be proud of her. She expected me to follow her to the window, for from between the great purple rhododendrons she waved me a lace mitten, then glinted on like a flower moving brightly through the green hazels. Her path lay through the wood in the opposite direction from Strelley Mill, down the red drive across the tree-scattered space to the highroad. This road ran along the end of our lakelet, Nethermere, for about a quarter of a mile. Nethermere is the lowest in a chain of three ponds. The other two are the upper and lower mill ponds at Strelley: this is the largest and most charming piece of water, a mile long and about a quarter of a mile in width. Our wood runs down to the water's edge. On the opposite side, on a hill beyond the farthest corner of the lake, stands Highclose. It looks across the water at us in Woodside with one eye as it were, while our cottage casts a side-long glance back again at the proud house, and peeps coyly through the trees.

I could see Lettie like a distant sail stealing along the water's edge, her parasol flowing above. She turned through the wicket under the pine clump, climbed the steep field, and was enfolded again in the trees beside Highclose.

Leslie was sprawled on a camp chair, under a copper beech on the lawn, his cigar glowing. He watched the ash grow strange and grey in the warm daylight, and he felt sorry for poor Nell Wycherley, whom he had driven that morning to the station, for would she not be frightfully cut up as the train whirled her further and further away? These girls are so daft with a fellow! But she was a nice little thing – he'd get Marie to write to her.

At this point he caught sight of a parasol fluttering along the drive, and immediately he fell into a deep sleep, with just a tiny slit in his slumber to allow him to see Lettie approach. She, finding her watchman ungallantly asleep, and his cigar, instead of his lamp, untrimmed, broke off a twig of syringa whose ivory buds had not yet burst with luscious scent. I know not how the end of his nose tickled in anticipation before she tickled him in reality, but he kept bravely still until the petals swept him. Then, starting from his sleep, he exclaimed:

'Lettie! I was dreaming of kisses!'

'On the bridge of your nose?' laughed she – 'But whose were the kisses?'

'Who produced the sensation?' he smiled.

'Since I only tapped your nose you should dream of –'

'Go on!' said he, expectantly.

'Of Doctor Slop,' she replied, smiling to herself as she closed her parasol.

'I do not know the gentleman,' he said, afraid that she was laughing at him.

'No – your nose is quite classic,' she answered, giving him one of those brief intimate glances with which women flatter men so cleverly. He radiated with pleasure.

CHAPTER II

Dangling the Apple

THE long-drawn booming of the wind in the wood and the sobbing and moaning in the maples and oaks near the house, had made Lettie restless. She did not want to go anywhere, she did not want to do anything, so she insisted on my just going out with her as far as the edge of the water. We crossed the tangle of fern and bracken, bramble and wild raspberry canes that spread in the open space before the house, and we went down the grassy slope to the edge of Nethermere. The wind whipped up noisy little wavelets, and the cluck and clatter of these among the pebbles, the swish of the rushes and the freshening of the breeze against our faces, roused us.

The tall meadow-sweet was in bud along the tiny beach and we walked knee-deep among it, watching the foamy race of the ripples and the whitening of the willows on the far shore. At the place where Nethermere narrows to the upper end, and receives the brook from Strelley, the wood sweeps down and stands with its feet washed round with waters. We broke our way along the shore, crushing the sharp-scented wild mint, whose odour checks the breath, and examining here and there among the marshy places ragged nests of water-fowl, now deserted. Some slim young lapwings started at our approach, and sped lightly from us, their necks outstretched in straining fear of that which could not hurt them. One, two, fled cheeping into cover of the wood; almost instantly they coursed back again to where we stood, to dart off from us at an angle, in an ecstasy of bewilderment and terror.

'What has frightened the crazy little things?' asked Lettie.

'I don't know. They've cheek enough sometimes; then they go whining, skelping off from a fancy as if they had a snake under their wings.'

Lettie however paid small attention to my eloquence. She

pushed aside an elder bush, which graciously showered down upon her myriad crumbs from its flowers like slices of bread, and bathed her in a medicinal scent. I followed her, taking my dose, and was startled to hear her sudden, 'Oh, Cyril!'

On the bank before us lay a black cat, both hind-paws torn and bloody in a trap. It had no doubt been bounding forward after its prey when it was caught. It was gaunt and wild; no wonder it frightened the poor lapwings into cheeping hysteria. It glared at us fiercely, growling low.

'How cruel – oh, how cruel!' cried Lettie, shuddering.

I wrapped my cap and Lettie's scarf over my hands and bent to open the trap. The cat struck with her teeth, tearing the cloth convulsively. When it was free, it sprang away with one bound, and fell panting, watching us.

I wrapped the creature in my jacket, and picked her up, murmuring.

'Poor Mrs Nickie Ben – we always prophesied it of you.'

'What will you do with it?' asked Lettie.

'It is one of the Strelley Mill cats,' said I, 'and so I'll take her home.'

The poor animal moved and murmured as I carried her, but we brought her home. They stared, on seeing me enter the kitchen coatless, carrying a strange bundle, while Lettie followed me.

'I have brought poor Mrs Nickie Ben,' said I, unfolding my burden.

'Oh, what a shame!' cried Emily, putting out her hand to touch the cat, but drawing quickly back, like the peewits.

'This is how they all go,' said the mother.

'I wish keepers had to sit two or three days with their bare ankles in a trap,' said Mollie in vindictive tones.

We laid the poor brute on the rug and gave it warm milk. It drank very little, being too feeble. Mollie, full of anger, fetched Mr Nickie Ben, another fine black cat, to survey his crippled mate. Mr Nickie Ben looked, shrugged his sleek shoulders, and walked away with high steps. There was a general feminine outcry on masculine callousness.

George came in for hot water. He exclaimed in surprise on seeing us, and his eyes became animated.

'Look at Mrs Nickie Ben,' cried Mollie. He dropped on his knees on the rug and lifted the wounded paws.

'Broken,' said he.

'How awful!' said Emily, shuddering violently, and leaving the room.

'Both?' I said.

'Only one – look!'

'You are hurting her!' cried Lettie.

'It's no good,' said he.

Mollie and the mother hurried out of the kitchen into the parlour.

'What are you going to do?' asked Lettie.

'Put her out of her misery,' he replied, taking up the poor cat. We followed him into the barn.

'The quickest way,' said he, 'is to swing her round and knock her head against the wall.'

'You make me sick,' exclaimed Lettie.

'I'll drown her then,' he said with a smile. We watched him morbidly, as he took a length of twine and fastened a noose round the animal's neck, and near it an iron goose; he kept a long piece of cord attached to the goose.

'You're not coming, are you?' said he. Lettie looked at him; she had grown rather white.

'It'll make you sick,' he said. She did not answer, but followed him across the yard to the garden. On the bank of the lower mill-pond he turned again to us and said:

'Now for it! – you are chief mourners.' As neither of us replied, he smiled, and dropped the poor writhing cat into the water, saying, 'Good-bye, Mrs Nickie Ben.'

We waited on the bank some time. He eyed us curiously.

'Cyril,' said Lettie quietly, 'isn't it cruel? – isn't it awful?' I had nothing to say.

'Do you mean me?' asked George.

'Not you in particular – everything! If we move the blood rises in our heel-prints.'

He looked at her seriously, with dark eyes.

'I had to drown her out of mercy,' said he, fastening the cord he held to an ash-pole. Then he went to get a spade, and with it, he dug a grave in the old black earth.

'If,' said he, 'the poor old cat had made a prettier corpse, you'd have thrown violets on her.'

He had struck the spade into the ground, and hauled up the cat and the iron goose.

'Well,' he said, surveying the hideous object, 'haven't her good looks gone! She was a fine cat.'

'Bury it and have done,' Lettie replied.

He did so asking: 'Shall you have bad dreams after it?'

'Dreams do not trouble me,' she answered, turning away.

We went indoors, into the parlour, where Emily sat by a window, biting her finger. The room was long and not very high; there was a great rough beam across the ceiling. On the mantel-piece, and in the fireplace, and over the piano were wild flowers and fresh leaves plentifully scattered; the room was cool with the scent of the woods.

'Has he done it?' asked Emily – 'and did you watch him? If I had seen it I should have hated the sight of him, and I'd rather have touched a maggot than him.'

'I shouldn't be particularly pleased if he touched me,' said Lettie.

'There is something so loathsome about callousness and brutality,' said Emily. 'He fills me with disgust.'

'Does he?' said Lettie, smiling coldly. She went across to the old piano. 'He's only healthy. He's never been sick, not anyway, yet.' She sat down and played at random, letting the numbed notes fall like dead leaves from the haughty, ancient piano.

Emily and I talked on by the window, about books and people. She was intensely serious, and generally succeeded in reducing me to the same state.

After a while, when the milking and feeding were finished, George came in. Lettie was still playing the piano. He asked her why she didn't play something with a tune in it, and this caused her to turn round in her chair to give him a withering answer. His appearance, however, scattered her words like startled birds. He had come straight from washing in the scullery, to the parlour, and he stood behind Lettie's chair unconcernedly wiping the moisture from his arms. His sleeves were rolled up to the shoulder, and his shirt was opened wide at the breast. Lettie was somewhat taken aback by the sight of him standing with legs apart, dressed in dirty leggings and boots, and breeches torn at the knee, naked at the breast and arms.

'Why don't you play something with a tune in it?' he repeated, rubbing the towel over his shoulders beneath the shirt.

'A tune?' she echoed, watching the swelling of his arms as he moved them, and the rise and fall of his breasts, wonderfully solid and white. Then having curiously examined the sudden meeting of the sun-hot skin with the white flesh in his throat, her eyes met his, and she turned again to the piano, while the colour grew in her ears, mercifully sheltered by a profusion of bright curls.

'What shall I play?' she asked, fingering the keys somewhat confusedly.

He dragged out a book of songs from a little heap of music, and set it before her.

'Which do you want to sing?' she asked thrilling a little as she felt his arms so near her.

'Anything you like.'

'A love song?' she said.

'If you like – yes, a love song –' he laughed with clumsy insinuation that made the girl writhe.

She did not answer, but began to play Sullivan's 'Tit Willow'. He had a passable bass voice, not of any great depth, and he sang with gusto. Then she gave him, 'Drink to me only with thine eyes'. At the end she turned and asked him if he liked the words. He replied that he thought them rather daft. But he looked at her with glowing brown eyes, as if in hesitating challenge.

'That's because you have no wine in your eyes to pledge with,' she replied, answering his challenge with a blue blaze of her eyes. Then her eyelashes drooped on to her cheek. He laughed with a faint ring of consciousness, and asked her how could she know.

'Because,' she said slowly, looking up at him with pretended scorn, 'because there's no change in your eyes when I look at you. I always think people who are worth much talk with their eyes. That's why you are forced to respect many quite uneducated people. Their eyes are so eloquent, and full of knowledge.'

She had continued to look at him as she spoke – watching his faint appreciation of her upturned face, and her hair, where the light was always tangled, watching his brief self-examination to see if he could feel any truth in her words, watching till he broke into a little laugh which was rather more awkward and less satisfied than usual. Then she turned away, smiling also.

'There's nothing in this book nice to sing,' she said, turning over the leaves discontentedly. I found her a volume, and she sang 'Should he upbraid'. She had a fine soprano voice, and the song delighted him. He moved nearer to her, and when at the finish she looked round with a flashing, mischievous air, she found him pledging her with wonderful eyes.

'You like that,' said she with the air of superior knowledge, as if, dear me, all one had to do was to turn over to the right page of the vast volume of one's soul to suit these people.

'I do,' he answered emphatically, thus acknowledging her triumph.

'I'd rather "dance and sing" round "wrinkled care" than carefully shut the door on him, while I slept in the chimney seat – wouldn't you?' she asked.

He laughed, and began to consider what she meant before he replied.

'As you do,' she added.

'What?' he asked.

'Keep half your senses asleep – half alive.'

'Do I?' he asked.

'Of course you do; – "bos – bovis; an ox." You are like a stalled ox, food and comfort, no more. Don't you love comfort?' she smiled.

'Don't you?' he replied, smiling shamefaced.

'Of course. Come and turn over for me while I play this piece. Well, I'll nod when you must turn – bring a chair.'

She began to play a romance of Schubert's. He leaned nearer to her to take hold of the leaf of music; she felt her loose hair touch his face, and turned to him a quick, laughing glance, while she played. At the end of the page she nodded, but he was oblivious; 'Yes!' she said, suddenly impatient, and he tried to get the leaf over; she quickly pushed his hand aside, turned the page herself and continued playing.

'Sorry!' said he, blushing actually.

'Don't bother,' she said, continuing to play without observing him. When she had finished:

'There!' she said, 'now tell me how you felt while I was playing.'

'Oh – a fool!' – he replied, covered with confusion.

'I'm glad to hear it,' she said – 'but I didn't mean that. I meant how did the music make you feel?'

'I don't know – whether – it made me feel anything,' he replied deliberately, pondering over his answer, as usual.

'I tell you,' she declared, 'you're either asleep or stupid. Did you really see nothing in the music? But what did you think about?'

He laughed – and thought awhile – and laughed again.

'Why!' he admitted, laughing, and trying to tell the exact truth, 'I thought how pretty your hands are – and what they are like to touch – and I thought it was a new experience to feel somebody's hair tickling my cheek.' When he had finished his deliberate account she gave his hand a little knock, and left him saying:

'You are worse and worse.'

She came across the room to the couch where I was sitting talking to Emily, and put her arm around my neck.

'Isn't it time to go home, Pat?' she asked.

'Half-past eight – quite early,' said I.

'But I believe – I think I ought to be home now,' she said.

'Don't go,' said he.

'Why?' I asked.

'Stay to supper,' urged Emily.

'But I believe –' she hesitated.

'She has another fish to fry,' I said.

'I am not sure –' she hesitated again. Then she flashed into sudden wrath, exclaiming, 'Don't be so mean and nasty, Cyril!'

'Were you going somewhere?' asked George humbly.

'Why – no!' she said, blushing.

'Then stay to supper – will you?' he begged. She laughed, and yielded. We went into the kitchen. Mr Saxton was sitting reading. Trip, the big bull terrier, lay at his feet pretending to sleep; Mr Nickie Ben reposed calmly on the sofa; Mrs Saxton and Mollie were just going to bed. We bade them good-night, and sat down. Annie, the servant, had gone home, so Emily prepared the supper.

'Nobody can touch that piano like you,' said Mr Saxton to Lettie, beaming upon her with admiration and deference. He was proud of the stately, mumbling old thing, and used to say that it was full of music for those that liked to ask for it. Lettie laughed, and said that so few folks ever tried it, that her honour was not great.

'What do you think of our George's singing?' asked the father proudly, but with a deprecating laugh at the end.

'I tell him, when he's in love he'll sing quite well,' she said.

'When he's in love!' echoed the father, laughing aloud, very pleased.

'Yes,' she said, 'when he finds out something he wants and can't have.'

George thought about it, and he laughed also.

Emily, who was laying the table, said, 'There is hardly any water in the pippin, George.'

'Oh, dash!' he exclaimed, 'I've taken my boots off.'

'It's not a very big job to put them on again,' said his sister.

'Why couldn't Annie fetch it – what's she here for?' he said angrily.

Emily looked at us, tossed her head, and turned her back on him.

'I'll go, I'll go, after supper,' said the father in a comforting tone.

'After supper!' laughed Emily.

George got up and shuffled out. He had to go into the spinney near the house to a well, and being warm disliked turning out.

We had just sat down to supper when Trip rushed barking to the door. 'Be quiet,' ordered the father, thinking of those in bed, and he followed the dog.

It was Leslie. He wanted Lettie to go home with him at once. This she refused to do, so he came indoors, and was persuaded to sit down at table. He swallowed a morsel of bread and cheese, and a cup of coffee, talking to Lettie of a garden party which was going to be arranged at Highclose for the following week.

'What is it for then?' interrupted Mr Saxton.

'For?' echoed Leslie.

'Is it for the missionaries, or the unemployed, or something?' explained Mr Saxton.

'It's a garden-party, not a bazaar,' said Leslie.

'Oh – a private affair. I thought it would be some church matter of your mother's. She's very big at the church, isn't she?'

'She is interested in the church – yes!' said Leslie, then proceeding to explain to Lettie that he was arranging a tennis tournament in which she was to take part. At this point he became aware that he was monopolizing the conversation, and turned to George, just as the latter was taking a piece of cheese from his knife with his teeth, asking:

'Do you play tennis, Mr Saxton? – I know Miss Saxton does not.'

'No,' said George, working the piece of cheese into his cheek. 'I never learned any ladies' accomplishments.'

Leslie turned to Emily, who had nervously been pushing two plates over a stain in the cloth, and who was very startled when she found herself addressed.

'My mother would be so glad if you would come to the party, Miss Saxton.'

'I cannot. I shall be at school. Thanks very much.'

'Ah – it's very good of you,' said the father, beaming. But George smiled contemptuously.

When supper was over Leslie looked at Lettie to inform her that he was ready to go. She, however, refused to see his look, but talked brightly to Mr Saxton, who was delighted. George, flattered, joined in the talk with gusto. Then Leslie's angry silence began to tell on us all. After a dull lapse, George lifted his head and said to his father:

'Oh, I shouldn't be surprised if that little red heifer calved tonight.'

Lettie's eyes flashed with a sparkle of amusement at this thrust.

'No,' assented the father, 'I thought so myself.'

After a moment's silence, George continued deliberately, 'I felt her gristles –'

'George!' said Emily sharply.

'We will go,' said Leslie.

George looked up sideways at Lettie and his black eyes were full of sardonic mischief.

'Lend me a shawl, will you, Emily?' said Lettie. 'I brought nothing, and I think the wind is cold.'

Emily, however, regretted that she had no shawl, and so Lettie must needs wear a black coat over her summer dress. It fitted so absurdly that we all laughed, but Leslie was very angry that she should appear ludicrous before them. He showed her all the polite attentions possible, fastened the neck of her coat with his pearl scarf-pin, refusing the pin Emily discovered, after some search. Then we sallied forth.

When we were outside, he offered Lettie his arm with an air of injured dignity. She refused it and began to remonstrate.

'I consider you ought to have been home as you promised.'

'Pardon me,' she replied, 'but I did not promise.'

'But you knew I was coming,' said he.

'Well – you found me,' she retorted.

'Yes,' he assented. 'I did find you; flirting with a common fellow,' he sneered.

'Well,' she returned. 'He did – it is true – call a heifer, a heifer.'

'And I should think you liked it,' he said.

'I didn't mind,' she said, with galling negligence.

'I thought your taste was more refined,' he replied, sarcastically. 'But I suppose you thought it romantic.'

'Very! Ruddy, dark, and really thrilling eyes,' said she.

'I hate to hear a girl talk rot,' said Leslie. He himself had crisp hair of the 'ginger' class.

'But I mean it,' she insisted, aggravating his anger.

Leslie was angry. 'I'm glad he amuses you!'

'Of course, I'm not hard to please,' she said pointedly. He was stung to the quick.

'Then there's some comfort in knowing I don't please you,' he said coldly.

'Oh! but you do! You amuse me also,' she said.

After that he would not speak, preferring, I suppose, *not* to amuse her.

Lettie took my arm, and with her disengaged hand held her

skirts above the wet grass. When he had left us at the end of
the riding in the wood, Lettie said:

'What an infant he is!'

'A bit of an ass,' I admitted.

'But really!' she said, 'he's more agreeable on the whole
than – than my Taurus.'

'Your bull!' I repeated laughing.

CHAPTER III

A Vendor of Visions

THE Sunday following Lettie's visit to the mill, Leslie came up in the morning, admirably dressed, and perfected by a grand air. I showed him into the dark drawing-room, and left him. Ordinarily he would have wandered to the stairs, and sat there calling to Lettie; today he was silent. I carried the news of his arrival to my sister, who was pinning on her brooch.

'And how is the dear boy?' she asked.

'I have not inquired,' said I.

She laughed, and loitered about till it was time to set off for church before she came downstairs. Then she also assumed the grand air and bowed to him with a beautiful bow. He was somewhat taken aback and had nothing to say. She rustled across the room to the window, where the white geraniums grew magnificently. 'I must adorn myself,' she said.

It was Leslie's custom to bring her flowers. As he had not done so this day, she was piqued. He hated the scent and chalky whiteness of the geraniums. So she smiled at him as she pinned them into the bosom of her dress, saying:

'They are very fine, are they not?'

He muttered that they were. Mother came downstairs, greeted him warmly, and asked him if he would take her to church.

'If you will allow me,' said he.

'You are modest today,' laughed mother.

'Today!' he repeated.

'I hate modesty in a young man,' said mother – 'Come, we shall be late.' Lettie wore the geraniums all day – till evening. She brought Alice Gall home to tea, and bade me bring up 'Mon Taureau', when his farm work was over.

The day had been hot and close. The sun was reddening in the west as we leaped across the lesser brook. The evening scents began to awake, and wander unseen through the still air. An occasional yellow sunbeam would slant through the thick roof of leaves and cling passionately to the orange clusters of mountain-ash berries. The trees were silent, drawing together to sleep. Only a few pink orchids stood palely by the path, looking wistfully out at the ranks of red-purple bugle, whose last flowers, glowing from the top of the bronze column, yearned darkly for the sun.

We sauntered on in silence, not breaking the first hush of the woodlands. As we drew near home we heard a murmur from among the trees, from the lover's seat, where a great tree had fallen and remained mossed and covered with fragile growth. There a crooked bough made a beautiful seat for two.

'Fancy being in love and making a row in such a twilight,' said I as we continued our way. But when we came opposite the fallen tree, we saw no lovers there, but a man sleeping, and muttering through his sleep. The cap had fallen from his grizzled hair, and his head leaned back against a profusion of the little wild geraniums that decorated the dead bough so delicately. The man's clothing was good, but slovenly and neglected. His face was pale and worn with sickness and dissipation. As he slept, his grey beard wagged, and his loose unlovely mouth moved in indistinct speech. He was acting over again some part of his life, and his features twitched during the unnatural sleep. He would give a little groan, gruesome to hear, and then talk to some woman. His features twitched as if with pain, and he moaned slightly.

The lips opened in a grimace showing the yellow teeth behind the beard. Then he began again talking in his throat, thickly, so that we could only tell part of what he said. It was very unpleasant. I wondered how we should end it. Suddenly through the gloom of the twilight-haunted woods came the scream of a rabbit caught by a weasel. The man awoke with a sharp 'Ah!' – he looked round in consternation, then sinking down again wearily, said, 'I was dreaming again.'

'You don't seem to have nice dreams,' said George.

The man winced, then looking at us said, almost sneering: 'And who are you?'

We did not answer, but waited for him to move. He sat still, looking at us.

'So!' he said at last, wearily, 'I do dream. I do, I do.' He sighed heavily. Then he added, sarcastically: 'Were you interested?'

'No,' said I. 'But you are out of your way surely. Which road did you want?'

'You want me to clear out,' he said.

'Well,' I said laughing in deprecation. 'I don't mind your dreaming. But this is not the way to anywhere.'

'Where may you be going then?' he asked.

'I? Home,' I replied with dignity.

'You are a Beardsall?' he queried, eyeing me with bloodshot eyes.

'I am!' I replied with more dignity, wondering who the fellow could be.

He sat a few moments looking at me. It was getting dark in the wood. Then he took up an ebony stick with a gold head, and rose. The stick seemed to catch at my imagination. I watched it curiously as we walked with the old man along the path to the gate. We went with him into the open road. When we reached the clear sky where the light from the west fell full on our faces, he turned again and looked at us closely. His mouth opened sharply, as if he would speak, but he stopped himself, and only said 'Good-bye – Good-bye.'

'Shall you be all right?' I asked, seeing him totter.

'Yes – all right – good-bye, lad.'

He walked away feebly into the darkness. We saw the lights of a vehicle on the high-road: after a while we heard the bang of a door, and a cab rattled away.

'Well – whoever's he?' said George laughing.

'Do you know,' said I, 'it's made me feel a bit rotten.'

'Ay?' he laughed, turning up the end of the exclamation with indulgent surprise.

We went back home, deciding to say nothing to the women. They were sitting in the window seat watching for us, mother and Alice and Lettie.

'You *have* been a long time!' said Lettie. 'We've watched the sun go down – it set splendidly – look – the rim of the hill is smouldering yet. What have you been doing?'

'Waiting till your Taurus finished work.'

'Now be quiet,' she said hastily, and – turning to him, 'You have come to sing hymns?'

'Anything you like,' he replied.

'How nice of you, George!' exclaimed Alice, ironically. She was a short, plump girl, pale, with daring, rebellious eyes. Her mother was a Wyld, a family famous either for shocking lawlessness, or for extreme uprightness. Alice, with an admirable father, and a mother who loved her husband passionately, was wild and lawless on the surface, but at heart very upright and amenable. My mother and she were fast friends, and Lettie had a good deal of sympathy with her. But Lettie generally deplored Alice's outrageous behaviour, though she relished it –if 'superior' friends were not present. Most men enjoyed Alice in company, but they fought shy of being alone with her.

'Would you say the same to me?' she asked.

'It depends what you'd answer,' he said, laughingly.

'Oh, you're so bloomin' cautious. I'd rather have a tack in my shoe than a cautious man, wouldn't you, Lettie?'

'Well – it depends how far I had to walk,' was Lettie's reply – 'but if I hadn't to limp too far –'

Alice turned away from Lettie, whom she often found rather irritating.

'You do look glum, Sybil,' she said to me, 'did somebody want to kiss you?'

I laughed – on the wrong side, understanding her malicious feminine reference – and answered:

'If they had, I should have looked happy.'

'Dear boy, smile now then,' – and she tipped me under the chin. I drew away.

'Oh, Gum – we are solemn! What's the matter with you? Georgie – say something – else I's'll begin to feel nervous.'

'What shall I say?' he asked, shifting his feet and resting his elbows on his knees. 'Oh, Lor!' she cried in great impatience. He did not help her, but sat clasping his hands, smiling on one side of his face. He was nervous. He looked at the pictures, the ornaments, and everything in the room; Lettie got up to settle some flowers on the mantelpiece, and he scrutinized her closely. She was dressed in some blue foulard stuff, with lace at the throat, and lace cuffs to the elbow. She was tall and supple; her hair had a curling fluffiness very charming. He was no taller than she, and looked shorter, being strongly built. He too had a grace of his own, but not as he sat stiffly on a horse-hair chair. She was elegant in her movements.

After a little while mother called us in to supper.

'Come,' said Lettie to him, 'take me in to supper.'

He rose, feeling very awkward.

'Give me your arm,' said she to tease him. He did so, and flushed under his tan, afraid of her round arm half hidden by lace, which lay among his sleeve.

When we were seated she flourished her spoon and asked him what he would have. He hesitated, looked at the strange dishes and said he would have some cheese. They insisted on his eating new, complicated meats.

'I'm sure you like tantafflins, don't you Georgie?' said Alice, in her mocking fashion. He was *not* sure. He could not analyse the flavours, he felt confused and bewildered even through his sense of taste! Alice begged him to have salad.

'No, thanks,' said he. 'I don't like it.'

'Oh, George!' she said, 'How *can* you say so when I'm *offering* it you.'

'Well – I've only had it once,' said he, 'and that was when I was working with Flint, and he gave us fat bacon and bits of lettuce soaked in vinegar – "'Ave a bit more salit," he kept saying, but I'd had enough.'

'But all our lettuce,' said Alice with a wink, 'is as sweet as a nut, no vinegar about our lettuce.' George laughed in much confusion at her pun on my sister's name.

'I believe you,' he said, with pompous gallantry.

'Think of that!' cried Alice. 'Our Georgie believes me. Oh, I am so, so pleased!'

He smiled painfully. His hand was resting on the table, the thumb tucked tight under the fingers, his knuckles white as he nervously gripped his thumb. At last supper was finished, and he picked up his serviette from the floor and began to fold it. Lettie also seemed ill at ease. She had teased him till the sense of his awkwardness had become uncomfortable. Now she felt sorry, and a trifle repentant, so she went to the piano, as she always did to dispel her moods. When she was angry she played tender fragments of Tschaikowsky, when she was miserable, Mozart. Now she played Handel in a manner that suggested the plains of heaven in the long notes, and in the little trills as if she were waltzing up the ladder of Jacob's dream like the damsels in Blake's pictures. I often told her she flattered herself scandalously through the piano; but generally she pretended not to understand me, and occasionally she surprised me by a sudden rush of tears to her eyes. For George's sake, she played Gounod's 'Ave Maria', knowing that the sentiment of the chant would appeal to him, and make him sad, forgetful of the petty evils of this life. I smiled as I watched the cheap spell working. When she had finished, her fingers lay motionless for a minute on the keys, then she spun round, and looked him straight in the eyes, giving promise of a smile. But she glanced down at her knee.

'You are tired of music,' she said.

'No,' he replied, shaking his head.

'Like it better than salad?' she asked with a flash of raillery.

He looked up at her with a sudden smile, but did not reply. He was not handsome; his features were too often in a heavy repose; but when he looked up and smiled unexpectedly, he flooded her with an access of tenderness.

'Then you'll have a little more,' said she, and she turned again to the piano. She played soft, wistful morsels, then suddenly broke off in the midst of one sentimental plaint, and left the piano, dropping into a low chair by the fire. There she sat and looked at him. He was conscious that her eyes were fixed on him, but he dared not look back at her, so he pulled his moustache.

'You are only a boy, after all,' she said to him quietly. Then he turned and asked her why.

'It is a boy that you are,' she repeated, leaning back in her chair, and smiling lazily at him.

'I never thought so,' he replied seriously.

'Really?' she said, chuckling.

'No,' said he, trying to recall his previous impressions.

She laughed heartily, saying:

'You're growing up.'

'How?' he asked.

'Growing up,' she repeated, still laughing.

'But I'm sure I was never boyish,' said he.

'I'm teaching you,' said she, 'and when you're boyish you'll be a very decent man. A mere man daren't be a boy for fear of tumbling off his manly dignity, and then he'd be a fool, poor thing.'

He laughed, and sat still to think about it, as was his way.

'Do you like pictures?' she asked suddenly, being tired of looking at him.

'Better than anything,' he replied.

'Except dinner, and a warm hearth and a lazy evening,' she said.

He looked at her suddenly, hardening at her insult, and biting his lips at the taste of this humiliation. She repented, and smiled her plaintive regret to him.

'I'll show you some,' she said, rising and going out of the room. He felt he was nearer her. She returned, carrying a pile of great books.

'Jove – you're pretty strong!' said he.

'You are charming in your compliment,' she said.

He glanced at her to see if she were mocking.

'That's the highest you could say of me, isn't it?' she insisted.

'Is it?' he asked, unwilling to compromise himself.

'For sure,' she answered – and then, laying the books on the table, 'I know how a man will compliment me by the way he looks at me' – she kneeled before the fire. 'Some look at my hair, some watch the rise and fall of my breathing, some look at my neck, and a few – not you among them – look me in the eyes for my thoughts. To you, I'm a fine specimen, strong! Pretty strong! You primitive man!'

He sat twisting his fingers; she was very contrary.

'Bring your chair up,' she said, sitting down at the table and opening a book. She talked to him of each picture, insisting on hearing his opinion. Sometimes he disagreed with her and would not be persuaded. At such times she was piqued.

'If,' said she, 'an ancient Briton in his skins came and contradicted me as you do, wouldn't you tell him not to make an ass of himself?'

'I don't know,' he said.

'Then you ought to,' she replied. 'You know nothing.'

'How is it you ask me then?' he said.

She began to laugh.

'Why – that's a pertinent question. I think you might be rather nice, you know.'

'Thank you,' he said, smiling ironically.

'Oh!' she said. 'I know, you think you're perfect, but you're not, you're very annoying.'

'Yes,' exclaimed Alice, who had entered the room again, dressed ready to depart. 'He's so blooming slow! Great whizz! Who wants fellows to carry cold dinners? Shouldn't you like to shake him, Lettie?'

'I don't feel concerned enough,' replied the other, calmly.

'Did you ever carry a boiled pudding, Georgy?' asked Alice with innocent interest, punching me slyly.

'Me! – why? – what makes you ask?' he replied, quite at a loss.

'Oh, I only wondered if your people needed any indigestion mixture – pa mixes it – 1s. 1½d. a bottle.'

'I don't see –' he began.

'Ta – ta, old boy, I'll give you time to think about it. Good-night, Lettie. Absence makes the heart grow fonder – Georgy – of someone else. Farewell. Come along, Sybil love, the moon is shining – Good night all, good night!'

I escorted her home, while they continued to look at the pictures. He was a romanticist. He liked Copley, Fielding, Cattermole and Birket Foster; he could see nothing whatsoever in Girtin or David Cox. They fell out decidedly over George Clausen.

'But,' said Lettie, 'he is a real realist, he makes common things beautiful, he sees the mystery and magnificence that envelops us even when we work menially. I *do* know and I *can* speak. If I hoed in the fields beside you –' This was a very new idea for him, almost a shock to his imagination, and she talked unheeded. The picture under discussion was a water colour – 'Hoeing' by Clausen.

'You'd be just that colour in the sunset,' she said, thus bringing him back to the subject, 'and if you looked at the ground you'd find there was a sense of warm gold fire in it, and once you'd perceived the colour, it would strengthen till you'd see nothing else. You are blind; you are only half-born; you are gross with good living and heavy sleeping. You are a piano which will only play a dozen common notes. Sunset is nothing to you – it merely happens anywhere. Oh, but you make me feel as if I'd like to make you suffer. If you'd ever been sick; if you'd ever been born into a home where there was something oppressed you, and you couldn't understand; if ever you'd believed, or even doubted, you might have been a man by now. You never grow up, like bulbs which spend all summer getting fat and fleshy, but never wakening the germ of a flower. As for me, the flower is born in me, but it wants bringing forth. Things don't flower if they're overfed. You have to suffer before you blossom in this life. When death is just touching a plant, it forces it into a passion of flowering. You wonder how I have touched death. You don't know. There's always a sense of death in this home. I believe my mother hated my father before I was born. That was death in her veins for me before I was born. It makes a difference –'

As he sat listening, his eyes grew wide and his lips were parted, like a child who feels the tale but does not understand the words. She, looking away from herself at last, saw him, began to laugh gently, and patted his hand saying:

'Oh! my dear heart, are you bewildered? How amiable of you to listen to me – there isn't any meaning in it all – there isn't really!'

'But,' said he, 'why do you say it?'

'Oh, the question!' she laughed. 'Let us go back to our muttons, we're gazing at each other like two dazed images.'

They turned on, chatting casually, till George suddenly exclaimed, 'There!'

It was Maurice Greiffenhagen's 'Idyll'.

'What of it?' she asked, gradually flushing. She remembered her own enthusiasm over the picture.

'Wouldn't it be fine?' he exclaimed, looking at her with glowing eyes, his teeth showing white in a smile that was not amusement.

'What?' she asked, dropping her head in confusion.

'That – a girl like that – half afraid – and passion!' He lit up curiously.

'She may well be half afraid, when the barbarian comes out in his glory, skins and all.'

'But don't you like it?' he asked.

She shrugged her shoulders, saying, 'Make love to the next girl you meet, and by the time the poppies redden the field, she'll hang in your arms. She'll have need to be more than half afraid, won't she?'

She played with the leaves of the book, and did not look at him.

'But,' he faltered, his eyes glowing, 'it would be – rather –'

'Don't, sweet lad, don't!' she cried laughing.

'But I shouldn't' – he insisted, 'I don't know whether I should like any girl I know to –'

'Precious Sir Galahad,' she said in a mock caressing voice, and stroking his cheek with her finger, 'You ought to have been a monk – a martyr, a Carthusian.'

He laughed, taking no notice. He was breathlessly quivering under the new sensation of heavy, unappeased fire in his breast and in the muscles of his arms. He glanced at her bosom and shivered.

'Are you studying just how to play the part?' she asked.

'No – but –' he tried to look at her, but failed. He shrank, laughing, and dropped his head.

'What?' she asked with vibrant curiosity.

Having become a few degrees calmer, he looked up at her now, his eyes wide and vivid with a declaration that made her shrink back as if flame had leaped towards her face. She bent down her head, and picked at her dress.

'Didn't you know the picture before?' she said, in a low toneless voice.

He shut his eyes and shrank with shame.

'No, I've never seen it before,' he said.

'I'm surprised,' she said. 'It is a very common one.'

'Is it?' he answered, and this make-believe conversation fell. She looked up, and found his eyes. They gazed at each other for a moment before they hid their faces again. It was a torture to each of them to look thus nakedly at the other, a dazzled, shrinking pain that they forced themselves to undergo for a moment, that they might the moment after tremble with a fierce sensation that filled their veins with fluid, fiery electricity. She sought almost in panic, for something to say.

'I believe it's in Liverpool, the picture,' she contrived to say.

He dared not kill this conversation, he was too self-conscious. He forced himself to reply, 'I didn't know there was a gallery in Liverpool.'

'Oh, yes, a very good one,' she said.

Their eyes met in the briefest flash of a glance, then both turned their faces aside. Thus averted, one from the other, they made talk. At last she rose, gathered the books together, and carried them off. At the door she turned. She must steal another keen moment: 'Are you admiring my strength?' she asked. Her pose was fine. With her head thrown back, the roundness of her throat ran finely down to the bosom which swelled above the pile of books, held by her straight arms. He looked at her. Their lips smiled curiously. She put back her throat as if she were drinking. They felt the blood beating madly in their necks. Then, suddenly breaking into a slight trembling, she turned round and left the room.

While she was out, he sat twisting his moustache. She came back along the hall talking madly to herself in French. Having been much impressed by Sarah Bernhardt's 'Dame aux Camelias' and 'Adrienne Lecouvreur', Lettie had caught something of the weird tone of this great actress, and her raillery and mockery came out in little wild waves. She laughed at him, and at herself, and at men in general, and at love in particular. Whatever he said to her, she answered in the same mad clatter of French, speaking high and harshly. The sound was strange and uncomfortable. There was a painful perplexity in his brow, such as I often perceived afterwards, a sense of something hurting, something he could not understand.

'Well, well, well, well!' she exclaimed at last. 'We must be mad sometimes, or we should be getting aged. Hein?'

'I wish I could understand,' he said plaintively.

'Poor dear?' she laughed. 'How sober he is! And will you really go? They will think we've given you no supper, you look so sad.'

'I have supped – full –' he began, his eyes dancing with a smile as he ventured upon a quotation. He was very much excited.

'Of horrors!' she cried completing it. 'Now that is worse than anything I have given you.'

'Is it?' he replied, and they smiled at each other.

'Far worse,' she answered. They waited in suspense for some moments. He looked at her.

'Good-bye,' she said, holding out her hand. Her voice was full of insurgent tenderness. He looked at her again, his eyes flickering. Then he took her hand. She pressed his fingers, holding them a little while. Then ashamed of her display of feeling, she looked down. He had a deep cut across his thumb.

'What a gash!' she exclaimed, shivering, and clinging a little tighter to his fingers before she released them. He gave a little laugh.

'Does it hurt you?' she asked very gently.

He laughed again – 'No!' he said softly, as if his thumb were not worthy of consideration.

They smiled again at each other, and, with a blind movement, he broke the spell and was gone.

CHAPTER IV

The Father

AUTUMN set in, and the red dahlias which kept the warm light alive in their bosoms so late into the evening died in the night, and the morning had nothing but brown balls of rottenness to show.

They called me as I passed the post-office door in Eberwich one evening, and they gave me a letter for my mother. The distorted, sprawling handwriting perplexed me with a dim uneasiness; I put the letter away, and forgot it. I remembered it later in the evening, when I wished to recall something to interest my mother. She looked at the handwriting, and began hastily and nervously to tear open the envelope; she held it away from her in the light of the lamp, and with eyes drawn half closed, tried to scan it. So I found her spectacles, but she did not speak her thanks, and her hand trembled. She read the short letter quickly; then she sat down, and read it again, and continued to look at it.

'What is it, mother?' I asked.

She did not answer, but continued staring at the letter. I went up to her, and put my hand on her shoulder, feeling very uncomfortable. She took no notice of me, beginning to murmur: 'Poor Frank – Poor Frank.' That was my father's name.

'But what is it, mother? – tell me what's the matter!'

She turned and looked at me as if I were a stranger; she got up, and began to walk about the room; then she left the room, and I heard her go out of the house.

The letter had fallen on to the floor. I picked it up. The handwriting was very broken. The address gave a village some few miles away; the date was three days before.

My Dear Lettice:

You will want to know I am gone. I can hardly last a day or two – my kidneys are nearly gone.

I came over one day. I didn't see you, but I saw the girl by the window, and I had a few words with the lad. He never knew, and he felt nothing. I think the girl might have done. If you knew how awfully lonely I am, Lettice – how awfully I have been, you might feel sorry.

I have saved what I could, to pay you back. I have had the worst of it, Lettice and I'm glad the end has come I have had the worst of it

Good-bye – for ever – your husband,
FRANK BEARDSALL

I was numbed by this letter of my father's. With almost agonized effort I strove to recall him, but I knew that my image of a tall, handsome, dark man with pale grey eyes was made up from my mother's few words, and from a portrait I had once seen.

The marriage had been unhappy. My father was of frivolous, rather vulgar character, but plausible, having a good deal of charm. He was a liar, without notion of honesty, and he had deceived my mother thoroughly. One after another she discovered his mean dishonesties and deceits, and her soul revolted from him, and because the illusion of him had broken into a thousand vulgar fragments, she turned away with the scorn of a woman who finds her romance has been a trumpery tale. When he left her for other pleasures – Lettie being a baby of three years, while I was five – she rejoiced bitterly. She had heard of him indirectly – and of him nothing good, although he prospered – but he had never come to see her or written to her in all the eighteen years.

In a while my mother came in. She sat down, pleating up the hem of her black apron, and smoothing it out again.

'You know,' she said, 'he had a right to the children, and I've kept them all the time.'

'He could have come,' said I.

'I set them against him, I have kept them from him, and he wanted them. I ought to be by him now – I ought to have taken you to him long ago.'

'But how could you, when you knew nothing of him?'

'He would have come – he wanted to come – I have felt it for years. But I kept him away. I know I have kept him away.

I have felt it, and he has. Poor Frank – he'll see his mistakes now. He would not have been as cruel as I have been –'

'Nay, mother, it is only the shock that makes you say so.'

'This makes me know. I have felt in myself a long time that he was suffering; I have had the feeling of him in me. I knew, yes, I did know he wanted me, and you, I felt it. I have had the feeling of him upon me this last three months especially . . . I have been cruel to him.'

'Well – we'll go to him now, shall we?' I said.

'Tomorrow – tomorrow,' she replied, noticing me really for the first time. 'I'll go in the morning.'

'And I'll go with you.'

'Yes – in the morning. Lettie has her party to Chatsworth – don't tell her – we won't tell her.'

'No,' said I.

Shortly after, my mother went upstairs. Lettie came in rather late from Highclose; Leslie did not come in. In the morning they were going with a motor party into Matlock and Chatsworth, and she was excited, and did not observe anything.

After all, mother and I could not set out until the warm, tempered afternoon. The air was full of a soft yellowness when we stepped down from the train at Cossethay. My mother insisted on walking the long two miles to the village. We went slowly along the road, lingering over the little red flowers in the high hedge-bottom up the hillside. We were reluctant to come to our destination. As we came in sight of the little grey tower of the church, we heard the sound of braying, brassy music. Before us, filling a little croft, the Wakes was in full swing.

Some wooden horses careered gaily round, and the swing-boats leaped into the mild blue sky. We sat upon the stile, my mother and I, and watched. There were booths, and coconut shies and roundabouts scattered in the small field. Groups of children moved quietly from attraction to attraction. A deeply tanned man came across the field swinging two dripping buckets of water. Women looked from the doors of their brilliant caravans, and lean dogs rose lazily and settled down again under the steps. The fair moved slowly, for all its noise. A stout lady, with a husky masculine voice, invited the excited children into her peep show. A swarthy man stood with his thin legs astride on the platform of the roundabouts, and sloping backwards, his mouth distended with a row of fingers, he whistled astonishingly to the coarse row of the organ, and his whistle sounded clear like the flight of a wild goose high over the chimney tops, as he was carried round and round. A little fat man with an ugly swelling on his chest stood screaming from a filthy booth to a crowd of urchins, bidding them challenge a big, stolid young man who stood with folded arms, his fists pushing out his biceps. On being asked if he would undertake any of these prospective challenges, this young man nodded, not having yet attained a talking stage: – yes he would take two at a time, screamed the little fat man with the big excrescence on his chest, pointing at the cowering lads and girls. Further off, Punch's quaint voice could be heard when the coconut man ceased grinding out screeches from his rattle. The coconut man was wroth, for these youngsters would not risk a penny shy, and the rattle yelled like a fiend. A little girl came along to look at us, daintily licking an ice-cream sandwich. We were uninteresting, however, so she passed on to stare at the caravans.

We had almost gathered courage to cross the wakes, when the cracked bell of the church sent its note falling over the babble.

'One – two – three' – had it really sounded three! Then it rang on a lower bell – 'One – two – three.' A passing bell for a man! I looked at my mother – she turned away from me.

The organ flared on – the husky woman came forward to make another appeal. Then there was a lull. The man with the lump on his chest had gone inside the rag to spar with the solid fellow. The coconut man had gone to the Three Tuns in fury, and a brazen girl of seventeen or so was in charge of the nuts. The horses careered round, carrying two frightened boys.

Suddenly the quick, throbbing note of the low bell struck again through the din. I listened – but could not keep count. One, two, three, four – for the third time that great lad had determined to go on the horses, and they had started while his foot was on the step, and he had been foiled – eight, nine, ten – no wonder that whistling man had such a big Adam's apple – I wondered if it hurt his neck when he talked, being so pointed – nineteen, twenty – the girl was licking more ice-cream, with precious, tiny licks – twenty-five, twenty-six – I wondered if I did count to twenty-six mechanically. At this point I gave it up, and watched for Lord Tennyson's bald head to come spinning round on the painted rim of the round-abouts, followed by a red-faced Lord Roberts, and a villainous looking Disraeli.

'Fifty-one –' said my mother. 'Come – come along.'

We hurried through the fair, towards the church; towards a garden where the last red sentinels looked out from the top of the hollyhock spires. The garden was a tousled mass of faded pink chrysanthemums, and weak-eyed Michaelmas daisies, and spectre stalks of hollyhock. It belonged to a low, dark house, which crouched behind a screen of yews. We walked along to the front. The blinds were down, and in one room we could see the stale light of candles burning.

'Is this Yew Cottage?' asked my mother of a curious lad.

'It's Mrs May's,' replied the boy.

'Does she live alone?' I asked.

'She 'ad French Carlin – but he's dead – an' she's letten th' candles ter keep th' owd lad off'n 'im.'

We went to the house and knocked.

'An ye come about him?' hoarsely whispered a bent old woman, looking up with very blue eyes, nodding her old head with its velvet net significantly towards the inner room.

'Yes –' said my mother, 'we had a letter.'

'Ay, poor fellow – he's gone, missis,' and the old lady shook her head. Then she looked at us curiously, leaned forward, and, putting her withered old hand on my mother's arm, her hand with its dark blue veins, she whispered in confidence, 'and the candles 'as gone out twice. 'E wor a funny feller, very funny!'

'I must come in and settle things – I am his nearest relative,' said my mother, trembling.

'Yes – I must 'a dozed, for when I looked up, it wor black darkness. Missis, I dursn't sit up wi' 'im no more, an' many a a one I've laid out. Eh, but his sufferin's, Missis – poor feller – eh, Missis!' – she lifted her ancient hands, and looked up at my mother, with her eyes so intensely blue.

'Do you know where he kept his papers?' asked my mother.

'Yis, I axed Father Burns about it; he said we mun pray for 'im. I bought him candles out o' my own pocket. He wor a rum feller, he wor!' and again she shook her grey head mournfully. My mother took a step forward.

'Did ye want to see 'im?' asked the old woman with half timid questioning.

'Yes,' replied my mother, with a vigorous nod. She perceived now that the old lady was deaf.

We followed the woman into the kitchen, a long, low room, dark, with drawn blinds.

'Sit ye down,' said the old lady in the same low tone, as if she were speaking to herself:

'Ye are his sister, 'appen?'

My mother shook her head.

'Oh – his brother's wife!' persisted the old lady.

We shook our heads.

'Only a cousin?' she guessed, and looked at us appealingly. I nodded assent.

'Sit ye there a minute,' she said, and trotted off. She banged the door, and jarred a chair as she went. When she returned, she set down a bottle and two glasses with a thump on the table in front of us. Her thin, skinny wrist seemed hardly capable of carrying the bottle.

'It's one as he'd only just begun of – 'ave a drop to keep ye up – do now, poor thing,' she said, pushing the bottle to my mother, and hurrying off, returning with the sugar and the kettle. We refused.

' 'E won't want it no more, poor feller – an it's good, Missis, he allers drank it good. Ay – an' 'e 'adn't a drop the last three days, poor man, poor feller, not a drop. Come now, it'll stay ye, come now.' We refused.

' 'T's in there,' she whispered, pointing to a closed door in a dark corner of the gloomy kitchen. I stumbled up a little step, and went plunging against a rickety table on which was a candle in a tall brass candlestick. Over went the candle, and it rolled on the floor, and the brass holder fell with much clanging.

'Eh! – Eh! – Dear – Lord, Dear – Heart. Dear – Heart!' wailed the old woman. She hastened trembling round to the other side of the bed, and relit the extinguished candle at the taper which was still burning. As she returned, the light glowed on her old, wrinkled face, and on the burnished knobs of the dark mahogany bedstead, while a stream of wax dripped down on to the floor. By the glimmering light of the two tapers we could see the outlined form under the counterpane. She turned back the hem and began to make painful wailing sounds. My heart was beating heavily, and I felt choked. I did not want to look – but I must. It was the man I had seen in the woods – with the puffiness gone from his face. I felt the great wild pity, and a sense of terror, and a sense of horror, and a sense of awful littleness and loneliness among a great empty space. I felt beyond myself as if I were a mere fleck drifting unconsciously through the dark. Then I felt my mother's arm round my shoulders, and she cried pitifully, 'Oh, my son, my son!'

I shivered, and came back to myself. There were no tears in my mother's face, only a great pleading. 'Never mind, mother – never mind,' I said incoherently.

She rose and covered the face again, and went round to the old lady, and held her still, and stayed her little wailings. The woman wiped from her cheeks the few tears of old age, and pushed her grey hair smooth under the velvet network.

'Where are all his things?' asked mother.

'Eh?' said the old lady, lifting up her ear.

'Are all his things here?' repeated mother in a louder tone.

'Here?' – the woman waved her hand round the room. It contained the great mahogany bedstead, naked of hangings, a desk, and an oak chest, and two or three mahogany chairs. 'I couldn't get him upstairs; he's only been here about a three week.'

'Where's the key to the desk?' said my mother loudly in the woman's ear.

'Yes,' she replied – 'it's his desk.' She looked at us, perplexed and doubtful, fearing she had misunderstood us. This was dreadful.

'Key!' I shouted. 'Where is the key?'

Her old face was full of trouble as she shook her head. I took it that she did not know.

'Where are his clothes? *Clothes*,' I repeated pointing to my coat. She understood, and muttered, 'I'll fetch 'em ye.'

We should have followed her as she hurried upstairs through a door near the head of the bed, had we not heard a heavy footstep in the kitchen, and a voice saying: 'Is the old lady going to drink with the Devil? Hullo, Mrs May, come and drink with me!' We heard the tinkle of the liquor poured into a glass, and almost immediately the light tap of the empty tumbler on the table.

'I'll see what the old girl's up to,' he said, and the heavy tread came towards us. Like me, he stumbled at the little step, but escaped collision with the table.

'Damn that fool's step,' he said heartily. It was the doctor – for he kept his hat on his head, and did not hesitate to stroll about the house. He was a big, burly, red-faced man.

'I beg your pardon,' he said, observing my mother. My mother bowed.

'Mrs Beardsall?' he asked, taking off his hat.

My mother bowed.

'I posted a letter to you. You are a relative of his – of poor old Carlin's?' – he nodded sideways towards the bed.

'The nearest,' said my mother.

'Poor fellow – he was a bit stranded. Comes of being a bachelor, Ma'am.'

'I was very much surprised to hear from him,' said my mother.

'Yes, I guess he's not been much of a one for writing to his friends. He's had a bad time lately. You have to pay some time or other. We bring them on ourselves – silly devils as we are. – I beg your pardon.'

There was a moment of silence, during which the doctor sighed, and then began to whistle softly.

'Well – we might be more comfortable if we had the blind up,' he said, letting daylight in among the glimmer of the tapers as he spoke.

'At any rate,' he said, 'you don't have any trouble settling up – no debts or anything of that. I believe there's a bit to leave – so it's not so bad. Poor devil – he was very down at the last; but we have to pay at one end or the other. What on earth is the old girl after?' he asked, looking up at the raftered ceiling, which was rumbling and thundering with the old lady's violent rummaging.

'We wanted the key of his desk,' said my mother.

'Oh – I can find you that – and the will. He told me where they were, and to give them you when you came. He seemed to think a lot of you. Perhaps he might ha' done better for himself –'

Here we heard the heavy tread of the old lady coming downstairs. The doctor went to the foot of the stairs.

'Hello, now – be careful!' he bawled. The poor old woman did as he expected, and trod on the braces of the trousers she was trailing, and came crashing into his arms. He set her tenderly down, saying, 'Not hurt, are you ? – no!' and he smiled at her and shook his head.

'Eh, doctor – Eh, doctor — bless ye, I'm thankful ye've come. Ye'll see to 'em now, will ye ?'

'Yes –' he nodded in his bluff, winning way, and hurrying into the kitchen, he mixed her a glass of whisky, and brought one for himself, saying to her, 'There you are – 'twas a nasty shaking for you.'

The poor old woman sat in a chair by the open door of the staircase, the pile of clothing tumbled about her feet. She looked round pitifully, at us and at the daylight struggling among the candle-light, making a ghostly gleam on the bed where the rigid figure lay unmoved; her hand trembled so that she could scarcely hold her glass.

The doctor gave us the keys, and we rifled the desk and the drawers, sorting out all the papers. The doctor sat sipping and talking to us all the time.

'Yes,' he said, 'he's only been here about two years. Felt himself beginning to break up then, I think. He'd been a long time abroad; they always called him Frenchy.' The doctor sipped and reflected, and sipped again. 'Aye – he'd run the rig in his day – used to dream dreadfully. Good thing the old woman was so deaf. Awful, when a man gives himself away in his sleep; played the deuce with him, knowing it.' Sip, sip, sip – and more reflexions – and another glass to be mixed.

'But he was a jolly decent fellow – generous, open-handed. The folks didn't like him, because they couldn't get to the bottom of him; they always hate a thing they can't fathom. He was close, there's no mistake – save when he was asleep sometimes.' The doctor looked at his glass, and sighed.

'However – we shall miss him – shan't we, Mrs May?' he bawled suddenly, startling us, making us glance at the bed.

He lit his pipe and puffed voluminously in order to obscure the attraction of his glass. Meanwhile we examined the papers. There were very few letters – one or two addressed to Paris. There were many bills, and receipts, and notes – business, all business.

There was hardly a trace of sentiment among all the litter. My mother sorted out such papers as she considered valuable; the others, letters and missives which she glanced at cursorily and put aside, she took into the kitchen and burned. She seemed afraid to find out too much.

The doctor continued to colour his tobacco smoke with a few pensive words.

'Ay,' he said, 'there are two ways. You can burn your lamp with a big draught, and it'll flare away, till the oil's gone, then it'll stink and smoke itself out. Or you can keep it trim on the kitchen table, dirty your fingers occasionally trimming it up, and it'll last a long time, and sink out mildly.' Here he turned to his glass, and finding it empty, was awakened to reality.

'Anything I can do, Madam?' he asked.

'No, thank you.'

'Ay, I don't suppose there's much to settle. Nor many tears to shed – when a fellow spends his years an' his prime on the Lord knows who, you can't expect those that remember him young to feel his loss too keenly. He'd had his fling in his day, though, ma'am. Ay – must ha' had some rich times. No lasting satisfaction in it though – always wanting, craving. There's nothing like marrying – you've got your dish before you then, and you've got to eat it.' He lapsed again into reflexion, from which he did not rouse till we had locked up the desk, burned the useless papers, put the others into my pockets and black bag, and were standing ready to depart. Then the doctor looked up suddenly and said:

'But what about the funeral?'

Then he noticed the weariness of my mother's look, and he jumped up, and quickly seized his hat, saying:

'Come across to my wife and have a cup of tea. Buried in

these dam holes a fellow gets such a boor. Do come – my little wife is lonely – come just to see her.'

My mother smiled and thanked him. We turned to go. My mother hesitated in her walk; on the threshold of the room she glanced round at the bed, but she went on.

Outside, in the fresh air of the fading afternoon, I could not believe it was true. It was not true, that sad, colourless face with grey beard, wavering in the yellow candle-light. It was a lie – that wooden bedstead, that deaf woman, they were fading phrases of the untruth. That yellow blaze of little sun-flowers was true, and the shadow from the sun-dial on the warm old almshouses – that was real. The heavy afternoon sunlight came round us warm and reviving; we shivered, and the untruth went out of our veins, and we were no longer chilled.

The doctor's house stood sweetly among the beech trees, and at the iron fence in front of the little lawn a woman was talking to a beautiful Jersey cow that pushed its dark nose through the fence from the field beyond. She was a little, dark woman with vivid colouring; she rubbed the nose of the delicate animal, peeped right into the dark eyes, and talked in a lovable Scottish speech; talked as a mother talks softly to her child.

When she turned round in surprise to greet us there was still the softness of a rich affection in her eyes. She gave us tea, and scones, and apple jelly, and all the time we listened with delight to her voice, which was musical as bees humming in the lime trees. Though she said nothing significant we listened to her attentively.

Her husband was merry and kind. She glanced at him with quick glances of apprehension, and her eyes avoided him. He, in his merry, frank way, chaffed her, and praised her extra-vagantly, and teased her again. Then he became a trifle uneasy. I think she was afraid he had been drinking; I think she was shaken with horror when she found him tipsy, and bewildered and terrified when she saw him drunk. They had no children. I noticed he ceased to joke when she became a little constrained. He glanced at her often, and looked somewhat pitiful when she avoided his looks, and he grew uneasy, and I could see he wanted to go away.

'I had better go with you to see the vicar, then,' he said to me, and we left the room, whose windows looked south, over the meadows, the room where dainty little water-colours, and beautiful bits of embroidery, and empty flower vases, and two dirty novels from the town library, and the closed piano, and the odd cups, and the chipped spout of the tea-pot causing stains on the cloth – all told one story.

We went to the joiner's and ordered the coffin, and the doctor had a glass of whisky on it; the graveyard fees were paid, and the doctor sealed the engagement with a drop of brandy; the vicar's port completed the doctor's joviality, and we went home.

This time the disquiet in the little woman's dark eyes could not dispel the doctor's merriment. He rattled away, and she nervously twisted her wedding ring. He insisted on driving us to the station, in spite of our alarm.

'But you will be quite safe with him,' said his wife, in her caressing Highland speech. When she shook hands at parting I noticed the hardness of the little palm; – and I have always hated an old, black alpaca dress.

It is such a long way home from the station at Eberwich. We rode part way in the bus; then we walked. It is a very long way for my mother, when her steps are heavy with trouble.

Rebecca was out by the rhododendrons looking for us. She hurried to us all solicitous, and asked mother if she had had tea.

'But you'll do with another cup,' she said, and ran back into the house.

She came into the dining-room to take my mother's bonnet and coat. She wanted us to talk; she was distressed on my mother's behalf; she noticed the blackness that lay under her eyes, and she fidgeted about, unwilling to ask anything, yet uneasy and anxious to know.

'Lettie has been home,' she said.

'And gone back again?' asked mother.

'She only came to change her dress. She put the green poplin on. She wondered where you'd gone.'

'What did you tell her?'

'I said you'd just gone out a bit. She said she was glad. She was as lively as a squirrel.'

Rebecca looked wistfully at my mother. At length the latter said:

'He's dead, Rebecca. I have seen him.'

'Now thank God for that – no more need to worry over him.'

'Well! – He died all alone, Rebecca – all alone.'

'He died as you've lived,' said Becky with some asperity.

'But I've had the children, I've had the children – we won't tell Lettie, Rebecca.'

'No 'm.' Rebecca left the room.

'You and Lettie will have the money,' said mother to me. There was a sum of four thousand pounds or so. It was left to my mother; or, in default, to Lettie and me.

'Well, mother – if it's ours, it's yours.'

There was silence for some minutes, then she said, 'You might have had a father –'

'We're thankful we hadn't, mother. You spared us that.'

'But how can you tell?' said my mother.

'I can,' I replied. 'And I am thankful to you.'

'If ever you feel scorn for one who is near you rising in your throat, try and be generous, my lad.'

'Well –' said I.

'Yes,' she replied, 'we'll say no more. Sometime you must tell Lettie – you tell her.'

I did tell her, a week or so afterwards.

'Who knows?' she asked, her face hardening.

'Mother, Becky, and ourselves.'

'Nobody else?'

'No.'

'Then it's a good thing he is out of the way if he was such a nuisance to mother. Where is she?'

'Upstairs.'

Lettie ran to her.

CHAPTER V

The Scent of Blood

THE death of the man who was our father changed our lives. It was not that we suffered a great grief; the chief trouble was the unanswered crying of failure. But we were changed in our feelings and in our relations; there was a new consciousness, a new carefulness.

We had lived between the woods and the water all our lives, Lettie and I, and she had sought the bright notes in everything. She seemed to hear the water laughing, and the leaves tittering and giggling like young girls; the aspen fluttered like the draperies of a flirt, and the sound of the wood-pigeons was almost foolish in its sentimentality.

Lately, however, she had noticed again the cruel pitiful crying of a hedgehog caught in a gin, and she had noticed the traps for the fierce little murderers, traps walled in with a small fence of fir, and baited with the guts of a killed rabbit.

On an afternoon a short time after our visit to Cossethay, Lettie sat in the window seat. The sun clung to her hair, and kissed her with passionate splashes of colour brought from the vermilion, dying creeper outside. The sun loved Lettie, and was loath to leave her. She looked out over Nethermere to Highclose, vague in the September mist. Had it not been for the scarlet light on her face, I should have thought her look was sad and serious. She nestled up to the window, and leaned her head against the wooden shaft. Gradually she drooped into sleep. Then she became wonderfully childish again – it was the girl of seventeen sleeping there, with her full pouting lips slightly apart, and the breath coming lightly. I felt the old feeling of responsibility; I must protect her, and take care of her.

There was a crunch of the gravel. It was Leslie coming. He lifted his hat to her, thinking she was looking. He had that fine, lithe physique, suggestive of much animal vigour; his person was exceedingly attractive; one watched him move about, and felt pleasure. His face was less pleasing than his person. He was not handsome; his eyebrows were too light, his nose was large and ugly, and his forehead, though high and fair, was without dignity. But he had a frank, good-natured expression, and a fine, wholesome laugh.

He wondered why she did not move. As he came nearer he saw. Then he winked at me and came in. He tip-toed across the room to look at her. The sweet carelessness of her attitude, the appealing, half-pitiful girlishness of her face touched his responsive heart, and he leaned forward and kissed her cheek where already was a crimson stain of sunshine.

She roused half out of her sleep with a little, petulant 'Oh!' as an awakened child. He sat down behind her, and gently drew her head against him, looking down at her with a tender, soothing smile. I thought she was going to fall asleep thus. But her eyelids quivered, and her eyes beneath them flickered into consciousness.

'Leslie! – oh! – Let me go!' she exclaimed, pushing him away. He loosed her, and rose, looking at her reproachfully. She shook her dress, and went quickly to the mirror to arrange her hair.

'You are mean!' she exclaimed, looking very flushed, vexed, and dishevelled.

He laughed indulgently, saying, 'You shouldn't go to sleep then and look so pretty. Who could help?'

'It is not nice!' she said, frowning with irritation.

'We are not "nice" – are we? I thought we were proud of our unconventionality. Why shouldn't I kiss you?'

'Because it is a question of me, not of you alone.'

'Dear me, you *are* in a way!'

'Mother is coming.'

'Is she? You had better tell her.'

Mother was very fond of Leslie.

'Well, sir,' she said, 'why are you frowning?'

He broke into a laugh.

'Lettie is scolding me for kissing her when she was playing "Sleeping Beauty".'

'The conceit of the boy, to play Prince!' said my mother.

'Oh, but it appears I was sadly out of character,' he said rue-fully.

Lettie laughed and forgave him.

'Well,' he said, looking at her, and smiling, 'I came to ask you to go out.'

'It is a lovely afternoon,' said mother.

She glanced at him, and said:

'I feel dreadfully lazy.'

'Never mind!' he replied, 'you'll wake up. Go and put your hat on.'

He sounded impatient. She looked at him.

He seemed to be smiling peculiarly.

She lowered her eyes and went out of the room.

'She'll come all right,' he said, to himself, and to me. 'She likes to play you on a string.'

She must have heard him. When she came in again, drawing on her gloves, she said quietly:

'You come as well, Pat.'

He swung round and stared at her in angry amazement.

'I had rather stay and finish this sketch,' I said, feeling uncom-fortable.

'No, but do come, there's a dear.' She took the brush from my hand, and drew me from my chair. The blood flushed into his cheeks. He went quietly into the hall and brought my cap.

'All right!' he said angrily. 'Women like to fancy themselves Napoleons.'

'They do, dear Iron Duke, they do,' she mocked.

'Yet, there's a Waterloo in all their histories,' he said, since she had supplied him with the idea.

'Say Peterloo, my general, say Peterloo.'

'Ay, Peterloo,' he replied, with a splendid curl of the lip – 'Easy conquests!'

'"He came, he saw, he conquered,"' Lettie recited.

'Are you coming?' he said, getting more angry.

'When you bid me,' she replied, taking my arm.

We went through the wood, and through the dishevelled border-land to the high road, through the border-land that should have been park-like, but which was shaggy with loose grass and yellow mole-hills, ragged with gorse and bramble and briar, with wandering old thorn-trees, and a queer clump of Scotch firs.

On the highway the leaves were falling, and they chattered under our steps. The water was mild and blue, and the corn stood drowsily in 'stook'.

We climbed the hill behind Highclose, and walked on along the upland, looking across towards the hills of arid Derbyshire, and seeing them not, because it was autumn. We came in sight of the head-stocks of the pit at Selsby, and of the ugly village standing blank and naked on the brow of the hill.

Lettie was in very high spirits. She laughed and joked continually. She picked bunches of hips and stuck them in her dress. Having got a thorn in her finger from a spray of blackberries, she went to Leslie to have it squeezed out. We were all quite gay as we turned off the high road and went along the bridle path, with the woods on our right, the high Strelley hills shutting in our small valley in front, and the fields and the common to the left. About half way down the lane we heard the slurr of the scythestone on the scythe. Lettie went to the hedge to see. It was George mowing the oats on the steep hillside where the machine could not go. His father was tying up the corn into sheaves.

Straightening his back, Mr Saxton saw us, and called to us to come and help. We pushed through a gap in the hedge and went up to him.

'Now then,' said the father to me, 'take that coat off,' and to Lettie: 'Have you brought us a drink? No; – come, that sounds bad! Going a walk, I guess. You see what it is to get fat,' and he pulled a wry face as he bent over to tie the corn. He was a man beautifully ruddy and burly, in the prime of life.

'Show me, I'll do some,' said Lettie.

'Nay,' he answered gently, 'it would scratch your wrists and break your stays. Hark at my hands' – he rubbed them together – 'like sand-paper!'

George had his back to us, and had not noticed us. He continued to mow. Leslie watched him.

'That's a fine movement!' he exclaimed.

'Yes,' replied the father, rising very red in the face from the tying, 'and our George enjoys a bit o' mowing. It puts you in fine condition when you get over the first stiffness.'

We moved across to the standing corn. The sun being mild, George had thrown off his hat, and his black hair was moist and twisted into confused half-curls. Firmly planted, he swung with a beautiful rhythm from the waist. On the hip of his belted breeches hung the scythestone; his shirt, faded almost white, was torn just above the belt, and showed the muscles of his back playing like lights upon the white sand of a brook. There was something exceedingly attractive in the rhythmic body.

I spoke to him, and he turned round. He looked straight at Lettie with a flashing, betraying smile. He was remarkably handsome. He tried to say some words of greeting, then he bent down and gathered an armful of corn, and deliberately bound it up.

Like him, Lettie had found nothing to say. Leslie, however, remarked:

'I should think mowing is a nice exercise.'

'It is,' he replied, and continued, as Leslie picked up the scythe, 'but it will make you sweat, and your hands will be sore.'

Leslie tossed his head a little, threw off his coat, and said briefly:

'How do you do it?' Without waiting for a reply he proceeded. George said nothing, but turned to Lettie.

'You are picturesque,' she said, a trifle awkwardly. 'Quite fit for an Idyll.'

'And you?' he said.

She shrugged her shoulders, laughed, and turned to pick up a scarlet pimpernel.

'How do you bind the corn?' she asked.

He took some long straws, cleaned them, and showed her the way to hold them. Instead of attending, she looked at his hands, big, hard, inflamed by the snaith of the scythe.

'I don't think I could do it,' she said.

'No,' he replied quietly, and watched Leslie mowing. The latter, who was wonderfully ready at everything, was doing fairly well, but he had not the invincible sweep of the other, nor did he make the same crisp crunching music.

'I bet he'll sweat,' said George.

'Don't you?' she replied.

'A bit – but I'm not dressed up.'

'Do you know,' she said suddenly, 'your arms tempt me to touch them. They are such a fine brown colour, and they look so hard.'

He held out one arm to her. She hesitated, then she swiftly put her finger-tips on the smooth brown muscle, and drew them along. Quickly she hid her hand into the folds of her skirt, blushing.

He laughed a low, quiet laugh, at once pleasant and startling to hear.

'I wish I could work here,' she said, looking away at the standing corn, and the dim blue woods. He followed her look, and laughed quietly, with indulgent resignation.

'I do!' she said emphatically.

'You feel so fine,' he said, pushing his hand through his open shirt front, and gently rubbing the muscles of his side. 'It's a pleasure to work or to stand still. It's a pleasure to yourself – your own physique.'

She looked at him, full at his physical beauty, as if he were some great firm bud of life.

Leslie came up, wiping his brow.

'Jove,' said he, 'I do perspire.'

George picked up his coat and helped him into it, saying:

'You may take a chill.'

'It's a jolly nice form of exercise,' said he.

George, who had been feeling one finger-tip, now took out his pen-knife and proceeded to dig a thorn from his hand.

'What a hide you must have,' said Leslie.

Lettie said nothing, but she recoiled slightly.

The father, glad of an excuse to straighten his back and to chat, came to us.

'You'd soon had enough,' he said, laughing, to Leslie.

George startled us with a sudden 'Holloa'. We turned, and saw a rabbit, which had burst from the corn, go coursing through the hedge, dodging and bounding in the sheaves. The standing corn was a patch along the hill-side some fifty paces in length, and ten or so in width.

'I didn't think there'd have been any in,' said the father, picking up a short rake, and going to the low wall of the corn. We all followed.

'Watch!' said the father, 'if you see the heads of the corn shake!'

We prowled round the patch of corn.

'Hold! Look out!' shouted the father excitedly, and immediately after a rabbit broke from the cover.

'Ay – Ay – Ay,' was the shout, 'turn him – turn him!' We set off full pelt. The bewildered little brute, scared by Leslie's wild running and crying, turned from its course, and dodged across the hill, threading its terrified course through the maze of lying sheaves, spurting on in a painful zigzag, now bounding over an untied bundle of corn, now swerving from the sound of a shout. The little wretch was hard pressed; George rushed upon it. It darted into some fallen corn, but he had seen it, and had fallen on it. In an instant he was up again, and the little creature was dangling from his hand.

We returned, panting, sweating, our eyes flashing, to the edge of the standing corn. I heard Lettie calling, and turning round saw Emily and the two children entering the field as they passed from school.

'There's another!' shouted Leslie.

I saw the oat-tops quiver. 'Here! Here!' I yelled. The animal leaped out, and made for the hedge. George and Leslie, who were on that side, dashed off, turned him, and he coursed back our way. I headed him off to the father who swept in pursuit for a short distance, but who was too heavy for the work. The little beast made towards the gate, but this time Mollie, with her hat in her hand and her hair flying, whirled upon him, and she and the little fragile lad sent him back again. The rabbit was getting tired. It dodged the sheaves badly, running towards the top hedge. I went after it. If I could have let myself fall on it I could have caught it, but this was impossible to me, and I merely prevented its dashing through the hole into safety. It raced along the hedge bottom. George tore after it. As he was upon it, it darted into the hedge. He fell flat, and shot his hand into the gap. But it had escaped. He lay there, panting in great sobs, and looking at me with eyes in which excitement and exhaustion struggled like flickering light and darkness. When he could speak, he said, 'Why didn't you fall on top of it?'

'I couldn't,' said I.

We returned again. The two children were peering into the thick corn also. We thought there was nothing more. George began to mow. As I walked round I caught sight of a rabbit skulking near the bottom corner of the patch. Its ears lay pressed against its back; I could see the palpitation of the heart under the brown fur, and I could see the shining dark eyes looking at me. I felt no pity for it, but still I could not actually hurt it. I beckoned to the father. He ran up, and aimed a blow with the rake. There was a sharp little cry which sent a hot pain through me as if I had been cut. But the rabbit ran out, and instantly I forgot the cry, and gave pursuit, fairly feeling my fingers stiffen to choke it. It was all lame. Leslie was upon it in a moment, and he almost pulled its head off in his excitement to kill it.

I looked up. The girls were at the gate, just turning away.

'There are no more,' said the father.

At that instant Mary shouted:

'There's one down this hole.'

The hole was too small for George to get his hand in, so we dug it out with the rake handle. The stick went savagely down the hole, and there came a squeak.

'Mice!' said George, and as he said it the mother slid out. Somebody knocked her on the back, and the hole was opened out. Little mice seemed to swarm everywhere. It was like killing insects. We counted nine little ones lying dead.

'Poor brute,' said George, looking at the mother. 'What a job she must have had rearing that lot!' He picked her up, handled her curiously and with pity. Then he said, 'Well, I may as well finish this tonight!'

His father took another scythe from off the hedge, and together they soon laid the proud, quivering heads low. Leslie and I tied up as they mowed, and soon all was finished.

The beautiful day was flushing to die. Over in the west the mist was gathering bluer. The intense stillness was broken by the rhythmic hum of the engines at the distant coal-mine, as they drew up the last bantles of men. As we walked across the fields the tubes of stubble tinkled like dulcimers. The scent of the corn began to rise gently. The last cry of the pheasants came from the wood, and the little clouds of birds were gone.

I carried a scythe, and we walked, pleasantly weary, down the hill towards the farm. The children had gone home with the rabbits.

When we reached the mill, we found the girls just rising from the table. Emily began to carry away the used pots, and to set clean ones for us. She merely glanced at us and said her formal greeting. Lettie picked up a book that lay in the ingle seat, and went to the window. George dropped into a chair. He had flung off his coat, and had pushed back his hair. He rested his great brown arms on the table and was silent for a moment.

'Running like that,' he said to me, passing his hand over his eyes, 'makes you more tired than a whole day's work. I don't think I shall do it again.'

'The sport's exciting while it lasts,' said Leslie.

'It does you more harm than the rabbits do us good,' said Mrs Saxton.

'Oh, I don't know, mother,' drawled her son, 'it's a couple of shillings.'

'And a couple of days off your life.'

'What be that!' he replied, taking a piece of bread and butter, and biting a large piece from it.

'Pour us a drop of tea,' he said to Emily.

'I don't know that I shall wait on such brutes,' she replied, relenting, and flourishing the teapot.

'Oh,' said he, taking another piece of bread and butter, 'I'm not all alone in my savageness this time.'

'Men are all brutes,' said Lettie, hotly, without looking up from her book.

'You can tame us,' said Leslie, in mighty good humour.

She did not reply. George began, in that deliberate voice that so annoyed Emily:

'It does make you mad, though, to touch the fur, and not be able to grab him' – he laughed quietly.

Emily moved off in disgust. Lettie opened her mouth sharply to speak, but remained silent.

'I don't know,' said Leslie. 'When it comes to killing it goes against the stomach.'

'If you can run,' said George, 'you should be able to run to death. When your blood's up, you don't hang half way.'

'I think a man is horrible,' said Lettie, 'who can tear the head off a little mite of a thing like a rabbit, after running it in torture over a field.'

'When he is nothing but a barbarian to begin with –' said Emily.

'If you began to run yourself – you'd be the same,' said George.

'Why, women are cruel enough,' said Leslie, with a glance at Lettie. 'Yes,' he continued, 'they're cruel enough in their way' – another look, and a comical little smile.

'Well,' said George, 'what's the good finicking! If you feel like doing a thing – you'd better do it.'

'Unless you haven't courage,' said Emily, bitingly.

He looked up at her with dark eyes, suddenly full of anger.

'But,' said Lettie – she could not hold herself from asking. 'Don't you think it's brutal, now – now that you *do* think – isn't it degrading and mean to run the poor little things down?'

'Perhaps it is,' he replied, 'but it wasn't an hour ago.'

'You have no feeling,' she said bitterly.

He laughed deprecatingly, but said nothing.

We finished tea in silence. Lettie reading, Emily moving about the house. George got up and went out at the end. A moment or two after we heard him across the yard with the milk-buckets, singing: 'The Ash Grove'.

'He doesn't care a scrap for anything,' said Emily with accumulated bitterness. Lettie looked out of the window across the yard, thinking. She looked very glum.

After a while we went out also, before the light faded altogether from the pond. Emily took us into the lower garden to get some ripe plums. The old garden was very low. The soil was black. The cornbind and goosegrass were clutching at the ancient gooseberry bushes, which sprawled by the paths. The garden was not very productive, save of weeds, and perhaps, tremendous lank artichokes or swollen marrows. But at the bottom, where the end of the farm buildings rose high and grey, there was a plum-tree which had been crucified to the wall, and which had broken away and leaned forward from bondage. Now under the boughs were hidden great mist-bloomed, crimson treasures, splendid globes. I shook the old, ragged trunk, green, with even the fresh gum dulled over, and the treasures fell heavily, thudding down among the immense rhubarb leaves below. The girls laughed, and we divided the spoil, and turned back to the yard. We went down to the edge of the garden, which skirted the bottom pond, a pool chained in heavy growth of weeds. It was moving with rats, the father had said. The rushes were thick below us; opposite, the great bank fronted us, with orchard trees climbing it like a hillside. The lower pond received the overflow from the upper by a tunnel from the deep black sluice.

Two rats ran into the black culvert at our approach. We sat on some piled, mossy stones, to watch. The rats came out again, ran a little way, stopped, ran again, listened, were reassured, and slid about freely, dragging their long naked tails. Soon six or seven grey beasts were playing round the mouth of the culvert, in the gloom. They sat and wiped their sharp faces, stroking their whiskers. Then one would give a little rush and a little squirm of excitement and would jump vertically into the air, alighting on four feet, running, sliding into the black shadow. One dropped with an ugly plop into the water, and swam towards us, the hoary imp, his sharp snout and his wicked little eyes moving at us. Lettie shuddered. I threw a stone into the dead pool, and frightened them all. But we had frightened ourselves more, so we hurried away, and stamped our feet in relief on the free pavement of the yard.

Leslie was looking for us. He had been inspecting the yard and the stock under Mr Saxton's supervision.

'Were you running away from me?' he asked.

'No,' she replied. 'I have been to fetch you a plum. Look!' And she showed him two in a leaf.

'They are too pretty to eat!' said he.

'You have not tasted yet,' she laughed.

'Come,' he said, offering her his arm. 'Let us go up to the water.' She took his arm.

It was a splendid evening, with the light all thick and yellow lying on the smooth pond. Lettie made him lift her on to a leaning bough of willow. He sat with his head resting against her skirts. Emily and I moved on. We heard him murmur something, and her voice reply, gently, caressingly:

'No – let us be still – it is all so still – I love it best of all now.'

Emily and I talked, sitting at the base of the alders, a little way on. After an excitement, and in the evening, especially in autumn, one is inclined to be sad and sentimental. We had forgotten that the darkness was weaving. I heard in the little distance Leslie's voice begin to murmur like a flying beetle that comes not too near. Then, away down in the yard George began singing the old song, 'I sowed the seeds of love'.

This interrupted the flight of Leslie's voice, and as the singing came nearer, the hum of low words ceased. We went forward to meet George. Leslie sat up, clasping his knees, and did not speak. George came near, saying:

'The moon is going to rise.'

'Let me get down,' said Lettie, lifting her hands to him to help her. He, mistaking her wish, put his hands under her arms, and set her gently down, as one would a child. Leslie got up quickly, and seemed to hold himself separate, resenting the intrusion.

'I thought you were all four together,' said George quietly. Lettie turned quickly at the apology:

'So we were. So we were – five now. Is it there the moon will rise?'

'Yes – I like to see it come over the wood. It lifts slowly up to stare at you. I always think it wants to know something, and I always think I have something to answer, only I don't know what it is,' said Emily.

Where the sky was pale in the east over the rim of wood came the forehead of the yellow moon. We stood and watched in silence. Then, as the great disc, nearly full, lifted and looked straight upon us, we were washed off our feet in a vague sea of moonlight. We stood with the light like water on our faces. Lettie was glad, a little bit exalted; Emily was passionately troubled; her lips were parted, almost beseeching; Leslie was frowning, oblivious, and George was thinking, and the terrible, immense moonbeams braided through his feeling. At length Leslie said softly, mistakenly:

'Come along, dear' – and he took her arm.

She let him lead her along the bank of the pond, and across the plank over the sluice.

'Do you know,' she said, as we were carefully descending the steep bank of the orchard, 'I feel as if I wanted to laugh, or dance – something rather outrageous.'

'Surely not like that *now*,' Leslie replied in a low voice, feeling really hurt.

'I do though! I will race you to the bottom.'

'No, no, dear!' He held her back. When he came to the wicket leading on to the front lawns, he said something to her softly, as he held the gate.

I think he wanted to utter his half-finished proposal, and so bind her.

She broke free, and, observing the long lawn which lay in grey shadow between the eastern and western glows, she cried:

'Polka! – a polka – one can dance a polka when the grass is smooth and short – even if there are some fallen leaves. Yes, yes – how jolly!'

She held out her hand to Leslie, but it was too great a shock to his mood. So she called to me, and there was a shade of anxiety in her voice, lest after all she should be caught in the toils of the night's sentiment.

'Pat – you'll dance with me – Leslie hates a polka.' I danced with her. I do not know the time when I could not polka – it seems innate in one's feet, to dance that dance. We went flying round, hissing through the dead leaves. The night, the low-hung yellow moon, the pallor of the west, the blue cloud of evening overhead went round and through the fantastic branches of the old laburnum, spinning a little madness. You cannot tire Lettie; her feet are wings that beat the air. When at last I stayed her she laughed as fresh as ever, as she bound her hair.

'There!' she said to Leslie, in tones of extreme satisfaction, 'that was lovely. Do you come and dance now.'

'Not a polka,' said he, sadly, feeling the poetry in his heart insulted by the jigging measure.

'But one cannot dance anything else on wet grass, and through shuffling dead leaves. You, George?'

'Emily says I jump,' he replied.

'Come on – come on' – and in a moment they were bounding across the grass. After a few steps she fell in with him, and they spun round the grass. It was true, he leaped, sprang with large strides, carrying her with him. It was a tremendous, irresistible dancing. Emily and I must join, making an inner ring. Now and again there was a sense of something white flying near, and wild rustle of draperies, and a swish of disturbed leaves as they whirled past us. Long after we were tired they danced on.

At the end, he looked big, erect, nerved with triumph, and she was exhilarated like a Bacchante.

'Have you finished?' Leslie asked.

She knew she was safe from his question that day.

'Yes,' she panted. 'You should have danced. Give me my hat, please. Do I look very disgraceful?'

He took her hat and gave it to her.

'Disgraceful?' he repeated.

'Oh, you *are* solemn tonight! What is it?'

'Yes, what is it?' he repeated ironically.

'It must be the moon. Now, is my hat straight? Tell me now – you're not looking. Then put it level. Now then! Why, your hands are quite cold, and mine so hot! I feel so impish,' and she laughed.

'There – now I'm ready. Do you notice these little chrysanthemums trying to smell sadly; when the old moon is laughing and winking through those boughs? What business have they with their sadness!' She took a handful of petals and flung them into the air: 'There – if they sigh they ask for sorrow – I like things to wink and look wild.'

CHAPTER VI

The Education of George

As I have said, Strelley Mill lies at the north end of the long Nethermere valley. On the northern slopes lay its pasture and arable lands. The shaggy common, now closed and part of the estate, covered the western slope, and the cultivated land was bounded on the east by the sharp dip of the brook course, a thread of woodland broadening into a spinney and ending at the upper pond; beyond this, on the east, rose the sharp, wild, grassy hillside, scattered with old trees, ruinous with the gaunt, ragged bones of old hedge-rows, grown into thorn trees. Along the rim of the hills, beginning in the northwest, were dark woodlands, which swept round east and south till they raced down in riot to the very edge of southern Nethermere, surrounding our house. From the eastern hill crest, looking straight across, you could see the spire of Selsby Church, and a few roofs, and the head-stocks of the pit.

So on three sides the farm was skirted by woods, the dens of rabbits, and the common held another warren.

Now the squire of the estate, head of an ancient, once even famous, but now decayed house, loved his rabbits. Unlike the family fortunes, the family tree flourished amazingly; Sherwood could show nothing comparable. Its ramifications were stupendous; it was more like a banyan than a British oak. How was the good squire to nourish himself and his lady, his name, his tradition, and his thirteen lusty branches on his meagre estates? An evil fortune discovered to him that he could sell each of his rabbits, those bits of furry vermin, for a shilling or thereabouts in Nottingham; since which time the noble family subsisted by rabbits.

Farms were gnawed away; corn and sweet grass departed from the face of the hills; cattle grew lean, unable to eat the defiled herbage. Then the farm became the home of a keeper, and the country was silent, with no sound of cattle, no clink of horses, no barking of lusty dogs.

But the squire loved his rabbits. He defended them against the snares of the despairing farmer, protected them with gun and notices to quit. How he glowed with thankfulness as he saw the dishevelled hillside heave when the gnawing hosts moved on!

'Are they not quails and manna?' said he to his sporting guest, early one Monday morning, as the high meadow broke into life at the sound of his gun. 'Quails and manna – in this wilderness?'

'They are, by Jove!' assented the sporting guest as he took another gun, while the saturnine keeper smiled grimly.

Meanwhile, Strelley Mill began to suffer under this gangrene. It was the outpost in the wilderness. It was an understood thing that none of the squire's tenants had a gun.

'Well,' said the squire to Mr Saxton, 'you have the land for next to nothing – next to nothing – at a rent really absurd. Surely the little that the rabbits eat –'

'It's not a little – come and look for yourself,' replied the farmer. The squire made a gesture of impatience.

'What *do* you want?' he inquired.

'Will you wire me off?' was the repeated request.

'Wire is – what does Halkett say – so much per yard – and it would come to – what did Halkett tell me now? – but a large sum. No, I can't do it.'

'Well, I can't live like this.'

'Have another glass of whisky? Yes, yes, I want another glass myself, and I can't drink alone – so if I am to enjoy my glass. – That's it! Now surely you exaggerate a little. It's not so bad.'

'I can't go on like it, I'm sure.'

'Well, we'll see about compensation – we'll see. I'll have a talk with Halkett, and I'll come down and have a look at you. We all find a pinch somewhere – it's nothing but humanity's heritage.'

*

I was born in September, and love it best of all the months.

There is no heat, no hurry, no thirst and weariness in corn harvest as there is in the hay. If the season is late, as is usual with us, then mid-September sees the corn still standing in stook. The mornings come slowly. The earth is like a woman married and fading; she does not leap up with a laugh for the first fresh kiss of dawn, but slowly, quietly, unexpectantly lies watching the waking of each new day. The blue mist, like memory in the eyes of a neglected wife, never goes from the wooded hill, and only at noon creeps from the near hedges. There is no bird to put a song in the throat of morning; only the crow's voice speaks during the day. Perhaps there is the regular breathing hush of the scythe – even the fretful jar of the mowing machine. But next day, in the morning, all is still again. The lying corn is wet, and when you have bound it, and lift the heavy sheaf to make the stook, the tresses of oats wreathe round each other and droop mournfully.

As I worked with my friend through the still mornings we talked endlessly. I would give him the gist of what I knew of chemistry, and botany, and psychology. Day after day I told him what the professors had told me; of life, of sex and its origins; of Schopenhauer and William James. We had been friends for years, and he was accustomed to my talk. But this autumn fruited the first crop of intimacy between us. I talked a great deal of poetry to him, and of rudimentary metaphysics. He was very good stuff. He had hardly a single dogma, save that of pleasing himself. Religion was nothing to him. So he heard all I had to say with an open mind, and understood the drift of things very rapidly, and quickly made these ideas part of himself.

We tramped down to dinner with only the clinging warmth of the sunshine for a coat. In this still, enfolding weather a quiet companionship is very grateful. Autumn creeps through everything. The little damsons in the pudding taste of September, and are fragrant with memory. The voices of those at table are softer and more reminiscent than at haytime.

Afternoon is all warm and golden. Oat sheaves are lighter; they whisper to each other as they freely embrace. The long, stout stubble tinkles as the foot brushes over it; the scent of the straw is sweet. When the poor, bleached sheaves are lifted out of the hedge, a spray of nodding wild raspberries is disclosed, with belated berries ready to drop; among the damp grass lush blackberries may be discovered. Then one notices that the last bell hangs from the ragged spire of foxglove. The talk is of people, an odd book; of one's hopes – and the future; of Canada, where work is strenuous, but not life; where the plains are wide, and one is not lapped in a soft valley, like an apple that falls in a secluded orchard. The mist steals over the face of the warm afternoon. The tying-up is all finished, and it only remains to rear up the fallen bundles into shocks. The sun sinks into a golden glow in the west. The gold turns to red, the red darkens, like a fire burning low, the sun disappears behind the bank of milky mist, purple like the pale bloom on blue plums, and we put on our coats and go home.

*

In the evening, when the milking was finished, and all the things fed, then we went out to look at the snares. We wandered on across the stream and up the wild hillside. Our feet rattled through black patches of devil's-bit scabious; we skirted a swim of thistle-down, which glistened when the moon touched it. We stumbled on through wet, coarse grass, over soft mole-hills and black rabbit-holes. The hills and woods cast shadows; the pools of mist in the valleys gathered the moonbeams in cold, shivery light.

We came to an old farm that stood on the level brow of the hill. The woods swept away from it, leaving a great clearing of what was once cultivated land. The handsome chimneys of the house, silhouetted against a light sky, drew my admiration. I noticed that there was no light or glow in any window, though the house had only the width of one room, and though the night was only at eight o'clock. We looked at the long, impressive front. Several of the windows had been bricked in, giving a pitiful impression of blindness; the places where the plaster had fallen off the walls showed blacker in the shadow. We pushed open the gate, and as we walked down the path weeds and dead plants brushed our ankles. We looked in at a window. The room was lighted also by a window from the other side, through which the moonlight streamed on to the flagged floor, dirty, littered with paper, and wisps of straw. The hearth lay in the light, with all its distress of grey ashes, and piled cinders of burnt paper, and a child's headless doll, charred and pitiful. On the border-line of shadow lay a round fur cap – a gamekeeper's cap. I blamed the moonlight for entering the desolate room; the dark-ness alone was decent and reticent. I hated the little roses on the illuminated piece of wallpaper, I hated that fireside.

With farmer's instinct George turned to the out-house. The cow-yard startled me. It was a forest of the tallest nettles I have ever seen – nettles far taller than my six feet. The air was sod-dened with the dank scent of nettles. As I followed George along the obscure brick path, I felt my flesh creep. But the buildings, when we entered them, were in splendid condition; they had been restored within a small number of years; they were well-timbered, neat, and cosy. Here and there we saw feathers, bits of animal wreckage, even the remnants of a cat, which we hastily examined by the light of a match. As we entered the stable there was an ugly noise, and three great rats half rushed at us and threatened us with their vicious teeth. I shuddered, and hurried back, stumbling over a bucket, rotten with rust, and so filled with weeds that I thought it part of the jungle. There was a silence made horrible by the faint noises that rats and flying bats give out. The place was bare of any vestige of corn or straw or hay, only choked with a growth of abnormal weeds. When I found myself free in the orchard I could not stop shivering. There were no apples to be seen overhead between us and the clear sky. Either the birds had caused them to fall, when the rab-bits had devoured them, or someone had gathered the crop.

'This,' said George bitterly, 'is what the mill will come to.'

'After your time,' I said.

'My time – my time. I shall never have a time. And I shouldn't be surprised if father's time isn't short – with rabbits and one thing and another. As it is, we depend on the milk-round, and on the carting which I do for the council. You can't call it farm-ing. We're a miserable mixture of farmer, milkman, green-grocer, and carting contractor. It's a shabby business.'

'You have to live,' I retorted.

'Yes – but it's rotten. And father won't move – and he won't change his methods.'

'Well – what about you?'

'Me! What should I change for? – I'm comfortable at home. As for my future, it can look after itself, so long as nobody depends on me.'

'*Laissez faire*,' I said, smiling.

'This is no *laissez faire*,' he replied, glancing round, 'this is pulling the nipple out of your lips, and letting the milk run away sour. Look there!'

Through the thin veil of moonlit mist that slid over the hillside we could see an army of rabbits bunched up, or hopping a few paces forward, feeding.

We set off at a swinging pace down the hill, scattering the hosts. As we approached the fence that bounded the Mill fields, he exclaimed, 'Hullo!' – and hurried forward. I followed him, and observed the dark figure of a man rise from the hedge. It was a game-keeper. He pretended to be examining his gun. As we came up he greeted us with a calm 'Good evenin'!'

George replied by investigating the little gap in the hedge.

'I'll trouble you for that snare,' he said.

'Will yer?' answered Annable, a broad, burly, black-faced fellow. 'An' *I* should like ter know what you're doin' on th' wrong side th' 'edge?'

'You can see what we're doing – hand over my snare – *and* the rabbit,' said George angrily.

'What rabbit?' said Annable, turning sarcastically to me.

'You know well enough – an' you can hand it over – or –' George replied.

'Or what? Spit it out! The sound won't kill me' – the man grinned with contempt.

'Hand over here!' said George, stepping up to the man in a rage.

'Now don't!' said the keeper, standing stock still, and looking unmovedly at the proximity of George:

'You'd better get off home – both you an' 'im. You'll get neither snare nor rabbit – see!'

'We *will* see!' said George, and he made a sudden move to get hold of the man's coat. Instantly he went staggering back with a heavy blow under the left ear.

'Damn brute!' I ejaculated, bruising my knuckles against the fellow's jaw. Then I too found myself sitting dazedly on the grass, watching the great skirts of his velveteens flinging round him as if he had been a demon, as he strode away. I got up, pressing my chest where I had been struck. George was lying in the hedge-bottom. I turned him over, and rubbed his temples, and shook the drenched grass on his face. He opened his eyes, and looked at me, dazed. Then he drew his breath quickly, and put his hand to his head.

'He – he nearly stunned me,' he said.

'The devil!' I answered.

'I wasn't ready.'

'No.'

'Did he knock me down?'

'Ay – me too.'

He was silent for some time, sitting limply. Then he pressed his hand against the back of his head, saying, 'My head does sing!' He tried to get up, but failed. 'Good God! – being knocked into this state by a damned keeper!'

'Come on,' I said, 'let's see if we can't get indoors.'

'No!' he said quickly, 'we needn't tell them – don't let them know.'

I sat thinking of the pain in my own chest, and wishing I could remember hearing Annable's jaw smash, and wishing that my knuckles were more bruised than they were – though that was bad enough. I got up, and helped George to rise. He swayed, almost pulling me over. But in a while he could walk unevenly.

'Am I,' he said, 'covered with clay and stuff?'

'Not much,' I replied, troubled by the shame and confusion with which he spoke.

'Get it off,' he said, standing still to be cleaned.

I did my best. Then we walked about the fields for a time, gloomy, silent, and sore.

Suddenly, as we went by the pond-side, we were startled by great, swishing black shadows that swept just above our heads. The swans were flying up for shelter, now that a cold wind had begun to fret Nethermere. They swung down on to the glassy mill-pond, shaking the moonlight in flecks across the deep shadows; the night rang with the clacking of their wings on the water; the stillness and calm were broken; the moonlight was furrowed and scattered, and broken. The swans, as they sailed into shadow, were dim, haunting spectres; the wind found us shivering.

'Don't – you won't say anything?' he asked as I was leaving him.

'No.'

'Nothing at all – not to anybody?'

'No.'

'Good night.'

*

About the end of September, our countryside was alarmed by the harrying of sheep by strange dogs. One morning, the squire, going the round of his fields as was his custom, to his grief and horror found two of his sheep torn and dead in the hedge-bottom, and the rest huddled in a corner swaying about in terror, smeared with blood. The squire did not recover his spirits for days.

There was a report of two grey wolvish dogs. The squire's keeper had heard yelping in the fields of Dr Collins, of the Abbey, about dawn. Three sheep lay soaked in blood when the labourer went to tend the flocks.

Then the farmers took alarm. Lord, of the White House farm, intended to put his sheep in pen, with his dogs in charge. It was Saturday, however, and the lads ran off to the little travelling theatre that had halted at Westwold. While they sat open-mouthed in the theatre, gloriously nicknamed the 'Blood-Tub', watching heroes die with much writhing, and heaving, and struggling up to say a word, and collapsing without having said it, six of their silly sheep were slaughtered in the field. At every house it was inquired of the dog; nowhere had one been loose.

Mr Saxton had some thirty sheep on the Common. George determined that the easiest thing was for him to sleep out with them. He built a shelter of hurdles interlaced with brushwood, and in the sunny afternoon we collected piles of bracken, browning to the ruddy winter-brown now. He slept there for a week, but that week aged his mother like a year. She was out in the cold morning twilight watching, with her apron over her head, for his approach. She did not rest with the thought of him out on the Common.

Therefore, on Saturday night he brought down his rugs, and took up Gyp to watch in his stead. For some time we sat looking at the stars over the dark hills. Now and then a sheep coughed, or a rabbit rustled beneath the brambles, and Gyp whined. The mist crept over the gorse-bushes, and the webs on the brambles were white; – the devil throws his net over the blackberries as soon as September's back is turned, they say.

'I saw two fellows go by with bags and nets,' said George, as we sat looking out of his little shelter.

'Poachers,' said I. 'Did you speak to them?'

'No – they didn't see me. I was dropping asleep when a rabbit rushed under the blanket, all of a shiver, and a whippet dog after it. I gave the whippet a punch in the neck, and he yelped off. The rabbit stopped with me quite a long time – then it went.'

'How did you feel?'

'I didn't care. I don't care much what happens just now. Father could get along without me, and mother has the children. I think I shall emigrate.'

'Why didn't you before?'

'Oh, I don't know. There are a lot of little comforts and interests at home that one would miss. Besides, you feel somebody in your own countryside, and you're nothing in a foreign part, I expect.'

'But you're going?'

'What is there to stop here for? The valley is all running wild and unprofitable. You've no freedom for thinking of what the other folks think of you, and everything round you keeps the same, and so you can't change yourself – because everything you look at brings up the same old feeling, and stops you from feeling fresh things. And what is there that's worth anything? – What's worth having in my life?'

'I thought,' said I, 'your comfort was worth having.'

He sat still and did not answer.

'What's shaken you out of your nest?' I asked.

'I don't know. I've not felt the same since that row with Annable. And Lettie said to me: "Here, you can't live as you like – in any way or circumstance. You're like a bit out of those coloured marble mosaics in the hall, you have to fit in your own set, fit into your own pattern, because you're put there from the first. But you don't want to be like a fixed bit of a mosaic – you want to fuse into life, and melt and mix with the rest of folk, to have some things burned out of you –" She was downright serious.'

'Well, you need not believe her. When did you see her?'

'She came down on Wednesday, when I was getting the apples in the morning. She climbed a tree with me, and there was a wind, that was why I was getting all the apples, and it rocked us, me right up at the top, she sitting half way down holding the basket. I asked her didn't she think that free kind of life was the best, and that was how she answered me. '

'You should have contradicted her.'

'It seemed true. I never thought of it being wrong, in fact.'

'Come – that sounds bad.'

'No – I thought she looked down on us – on our way of life. I thought she meant I was like a toad in a hole.'

'You should have shown her different.'

'How could I when I could see no different?'

'It strikes me you're in love.'

He laughed at the idea, saying, 'No, but it is rotten to find that there isn't a single thing you have to be proud of.'

'This is a new tune for you.'

He pulled the grass moodily.

'And when do you think of going?'

'Oh – I don't know – I've said nothing to mother. Not yet – at any rate not till spring.'

'Not till something has happened,' said I.

'What?' he asked.

'Something decisive.'

'I don't know what can happen – unless the Squire turns us out.'

'No?' I said.

He did not speak.

'You should make things happen,' said I.

'Don't make me feel a worse fool, Cyril,' he replied despairingly.

Gyp whined and jumped, tugging her chain to follow us.

The grey blurs among the blackness of the bushes were resting sheep. A chill, dim mist crept along the ground.

'But, for all that, Cyril,' he said, 'to have her laugh at you across the table; to hear her sing as she moves about, before you are washed at night, when the fire's warm, and you're tired; to have her sit by you on the hearth seat, close and soft ...'

'In Spain,' I said. 'In Spain.'

He took no notice, but turned suddenly, laughing.

'Do you know, when I was stooking up, lifting the sheaves, it felt like having your arm round a girl. It was quite a sudden sensation.'

'You'd better take care,' said I, 'you'll mesh yourself in the silk of dreams, and then –'

He laughed, not having heard my words.

'The time seems to go like lightning – thinking,' he confessed – 'I seem to sweep the mornings up in a handful.'

'Oh, Lord!' said I. 'Why don't you scheme for getting what you want, instead of dreaming fulfilments?'

'Well,' he replied. 'If it was a fine dream, wouldn't you want to go on dreaming?' and with that he finished, and I went home.

I sat at my window looking out, trying to get things straight. Mist rose, and wreathed round Nethermere, like ghosts meeting and embracing sadly. I thought of the time when my friend should not follow the harrow on our own snug valley side, and when Lettie's room next mine should be closed to hide its emptiness, not its joy. My heart clung passionately to the hollow which held us all; how could I bear that it should be desolate! I wondered what Lettie would do.

In the morning I was up early, when daybreak came with a shiver through the woods. I went out, while the moon still shone sickly in the west. The world shrank from the morning. It was then that the last of the summer things died. The wood was dark – and smelt damp and heavy with autumn. On the paths the leaves lay clogged.

As I came near the farm I heard the yelling of dogs. Running, I reached the Common, and saw the sheep huddled and scattered in groups, something leaped round them. George burst

into sight pursuing. Directly, there was the bang, bang of a
gun. I picked up a heavy piece of sandstone and ran forwards.
Three sheep scattered wildly before me. In the dim light I saw
their grey shadows move among the gorse bushes. Then a dog
leaped, and I flung my stone with all my might. I hit. There
came a high-pitched howling yelp of pain; I saw the brute make
off, and went after him, dodging the prickly bushes, leaping
the trailing brambles. The gunshots rang out again, and I heard
the men shouting with excitement. My dog was out of sight, but
I followed still, slanting down the hill. In a field ahead I saw
someone running. Leaping the low hedge, I pursued, and over-
took Emily, who was hurrying as fast as she could through the
wet grass. There was another gunshot and great shouting. Emily
glanced round, saw me, and started.

'It's gone to the quarries,' she panted. We walked on, without saying a word. Skirting the spinney, we followed the brook
course, and came at last to the quarry fence. The old excavations
were filled now with trees. The steep walls, twenty feet deep
in places, were packed with loose stones, and trailed with hanging brambles. We climbed down the steep bank of the brook,
and entered the quarries by the bed of the stream. Under the
groves of ash and oak a pale primrose still lingered, glimmering
wanly beside the hidden water. Emily found a smear of blood
on a beautiful trail of yellow convolvulus. We followed the tracks
on to the open, where the brook flowed on the hard rock bed,
and the stony floor of the quarry was only a tangle of gorse and
bramble and honeysuckle.

'Take a good stone,' said I, and we pressed on, where the
grove in the great excavation darkened again, and the brook
slid secretly under the arms of the bushes and the hair of the
long grass. We beat the cover almost to the road. I thought
the brute had escaped, and I pulled a bunch of mountain-ash
berries, and stood tapping them against my knee. I was startled
by a snarl and a little scream. Running forward, I came upon
one of the old, horse-shoe lime kilns that stood at the head of
the quarry. There, in the mouth of one of the kilns, Emily was
kneeling on the dog, her hands buried in the hair of its throat,
pushing back its head. The little jerks of the brute's body were
the spasms of death; already the eyes were turning inward,

and the upper lip was drawn from the teeth by pain.

'Good Lord, Emily! But he is dead!' I exclaimed.

'Has he hurt you?' I drew her away. She shuddered violently, and seemed to feel a horror of herself.

'No – no,' she said, looking at herself, with blood all on her skirt, where she had knelt on the wound which I had given the dog, and pressed the broken rib into the chest. There was a trickle of blood on her arm.

'Did he bite you?' I asked, anxious.

'No – oh, no – I just peeped in, and he jumped. But he had no strength, and I hit him back with my stone, and I lost my balance, and fell on him.'

'Let me wash your arm.'

'Oh!' she exclaimed, 'isn't it horrible! Oh, I think it is so awful.'

'What?' said I, busy bathing her arm in the cold water of the brook.

'This – this whole brutal affair.'

'It ought to be cauterized,' said I, looking at a score on her arm from the dog's tooth.

'That scratch – that's nothing! Can you get that off my skirt – I feel hateful to myself.'

I washed her skirt with my handkerchief as well as I could, saying:

'Let me just sear it for you; we can go to the Kennels. Do – you ought – I don't feel safe otherwise.'

'Really,' she said, glancing up at me, a smile coming into her fine dark eyes.

'Yes – come along.'

'Ha, ha!' she laughed. 'You look so serious.'

I took her arm, and drew her away. She linked her arm in mine, and leaned on me.

'It is just like Lorna Doone,' she said, as if she enjoyed it.

'But you will let me do it,' said I, referring to the cauterizing.

'You make me; but I shall feel – ugh, I daren't think of it. Get me some of those berries.'

I plucked a few bunches of guelder-rose fruits, transparent, ruby berries. She stroked them softly against her lips and cheek, caressing them. Then she murmured to herself:

'I have always wanted to put red berries in my hair.'

The shawl she had been wearing was thrown across her shoulders, and her head was bare, and her black hair, soft and short and ecstatic, tumbled wildly into loose light curls. She thrust the stalks of the berries under her combs. Her hair was not heavy or long enough to have held them. Then, with the ruby bunches glowing through the black mist of curls, she looked up at me, brightly, with wide eyes. I looked at her, and felt the smile winning into her eyes. Then I turned and dragged a trail of golden-leaved convolvulus from the hedge, and I twisted it into a coronet for her.

'There!' said I, 'you're crowned.'

She put back her head, and the low laughter shook in her throat.

'What?' she asked, putting all the courage and recklessness she had into the question, and in her soul trembling.

'Not Chloe, not Bacchante. You have always got your soul in your eyes, such an earnest, troublesome soul.'

The laughter faded at once, and her great seriousness looked out again at me, pleading.

'You are like Burne-Jones' damsels. Troublesome shadows are always crowding across your eyes, and you cherish them. You think the flesh of the apple is nothing, nothing. You only care for the eternal pips. Why don't you snatch your apple and eat it, and throw the core away?'

She looked at me sadly, not understanding, but believing that I in my wisdom spoke truth, as she always believed when I lost her in a maze of words. She stooped down, and the chaplet fell from her hair, and only one bunch of berries remained. The ground around us was strewn with the four-lipped burrs of beechnuts, and the quaint little nut-pyramids were scattered among the ruddy fallen leaves. Emily gathered a few nuts.

'I love beechnuts,' she said. 'but they make me long for my childhood again till I could almost cry out. To go out for beechnuts before breakfast; to thread them for necklaces before supper; – to be the envy of the others at school next day! There was as much pleasure in a beech necklace then, as there is in the whole autumn now – and no sadness. There are no more unmixed joys after you have grown up.' She kept her face to the ground as she spoke, and she continued to gather the fruits.

'Do you find any with nuts in?' I asked.

'Not many – here – here are two, three. You have them. No – I don't care about them.'

I stripped one of its horny brown coat and gave it to her. She opened her mouth slightly to take it, looking up into my eyes. Some people, instead of bringing with them clouds of glory, trail clouds of sorrow; they are born with 'the gift of sorrow'; 'sorrows' they proclaim 'alone are real. The veiled grey angels of sorrow work out slowly the beautiful shapes. Sorrow is beauty, and the supreme blessedness.' You read it in their eyes, and in the tones of their voices. Emily had the gift of sorrow. It fascinated me, but it drove me to rebellion.

We followed the soft, smooth-bitten turf road under the old beeches. The hillside fell away, dishevelled with thistles and coarse grass. Soon we were in sight of the Kennels, the red old Kennels which had been the scene of so much animation in the time of Lord Byron. They were empty now, overgrown with weeds. The barred windows of the cottage were grey with dust; there was no need now to protect the windows from cattle, dog or man. One of the three houses was inhabited. Clear water trickled through a wooden runnel into a great stone trough outside near the door.

'Come here,' said I to Emily. 'Let me fasten the back of your dress.'

'Is it undone?' she asked, looking quickly over her shoulder, and blushing.

As I was engaged in my task, a girl came out of the cottage with a black kettle and a tea-cup. She was so surprised to see me thus occupied, that she forgot her own duty, and stood open-mouthed.

'S'r Ann! S'r Ann,' called a voice from inside. 'Are ter goin' ter come in an' shut that door?'

Sarah Ann hastily poured a few cupfuls of water into the kettle, then she put down both utensils, and stood holding her bare arms to warm them. Her chief garment consisted of a grey bodice and red flannel skirt, very much torn. Her black hair hung in wild tails on to her shoulders.

'We must go in here,' said I, approaching the girl. She, however, hastily seized the kettle and ran indoors with an 'Oh, mother –!'

A woman came to the door. One breast was bare, and hung over her blouse, which, like a dressing-jacket, fell loose over her skirt. Her fading, red-brown hair was all frowsy from the bed. In the folds of her skirt clung a swarthy urchin with a shockingly short shirt. He stared at us with big black eyes, the only portion of his face undecorated with egg and jam. The woman's blue eyes questioned us languidly. I told her our errand.

'Come in – come in,' she said, 'but dunna look at th' 'ouse. Th' childers not been long up. Go in, Billy, wi' nowt on!'

We entered, taking the forgotten kettle lid. The kitchen was large, but scantily furnished; save, indeed, for children. The eldest, a girl of twelve or so, was standing toasting a piece of bacon with one hand, and holding back her nightdress in the other. As the toast hand got scorched, she transferred the bacon to the other, gave the hot fingers a lick to cool them, and then held back her nightdress again. Her auburn hair hung in heavy coils down her gown. A boy sat on the steel fender, catching the dropping fat on a piece of bread. 'One, two, three, four, five, six drops,' and he quickly bit off the tasty corner, and resumed the task with the other hand. When we entered he tried to draw his shirt over his knees, which caused the fat to fall wasted. A fat baby, evidently laid down from the breast, lay kicking on the squab, purple in the face, while another lad was pushing bread and butter into its mouth. The mother swept to the sofa, poked out the bread and butter, pushed her finger into the baby's throat, lifted the child up, punched its back, and was highly relieved when it began to yell. Then she administered a few sound spanks to the naked buttocks of the crammer. He began to howl, but stopped suddenly on seeing us laughing. On the sack-cloth which served as hearth-rug sat a beautiful child washing the face of a wooden doll with tea, and wiping it on her nightgown. At the table, an infant in a high chair sat sucking a piece of bacon, till the grease ran down his swarthy arms, oozing through his fingers. An older lad stood in the big arm-chair, whose back was hung with a calf-skin, and was industriously pouring the dregs of the teacups into a basin of milk. The mother whisked away the milk, and made a rush for the urchin, the baby hanging over her arm the while.

'I could half kill thee,' she said, but he had slid under the table – and sat serenely unconcerned.

'Could you' – I asked when the mother had put her bonny baby again to her breast – 'could you lend me a knitting needle?'

'Our S'r Ann, wheer's thy knittin' needles?' asked the woman, wincing at the same time, and putting her hand to the mouth of the sucking child. Catching my eye, she said:

'You wouldn't credit how he bites. 'E's nobbut two teeth, but they like six needles.' She drew her brows together, and pursed her lips, saying to the child, 'Naughty lad, naughty lad! Tha' shanna hae it, no, not if ter bites thy mother like that.'

The family interest was now divided between us and the private concerns in process when we entered; – save, however, that the bacon sucker had sucked on stolidly, immovable, all the time.

'Our Sam, wheer's my knittin', tha's 'ad it?' cried S'r Ann after a little search.

''A 'e na,' replied Sam from under the table.

'Yes, tha' 'as,' said the mother, giving a blind prod under the table with her foot.

''A 'e na then!' persisted Sam.

The mother suggested various possible places of discovery, and at last the knitting was found at the back of the table drawer, among forks and old wooden skewers.

'I 'an ter tell yer wheer ivrythink is,' said the mother in mild reproach. S'r Ann, however, gave no heed to her parent. Her heart was torn for her knitting, the fruit of her labours; it was a red woollen cuff for the winter; a corkscrew was bored through the web, and the ball of red wool was bristling with skewers.

'It's a' thee, our Sam,' she wailed. 'I know it's a' thee an' thy A. B. C.'

Samuel, under the table, croaked out in a voice of fierce monotony:

> 'P is for Porkypine, whose bristles so strong
> Kill the bold lion by pricking 'is tongue.'

The mother began to shake with quiet laughter.

'His father learnt him that – made it all up,' she whispered proudly to us – and to him.

'Tell us what "B" is, Sam.'

'Shonna,' grunted Sam.

'Go on, there's a duckie; an' I'll ma' 'e a treacle puddin'.'

'Today?' asked S'r Ann eagerly.

'Go on, Sam, my duck,' persisted the mother.

'Tha' 'as na got no treacle,' said Sam conclusively.

The needle was in the fire; the children stood about watching.

'Will you do it yourself?' I asked Emily.

'I!' she exclaimed, with wide eyes of astonishment, and she shook her head emphatically.

'Then I must.' I took out the needle, holding it in my handkerchief. I took her hand and examined the wound. But when she saw the hot glow of the needle, she snatched away her hand, and looked into my eyes, laughing in a half-hysterical fear and shame. I was very serious, very insistent. She yielded me her hand again, biting her lips in imagination of the pain, and looking at me. While my eyes were looking into hers she had courage; when I was forced to pay attention to my cauterizing, she glanced down, and with a sharp 'Ah!' ending in a little laugh, she put her hands behind her, and looked again up at me with wide brown eyes, all quivering with apprehension, and a little shame, and a laughter that held much pleading.

One of the children began to cry.

'It is no good,' said I, throwing the fast cooling needle on to the hearth.

I gave the girls all the pennies I had – then I offered Sam, who had crept out of the shelter of the table, a sixpence.

'Shonna a'e that,' he said, turning from the small coin.

'Well – I have no more pennies, so nothing will be your share.'

I gave the other boy a rickety knife I had in my pocket. Sam looked fiercely at me. Eager for revenge, he picked up the 'porkypine quill' by the hot end. He dropped it with a shout of rage, and, seizing a cup off the table, flung it at the fortunate Jack. It smashed against the fire-place. The mother grabbed at Sam, but he was gone. A girl, a little girl, wailed, 'Oh, that's my rosey mug – my rosey mug.' We fled from the scene of confusion. Emily had hardly noticed it. Her thoughts were of herself, and of me.

'I am an awful coward,' said she humbly.

'But I can't help it –' she looked beseechingly.

'Never mind,' said I.

'All my flesh seems to jump from it. You don't know how I feel.'

'Well – never mind.'

'I couldn't help it, not for my life.'

'I wonder,' said I, 'if anything could possibly disturb that young bacon-sucker? He didn't even look round at the smash.'

'No,' said she, biting the tip of her finger moodily.

Further conversation was interrupted by howls from the rear. Looking round we saw Sam careering after us over the close-bitten turf, howling scorn and derision at us. 'Rabbit-tail, rabbit-tail,' he cried, his bare little legs twinkling, and his little shirt fluttering in the cold morning air. Fortunately, at last he trod on a thistle or a thorn, for when we looked round again to see why he was silent, he was capering on one leg, holding his wounded foot in his hands.

CHAPTER VII

Lettie Pulls Down the Small Gold Grapes

DURING the falling of the leaves Lettie was very wilful. She uttered many banalities concerning men, and love, and marriage; she taunted Leslie and thwarted his wishes. At last he stayed away from her. She had been several times down to the mill, but because she fancied they were very familiar, receiving her on to their rough plane like one of themselves, she stayed away. Since the death of our father she had been restless; since inheriting her little fortune she had become proud, scornful, difficult to please. Difficult to please in every circumstance; she, who had always been so rippling in thoughtless life, sat down in the window sill to think, and her strong teeth bit at her handkerchief till it was torn in holes. She would say nothing to me; she read all things that dealt with modern woman.

One afternoon Lettie walked over to Eberwich. Leslie had not been to see us for a fortnight. It was a grey, dree afternoon. The wind drifted a clammy fog across the hills, and the roads were black and deep with mud. The trees in the wood slouched sulkily. It was a day to be shut out and ignored if possible. I heaped up the fire, and went to draw the curtains and make perfect the room. Then I saw Lettie coming along the path quickly, very erect. When she came in her colour was high.

'Tea not laid?' she said briefly.

'Rebecca has just brought in the lamp,' said I.

Lettie took off her coat and furs, and flung them on the couch. She went to the mirror, lifted her hair, all curled by the fog, and stared haughtily at herself. Then she swung round, looked at the bare table, and rang the bell.

It was so rare a thing for us to ring the bell from the dining-room, that Rebecca went first to the outer door. Then she came in the room saying:

'Did you ring?'

'I thought tea would have been ready,' said Lettie coldly. Rebecca looked at me, and at her, and replied:

'It is but half-past four. I can bring it in.'

Mother came down hearing the chink of the teacups.

'Well,' she said to Lettie, who was unlacing her boots, 'and did you find it a pleasant walk?'

'Except for the mud,' was the reply.

'Ah, I guess you wished you had stayed at home. What a state for your boots! – and your skirts too, I know. Here, let me take them into the kitchen.'

'Let Rebecca take them,' said Lettie – but mother was out of the room.

When mother had poured out the tea, we sat silently at table. It was on the tip of our tongues to ask Lettie what ailed her, but we were experienced and we refrained. After a while she said:

'Do you know, I met Leslie Tempest.'

'Oh,' said mother tentatively, 'Did he come along with you?'

'He did not look at me.'

'Oh!' exclaimed mother, and it was speaking volumes; then, after a moment, she resumed:

'Perhaps he did not see you.'

'Or was it a stony Britisher?' I asked.

'He saw me,' declared Lettie, 'or he wouldn't have made such a babyish show of being delighted with Margaret Raymond.'

'It may have been no show – he still may not have seen you.'

'I felt at once that he had; I could see his animation was extravagant. He need not have troubled himself, I was not going to run after him.'

'You seem very cross,' said I.

'Indeed I am not. But he knew I had to walk all this way home, and he could take up Margaret, who has only half the distance.'

'Was he driving?'

'In the dog-cart.' She cut her toast into strips viciously. We waited patiently.

'It was mean of him, wasn't it, mother?'

'Well, my girl, you have treated him badly.'

'What a baby! What a mean, manly baby! Men are great infants.'

'And girls,' said mother, 'do not know what they want.'

'A grown-up quality,' I added.

'Nevertheless,' said Lettie, 'he is a mean fop, and I detest him.'

She rose and sorted out some stitchery. Lettie never stitched unless she were in a bad humour. Mother smiled at me, sighed, and proceeded to Mr Gladstone for comfort; her breviary and missal were Morley's *Life of Gladstone*.

I had to take a letter to Highclose to Mrs Tempest – from my mother, concerning a bazaar in process at the church. 'I will bring Leslie back with me,' said I to myself.

The night was black and hateful. The lamps by the road from Eberwich ended at Nethermere; their yellow blur on the water made the cold, wet inferno of the night more ugly.

Leslie and Marie were both in the library – half a library, half a business office; used also as a lounge room, being cosy. Leslie lay in a great armchair by the fire, immune among clouds of blue smoke. Marie was perched on the steps, a great volume on her knee. Leslie got up in his cloud, shook hands, greeted me curtly, and vanished again. Marie smiled me a quaint, vexed smile, saying:

'Oh, Cyril, I'm so glad you've come. I'm so worried, and Leslie says he's not a pastry cook, though I'm sure I don't want him to be, only he need not be a bear.'

'What's the matter?'

She frowned, gave the big volume a little smack and said:

'Why, I do so much want to make some of those Spanish tartlets of your mother's that are so delicious, and of course Mabel knows nothing of them, and they're not in my cookery book, and I've looked through page upon page of the encyclopedia, right through "Spain", and there's nothing yet, and there are fifty pages more, and Leslie won't help me, though I've got a headache, because he's frabous about something.' She looked at me in comical despair.

'Do you want them for the bazaar?'

'Yes – for tomorrow. Cook has done the rest, but I had fairly set my heart on these. Don't you think they are lovely?'

'Exquisitely lovely. Suppose I go and ask mother.'

'If you would. But no, oh no, you can't make all that journey this terrible night. We are simply besieged by mud. The men are both out – William has gone to meet father – and mother has sent George to carry some things to the vicarage. I can't ask one of the girls on a night like this. I shall have to let it go – and the cranberry tarts too – it cannot be helped. I am so miserable.'

'Ask Leslie,' said I.

'He is too cross,' she replied, looking at him.

He did not deign a remark.

'Will you, Leslie?'

'What?'

'Go across to Woodside for me?'

'What for?'

'A recipe. Do, there's a dear boy.'

'Where are the men?'

'They are both engaged – they are out.'

'Send a girl, then.'

'At night like this? Who would go?'

'Cissy.'

'I shall not ask her. Isn't he mean, Cyril? Men are mean.'

'I will come back,' said I. 'There is nothing at home to do. Mother is reading, and Lettie is stitching. The weather disagrees with her, as it does with Leslie.'

'But it is not fair – ' she said, looking at me softly. Then she put away the great book, and climbed down.

'Won't you go, Leslie?' she said, laying her hand on his shoulder.

'Women!' he said, rising as if reluctantly. 'There's no end to their wants and their caprices.'

'I thought he would go,' said she warmly. She ran to fetch his overcoat. He put one arm slowly in the sleeve, and then the other, but he would not lift the coat on to his shoulders.

'Well!' she said, struggling on tiptoe, 'You are a great creature! Can't you get it on, naughty child?'

'Give her a chair to stand on,' he said.

She shook the collar of the coat sharply, but he stood like a sheep, impassive.

'Leslie, you are too bad. I can't get it on, you stupid boy.'

I took the coat and jerked it on.

'There,' she said, giving him his cap. 'Now don't be long.'

'What a damned dirty night!' said he, when we were out.

'It is,' said I.

'The town, anywhere's better than this hell of a country.'

'Ha! How did you enjoy yourself?'

He began a long history of three days in the metropolis. I listened, and heard little. I heard more plainly the cry of some night birds over Nethermere, and the peevish, wailing, yarling cry of some beast in the wood. I was thankful to slam the door behind me, to stand in the light of the hall.

'Leslie!' exclaimed mother, 'I am glad to see you.'

'Thank you,' he said, turning to Lettie, who sat with her lap full of work, her head busily bent.

'You see I can't get up,' she said, giving him her hand, adorned as it was by the thimble. 'How nice of you to come! We did not know you were back.'

'But!' he exclaimed, then he stopped.

'I suppose you enjoyed yourself,' she went on calmly.

'Immensely, thanks.'

Snap, snap, snap; went her needle through the new stuff. Then, without looking up, she said:

'Yes, no doubt. You have the air of a man who has been enjoying himself.'

'How do you mean?'

'A kind of guilty – or shall I say embarrassed – look. Don't you notice it, mother?'

'I do!' said my mother.

'I suppose it means we may not ask him questions,' Lettie concluded, always very busily sewing.

He laughed. She had broken her cotton, and was trying to thread the needle again.

'What have you been doing this miserable weather?' he inquired awkwardly.

'Oh, we have sat at home desolate. "Ever of thee I'm fo-o-ondly dreeaming" – and so on. Haven't we, mother?'

'Well,' said mother, 'I don't know. We imagined him all sorts of lions up there.'

'What a shame we may not ask him to roar his old roars over for us,' said Lettie.

'What are they like?' he asked.

'How should I know? Like a sucking dove, to judge from
your present voice. "A monstrous little voice".'

He laughed uncomfortably.

She went on sewing, suddenly beginning to sing to herself:

> 'Pussy cat, Pussy cat, where have you been?
> I've been up to London to see the fine queen:
> Pussy cat, Pussy cat, what did you there
> I frightened a little mouse under a stair.'

'I suppose,' she added, 'that may be so. Poor mouse! – But
I guess she's none the worse. You did not see the queen,
though?'

'She was not in London,' he replied, sarcastically.

'You don't –' she said, taking two pins from between her
teeth. 'I suppose you don't mean by that, she was in Eberwich
– your queen?'

'I don't know where she was,' he answered angrily.

'Oh!' she said, very sweetly, 'I thought perhaps you had
met her in Eberwich. When did you come back?'

'Last night,' he replied.

'Oh – why didn't you come and see us before?'

'I've been at the offices all day.'

'I've been up to Eberwich,' she said innocently.

'Have you!'

'Yes. And I feel so cross because of it. I thought I might
see you. I felt as if you were at home.'

She stitched a little, and glanced up secretly to watch his face
redden, then she continued innocently, 'Yes – I felt you had
come back. It is funny how one has a feeling occasionally that
someone is near; when it is someone one has a sympathy with.'
She continued to stitch, then she took a pin from her bosom,
and fixed her work, all without the least suspicion of guile.

'I thought I might meet you when I was out –' another pause,
another fixing, a pin to be taken from her lips – 'but I didn't.'

'I was at the office till rather late,' he said quickly.

She stitched away calmly, provokingly.

She took the pin from her mouth again, fixed down a fold
of stuff, and said softly:

'You little liar.'

Mother had gone out of the room for her recipe book.

He sat on his chair dumb with mortification. She stitched swiftly and unerringly. There was silence for some moments. Then he spoke:

'I did not know you wanted me for the pleasure of plucking this crow,' he said.

'I wanted you!' she exclaimed, looking up for the first time, 'Who said I wanted you?'

'No one. If you didn't want me I may as well go.'

The sound of stitching alone broke the silence for some moments, then she said deliberately:

'What made you think I wanted you?'

'I don't care a damn whether you wanted me, or whether you didn't.'

'It seems to upset you! And don't use bad language. It is the privilege of those near and dear to one.'

'That's why you begin it, I suppose.'

'I cannot remember –' she said, loftily.

He laughed sarcastically.

'Well – if you're so beastly cut up about it –' He put this tentatively, expecting the soft answer. But she refused to speak, and went on stitching. He fidgeted about, twisted his cap uncomfortably, and sighed. At last he said:

'Well – you – have we done then?'

She had the vast superiority, in that she was engaged in ostentatious work. She could fix the cloth, regard it quizzically, re-arrange it, settle down and begin to sew before she replied. This humbled him. At last she said:

'I thought so this afternoon.'

'But, good God, Lettie, can't you drop it?'

'And then?' – the question startled him.

'Why! – forget it,' he replied.

'Well?' – she spoke softly, gently. He answered to the call like an eager hound. He crossed quickly to her side as she sat sewing, and said, in a low voice:

'You do care something for me, don't you, Lettie?'

'Well,' – it was modulated kindly, a sort of promise of assent.

'You have treated me rottenly, you know, haven't you? You know I – well, I care a good bit.'

'It is a queer way of showing it.' Her voice was now a gentle reproof, the sweetest of surrenders and forgiveness. He leaned forward, took her face in his hands, and kissed her, murmuring:

'You are a little tease.'

She laid her sewing in her lap, and looked up.

*

The next day, Sunday, broke wet and dreary. Breakfast was late, and about ten o'clock we stood at the window looking upon the impossibility of our going to church.

There was a driving drizzle of rain, like a dirty curtain before the landscape. The nasturtium leaves by the garden walk had gone rotten in a frost, and the gay green discs had given place to the first black flags of winter, hung on flaccid stalks, pinched at the neck. The grass plot was strewn with fallen leaves, wet and brilliant: scarlet splashes of Virginia creeper, golden drift from the limes, ruddy brown shawls under the beeches, and away back in the corner, the black mat of maple leaves, heavy soddened; they ought to have been a vivid lemon colour. Occasionally one of these great black leaves would loose its hold, and zigzag down, staggering in the dance of death.

'There now!' said Lettie suddenly.

I looked up in time to see a crow close his wings and clutch the topmost bough of an old grey holly tree on the edge of the clearing. He flapped again, recovered his balance, and folded himself up in black resignation to the detestable weather.

'Why has the old wretch settled just over our noses,' said Lettie petulantly. 'Just to blot the promise of a sorrow.'

'Yours or mine?' I asked.

'He is looking at me, I declare.'

'You can see the wicked pupil of his eye at this distance,' I insinuated.

'Well,' she replied, determined to take this omen unto herself. 'I saw him first.

> One for sorrow, two for joy,
>   Three for a letter, four for a boy,
>   Five for silver, six for gold,
>   And seven for a secret never told.

– You may bet he's only a messenger in advance. There'll be three more shortly, and you'll have your four,' said I, comforting.

'Do you know,' she said, 'it is very funny, but whenever I've particularly noticed one crow, I've had some sorrow or other.'

'And when you notice four?' I asked.

'You should have heard old Mrs Wagstaffe,' was her reply. 'She declares an old crow croaked in their apple tree every day for a week before Jerry got drowned.'

'Great sorrow for her,' I remarked.

'Oh, but she wept abundantly. I felt like weeping too, but somehow I laughed. She hoped he had gone to heaven – but – I'm sick of that word "but" – it is always tangling one's thoughts.'

'But, Jerry!' I insisted.

'Oh, she lifted up her forehead, and the tears dripped off her nose. He must have been an old nuisance, Syb. I can't understand why women marry such men. I felt downright glad to think of the drunken old wretch toppling into the canal out of the way.'

She pulled the thick curtain across the window, and nestled down in it, resting her cheek against the edge, protecting herself from the cold window pane. The wet, grey wind shook the half-naked trees, whose leaves dripped and shone sullenly. Even the trunks were blackened, trickling with the rain which drove persistently.

Whirled down the sky like black maple leaves caught up aloft, came two more crows. They swept down and clung hold of the trees in front of the house, staying near the old forerunner. Lettie watched them, half amused, half melancholy. One bird was carried past. He swerved round and began to battle up the wind, rising higher, and rowing laboriously against the driving wet current.

'Here comes your fourth,' said I.

She did not answer but continued to watch. The bird wrestled heroically, but the wind pushed him aside, tilted him, caught him under his broad wings and bore him down. He swept in level flight down the stream, outspread and still, as if fixed in despair. I grieved for him. Sadly two of his fellows rose and were carried away after him, like souls hunting for a body to inhabit, and despairing. Only the first ghoul was left on the withered, silver-grey skeleton of the holly.

'He won't even say "Nevermore",' I remarked.

'He has more sense,' replied Lettie. She looked a trifle lugubrious. Then she continued: 'Better say "Nevermore" than "Evermore".'

'Why?' I asked.

'Oh, I don't know. Fancy this "Evermore".'

She had been sure in her own soul that Leslie would come – now she began to doubt: – things were very perplexing.

The bell in the kitchen jangled; she jumped up. I went and opened the door. He came in. She gave him one bright look of satisfaction. He saw it, and understood.

'Helen has got some people over – I have been awfully rude to leave them now,' he said quietly.

'What a dreadful day!' said mother.

'Oh, fearful! Your face *is* red, Lettie! What have you been doing?'

'Looking into the fire.'

'What did you see?'

'The pictures wouldn't come plain – nothing.'

He laughed. We were silent for some time.

'You were expecting me?' he murmured.

'Yes – I knew you'd come.'

They were left alone. He came up to her and put his arm around her, as she stood with her elbow on the mantelpiece.

'You do want me,' he pleaded softly.

'Yes,' she murmured.

He held her in his arms and kissed her repeatedly, again and again, till she was out of breath and put up her hand, and gently pushed her face away.

'You are a cold little lover – you are a shy bird,' he said, laughing into her eyes. He saw her tears rise, swimming on her lids, but not falling.

'Why, my love, my darling – why!' – he put his face to hers, and took the tear on his cheek:

'I know you love me,' he said, gently, all tenderness.

'Do you know,' he murmured. 'I can positively feel the tears rising up from my heart and throat. They are quite painful gathering, my love. There – you can do anything with me.'

They were silent for some time. After a while, a rather long while, she came upstairs and found mother – and at the end of some minutes I heard my mother go to him.

I sat by my window and watched the low clouds reel and stagger past. It seemed as if everything were being swept along – I myself seem to have lost my substance, to have become detached from concrete things and the firm trodden pavement of everyday life. Onward, always onward, not knowing where, nor why, the wind, the clouds, the rain and the birds and the leaves, everything whirling along – why?

All this time the old crow sat motionless, though the clouds tumbled, and were rent and piled, though the trees bent, and the window-pane shivered with running water. Then I found it had ceased to rain; that there was a sickly yellow gleam of sunlight, brightening on some great elm-leaves near at hand till they looked like ripe lemons hanging. The crow looked at me – I was certain he looked at me.

'What do you think of it all?' I asked him.

He eyed me with contempt, great featherless, half-winged bird as I was, incomprehensible, contemptible, but awful. I believe he hated me.

'But,' said I, 'if a raven could answer, why won't you?'

He looked wearily away. Nevertheless my gaze disquieted him. He turned uneasily; he rose, waved his wings as if for flight, then settled defiantly down again.

'You are no good,' said I, 'you won't help even with a word.'

He sat stolidly unconcerned. Then I heard the lapwings in the meadow crying, crying. They seemed to seek the storm, yet to rail at it. They wheeled in the wind, yet never ceased to complain of it. They enjoyed the struggle, and lamented it in wild lament, through which came a sound of exultation. All the lapwings cried, cried the same tale, 'Bitter, bitter, the struggle – for nothing, nothing, nothing,' – and all the time they swung about on their broad wings, revelling.

'There,' said I to the crow, 'they try it, and find it bitter, but they wouldn't like to miss it, to sit still like you, you old corpse.'

He could not endure this. He rose in defiance, flapped his wings, and launched off, uttering one 'Caw' of sinister foreboding. He was soon whirled away.

I discovered that I was very cold, so I went downstairs.

Twisting a curl round his finger, one of those loose curls that always dance free from the captured hair, Leslie said:

'Look how fond your hair is of me; look how it twines round my finger. Do you know, your hair – the light in it is like – oh – buttercups in the sun.'

'It is like me – it won't be kept in bounds,' she replied.

'Shame if it were – like this, it brushes my face – so – and sets me tingling like music.'

'Behave! Now be still, and I'll tell you what sort of music you make.'

'Oh – well – tell me.'

'Like the calling of throstles and blackies, in the evening, frightening the pale little wood-anemones, till they run panting and swaying right up to our wall. Like the ringing of bluebells when the bees are at them; like Hippomenes, out-of-breath, laughing because he'd won.'

He kissed her with rapturous admiration.

'Marriage music, sir,' she added.

'What golden apples did I throw?' he asked lightly.

'What!' she exclaimed, half mocking.

'This Atlanta,' he replied, looking lovingly upon her, 'this Atlanta – I believe she just lagged at last on purpose.'

'You have it,' she cried, laughing, submitting to his caresses. 'It was you – the apples of your firm heels – the apples of your eyes – the apples Eve bit – that won me – hein!'

'That was it – you are clever, you are rare. And I've won, won the ripe apples of your cheeks, and your breasts, and your very fists – they can't stop me – and – and – all your roundness and warmness and softness – I've won you, Lettie.'

She nodded wickedly, saying:

'All those – those – yes.'

'All – she admits it – everything!'

'Oh! – but let me breathe. Did you claim everything?'

'Yes, and you gave it me.'

'Not yet. Everything though?'

'Every atom.'

'But – now you look –'

'Did I look aside?'

'With the inward eye. Suppose now we were two angels –'

'Oh, dear – a sloppy angel!'

'Well – don't interrupt now – suppose I were one – like the "Blessed Damosel".'

'With a warm bosom –!'

'Don't be foolish, now – I a "Blessed Damosel" and you kicking the brown beech leaves below thinking –'

'What *are* you driving at?'

'Would you be thinking – thoughts like prayers?'

'What on earth do you ask that for? Oh – I think I'd be cursing – eh?'

'No – saying fragrant prayers – that your thin soul might mount up –'

'Hang thin souls, Lettie! I'm not one of your souly sort. I can't stand Pre-Raphaelities. You – You're not a Burne-Jonesess — you're an Albert Moore. I think there's more in the warm touch of a soft body than in a prayer. I'll pray with kisses.'

'And when you can't?'

'I'll wait till prayer-time again. By Jove, I'd rather feel my arms full of you; I'd rather touch that red mouth – you grudger! – than sing hymns with you in any heaven.'

'I'm afraid you'll never sing hymns with me in heaven.'

'Well – I have you here – yes, I have you now.'

'Our life is but a fading dawn?'

'Liar! – Well, you called me! Besides, I don't care; *Carpe diem*, my rosebud, my fawn. There's a nice Carmen about a fawn. "Time to leave its mother, and venture into a warm embrace." Poor old Horace – I've forgotten him.'

'Then poor old Horace.'

'Ha! Ha! – Well, I shan't forget *you*. What's that queer look in your eyes?'

'What is it?'

'Nay – you tell me. You are such a tease, there's no getting to the bottom of you.'

'You can fathom the depth of a kiss –'

'I will – I will –'

After a while he asked:

'When shall we be properly engaged, Lettie?'

'Oh, wait till Christmas – till I am twenty-one.'

'Nearly three months! Why on earth –!'

'It will make no difference. I shall be able to choose thee of my own free choice then.'

'But three months!'

'I shall consider thee engaged – it doesn't matter about other people.'

'I thought we should be married in three months.'

'Ah – married in haste – . But what will your mother say?'

'Say! Oh, she'll say it's the first wise thing I've done. You'll make a fine wife, Lettie, able to entertain, and all that.'

'You will flutter brilliantly.'

'We will.'

'No – you'll be the moth – I'll paint your wings – gaudy feather-dust. Then when you lose your coloured dust, when you fly too near the light, or when you play dodge with a butterfly net – away goes my part – you can't fly – I – alas, poor me! What becomes of the feather-dust when the moth brushes his wings against a butterfly net?'

'What are you making so many words about? You don't know now, do you?'

'No – that I don't.'

'Then just be comfortable. Let me look at myself in your eyes.'

'Narcissus, Narcissus! – Do you see yourself well? Does the image flatter you? – Or is it a troubled stream, distorting your fair lineaments.'

'I can't see anything – only feel you looking – you are laughing at me – What have you behind there – what joke?'

'I – I'm thinking you're just like Narcissus – a sweet, beautiful youth.'

'Be serious – do.'

'It would be dangerous. You'd die of it, and I – I should –'

'What!'

'Be just like I am now – serious.'

He looked proudly, thinking she referred to the earnestness of her love.

*

In the wood the wind rumbled and roared hoarsely overhead, but not a breath stirred among the saddened bracken. An occasional raindrop was shaken out of the trees; I slipped on the wet paths. Black bars striped the grey tree-trunks, where water had trickled down; the bracken was overthrown, its yellow ranks broken. I slid down the steep path to the gate, out of the wood.

Armies of cloud marched in rank across the sky, heavily laden, almost brushing the gorse on the common. The wind was cold and disheartening. The ground sobbed at every step. The brook was full, swirling along, hurrying, talking to itself, in absorbed intent tones. The clouds darkened; I felt the rain. Careless of the mud, I ran, and burst into the farm kitchen.

The children were painting, and they immediately claimed my help.

'Emily – and George – are in the front room,' said the mother, quietly, for it was Sunday afternoon. I satisfied the little ones; I said a few words to the mother, and sat down to take off my clogs.

In the parlour, the father, big and comfortable, was sleeping in an arm-chair. Emily was writing at the table – she hurriedly hid her papers when I entered. George was sitting by the fire, reading. He looked up as I entered, and I loved him when he looked up at me, and as he lingered on his quiet 'Hullo!' His eyes were beautifully eloquent – as eloquent as a kiss.

We talked in subdued murmurs, because the father was asleep, opulently asleep, his tanned face as still as a brown pear against the wall. The clock itself went slowly, with languid throbs. We gathered round the fire, and talked quietly, about nothing – blissful merely in the sound of our voices, a murmured, soothing sound – a grateful, dispassionate love trio.

At last George rose, put down his book – looked at his father – and went out.

In the barn there was a sound of the pulper crunching the

turnips. The crisp strips of turnip sprinkled quietly down on to a heap of gold which grew beneath the pulper. The smell of pulped turnips, keen and sweet, brings back to me the feeling of many winter nights, when frozen hoof-prints crunch in the yard, and Orion is in the south; when a friendship was at its mystical best.

'Pulping on Sunday!' I exclaimed.

'Father didn't do it yesterday; it's his work; and I didn't notice it. You know – Father often forgets – he doesn't like to have to work in the afternoon, now.'

The cattle stirred in their stalls; the chains rattled round the posts; a cow coughed noisily. When George had finished pulping, and it was quiet enough to talk, just as he was spreading the first layers of chop and turnip and meal – in ran Emily, with her hair in silken, twining confusion, her eyes glowing – to bid us go into tea before the milking was begun. It was the custom to milk before tea on Sunday – but George abandoned it without demur – his father willed it so, and his father was master, not to be questioned on farm matters, however one disagreed.

The last day in October had been dreary enough; the night could not come too early. We had tea by lamplight, merrily, with the father radiating comfort as the lamp shone yellow light. Sunday tea was imperfect without a visitor; with me, they always declared, it was perfect. I loved to hear them say so. I smiled, rejoicing quietly into my teacup when the Father said:

'It seems proper to have Cyril here at Sunday tea, it seems natural.'

He was most loath to break the delightful bond of the lamp-lit tea-table; he looked up with a half-appealing glance when George at last pushed back his chair and said he supposed he'd better make a start.

'Ay,' said the father in a mild, conciliatory tone, 'I'll be out in a minute.'

The lamp hung against the barn-wall, softly illuminating the lower part of the building, where bits of hay and white dust lay in the hollows between the bricks, where the curled chips of turnip scattered orange gleams over the earthen floor; the lofty roof, with its swallows' nests under the tiles, was deep in shadow, and the corners were full of darkness, hiding, half hiding, the hay, the chopper, the bins. The light shone along the passages before the stalls, glistening on the moist noses of the cattle, and on the whitewash of the walls.

George was very cheerful; but I wanted to tell him my message. When he had finished the feeding, and had at last sat down to milk, I said:

'I told you Leslie Tempest was at our house when I came away.'

He sat with the bucket between his knees, his hands at the cow's udder, about to begin to milk. He looked up a question at me.

'They are practically engaged now,' I said.

He did not turn his eyes away, but he ceased to look at me. As one who is listening for a far-off noise, he sat with his eyes fixed. Then he bent his head, and leaned it against the side of the cow, as if he would begin to milk. But he did not. The cow looked round and stirred uneasily. He began to draw the milk, and then to milk mechanically. I watched the movement of his hands, listening to the rhythmic clang of the jets of milk on the bucket, as a relief. After a while the movement of his hands became slower, thoughtful – then stopped.

'She has really said yes?'

I nodded.

'And what does your mother say?'

'She is pleased.'

He began to milk again. The cow stirred uneasily, shifting her legs. He looked at her angrily, and went on milking. Then, quite upset, she shifted again, and swung her tail in his face.

'Stand still!' he shouted, striking her on the haunch. She seemed to cower like a beaten woman. He swore at her, and continued to milk. She did not yield much that night; she was very restive; he took the stool from beneath him and gave her a good blow; I heard the stool knock on her prominent hip bone. After that she stood still, but her milk soon ceased to flow.

When he stood up, he paused before he went to the next beast, and I thought he was going to talk. But just then the father came along with his bucket. He looked in the shed, and, laughing in his mature, pleasant way, said:

'So you're an onlooker today, Cyril – I thought you'd have milked a cow or two for me by now.'

'Nay,' said I, 'Sunday is a day of rest – and milking makes your hands ache.'

'You only want a bit more practice,' he said, joking in his ripe fashion. 'Why George, is that all you've got from Julia?'

'It is.'

'H'm – she's soon going dry. Julia, old lady, don't go and turn skinny.'

When he had gone, and the shed was still, the air seemed colder. I heard his good-humoured 'Stand over, old lass,' from the other shed, and the drum-beats of the first jets of milk on the pail.

'He has a comfortable time,' said George, looking savage. I laughed. He still waited.

'You really expected Lettie to have *him*,' I said.

'I suppose so,' he replied, 'then she'd made up her mind to it. It didn't matter – what she wanted – at the bottom.'

'You?' said I.

'If it hadn't been that he was a prize – with a ticket – she'd have had –'

'You!' said I.

'She was afraid – look how she turned and kept away –'

'From you?' said I.

'I should like to squeeze her till she screamed.'

'You should have gripped her before, and kept her,' said I.

'She – she's like a woman, like a cat – running to comforts – she strikes a bargain. Women are all tradesmen.'

'Don't generalize, it's no good.'

'She's like a prostitute –'

'It's banal! I believe she loves him.'

He started, and looked at me queerly. He looked quite childish in his doubt and perplexity.

'She, what –?'

'Loves him – honestly.'

'She'd 'a loved me better,' he muttered, and turned to his milking. I left him and went to talk to his father. When the latter's four beasts were finished, George's light still shone in the other shed.

I went and found him at the fifth, the last cow. When at length he had finished he put down his pail, and going over to poor Julia, stood scratching her back, and her poll, and her nose, looking into her big, startled eye and murmuring. She was afraid; she jerked her head, giving him a good blow on the cheek with her horn.

'You can't understand them,' he said sadly, rubbing his face, and looking at me with his dark, serious eyes.

'I never knew I couldn't understand them. I never thought about it – till –. But you know, Cyril, she led me on.'

I laughed at his rueful appearance.

CHAPTER VIII

The Riot of Christmas

FOR some weeks, during the latter part of November and the beginning of December, I was kept indoors by a cold. At last came a frost which cleared the air and dried the mud. On the second Saturday before Christmas the world was transformed; tall, silver and pearl-grey trees rose pale against a dim-blue sky, like trees in some rare, pale Paradise; the whole woodland was as if petrified in marble and silver and snow; the holly-leaves and long leaves of the rhododendron were rimmed and spangled with delicate tracery.

When the night came clear and bright, with a moon among the hoar-frost, I rebelled against confinement, and the house. No longer the mists and dank weather made the home dear; tonight even the glare of the distant little iron works was not visible, for the low clouds were gone, and pale stars blinked from beyond the moon.

Lettie was staying with me; Leslie was in London again. She tried to remonstrate in a sisterly fashion when I said I would go out.

'Only down to the Mill,' said I. Then she hesitated a while – said she would come too. I suppose I looked at her curiously, for she said:

'Oh – if you would rather go alone – !'

'Come – come – yes, come !' said I, smiling to myself.

Lettie was in her old animated mood. She ran, leaping over rough places, laughing, talking to herself in French. We came to the Mill. Gyp did not bark. I opened the outer door and we crept softly into the great dark scullery, peeping into the kitchen through the crack of the door.

The mother sat by the hearth, where was a big bath half full of soapy water, and at her feet, warming his bare legs at the fire, was David, who had just been bathed. The mother was gently rubbing his fine fair hair into a cloud. Mollie was combing out her brown curls, sitting by her father, who, in the fire-seat, was reading aloud in a hearty voice, with quaint precision. At the table sat Emily and George: she was quickly picking over a pile of little yellow raisins, and he, slowly, with his head sunk, was stoning the large raisins. David kept reaching forward to play with the sleepy cat – interrupting his mother's rubbing. There was no sound but the voice of the father, full of zest; I am afraid they were not all listening carefully. I clicked the latch and entered.

'Lettie!' exclaimed George.

'Cyril!' cried Emily.

'Cyril, 'ooray!' shouted David.

'Hullo, Cyril!' said Mollie.

Six large brown eyes, round with surprise, welcomed me. They overwhelmed me with questions, and made much of us. At length they were settled and quiet again.

'Yes, I am a stranger,' said Lettie, who had taken off her hat and furs and coat. 'But you do not expect me often, do you? I may come at times, eh?'

'We are only too glad,' replied the mother. 'Nothing all day long but the sound of the sluice – and mists, and rotten leaves. I am thankful to hear a fresh voice.'

'Is Cyril really better, Lettie?' asked Emily softly.

'He's a spoiled boy – I believe he keeps a little bit ill so that we can cade him. Let me help you – let me peel the apples – yes, yes – I will.'

She went to the table, and occupied one side with her apple-peeling. George had not spoken to her. So she said:

'I won't help you – George, because I don't like to feel my fingers so sticky, and because I love to see you so domesticated.'

'You'll enjoy the sight a long time, then, for these things are numberless.'

'You should eat one now and then – I always do.'

'If I ate one I should eat the lot.'

'Then you may give me your one.'

He passed her a handful without speaking.

'That is too many, your mother is looking. Let me just finish this apple. There, I've not broken the peel!'

She stood up, holding up a long curling strip of peel.

'How many times must I swing it, Mrs Saxton?'

'Three times – but it's not All Hallows' Eve.'

'Never mind! Look! –' she carefully swung the long band of green peel over her head three times, letting it fall the third. The cat pounced on it, but Mollie swept him off again.

'What is it?' cried Lettie, blushing.

'G,' said the father, winking and laughing – the mother looked daggers at him.

'It isn't nothink,' said David naively, forgetting his confusion at being in the presence of a lady in his shirt. Mollie remarked in her cool way:

'It might be a "hess" – if you couldn't write.'

'Or an "L",' I added. Lettie looked over at me imperiously, and I was angry.

'What do you say, Emily?' she asked.

'Nay,' said Emily, 'It's only you can see the right letter.'

'Tell us what's the right letter,' said George to her.

'I!' exclaimed Lettie, 'who can look into the seeds of Time?'

'Those who have set 'em and watched 'em sprout,' said I.

She flung the peel into the fire, laughing a short laugh and went on with her work.

Mrs Saxton leaned over to her daughter and said softly, so that he should not hear, that George was pulling the flesh out of the raisins.

'George!' said Emily sharply, 'You're leaving nothing but the husks.'

He too was angry:

'"And he would fain fill his belly with the husks that the swine did eat,"' he said quietly, taking a handful of the fruit he had picked and putting some in his mouth. Emily snatched away the basin:

'It is too bad!' she said.

'Here,' said Lettie, handing him an apple she had peeled. 'You may have an apple, greedy boy.'

He took it and looked at it. Then a malicious smile twinkled round his eyes – as he said:

'If you give me the apple, to whom will you give the peel?'

'The swine,' she said, as if she only understood his first reference to the Prodigal Son. He put the apple on the table.

'Don't you want it?' she said.

'Mother,' he said, comically, as if jesting. 'She is offering me the apple like Eve.'

Like a flash, she snatched the apple from him, hid it in her skirts a moment, looking at him with dilated eyes, and then she flung it at the fire. She missed, and the father leaned forward and picked it off the hob, saying:

'The pigs may as well have it. You were slow, George – when a lady offers you a thing you don't have to make mouths.'

'*À ce qu'il paraît*,' she cried, laughing now at her ease, boisterously.

'Is she making love, Emily?' asked the father, laughing suggestively.

'She says it too fast for me,' said Emily.

George was leaning back in his chair, his hands in his breeches pockets.

'We shall have to finish his raisins after all, Emily,' said Lettie brightly. 'Look what a lazy animal he is.'

'He likes his comfort,' said Emily, with irony.

'The picture of content – solid, healthy, easy-moving content –' continued Lettie. As he sat thus, with his head thrown back against the end of the ingle-seat, coatless, his red neck seen in repose, he did indeed look remarkably comfortable.

'I shall never fret my fat away,' he said stolidly.

'No – you and I – we are not like Cyril. We do not burn our bodies in our heads – or our hearts, do we?'

'We have it in common,' said he, looking at her indifferently beneath his lashes, as his head was tilted back.

Lettie went on with the paring and coring of her apples – then she took the raisins. Meanwhile, Emily was making the house ring as she chopped the suet in a wooden bowl. The children were ready for bed. They kissed us all 'Good night' – save George. At last they were gone, accompanied by their mother. Emily put down her chopper, and sighed that her arm was aching, so I relieved her. The chopping went on for a long time, while the father read, Lettie worked, and George sat tilted back looking on. When at length the mincemeat was finished we were all out of work. Lettie helped to clear away – sat down – talked a little with effort – jumped up and said:

'Oh, I'm too excited to sit still – it's so near Christmas – let us play at something.'

'A dance?' said Emily.

'A dance – a dance!'

He suddenly sat straight and got up:

'Come on!' he said.

He kicked off his slippers, regardless of the holes in his stockinged feet, and put away the chairs. He held out his arm to her – she came with a laugh, and away they went, dancing over the great flagged kitchen at an incredible speed. Her light flying steps followed his leaps; you could hear the quick light tap of her toes more plainly than the thud of his stockinged feet. Emily and I joined in. Emily's movements are naturally slow, but we danced at great speed. I was hot and perspiring, and she was panting, when I put her in a chair. But they whirled on in the dance, on and on till I was giddy, till the father, laughing, cried that they should stop. But George continued the dance; her hair was shaken loose, and fell in a great coil down her back; her feet began to drag; you could hear a light slur on the floor; she was panting – I could see her lips murmur to him, begging him to stop; he was laughing with open mouth, holding her tight; at last her feet trailed; he lifted her, clasping her tightly, and danced twice round the room with her thus. Then he fell with a crash on the sofa, pulling her beside him. His eyes glowed like coals; he was panting in sobs, and his hair was wet and glistening. She lay back on the sofa, with his arm still around her, not moving; she was quite overcome. Her hair was wild about her face. Emily was anxious; the father said, with a shade of inquietude:

'You've overdone it – it is very foolish.'

When at last she recovered her breath and her life, she got up, and laughing in a queer way, began to put up her hair. She went into the scullery where were the brush and combs, and Emily followed with a candle. When she returned, ordered once more, with a little pallor succeeding the flush, and with a great black stain of sweat on her leathern belt where his hand had held her, he looked up at her from his position on the sofa, with a peculiar glance of triumph, smiling.

'You great brute,' she said, but her voice was not as harsh as her words. He gave a deep sigh, sat up, and laughed quietly.

'*Another*?' he said.

'Will you dance with *me*?'

'At your pleasure.'

'Come then – a minuet.'

'Don't know it.'

'Nevertheless, you must dance it. Come along.'

He reared up, and walked to her side. She put him through the steps, even dragging him round the waltz. It was very ridiculous. When it was finished she bowed him to his seat, and, wiping her hands on her handkerchief, because his shirt, where her hand had rested on his shoulders, was moist, she thanked him.

'I hope you enjoyed it,' he said.

'Ever so much,' she replied.

'You made me look a fool – so no doubt you did.'

'Do you think you could look a fool? Why, you are ironical! *Ça marche!* In other words, you have come on. But it is a sweet dance.'

He looked at her, lowered his eyelids, and said nothing.

'Ah, well,' she laughed, 'some are bred for the minuet, and some for –'

'– Less tomfoolery,' he answered.

'Ah – you call it tomfoolery because you cannot do it. Myself, I like it – so –'

'And I can't do it?'

'Could you? Did you? You are not built that way.'

'Sort of Clarence MacFadden,' he said, lighting a pipe as if the conversation did not interest him.

'Yes – what ages since we sang that!

> Clarence MacFadden he wanted to dance
> But his feet were not gaited that way ...

I remember we sang it after one corn harvest – we had a fine time. I never thought of you before as Clarence. It is very funny. By the way – will you come to our party at Christmas?'

'When? Who's coming?'

'The twenty-sixth. – Oh! – only the old people – Alice – Tom Smith – Fanny – those from Highclose.'

'And what will you do?'

'Sing charades – dance a little – anything you like.'

'Polka?'

'And minuets – and valetas. Come and dance a valeta, Cyril.'

She made me take her through a valeta, a minuet, a mazurka, and she danced elegantly, but with a little of Carmen's ostentation – her dash and devilry. When we had finished, the father said:

'Very pretty – very pretty, indeed! They do look nice, don't they, George? I wish I was young.'

'As I am –' said George, laughing bitterly.

'Show me how to do them – some time, Cyril,' said Emily, in her pleading way, which displeased Lettie so much.

'Why don't you ask me?' said the latter quickly.

'Well – but you are not often here.'

'I am here now. Come –' and she waved Emily imperiously to the attempt.

Lettie, as I have said, is tall, approaching six feet; she is lissom, but firmly moulded, by nature graceful; in her poise and harmonious movement are revealed the subtle sympathies of her artist's soul. The other is shorter, much heavier. In her every motion you can see the extravagance of her emotional nature. She quivers with feeling; emotion conquers and carries havoc through her, for she has not a strong intellect, nor a heart of light humour; her nature is brooding and defenceless; she knows herself powerless in the tumult of her feelings, and adds to her misfortunes a profound mistrust of herself.

As they danced together, Lettie and Emily, they showed in striking contrast. My sister's ease and beautiful poetic movement was exquisite; the other could not control her movements, but repeated the same error again and again. She gripped Lettie's hand fiercely, and glanced up with eyes full of humiliation and terror of her continued failure, and passionate, trembling, hopeless desire to succeed. To show her, to explain, made matters worse. As soon as she trembled on the brink of an action, the terror of not being able to perform it properly blinded her, and

she was conscious of nothing but that she must do something –
in a turmoil. At last Lettie ceased to talk, and merely swung her
through the dances haphazard. This way succeeded better. So
long as Emily need not think about her actions, she had a large,
free grace; and the swing and rhythm and time were imparted
through her senses rather than through her intelligence.

It was time for supper. The mother came down for a while,
and we talked quietly, at random. Lettie did not utter a word
about her engagement, not a suggestion. She made it seem as if
things were just as before, although I am sure she had discovered
that I had told George. She intended that we should play as if
ignorant of her bond.

After supper, when we were ready to go home, Lettie said to
him:

'By the way – you must send us some mistletoe for the party –
with plenty of berries, you know. Are there many berries on
your mistletoe this year?'

'I do not know – I have never looked. We will go and see – if
you like,' George answered.

'But will you come out into the cold?'

He pulled on his boots, and his coat, and twisted a scarf round
his neck. The young moon had gone. It was very dark – the
liquid stars wavered. The great night filled us with awe. Lettie
caught hold of my arm, and held it tightly. He passed on in
front to open the gates. We went down into the front garden,
over the turf bridge where the sluice rushed coldly under, on
to the broad slope of the bank. We could just distinguish the
gnarled old apple trees leaning about us. We bent our heads to
avoid the boughs, and followed George. He hesitated a moment,
saying:

'Let me see – I think they are there – the two trees with mistletoe on.'

We again followed silently.

'Yes,' he said, 'Here they are!'

We went close and peered into the old trees. We could just
see the dark bush of the mistletoe between the boughs of the
tree. Lettie began to laugh.

'Have we come to count the berries?' she said. 'I can't even
see the mistletoe.'

She leaned forwards and upwards to pierce the darkness; he, also straining to look, felt her breath on his cheek, and turning, saw the pallor of her face close to his, and felt the dark glow of her eyes. He caught her in his arms, and held her mouth in a kiss. Then, when he released her, he turned away, saying something incoherent about going to fetch the lantern to look. She remained with her back towards me, and pretended to be feeling among the mistletoe for the berries. Soon I saw the swing of the hurricane lamp below.

'He is bringing the lantern,' said I.

When he came up, he said, and his voice was strange and subdued:

'Now we can see what it's like.'

He went near, and held up the lamp, so that it illuminated both their faces, and the fantastic boughs of the trees, and the weird bush of mistletoe sparsely pearled with berries. Instead of looking at the berries they looked into each other's eyes; his lids flickered, and he flushed, in the yellow light of the lamp looking warm and handsome; he looked upwards in confusion and said: 'There are plenty of berries.'

As a matter of fact there were very few.

She too looked up, and murmured her assent. The light seemed to hold them as in a globe, in another world apart from the night in which I stood. He put up his hand and broke off a sprig of mistletoe, with berries, and offered it to her. They looked into each other's eyes again. She put the mistletoe among her furs, looking down at her bosom. They remained still, in the centre of light, with the lamp uplifted; the red and black scarf wrapped loosely round his neck gave him a luxurious, generous look. He lowered the lamp and said, affecting to speak naturally:

'Yes – there is plenty this year,'

'You will give me some,' she replied, turning away and finally breaking the spell.

'When shall I cut it?' – He strode beside her, swinging the lamp, as we went down the bank to go home. He came as far as the brooks without saying another word. Then he bade us good night. When he had lighted her over the stepping-stones, she did not take my arm as we walked home.

During the next two weeks we were busy preparing for Christmas, ranging the woods for the reddest holly, and pulling the gleaming ivy-bunches from the trees. From the farms around came the cruel yelling of pigs, and in the evening, later, was a scent of pork-pies. Far off on the highway could be heard the sharp trot of ponies hastening with Christmas goods.

There the carts of the hucksters dashed by to the expectant villagers, triumphant with great bunches of light foreign mistletoe, gay with oranges peeping through the boxes, and scarlet intrusion of apples, and wild confusion of cold, dead poultry. The hucksters waved their whips triumphantly, the little ponies rattled bravely under the sycamores, towards Christmas.

In the late afternoon of the twenty-fourth, when dust was rising under the hazel brake, I was walking with Lettie. All among the mesh of twigs overhead was tangled a dark red sky. The boles of the trees grew denser – almost blue.

Tramping down the riding we met two boys, fifteen or sixteen years old. Their clothes were largely patched with tough cotton moleskin; scarves were knotted round their throats, and in their pockets rolled tin bottles full of tea, and the white knobs of their knotted snap-bags.

'Why!' said Lettie. 'Are you going to work on Christmas Eve?'

'It looks like it, don't it?' said the elder.

'And what time will you be coming back?'

'About 'alf-past two.'

'Christmas morning!'

'You'll be able to look out for the herald Angels and the Star,' said I.

'They'd think we was two dirty little uns,' said the younger lad, laughing.

'They'll 'appen 'a done before we get up ter th' top,' added the elder boy – 'an' they'll none venture down th' shaft.'

'If they did,' put in the other, 'You'd ha'e ter bath 'em after. I'd gi'e 'em a bit o' my pasty.'

'Come on,' said the elder sulkily.

They tramped off, slurring their heavy boots.

'Merry Christmas!' I called after them.

'In th' mornin',' replied the elder.

'Same to you,' said the younger, and he began to sing with a tinge of bravado.

> 'In the fields with their flocks abiding.
> They lay on the dewy ground –'

'Fancy,' said Lettie, 'those boys are working for me!'

We were all going to the party at Highclose. I happened to go into the kitchen about half-past seven. The lamp was turned low, and Rebecca sat in the shadows. On the table, in the light of the lamp, I saw a glass vase with five or six very beautiful Christmas roses.

'Hullo, Becka, who's sent you these?' said I.

'They're not sent,' replied Rebecca from the depth of the shadow, with suspicion of tears in her voice.

'Why! I never saw them in the garden.'

'Perhaps not. But I've watched them these three weeks, and kept them under glass.'

'For Christmas? They are beauties. I thought someone must have sent them to you.'

'It's little as 'as ever been sent me,' replied Rebecca, 'an' less as will be.'

'Why – what's the matter?'

'Nothing. Who'm I, to have anything the matter! Nobody –nor ever was, nor ever will be. And I'm getting old as well.'

'Something's upset you, Becky.'

'What does it matter if it has? What are my feelings? A bunch o' fal-de-rol flowers as a gardener clips off wi' never a thought is preferred before mine as I've fettled after this three-week. I can sit at home to keep my flowers company – nobody wants 'em.'

I remembered that Lettie was wearing hot-house flowers; she was excited and full of the idea of the party at Highclose; I could imagine her quick 'Oh no thank you, Rebecca. I have had a spray sent to me –'

'Never mind, Becky,' said I, 'she is excited tonight.'

'An' I'm easy forgotten.'

'So are we all, Becky – *tant mieux.*'

At Highclose Lettie made a stir. Among the little belles of the countryside, she was decidedly the most distinguished. She was brilliant, moving as if in a drama. Leslie was enraptured, ostentatious in his admiration, proud of being so well infatuated. They looked into each other's eyes when they met, both triumphant, excited, blazing arch looks at one another. Lettie was enjoying her public demonstration immensely; it exhilarated her into quite a vivid love for him. He was magnificent in response. Meanwhile, the honoured lady of the house, pompous and ample, sat aside with my mother conferring her patronage on the latter amiable little woman, who smiled sardonically and watched Lettie. It was a splendid party; it was brilliant, it was dazzling.

I danced with several ladies, and honourably kissed each under the mistletoe – except that two of them kissed me first, it was all done in a most correct manner.

'You wolf,' said Miss Wookey archly. 'I believe you are a wolf – a veritable *rôdeur des femmes* – and you look such a lamb too – such a dear.'

'Even my bleat reminds you of Mary's pet.'

'But you are not my pet – at least – it is well that my Golaud doesn't hear you –'

'If he is so very big –' said I.

'He is really; he's beefy. I've engaged myself to him, somehow or other. One never knows how one does those things, do they?'

'I couldn't speak from experience,' said I.

'Cruel man! I suppose I felt Christmasy, and I'd just been reading Maeterlinck – and he really is big.'

'Who?' I asked.

'Oh – He, of course. My Golaud. I can't help admiring men who are a bit avoirdupoisy. It is unfortunate they can't dance.'

'Perhaps fortunate,' said I.

'I can see you hate him. Pity I didn't think to ask him if he danced – before –'

'Would it have influenced you very much?'

'Well – of course – one can be free to dance all the more with the really nice men whom one never marries.'

'Why not?'

'Oh – you can only marry one –'

'Of course.'

'There he is – he's coming for me! Oh, Frank, you leave me to the tender mercies of the world at large. I thought you'd forgotten me, dear.'

'I thought the same,' replied her Golaud, a great fat fellow with a childish bare face. He smiled awesomely, and one never knew what he meant to say.

We drove home in the early Christmas morning. Lettie, warmly wrapped in her cloak, had had a little stroll with her lover in the shrubbery. She was still brilliant, flashing in her movements. He, as he bade her good-bye, was almost beautiful in his grace and his low musical tone. I nearly loved him myself. She was very fond towards him. As we came to the gate where the private road branched from the highway, we heard John say 'Thank you' – and looking out, saw our two boys returning from the pit. They were very grotesque in the dark night as the lamp-light fell on them, showing them grimy, flecked with bits of snow. They shouted merrily their good wishes. Lettie leaned out and waved to them, and they cried 'ooray!' Christmas came in with their acclamations.

CHAPTER IX

Lettie Comes of Age

LETTIE was twenty-one on the day after Christmas. She woke me in the morning with cries of dismay. There was a great fall of snow, multiplying the cold morning light, startling the slow-footed twilight. The lake was black like the open eyes of a corpse; the woods were black like the beard on the face of a corpse. A rabbit bobbed out, and floundered in much consternation; little birds settled into the depth, and rose in a dusty whirr, much terrified at the universal treachery of the earth. The snow was eighteen inches deep, and drifted in places.

'They will never come!' lamented Lettie, for it was the day of her party.

'At any rate – Leslie will,' said I.

'One!' she exclaimed.

'That one is all, isn't it?' said I. 'And for sure George will come though I've not seen him this fortnight. He's not been in one night, they say, for a fortnight.'

'Why not?'

'I cannot say.'

Lettie went away to ask Rebecca for the fiftieth time if she thought they would come. At any rate the extra woman-help came.

It was not more than ten o'clock when Leslie arrived, ruddy, with shining eyes, laughing like a boy. There was much stamping in the porch, and knocking of leggings with his stick, and crying of Lettie from the kitchen to know who had come, and loud, cheery answers from the porch bidding her come and see. She came, and greeted him with effusion.

'Ha, my little woman!' he said kissing her. 'I declare you are a woman. Look at yourself in the glass now –' She did so – 'What do you see?' he asked laughing.

'You – mighty gay, looking at me.'

'Ah but look at yourself. There! I declare you're more afraid of your own eyes than of mine, aren't you?'

'I am,' she said, and he kissed her with rapture.

'It's your birthday,' he said.

'I know,' she replied.

'So do I. You promised me something.'

'What?' she asked.

'Here – see if you like it,' – he gave her a little case. She opened it, and instinctively slipped the ring on her finger. He made a movement of pleasure. She looked up, laughing breathlessly at him.

'Now!' said he, in tones of finality.

'Ah!' she exclaimed in a strange, thrilled voice.

He caught her in his arms.

After a while, when they could talk rationally again, she said:

'Do you think they will come to my party?'

'I hope not – By Heaven!'

'But – oh, yes! We have made all preparations.'

'What does that matter! Ten thousand folks here today –.'

'Not ten thousand – only five or six. I shall be wild if they can't come.'

'You want them?'

'We have asked them – and everything is ready – and I do want us to have a party one day.'

'But today – damn it all, Lettie!'

'But I did want my party today. Don't you think they'll come?'

'They won't if they've any sense!'

'You might help me –' she pouted.

'Well I'll be – ! and you've set your mind on having a houseful of people today?'

'You know how we look forward to it – my party. At any rate – I know Tom Smith will come – and I'm almost sure Emily Saxton will.'

He bit his moustache angrily, and said at last:

'Then I suppose I'd better send John round for the lot.'

'It wouldn't be much trouble, would it?'

'No *trouble* at all.'

'Do you know,' she said, twisting the ring on her finger. 'It

makes me feel as if I tied something round my finger to remember by. It somehow remains in my consciousness all the time.'

'At any rate,' said he, 'I have got you.'

After dinner, when we were alone, Lettie sat at the table,
nervously fingering her ring.

'It is pretty, mother, isn't it?' she said a trifle pathetically.

'Yes, very pretty. I have always liked Leslie,' replied my
mother.

'But it feels so heavy – it fidgets me. I should like to take
it off.'

'You are like me, I never could wear rings. I hated my
wedding ring for months.'

'Did you, mother?'

'I longed to take it off and put it away. But after a while I
got used to it.'

'I'm glad this isn't a wedding ring.'

'Leslie says it is as good,' said I.

'Ah, well, yes! But still it is different –' She put the jewels
round under her finger, and looked at the plain gold band –
then she twisted it back quickly, saying:

'I'm glad it's not – not yet. I begin to feel a woman, little
mother – I feel grown up today.'

My mother got up suddenly, and went and kissed Lettie
fervently.

'Let me kiss my girl good-bye,' she said, and her voice
was muffled with tears. Lettie clung to my mother, and sobbed
a few quiet sobs, hidden in her bosom. Then she lifted her
face, which was wet with tears, and kissed my mother, murmuring:

'No, mother – no – o – !'

About three o'clock the carriage came with Leslie and Marie.
Both Lettie and I were upstairs, and I heard Marie come
tripping up to my sister.

'Oh, Lettie, he is in such a state of excitement, you never
knew. He took me with him to buy it – let me see it on. I
think it's awfully lovely. Here, let me help you to do your
hair – all in those little rolls – it will look charming. You've
really got beautiful hair – there's so much life in it – it's a
pity to twist it into a coil as you do. I wish my hair were a

bit longer – though really, it's all the better for this fashion – don't you like it? – it's so "chic" – I think these little puffs are just fascinating – it is rather long for them – but it will look ravishing. Really, my eyes, and eyebrows, and eyelashes are my best features, don't you think?'

Marie, the delightful, charming little creature, twittered on. I went downstairs.

Leslie started when I entered the room, but seeing only me, he leaned forward again, resting his arms on his knees, looking in the fire.

'What the dickens is she doing?' he asked.

'Dressing.'

'Then we may keep on waiting. Isn't it a deuced nuisance these people coming?'

'Well, we generally have a good time.'

'Oh – it's all very well – we're not in the same boat, you and me.'

'Fact,' said I laughing.

'By Jove, Cyril, you don't know what it is to be in love. I never thought – I couldn't ha' believed I should be like it. All the time when it isn't at the top of your blood, it's at the bottom: – "the Girl, the Girl".'

He stared into the fire.

'It seems pressing you, pressing you on. Never leaves you alone a moment.'

Again he lapsed into reflexion.

'Then, all at once, you remember how she kissed you, and all your blood jumps afire.'

He mused again for awhile – or rather, he seemed fiercely to con over his sensations.

'You know,' he said, 'I don't think she feels for me as I do for her.'

'Would you want her to?' said I.

'I don't know. Perhaps not – but – still I don't think she feels –'

At this he lighted a cigarette to soothe his excited feelings, and there was silence for some time. Then the girls came down. We could hear their light chatter. Lettie entered the room. He jumped up and surveyed her. She was dressed in soft, creamy, silken stuff; her neck was quite bare; her hair was, as Marie promised, fascinating; she was laughing nervously. She grew warm, like a blossom in the sunshine, in the glow of his admiration. He went forward and kissed her.

'You are splendid!' he said.

She only laughed for answer. He drew her away to the great arm-chair, and made her sit in it beside him. She was indulgent and he radiant. He took her hand and looked at it. and at his ring which she wore.

'It looks all right!' he murmured.

'Anything would,' she replied.

'What do they mean – sapphires and diamonds – for I don't know?'

'Nor do I. Blue for hope, because Speranza in *Fairy Queen* had a blue gown – and diamonds for – the crystalline clearness of my nature.'

'Its glitter and hardness, you mean – You are a hard little mistress. But why Hope?'

'Why? – No reason whatever, like most things. No, that's not right. Hope! Oh – Blindfolded – hugging a silly harp with no strings. I wonder why she didn't drop her harp framework over the edge of the glove, and take the handkerchief off her eyes, and have a look round! But of course she was a woman – and a man's woman. Do you know I believe most women can sneak a look down their noses from underneath the handkerchief of hope they've tied over their eyes. They could take the whole muffler off – but they don't do it, the dears.'

'I don't believe you know what you're talking about, and I'm sure I don't. Sapphires reminded me of your eyes – and – isn't it "Blue that kept faith"? I remember something about it.'

'Here,' said she, pulling off the ring, 'you ought to wear it yourself, Faithful One, to keep me in constant mind.'

'Keep it on, keep it on. It holds you faster than that fair damsel tied to a tree in Millais' picture – I believe it's Millais.'

She sat shaking with laughter.

'What a comparison! Who'll be the brave knight to rescue me – discreetly – from behind?'

'Ah,' he answered, 'it doesn't matter. You don't want rescuing, do you?'

'Not yet,' she replied, teasing him.

They continued to talk half nonsense, making themselves eloquent by quick looks and gestures, and communion of warm closeness. The ironical tones went out of Lettie's voice, and they made love.

Marie drew me away into the dining-room, to leave them alone.

*

Marie is a charming little maid whose appearance is neatness, whose face is confident little goodness. Her hair is dark, and lies low upon her neck in wavy coils. She does not affect the fashion in coiffure, and generally is a little behind the fashion in dress. Indeed she is a half-opened bud of a matron, conservative, full of proprieties, and of gentle indulgence. She now smiled at me with a warm delight in the romance upon which she had just shed her grace, but her demureness allowed nothing to be said. She glanced round the room, and out of the window, and observed:

'I always love Woodside, it is restful – there is something about it – oh – assuring – really – it comforts one – I've been reading Maxim Gorky.'

'You shouldn't,' said I.

'Dadda reads them – but I don't like them – I shall read no more. I like Woodside – it makes you feel – really at home – it soothes one like the old wood does. It seems right – life is proper here – not ulcery –'

'Just healthy living flesh,' said I.

'No, I don't mean that, because one feels – oh, as if the world were old and good, not old and bad.'

'Young and undisciplined, and mad,' said I.

'No – but here, you, and Lettie, and Leslie, and me – it is so nice for us, and it seems so natural and good. Woodside is so old, and so sweet and serene – it does reassure one.'

'Yes,' said I, 'we just live, nothing abnormal, nothing cruel and extravagant – just natural – like doves in a dove-cote.'

'Oh! – doves! – they are so – so mushy.'

'They are dear little birds, doves. You look like one yourself, with the black band round your neck. You a turtle-dove, and Lettie a wood-pigeon.'

'Lettie is splendid, isn't she? What a swing she has – what a mastery! I wish I had her strength – she just marches straight through in the right way – I think she's fine.'

I laughed to see her so enthusiastic in her admiration of my sister. Marie is such a gentle, serious little soul. She went to the window. I kissed her, and pulled two berries off the mistletoe. I made her a nest in the heavy curtains, and she sat there looking out on the snow.

'It is lovely,' she said reflectively. 'People must be ill when they write like Maxim Gorky.'

'They live in town,' said I.

'Yes – but then look at Hardy – life seems so terrible – it isn't, is it?'

'If you don't feel it, it isn't – if you don't see it. I don't see it for myself.'

'It's lovely enough for heaven.'

'Eskimo's heaven perhaps. And we're the angels, eh? And I'm an archangel.'

'No, you're a vain, frivolous man. Is that – ? What is that moving through the trees?'

'Somebody coming,' said I.

*

It was a big, burly fellow moving curiously through the bushes.

'Doesn't he walk funnily?' exclaimed Marie. He did. When he came near enough we saw he was straddled upon Indian snow-shoes. Marie peeped, and laughed, and peeped, and hid again in the curtains laughing. He was very red, and looked very hot, as he hauled the great meshes, shuffling over the snow; his body rolled most comically. I went to the door and admitted him, while Marie stood stroking her face with her hands to smooth away the traces of her laughter.

He grasped my hand in a very large and heavy glove, with which he then wiped his perspiring brow.

'Well, Beardsall, old man,' he said, 'and how's things? God, I'm not 'alf hot! Fine idea though –' He showed me his snow-shoes.

'Ripping! ain't they? I've come like an Indian brave –' He rolled his 'r's', and lengthened out his 'ah's' tremendously – 'brra-ave.'

'Couldn't resist it though,' he continued.

'Remember your party last year – Girls turned up? On the war-path, eh?' He pursed up his childish lips, and rubbed his fat chin.

Having removed his coat, and the white wrap which protected his collar, not to mention the snow-flakes, which Rebecca took almost as an insult to herself – he seated his fat, hot body on a chair, and proceeded to take off his gaiters and his boots. Then he donned his dancing pumps, and I led him upstairs.

'Lord, I skimmed here like a swallow!' he continued – and I looked at his corpulence.

'Never met a soul, though they've had a snow-plough down the road. I saw the marks of a cart up the drive, so I guessed the Tempests were here. So Lettie's put her nose in Tempest's nosebag – leaves nobody a chance, that – some women have rum taste – only they're like ravens, they go for the gilding – don't blame 'em – only it leaves nobody a chance. Madie Howitt's coming, I suppose?'

I ventured something about the snow.

'She'll come,' he said, 'if it's up to the neck. Her mother saw me go past.'

He proceeded with his toilet. I told him that Leslie had sent the carriage for Alice and Madie. He slapped his fat legs, and exclaimed:

'Miss Gall – I smell sulphur! Beardsall, old boy, there's fun in the wind. Madie, and the coy little Tempest, and –' he hissed a line of a music-hall song through his teeth.

During all this he had straightened his cream and lavender waistcoat:

'Little pink of a girl worked it for me – a real juicy little peach – chipped somehow or other' – he had arranged his white bow – he had drawn forth two rings, one a great signet, the other gorgeous with diamonds, and had adjusted them on his fat white fingers; he had run his fingers delicately through his hair, which rippled backwards a trifle tawdrily – being fine and somewhat sapless; he had produced a box, containing a cream carnation with suitable greenery; he had flicked himself with a silk handkerchief, and had dusted his patent-leather shoes; lastly, he had pursed up his lips and surveyed himself with great satisfaction in the mirror. Then he was ready to be presented.

'Couldn't forget today, Lettie. Wouldn't have let old Pluto and all the bunch of 'em keep me away. I skimmed here like a "Brra-ave" on my snow-shoes, like Hiawatha coming to Minnehaha.'

'Ah – that was famine,' said Marie softly.

'And this is a feast, a gorgeous feast, Miss Tempest,' he said, bowing to Marie, who laughed.

'You have brought some music?' asked mother.

'Wish I was Orpheus,' he said, uttering his words with exaggerated enunciation, a trick he had caught from his singing, I suppose.

'I see you're in full feather, Tempest. "Is she kind as she is fair?"'

'Who?'

Will pursed up his smooth sensuous face that looked as if it had never needed shaving. Lettie went out with Marie, hearing the bell ring.

'She's an houri!' exclaimed William. 'Gad, I'm almost done for! She's a lotus-blossom! – But is that your ring she's wearing, Tempest?'

'Keep off,' said Leslie.

'And don't be a fool,' said I.

'Oh, O-O-Oh?' drawled Will, 'so we must look the other way! *Le bel homme sans merci!*'

He sighed profoundly, and ran his fingers through his hair, keeping one eye on himself in the mirror as he did so. Then he adjusted his rings and went to the piano. At first he only splashed about brilliantly. Then he sorted the music, and took a volume of Tchaikowsky's songs. He began the long opening of one song, was unsatisfied, and found another, a serenade of Don Juan. Then at last he began to sing.

His voice is a beautiful tenor, softer, more mellow, less strong and brassy than Leslie's. Now it was raised that it might be heard upstairs. As the melting gush poured forth, the door opened. William softened his tones, and sang *dolce,* but he did not glance round.

'Rapture! – Choir of Angels,' exclaimed Alice, clasping her hands and gazing up at the lintel of the door like a sainted virgin.

'Persephone – Europa –' murmured Madie, at her side getting tangled in her mythology.

Alice pressed her clasped hands against her bosom in ecstasy as the notes rose higher.

'Hold me, Madie, or I shall rush to extinction in the arms of this siren.' She clung to Madie. The song finished, and Will turned round.

'Take it calmly, Miss Gall,' he said. 'I hope you're not hit too badly.'

'Oh – how can you say "take it calmly" – how can the savage beast be calm!'

'I'm sorry for you,' said Will.

'You are the cause of my trouble, dear boy,' replied Alice.

'I never thought you'd come,' said Madie.

'Skimmed here like an Indian "brra-ave".' said Will. 'Like Hiawatha towards Minnehaha. I knew you were coming.'

'You know,' simpered Madie, 'It gave me quite a flutter when I heard the piano. It is a year since I saw you. How did you get here?'

'I came on snow-shoes,' said he. 'Real Indian, – came from Canada – they're just ripping.'

'Oh – Aw-w *do* go and put them on and show us –*do!* – *do* perform for us, Billy dear!' cried Alice.

'Out in the cold and driving sleet – no fear,' said he, and he turned to talk to Madie. Alice sat chatting with mother. Soon Tom Smith came, and took a seat next to Marie; and sat quietly looking over his spectacles with his sharp brown eyes, full of scorn for William, full of misgiving for Leslie and Lettie.

Shortly after, George and Emily came in. They were rather nervous. When they had changed their clogs, and Emily had taken off her brown-paper leggings, and he his leather ones, they were not anxious to go into the drawing-room. I was surprised – and so was Emily – to see that he had put on dancing shoes.

Emily, ruddy from the cold air, was wearing a wine-coloured dress, which suited her luxurious beauty. George's clothes were well made – it was a point on which he was particular, being somewhat self-conscious. He wore a jacket, and a dark bow. The other men were in evening dress.

We took them into the drawing-room, where the lamp was not lighted, and the glow of the fire was becoming evident in the dusk. We had taken up the carpet – the floor was all polished – and some of the furniture was taken away – so that the room looked large and ample.

There was general hand-shaking, and the new-comers were seated near the fire. First mother talked to them – then the candles were lighted at the piano, and Will played to us. He is an exquisite pianist, full of refinement and poetry. It is astonishing, and it is a fact. Mother went out to attend to the tea, and after a while, Lettie crossed over to Emily and George, and, drawing up a low chair, sat down to talk to them. Leslie stood in the window bay, looking out on the lawn where the snow grew bluer and bluer and the sky almost purple.

Lettie put her hands on Emily's lap, and said softly, 'Look – do you like it?'

'What! engaged?' exclaimed Emily.

'I am of age, you see,' said Lettie.

'It is a beauty, isn't it. Let me try it on, will you? Yes, I've never had a ring. There, it won't go over my knuckle – no I thought not. Aren't my hands red? – it's the cold – yes, it's too small for me. I do like it.'

George sat watching the play of the four hands in his sister's lap, two hands moving so white and fascinating in the twilight, the other two rather red, with rather large bones, looking so nervous, almost hysterical. The ring played between the four hands, giving an occasional flash from the twilight or candle-light.

'You must congratulate me,' she said, in a very low voice, and two of us knew she spoke to him.

'Ah, yes,' said Emily, 'I do.'

'And you?' she said, turning to him who was silent.

'What do you want me to say?' he asked.

'Say what you like.'

'Sometime, when I've thought about it.'

'Cold dinners!' laughed Lettie, awaking Alice's old sarcasm at his slowness.

'What?' he exclaimed, looking up suddenly at her taunt. She knew she was playing false; she put the ring on her finger and went across the room to Leslie, laying her arm over his shoulder, and leaning her head against him, murmuring softly to him. He, poor fellow, was delighted with her, for she did not display her fondness often.

We went in to tea. The yellow shaded lamp shone softly over the table, where Christmas roses spread wide open among some dark-coloured leaves; where the china and silver and the coloured dishes shone delightfully. We were all very gay and bright; who could be otherwise, seated round a well-laid table, with young company, and the snow outside. George felt awkward when he noticed his hands over the table, but for the rest, we enjoyed ourselves exceedingly.

The conversation veered inevitably to marriage.

'But what have you to say about it, Mr Smith?' asked little Marie.

'Nothing yet,' replied he in his peculiar grating voice. 'My marriage is in the unanalysed solution of the future – when I've done the analysis I'll tell you.'

'But what do you think about it –?'

'Do you remember, Lettie,' said Will Bancroft, 'that little red-haired girl who was in our year at college? She has just married old Craven out of Physics department.'

'I wish her joy of it!' said Lettie; 'wasn't she an old flame of yours?'

'Among the rest,' he replied smiling. 'Don't you remember you were one of them; you had your day.'

'What a joke that was!' exclaimed Lettie, 'we used to go in the arboretum at dinner-time. You lasted half one autumn. Do you remember when we gave a concert, you and I, and Frank Wishaw, in the small lecture theatre?'

'When the Prinny was such an old buck, flattering you,'

continued Will. 'And that night Wishaw took you to the station – sent old Gettim for a cab and saw you in, large as life – never was such a thing before. Old Wishaw won you with that cab, didn't he?'

'Oh, how I swelled!' cried Lettie. 'There were you all at the top of the steps gazing with admiration! But Frank Wishaw was not a nice fellow, though he played the violin beautifully. I never liked his eyes –'

'No,' added Will. 'He didn't last long, did he? – though long enough to oust me. We had a giddy ripping time in Coll., didn't we?'

'It was not bad,' said Lettie. 'Rather foolish. I'm afraid I wasted my three years.'

'I think,' said Leslie, smiling, 'you improved the shining hours to great purpose.'

It pleased him to think what a flirt she had been, since the flirting had been harmless, and only added to the glory of his final conquest. George felt very much left out during these reminiscences.

*

When we had finished tea, we adjourned to the drawing-room. It was in darkness, save for the fire-light. The mistletoe had been discovered, and was being appreciated.

'Georgie, Sybil, Sybil, Georgie, come and kiss me,' cried Alice.

Will went forward to do her the honour. She ran to me, saying, 'Get away, you fat fool – keep on your own preserves. Now Georgie dear, come and kiss me, 'cause you haven't got nobody else but me, no y'aven't. Do you want to run away, like Georgy-Porgy apple-pie? Shan't cry, sure I shan't, if you are ugly.'

She took him and kissed him on either cheek, saying softly, 'You shan't be so serious, old boy – buck up, there's a good fellow.'

We lighted the lamp, and charades were proposed. Leslie and Lettie, Will and Madie and Alice went out to play. The first scene was an elopement to Gretna Green – with Alice a maid servant, a part that she played wonderfully well as a caricature. It was very noisy, and extremely funny. Leslie was in high spirits. It was remarkable to observe that, as he became more animated, more abundantly energetic, Lettie became quieter. The second scene, which they were playing as excited melodrama, she turned into small tragedy with her bitterness. They went out, and Lettie blew us kisses from the doorway.

'Doesn't she act well?' exclaimed Marie, speaking to Tom.

'Quite realistic,' said he.

'She could always play a part well,' said mother.

'I should think,' said Emily, 'she could take a role in life and play up to it.'

'I believe she could,' mother answered, 'there would only be intervals when she would see herself in a mirror acting.'

'And what then?' said Marie.

'She would feel desperate, and wait till the fit passed off,' replied my mother, smiling significantly.

The players came in again. Lettie kept her part subordinate. Leslie played with brilliance; it was rather startling how he excelled. The applause was loud – but we could not guess the word. Then they laughed, and told us. We clamoured for more.

'Do go, dear,' said Lettie to Leslie, 'and I will be helping to arrange the room for the dances. I want to watch you – I am rather tired – it is so exciting – Emily will take my place.'

They went. Marie and Tom, and Mother and I played bridge in one corner. Lettie said she wanted to show George some new pictures, and they bent over a portfolio for some time. Then she bade him help her to clear the room for the dances.

'Well, you have had time to think,' she said to him.

'A short time,' he replied. 'What shall I say?'

'Tell me what you've been thinking.'

'Well – about you –' he answered, smiling foolishly.

'What about me?' she asked, venturesome.

'About you, how you were at College,' he replied.

'Oh! I had a good time. I had plenty of boys. I liked them all, till I found there was nothing in them; then they tired me.'

'Poor boys!' he said laughing. 'Were they all alike?'

'All alike,' she replied, 'and they are still.'

'Pity,' he said, smiling. 'It's hard lines on you.'

'Why?' she asked.

'It leaves you nobody to care for –' he replied.

'How very sarcastic you are. You make one reservation.'

'Do I?' he answered, smiling. 'But you fire sharp into the air, and then say we're all blank cartridges – except one, of course.'

'You?' she queried, ironically – 'oh, you would forever hang fire.'

'"Cold dinners!"' he quoted in bitterness. 'But you knew I loved you. You knew well enough.'

'Past tense,' she replied, 'thanks – make it perfect next time.'

'It's you who hang fire – it's you who make me,' he said.

'"And so from the retort circumstantial to the retort direct,"' she replied, smiling.

'You see – you put me off,' he insisted, growing excited. For reply, she held out her hand and showed him the ring. She smiled very quietly. He stared at her with darkening anger.

'Will you gather the rugs and stools together, and put them in that corner?' she said.

He turned away to do so, but he looked back again, and said, in low, passionate tones:

'You never counted me. I was a figure naught in the counting all along.'

'See – there is a chair that will be in the way,' she replied calmly; but she flushed, and bowed her head. She turned away, and he dragged an armful of rugs into a corner.

When the actors came in, Lettie was moving a vase of flowers. While they played, she sat looking on, smiling, clapping her hands. When it was finished Leslie came and whispered to her, whereon she kissed him unobserved, delighting and exhilarating him more than ever. Then they went out to prepare the next act.

George did not return to her till she called him to help her. Her colour was high in her cheeks.

'How do you know you did not count?' she said, nervously, unable to resist the temptation to play this forbidden game.

He laughed, and for a moment could not find any reply.

'I do!' he said. 'You knew you could have me any day, so you didn't care.'

'Then we're behaving in quite the traditional fashion,' she answered with irony.

'But you know,' he said, 'you began it. You played with me,

and showed me heaps of things – and those mornings – when I was binding corn, and when I was gathering the apples, and when I was finishing the straw-stack – you came then – I can never forget those mornings – things will never be the same – You have awakened my life – I imagine things that I couldn't have done.'

'Ah! – I am very sorry, I am so sorry.'

'Don't be! – don't say so. But what of me?'

'What?' she asked rather startled. He smiled again; he felt the situation, and was a trifle dramatic, though deadly in earnest.

'Well,' said he, 'you start me off – then leave me at a loose end. What am I going to do?'

'You are a man,' she replied.

He laughed. 'What does that mean?' he said contemptuously.

'You can go on – which way you like,' she answered.

'Oh, well,' he said, 'we'll see.'

'Don't you think so?' she asked, rather anxious.

'I don't know – we'll see,' he replied.

They went out with some things. In the hall, she turned to him, with a break in her voice, saying: 'Oh, I am so sorry – I am so sorry.'

He said, very low and soft, – 'Never mind – never mind.'

She heard the laughter of those preparing the charade. She drew away and went in the drawing-room, saying aloud:

'Now I think everything is ready – we can sit down now.'

After the actors had played the last charade, Leslie came and claimed her.

'Now, Madam – are you glad to have me back?'

'That I am,' she said. 'Don't leave me again, will you?'

'I won't,' he replied, drawing her beside him. 'I have left my handkerchief in the dining-room,' he continued; and they went out together.

Mother gave me permission for the men to smoke.

'You know,' said Marie to Tom, 'I am surprised that a scientist should smoke. Isn't it a waste of time?'

'Come and light me,' he said.

'Nay,' she replied, 'let science light you.'

'Science does – Ah, but science is nothing without a girl to set it going – Yes – Come on – now, don't burn my precious nose.'

'Poor George!' cried Alice. 'Does he want a ministering angel?'

He was half lying in a big arm chair.

'I do,' he replied. 'Come on, be my box of soothing ointment. My matches are all loose.'

'I'll strike it on my heel, eh? Now, rouse up, or I shall have to sit on your knee to reach you.'

'Poor dear – he shall be luxurious,' and the dauntless girl perched on his knee.

'What if I singe your whiskers – would you send an Armada? Aw – aw – pretty! – You do look sweet – doesn't he suck prettily?'

'Do you envy me?' he asked, smiling whimsically.

'Ra-ther!'

'Shame to debar you,' he said, almost with tenderness.

'Smoke with me.'

He offered her the cigarette from his lips. She was surprised, and exceedingly excited by his tender tone. She took the cigarette.

'I'll make a heifer – like Mrs Daws,' she said.

'Don't call yourself a cow,' he said.

'Nasty thing – let me go,' she exclaimed.

'No – you fit me – don't go,' he replied, holding her.

'Then you must have growed. Oh – what great hands – let go. Lettie, come and pinch him.'

'What's the matter?' asked my sister.

'He won't let me go.'

'He'll be tired first,' Lettie answered.

Alice was released, but she did not move. She sat with wrinkled forehead trying his cigarette. She blew out little tiny whiffs of smoke, and thought about it; she sent a small puff down her nostrils, and rubbed her nose.

'It's not as nice as it looks,' she said.

He laughed at her with masculine indulgence.

'Pretty boy,' she said, stroking his chin.

'Am I?' he murmured languidly.

'Cheek!' she cried, and she boxed his ears. Then 'Oh pore fing!' she said, and kissed him.

She turned round to wink at my mother and at Lettie. She found the latter sitting in the old position with Leslie, two in a chair. He was toying with her arm; holding it and stroking it.

'Isn't it lovely?' he said, kissing the forearm, 'so warm and yet so white. Io – it reminds one of Io.'

'Somebody else talking about heifers,' murmured Alice to George.

'Can you remember,' said Leslie, speaking low, 'that man in Merimée who wanted to bite his wife and taste her blood?'

'I do,' said Lettie. 'Have you a strain of wild beast too?'

'Perhaps,' he laughed, 'I wish these folks had gone. Your hair is all loose in your neck – it looks lovely like that though –'

Alice, the mocker, had unbuttoned the cuff of the thick wrist that lay idly on her knee, and had pushed his sleeve a little way.

'Ah!' she said. 'What a pretty arm, brown as an overbaked loaf!'.

He watched her smiling.

'Hard as a brick,' she added.

'Do you like it?' he drawled.

'No,' she said emphatically, in a tone that meant 'yes'. 'It makes me feel shivery.' He smiled again.

She superposed her tiny pale, flower-like hands on his.

He lay back looking at them curiously.

'Do you feel as if your hands were full of silver?' she asked almost wistfully, mocking.

'Better than that,' he replied gently.

'And your heart full of gold?' she mocked.

'Of hell!' he replied briefly.

Alice looked at him searchingly.

'And am I like a blue-bottle buzzing in your window to keep you company?' she asked.

He laughed.

'Good-bye,' she said, slipping down and leaving him.

'Don't go,' he said – but too late.

*

The irruption of Alice into the quiet, sentimental party was like taking a bright light into a sleeping hen-roost. Everybody jumped up and wanted to do something. They cried out for a dance.

'Emily – play a waltz – you won't mind, will you, George? What! You don't dance, Tom? Oh, Marie!'

'I don't mind, Lettie,' protested Marie.

'Dance with me, Alice,' said George, smiling, 'and Cyril will take Miss Tempest.'

'Glory! – come on – do or die!' said Alice.

We began to dance. I saw Lettie watching, and I looked round. George was waltzing with Alice, dancing passably, laughing at her remarks. Lettie was not listening to what her lover was saying to her; she was watching the laughing pair. At the end she went to George.

'Why!' she said, 'You can –'

'Did you think I couldn't?' he said. 'You are pledged for a minuet and a veleta with me – you remember?'

'Yes.'

'You promise?'

'Yes. But –'

'I went to Nottingham and learned.'

'Why – because? – Very well, Leslie, a mazurka. Will you play it, Emily? – Yes, it is quite easy. Tom, you look quite happy talking to the Mater.'

We danced the mazurka with the same partners. He did it better than I expected – without much awkwardness – but stiffly. However, he moved quietly through the dance, laughing and talking abstractedly all the time with Alice.

Then Lettie cried a change of partners, and they took their valeta. There was a little triumph in his smile.

'Do you congratulate me?' he said.

'I am surprised,' she answered.

'So am I. But I congratulate myself.'

'Do you? Well, so do I.'

'Thanks! You're beginning at last.'

'What?' she asked.

'To believe in me.'

'Don't begin to talk again,' she pleaded, sadly, 'nothing vital.'

'Do you like dancing with me?' he asked.

'Now, be quiet – *that's* real,' she replied.

'By heaven, Lettie, you make me laugh!'

'Do I?' she said – 'What if you married Alice – soon.'

'I – Alice! – Lettie!! Besides, I've only a hundred pounds in the world, and no prospects whatever. That's why – well – I shan't marry anybody – unless it's somebody with money.'

'I've a couple of thousand or so of my own –'

'Have you? It would have done nicely,' he said, smiling.

'You are different tonight,' she said, leaning on him.

'Am I?' he replied – 'It's because things are altered too. They're settled one way now – for the present at least.

'Don't forget the two steps this time,' said she, smiling, and adding seriously, 'You see, I couldn't help it.'

'No, why not?'

'Things! I have been brought up to expect it – everybody expected it – and you're bound to do what people expect you to do – you can't help it. We can't help ourselves, we're all chessmen,' she said.

'Ay,' he agreed, but doubtfully.

'I wonder where it will end,' she said.

'Lettie!' he cried, and his hand closed in a grip on hers.

'Don't – don't say anything – it's no good now, it's too late. It's done; and what is done, is done. If you talk any more, I shall say I'm tired and stop the dance. Don't say another word.'

He did not – at least to her. Their dance came to an end. Then he took Marie who talked winsomely to him. As he waltzed with Marie he regained his animated spirits. He was very lively the rest of the evening, quite astonishing and reckless. At supper he ate everything, and drank much wine.

'Have some more turkey, Mr Saxton.'

'Thanks – but give me some of that stuff in brown jelly, will you? It's new to me.'

'Have some of this trifle, Georgie?'

'I will – you are a jewel.'

'So will you be – a yellow topaz tomorrow!'

'Ah! tomorrow's tomorrow!'

After supper was over, Alice cried:

'George, dear – have you finished? – don't die the death of a king – King John – I can't spare you, pet.'

'Are you so fond of me?'

'I am – Aw! I'd throw my best Sunday hat under a milk-cart for you, I would!'

'No; throw yourself into the milk-cart – some Sunday, when I'm driving.'

'Yes – come and see us,' said Emily.

'How nice! Tomorrow you won't want me, Georgie dear, so I'll come. Don't you wish Pa would make Tono-Bungay? Wouldn't you marry me then?'

'I would,' said he.

When the cart came, and Alice, Madie, Tom and Will departed, Alice bade Lettie a long farewell – blew Georgie many kisses – promised to love him faithful and true – and was gone.

George and Emily lingered a short time.

Now the room seemed empty and quiet, and all the laughter seemed to have gone. The conversation dribbled away; there was an awkwardness.

'Well,' said George heavily, at last. 'Today is nearly gone – it will soon be tomorrow. I feel a bit drunk! We had a good time tonight.'

'I am glad,' said Lettie.

They put on their clogs and leggings, and wrapped themselves up, and stood in the hall.

'We must go,' said George, 'before the clock strikes, – like Cinderella – look at my glass slippers –' he pointed to his clogs. 'Midnight, and rags, and fleeing. Very appropriate. I shall call myself Cinderella who wouldn't fit. I believe I'm a bit drunk – the world looks funny.'

We looked out at the haunting wanness of the hills beyond Nethermere. 'Good-bye, Lettie; good-bye.'

They were out in the snow, which peered pale and eerily from the depths of the black wood.

'Good-bye,' he called out of the darkness. Leslie slammed the door, and drew Lettie away into the drawing-room. The sound of his low, vibrating satisfaction reached us, as he murmured to her, and laughed low. Then he kicked the door of the room shut. Lettie began to laugh and mock and talk in a high strained voice. The sound of their laughter mingled was strange and incongruous. Then her voice died down.

Marie sat at the little piano – which was put in the dining-room – strumming and tinkling the false, quavering old notes. It was a depressing jingling in the deserted remains of the feast, but she felt sentimental, and enjoyed it.

This was a gap between today and tomorrow, a dreary gap, where one sat and looked at the dreary comedy of yesterdays, and the grey tragedies of dawning tomorrows, vacantly, missing the poignancy of an actual today.

The cart returned.

'Leslie, Leslie, John is here, come along!' called Marie.

There was no answer.

'Leslie – John is waiting in the snow.'

'All right.'

'But you must come at once.' She went to the door and spoke to him. Then he came out looking rather sheepish, and rather angry at the interruption. Lettie followed, tidying her hair. She did not laugh and look confused, as most girls do on similar occasions; she seemed very tired.

At last Leslie tore himself away, and after more returns for a farewell kiss, mounted the carriage, which stood in a pool of yellow light, blurred and splotched with shadows, and drove away, calling something about tomorrow.

PART TWO

CHAPTER I

Strange Blossoms and Strange New Budding

WINTER lay a long time prostrate on the earth. The men in the mines of Tempest, Warrall and Co. came out on strike on a question of the re-arranging of the working system down below. The distress was not awful, for the men were on the whole wise and well-conditioned, but there was a dejection over the face of the country-side, and some suffered keenly. Everywhere, along the lanes and in the streets, loitered gangs of men, unoccupied and spiritless. Week after week went on, and the agents of the Miners' Union held great meetings, and the ministers held prayer-meetings, but the strike continued. There was no rest. Always the crier's bell was ringing in the street; always the servants of the company were delivering handbills, stating the case clearly, and always the people talked and filled the months with bitter, and then hopeless, resenting. Schools gave breakfasts, chapels gave soup, well-to-do people gave teas – the children enjoyed it. But we, who knew the faces of the old men and the privations of the women, breathed a cold, disheartening atmosphere of sorrow and trouble.

Determined poaching was carried on in the Squire's woods and warrens. Annable defended his game heroically. One man was at home with a leg supposed to be wounded by a fall on the slippery roads – but really, by a man-trap in the woods. Then Annable caught two men, and they were sentenced to two months' imprisonment.

On both the lodge gates of Highclose – on our side and on the far Eberwich side – were posted notices that trespassers on the drive or in the grounds would be liable to punishment. These posters were soon mudded over, and fresh ones fixed.

The men loitering on the road by Nethermere looked angrily at Lettie as she passed, in her black furs which Leslie had given her, and their remarks were pungent. She heard them, and they burned in her heart. From my mother she inherited democratic views, which she now proceeded to debate warmly with her lover.

Then she tried to talk to Leslie about the strike. He heard her with mild superiority, smiled, and said she did not know. Women jumped to conclusions at the first touch of feeling; men must look at a thing all round, then make a decision – nothing hasty and impetuous – careful, long-thought-out, correct decisions. Women could not be expected to understand these things, business was not for them; in fact, their mission was above business – etc., etc. Unfortunately Lettie was the wrong woman to treat thus.

'So!' said she, with a quiet, hopeless tone of finality.

'There now, you understand, don't you, Minnehaha, my Laughing Water – So laugh again, darling, and don't worry about these things. We will not talk about them any more, eh?'

'No more.'

'No more – that's right – you are as wise as an angel. Come here – pooh, the wood is thick and lonely! Look, there is nobody in the world but us, and you are my heaven and earth!'

'And hell?'

'Ah – if you are so cold – how cold you are! – it gives me little shivers when you look so – and I am always hot – Lettie!'

'Well?'

'You are cruel! Kiss me – now – No, I don't want your cheek – kiss me yourself. Why don't you say something?'

'What for? What's the use of saying anything when there's nothing immediate to say?'

'You are offended!'

'It feels like snow today,' she answered.

*

At last, however, winter began to gather her limbs, to rise, and drift with saddened garments northward.

The strike was over. The men had compromised. It was a gentle way of telling them they were beaten. But the strike was over.

The birds fluttered and dashed; the catkins on the hazel loosened their winter rigidity, and swung soft tassels. All through the day sounded long, sweet whistlings from the bushes; then later, loud, laughing shouts of bird triumph on every hand.

I remember a day when the breast of the hills was heaving in a last quick waking sigh, and the blue eyes of the waters opened bright. Across the infinite skies of March great rounded masses of cloud had sailed stately all day, domed with a white radiance, softened with faint, fleeting shadows as if companies of angels were gently sweeping past; adorned with resting, silken shadows like those of a full white breast. All day the clouds had moved on to their vast destination, and I had clung to the earth yearning and impatient. I took a brush and tried to paint them, then I raged at myself. I wished that in all the wild valley where cloud shadows were travelling like pilgrims, something would call me forth from my rooted loneliness. Through all the grandeur of the white and blue day, the poised cloud masses swung their slow flight, and left me unnoticed.

At evening, they were all gone, and the empty sky, like a blue bubble over us, swam on its pale bright rims.

Leslie came, and asked his betrothed to go out with him, under the darkening wonderful bubble. She bade me accompany her, and, to escape from myself, I went.

It was warm in the shelter of the wood and in the crouching hollows of the hills. But over the slanting shoulders of the hills the wind swept, whispering the redness into our faces.

'Get me some of those alder catkins, Leslie,' said Lettie, as we came down to the stream.

'Yes, those, where they hang over the brook. They are ruddy like new blood freshening under the skin. Look, tassels of crimson and gold!' She pointed to the dusty hazel catkins mingled with the alder on her bosom. Then she began to quote Christina Rossetti's *A Birthday*.

'I'm glad you came to take me for a walk,' she continued – 'Doesn't Strelley Mill look pretty? Like a group of orange and scarlet fungi in a fairy picture. Do you know, I haven't been, no, not for quite a long time. Shall we call now?'

'The daylight will be gone if we do. It is half-past five – more! I saw him – the son – the other morning.'

'Where?'

'He was carting manure – I made haste by.'

'Did he speak to you – did you look at him?'

'No, he said nothing. I glanced at him – he's just the same, brick colour – stolid. Mind that stone – it rocks. I'm glad you've got strong boots on.'

'Seeing that I usually wear them –'

She stood poised a moment on a large stone, the fresh spring brook hastening towards her, deepening, sidling round her.

'You won't call and see them, then?' she asked.

'No. I like to hear the brook tinkling, don't you?' he replied.

'Ah, yes – it's full of music.'

'Shall we go on?' he said, impatient but submissive.

'I'll catch up in a minute,' said I.

I went in and found Emily putting some bread in the oven.

'Come out for a walk,' said I.

'Now? Let me tell mother – I was longing –'

She ran and put on her long grey coat and her red tam-o-shanter. As we went down the yard, George called to me.

'I'll come back,' I shouted.

He came to the crew-yard gate to see us off. When we came out on to the path, we saw Lettie standing on the top bar of the stile, balancing with her hand on Leslie's head. She saw us, she saw George, and she waved to us. Leslie was looking up at her anxiously. She waved again, then we could hear her laughing, and telling him excitedly to stand still, and steady her while she turned. She turned round, and leaped with a great flutter, like a big bird launching, down from the top of the stile to the ground and into his arms. Then we climbed the steep hillside – Sunny Bank, that had once shone yellow with wheat, and now waved black tattered ranks of thistles where the rabbits ran. We passed the little cottages in the hollow scooped out of the hill, and gained the highlands that look out over Leicestershire to Charnwood on the left, and away into the mountain knob of Derbyshire straight in front and towards the right.

The upper road is all grassy, fallen into long disuse. It used to lead from the Abbey to the Hall; but now it ends blindly on the hill-brow. Half way along is the old White House farm, with its green mounting steps mouldering outside. Ladies have mounted here and ridden towards the Vale of Belvoir – but now a labourer holds the farm.

We came to the quarries, and looked in at the lime-kilns.

'Let us go right into the wood out of the quarry,' said Leslie. 'I have not been since I was a little lad.'

'It is trespassing,' said Emily.

'We don't trespass,' he replied grandiloquently.

So we went along by the hurrying brook, which fell over little cascades in its haste, never looking once at the primroses that were glimmering all along its banks. We turned aside, and climbed the hill through the woods. Velvety green sprigs of dog-mercury were scattered on the red soil. We came to the top of a slope, where the wood thinned. As I talked to Emily I became dimly aware of a whiteness over the ground. She exclaimed with surprise, and I found that I was walking, in the first shades of twilight, over clumps of snowdrops. The hazels were thin, and only here and there an oak tree uprose. All the ground was white with snowdrops, like drops of manna scattered over the red earth, on the grey-green cluster of leaves. There was a deep little dell, sharp sloping like a cup, and a white sprinkling of flowers all the way down, with white flowers showing pale among the first inpouring of shadow at the bottom. The earth was red and warm, pricked with the dark, succulent green of bluebell sheaths, and embroidered with grey-green clusters of spears, and many white flowerets. High above, above the light tracery of hazel, the weird oaks tangled in the sunset. Below, in the first shadows, drooped hosts of little white flowers, so silent and sad; it seemed like a holy communion of pure wild things, numberless, frail, and folded meekly in the evening light. Other flower companies are glad; stately barbaric hordes of blue-bells, merry-headed cowslip groups, even light, tossing wood anem-ones; but snowdrops are sad and mysterious. We have lost their meaning. They do not belong to us, who ravish them. The girls bent among them, touching them with their fingers, and symbolizing the yearning which I felt. Folded in the twilight, these conquered flowerets are sad like forlorn little friends of dryads.

'What do they mean, do you think?' said Lettie in a low voice, as her white fingers touched the flowers, and her black furs fell on them.

'There are not so many this year,' said Leslie.

'They remind me of mistletoe, which is never ours, though we wear it,' said Emily to me.

'What do you think they say – what do they make you think, Cyril?' Lettie repeated.

'I don't know. Emily says they belong to some old wild lost religion. They were the symbol of tears, perhaps, to some strange-hearted Druid folk before us.'

'More than tears,' said Lettie. 'More than tears, they are so still. Something out of an old religion, that we have lost. They make me feel afraid.'

'What should you have to fear?' asked Leslie.

'If I knew, I shouldn't fear,' she answered. 'Look at all the snowdrops' – they hung in dim, strange flecks among the dusky leaves – 'look at them – closed up, retreating, powerless. They belong to some knowledge we have lost, that I have lost and that I need. I feel afraid. They seem like something in fate. Do you think, Cyril, we can lose things off the earth – like mastodons, and those old monstrosities – but things that matter – wisdom?'

'It is against my creed,' said I.

'I believe I have lost something,' said she.

'Come,' said Leslie, 'don't trouble with fancies. Come with me to the bottom of this cup, and see how strange it will be, with the sky marked with branches like a filigree lid.'

She rose and followed him down the steep side of the pit, crying, 'Ah, you are treading on the flowers.'

'No,' said he, 'I am being very careful.'

They sat down together on a fallen tree at the bottom. She leaned forward, her fingers wandering white among the shadowed grey spaces of leaves, plucking, as if it were a rite, flowers here and there. He could not see her face.

'Don't you care for me?' he asked softly.

'You?' – she sat up and looked at him, and laughed strangely. 'You do not seem real to me,' she replied, in a strange voice.

For some time they sat thus, both bowed and silent. Birds 'skirred' off from the bushes, and Emily looked up with a great start as a quiet, sardonic voice said above us:

'A dove-cot, my eyes if it ain't! It struck me I 'eered a cooin', an' 'ere's th' birds. Come on, sweethearts, it's th' wrong place for billin' an' cooin', in th' middle o' these 'ere snowdrops. Let's 'ave yer names, come on.'

'Clear off, you fool!' answered Leslie from below, jumping up in anger.

We all four turned and looked at the keeper. He stood in the rim of light, darkly; fine, powerful form, menacing us. He did not move, but like some malicious Pan looked down on us and said:

'Very pretty – pretty! Two – and two makes four. 'Tis true, two and two makes four. Come on, come on out o' this 'ere bridal bed, an' let's 'ave a look at yer.'

'Can't you use your eyes, you fool,' replied Leslie, standing up and helping Lettie with her furs. 'At any rate you can see there are ladies here.'

'Very sorry, sir! You can't tell a lady from a woman at this distance at dusk. Who may you be, sir?'

'Clear out! Come along, Lettie, you can't stay here now.'

They climbed into the light.

'Oh, very sorry, Mr Tempest – when yer look down on a man he never looks the same. I thought it was some young fools come here dallyin' –'

'Damn you – shut up!' exclaimed Leslie – 'I beg your pardon, Lettie. Will you have my arm?'

They looked very elegant, the pair of them. Lettie was wearing a long coat which fitted close; she had a small hat whose feathers flushed straight back with her hair.

The keeper looked at them. Then, smiling, he went down the dell with great strides, and returned, saying, 'Well, the lady might as well take her gloves.'

She took them from him, shrinking to Leslie. Then she started, and said:

'Let me fetch my flowers.'

She ran for the handful of snowdrops that lay among the roots of the trees. We all watched her.

'Sorry I made such a mistake – a lady!' said Annable. 'But I've nearly forgot the sight o' one – save the squire's daughters, who are never out o' nights.'

'I should think you never have seen many – unless –! Have you ever been a groom?'

'No groom but a bridegroom, sir, and then I think I'd rather groom a horse than a lady, for I got well bit – if you will excuse me, sir.'

'And you deserved it – no doubt.'

'I got it – an' I wish you better luck, sir. One's more a man here in th' wood, though, than in my lady's parlour, it strikes me.'

'A lady's parlour !' laughed Leslie, indulgent in his amusement at the facetious keeper.

'Oh, yes ! "Will you walk into my parlour –"'

'You're very smart for a keeper.'

'Oh, yes sir – I was once a lady's man. But I'd rather watch th' rabbits an' th' birds; an' it's easier breeding brats in th' Kennels than in th' town.'

'They are yours, are they ?' said I.

'You know 'em, do you, Sir ? Aren't they a lovely little litter ? – aren't they a pretty bag o' ferrets ? – natural as weasels – that's what I said they should be – bred up like a bunch o' young foxes, to run as they would.'

Emily had joined Lettie, and they kept aloof from the man they instinctively hated.

'They'll get nicely trapped, one of these days,' said I.

'They're natural – they can fend for themselves like wild beasts do,' he replied, grinning.

'You are not doing your duty, it strikes me,' put in Leslie sententiously.

The man laughed.

'Duties of parents ! – tell me, I've need of it. I've nine – that is eight, and one not far off. She breeds well, the owd lass – one every two years – nine in fourteen years – done well, hasn't she ?'

'You've done pretty badly, I think.'

'I – why ? It's natural ! When a man's more than nature he's a devil. Be a good animal, says I, whether it's man or woman. You, sir, a good natural male animal; the lady there – a female un – that's proper – as long as yer enjoy it.'

'And what then ?'

'Do as th' animals do. I watch my brats – I let 'em grow. They're beauties, they are – sound as a young ash pole, every one. They shan't learn to dirty themselves wi' smirking deviltry

– not if I can help it. They can be like birds, or weasels, or vipers, or squirrels, so long as they ain't human rot, that's what I say.'

'It's one way of looking at things,' said Leslie.

'Ay. Look at the women looking at us. I'm something between a bull and a couple of worms stuck together, I am. See that spink!' he raised his voice for the girls to hear. 'Pretty, isn't he? What for? – And what for do you wear a fancy vest and twist your moustache, sir! What for, at the bottom! Ha – tell a woman not to come in a wood till she can look at natural things – she might see something – Good night, sir.'

He marched off into the darkness.

'Coarse fellow, that,' said Leslie when he had rejoined Lettie, 'but he's a character.'

'He makes you shudder,' she replied. 'But yet you are interested in him. I believe he has a history.'

'He seems to lack something,' said Emily.

'I thought him rather a fine fellow,' said I.

'Splendidly built fellow, but callous – no soul,' remarked Leslie, dismissing the question.

'No,' assented Emily. 'No soul – and among the snowdrops.'

Lettie was thoughtful, and I smiled.

It was a beautiful evening, still, with red, shaken clouds in the west. The moon in heaven was turning wistfully back to the east. Dark purple woods lay around us, painting out the distance. The near, wild, ruined land looked sad and strange under the pale afterglow. The turf path was fine and springy.

'Let us run!' said Lettie, and joining hands we raced wildly along, with a flutter and breathless laughter, till we were happy and forgetful. When we stopped we exclaimed at once, 'Hark!'

'A child!' said Lettie.

'At the Kennels,' said I.

We hurried forward. From the house came the mad yelling and yelping of children, and the wild hysterical shouting of a woman.

'Tha' little devil – tha' little devil – tha' shanna – that tha' shanna!' and this was accompanied by the hollow sound of blows, and a pandemonium of howling. We rushed in, and found the woman in a tousled frenzy belabouring a youngster with an enamelled pan. The lad was rolled up like a young hedgehog – the woman held him by the foot, and like a flail came the hollow utensil thudding on his shoulders and back. He lay in the firelight and howled, while scattered in various groups, with the leaping firelight twinkling over their tears and their open mouths, were the other children, crying too. The mother was in a state of hysteria; her hair streamed over her face, and her eyes were fixed in a stare of overwrought irritation. Up and down went her long arm like a windmill sail. I ran and held it. When she could hit no more, the woman dropped the pan from her nerveless hand, and staggered, trembling, to the squab. She looked desperately weary and fordone – she clasped and unclasped her hands continually. Emily hushed the children, while Lettie hushed the mother, holding her hard, cracked hands as she swayed to and fro. Gradually the mother became still, and sat staring in front of her; then aimlessly she began to finger the jewels on Lettie's finger.

Emily was bathing the cheek of a little girl, who lifted up her voice and wept loudly when she saw the speck of blood on the cloth. But presently she became quiet too, and Emily could empty the water from the late instrument of castigation, and at last light the lamp.

I found Sam under the table in a little heap. I put out my hand for him, and he wriggled away, like a lizard, into the passage. After a while I saw him in a corner, lying whimpering with little savage cries of pain. I cut off his retreat and captured him, bearing him struggling into the kitchen. Then, weary with pain, he became passive.

We undressed him, and found his beautiful white body all discoloured with bruises. The mother began to sob again, with a chorus of babies. The girls tried to soothe the weeping, while I rubbed butter into the silent, wincing boy. Then his mother caught him in her arms, and kissed him passionately, and cried with abandon. The boy let himself be kissed – then he too began to sob, till his little body was all shaken. They folded themselves together, the poor dishevelled mother and the half-naked boy, and wept themselves still. Then she took him to bed, and the girls helped the other little ones into their nightgowns, and soon the house was still.

'I canna manage 'em, I canna,' said the mother mournfully. 'They growin' beyont me – I dunna know what to do wi' 'em. An' niver a' 'and does 'e lift ter 'elp me – no – 'e cares not a thing for me – not a thing – nowt but makes a mock an' a sludge o' me.'

'Ah, baby,' said Lettie, setting the bonny boy on his feet, and holding up his trailing nightgown behind him, 'do you want to walk to your mother – go then – Ah!'

The child, a handsome little fellow of some sixteen months, toddled across to his mother, waving his hands as he went, and laughing, while his large hazel eyes glowed with pleasure. His mother caught him, pushed the silken brown hair back from his forehead, and laid his cheek against hers.

'Ah!' she said, 'Tha's got a funny Dad, tha' has, not like an-other man, no, my duckie. 'E's got no 'art ter care for nobody, 'e 'asna, ma pigeon – no, – lives like a stranger to his own flesh an' blood.'

The girl with the wounded cheek had found comfort in Leslie. She was seated on his knee, looking at him with solemn blue eyes, her solemnity increased by the quaint round head, whose black hair was cut short.

''S my chalk, yes it is, 'n our Sam says as it's 'issen, an' 'e ta'es it and marks it all gone, so I wouldn'a gie 't 'im,' – she clutched in her fat little hand a piece of red chalk. 'My Dad gen it me, ter mark my dolly's face red, what's on'y wood – I'll show yer.'

She wriggled down, and holding up her trailing gown with one hand, trotted to a corner piled with a child's rubbish, and hauled out a hideous carven caricature of a woman, and brought it to Leslie. The face of the object was streaked with red.

''Ere sh' is, my dolly, what my Dad make me – 'er name's Lady Mima.'

'Is it?' said Lettie, 'and are these her cheeks? She's not pretty, is she?'

'Um – sh' is. My Dad says sh' is – like a lady.'

'And he gave you her rouge, did he?'

'Rouge!' she nodded.

'And you wouldn't let Sam have it?'

'No – an' mi movver says, "Dun gie 't 'im" – 'n 'e bite me.'

'What will your father say?'

'Me Dad?'

''E'd nobbut laugh,' put in the mother, 'an' say as a bite's bett'r'n a kiss.'

'Brute!' said Leslie feelingly.

'No, but 'e never laid a finger on 'em – nor me neither. But 'e 's not like another man – niver tells yer nowt. He's more a stranger to me this day than 'e wor th' day I first set eyes on 'im.'

'Where was that?' asked Lettie.

'When I wor a lass at th' 'All – an' 'im a new man come – fair a gentleman, an' a, an' a! An even now can read an' talk like a gentleman – but 'e tells me nothing – Oh no – what am I in 'is eyes but a sludge bump? – 'e 's above me, 'e is, an' above 'is own childer. God a-mercy, 'e 'll be in in a minute. Come on 'ere!'

She hustled the children to bed, swept the litter into a corner, and began to lay the table. The cloth was spotless, and she put him a silver spoon in the saucer.

We had only just got out of the house when he drew near. I saw his massive figure in the doorway, and the big, prolific woman moved subserviently about the room.

'Hullo, Proserpine – had visitors?'

'I never axed 'em – they come in 'earin' th' childer cryin'. I never encouraged 'em –'

We hurried away into the night.

'Ah, it's always the woman bears the burden,' said Lettie bitterly.

'If he'd helped her – wouldn't she have been a fine woman now – splendid? But she's dragged to bits. Men are brutes – and marriage just gives scope to them,' said Emily.

'Oh you wouldn't take that as a fair sample of marriage,' replied Leslie. 'Think of you and me, Minnehaha.'

'Ay.'

'Oh – I meant to tell you – what do you think of Greymede old vicarage for us?'

'It's a lovely old place!' exclaimed Lettie, and we passed out of hearing.

We stumbled over the rough path. The moon was bright, and

we stepped apprehensively on the shadows thrown from the trees, for they lay so black and substantial. Occasionally a moon-beam would trace out a suave white branch that the rabbits had gnawed quite bare in the hard winter. We came out of the woods into the full heavens. The northern sky was full of a gush of green light; in front, eclipsed Orion leaned over his bed, and the moon followed.

'When the northern lights are up,' said Emily, 'I feel so strange – half eerie – they do fill you with awe, don't they?'

'Yes,' said I, 'they make you wonder, and look, and expect something.'

'What do you expect?' she said softly, and looked up, and saw me smiling, and she looked down again, biting her lips.

When we came to the parting of the roads, Emily begged them just to step into the mill – just for a moment – and Lettie consented.

The kitchen window was uncurtained, and the blind, as usual, was not drawn. We peeped in through the cords of budding honeysuckle. George and Alice were sitting at the table playing chess; the mother was mending a coat, and the father, as usual, was reading. Alice was talking quietly, and George was bent on the game. His arms lay on the table.

We made a noise at the door, and entered. George rose heavily, shook hands, and sat down again.

'Hullo, Lettie Beardsall, you are a stranger,' said Alice. 'Are you *so* much engaged?'

'Ay – we don't see much of her nowadays,' added the father in his jovial way.

'And isn't she a toff, in her fine hat and furs and snowdrops. Look at her, George, you've never looked to see what a toff she is.'

He raised his eyes, and looked at her apparel and at her flowers, but not at her face:

'Aye, she is fine,' he said, and returned to the chess.

'We have been gathering snowdrops,' said Lettie, fingering the flowers in her bosom.

'They are pretty – give me some, will you?' said Alice, holding out her hand. Lettie gave her the flowers.

'Check!' said George deliberately.

'Get out!' replied his opponent, 'I've got some snowdrops – don't they suit me, an innocent little soul like me? Lettie won't wear them – she's not meek and mild and innocent like me. Do you want some?'

'If you like – what for?'

'To make you pretty, of course, and to show you an innocent little meekling.'

'You're in check,' he said.

'Where can you wear them? – there's only your shirt. Aw! – there!' – she stuck a few flowers in his ruffled black hair – 'Look, Lettie, isn't he sweet?'

Lettie laughed with a strained little laugh:

'He's like Bottom and the ass's head,' she said.

'Then I'm Titania – don't I make a lovely fairy queen, Bully Bottom? – and who's jealous Oberon?'

'He reminds me of that man in *Hedda Gabler* – crowned with vine leaves – oh, yes, vine leaves,' said Emily.

'How's your mare's sprain, Mr Tempest?' George asked, taking no notice of the flowers in his hair.

'Oh – she'll soon be all right, thanks.'

'Ah – George told me about it,' put in the father, and he held Leslie in conversation.

'Am I in check, George?' said Alice, returning to the game. She knitted her brows and cogitated:

'Pooh!' she said, 'that's soon remedied!' – she moved her piece, and said triumphantly, 'Now, sir!'

He surveyed the game, and, with deliberation moved. Alice pounced on him; with a leap of her knight she called 'check!'

'I didn't see it – you may have the game now,' he said.

'Beaten, my boy! – don't crow over a woman any more. Stale-mate – with flowers in your hair!'

He put his hand to his head, and felt among his hair, and threw the flowers on the table.

'Would you believe it – !' said the mother, coming into the room from the dairy.

'What?' we all asked.

'Nickie Ben's been and eaten the sile cloth. Yes! When I went to wash it, there sat Nickie Ben gulping, and wiping the froth off his whiskers.'

George laughed loudly and heartily. He laughed till he was tired. Lettie looked and wondered when he would be done.

'I imagined,' he gasped, 'how he'd feel with half a yard of muslin creeping down his throttle.'

This laughter was most incongruous. He went off into another burst. Alice laughed too – it was easy to infect her with laughter. Then the father began – and in walked Nickie Ben, stepping disconsolately – we all roared again, till the rafters shook. Only Lettie looked impatiently for the end. George swept his bare arms across the table, and the scattered little flowers fell broken to the ground.

'Oh – what a shame!' exclaimed Lettie.

'What?' said he, looking round. 'Your flowers? Do you feel sorry for them? – you're too tender-hearted; isn't she, Cyril?'

'Always was – for dumb animals, and things,' said I.

'Don't you wish you was a little dumb animal, Georgie?' said Alice.

He smiled, putting away the chess-men.

'Shall we go, dear?' said Lettie to Leslie.

'If you are ready,' he replied, rising with alacrity.

'I am tired,' she said plaintively.

He attended to her with little tender solicitations.

'Have we walked too far?' he asked.

'No, it's not that. No – it's the snowdrops, and the man, and the children – and everything. I feel just a bit exhausted.'

She kissed Alice, and Emily, and the mother.

'Good night, Alice,' she said. 'It's not altogether my fault we're strangers. You know – really – I'm just the same – really. Only you imagine, and then what can I do?'

She said farewell to George, and looked at him through a quiver of suppressed tears.

George was somewhat flushed with triumph over Lettie. She had gone home with tears shaken from her eyes unknown to her lover; at the farm George laughed with Alice.

We escorted Alice home to Eberwich – 'Like a blooming little monkey dangling from two boughs,' as she put it, when we swung her along on our arms. We laughed and said many preposterous things. George wanted to kiss her at parting, but she tipped him under the chin and said, 'Sweet!' as one does to a canary. Then she laughed with her tongue between her teeth, and ran indoors.

'She is a little devil,' said he.

We took the long way home by Greymede, and passed the dark schools.

'Come on,' said he, 'let's go in the Ram Inn, and have a look at my cousin Meg.'

It was half-past ten when he marched me across the road and into the sanded passage of the little inn. The place had been an important farm in the days of George's grand-uncle, but since his decease it had declined, under the governance of the widow and a man-of-all-work. The old grand-aunt was propped and supported by a splendid grand-daughter. The near kin of Meg were all in California, so she, a bonny delightful girl of twenty-four, stayed near her grandma.

As we tramped grittily down the passage, the red head of Bill poked out of the bar, and he said as he recognized George:

'Good-ev'nin' – go forward – 'er's non abed yit.'

We went forward, and unlatched the kitchen door. The great-aunt was seated in her little, round-backed armchair, sipping her 'night-cap'.

'Well, George, my lad!' she cried, in her querulous voice. 'Tha' niver says it's thai, does ter? That's com'n for summat, for sure, else what brings thee ter see me?'

'No,' he said. 'Ah'n com ter see thee, nowt else. Wheer's Meg?'

'Ah! – Ha – Ha – Ah! – Me, did ter say? – come ter see me? – Ha – wheer's Meg! – an's who's this young gentleman?'

I was formally introduced, and shook the clammy corded hand of the old lady.

'Tha' looks delikit,' she observed, shaking her cap and its scarlet geraniums sadly: 'Cum now, sit thee down, an' dunna look so long o' th' leg.'

I sat down on the sofa, on the cushions covered with blue and red checks. The room was very hot, and I stared about uncomfortably. The old lady sat peering at nothing, in reverie. She was a hard-visaged, bosomless dame, clad in thick black cloth-like armour, and wearing an immense twisted gold brooch in the lace at her neck.

We heard heavy, quick footsteps above.

'Er's commin',' remarked the old lady, rousing from her apathy. The footsteps came downstairs – quickly, then cautiously round the bend. Meg appeared in the doorway. She started with surprise, saying:

'Well, I 'eered sumbody, but I never thought it was you.' More colour still flamed into her glossy cheeks, and she smiled in her fresh, frank way. I think I have never seen a woman who had more physical charm; there was a voluptuous fascination in her every outline and movement; one never listened to the words that came from her lips, one watched the ripe motion of those red fruits.

'Get 'em a drop o' whisky, Meg – you'll 'a'e a drop?'

I declined firmly, but did not escape.

'Nay,' declared the old dame. 'I s'll ha'e none o' thy no's. Should ter like it 'ot? – Say th' word, an' tha' 'as it.'

I did not say the word.

'Then gi'e 'im claret,' pronounced my hostess, 'though it's thin-bellied stuff ter go ter bed on' – and claret it was.

Meg went out again to see about closing. The grand-aunt sighed, and sighed again, for no perceptible reason but the whisky.

'It's well you've come ter see me now,' she moaned, 'for you'll none 'a'e a chance next time you come'n; – No – I'm all gone but my cap –' She shook that geraniumed erection, and I wondered what sardonic fate left it behind.

'An' I'm forced ter say it, I s'll be thankful to be gone,' she added, after a few sighs.

This weariness of the flesh was touching. The cruel truth is, however, that the old lady clung to life like a louse to a pig's back. Dying, she faintly, but emphatically declared herself, 'a bit better – a bit better. I s'll be up tomorrow.'

'I should a gone before now,' she continued, 'but for that blessed wench – I canna abear to think o' leavin' 'er – come drink up, my lad, drink up – nay, tha' 'rt nobbut young yet, tha' 'rt none topped up wi' a thimbleful.'

I took whisky in preference to the acrid stuff.

'Ay,' resumed the grand-aunt. 'I canna go in peace till 'er's settled – an' 'er's that tickle o' choosin'. Th' right sort 'asn't th' gumption ter ax 'er.'

She sniffed, and turned scornfully to her glass. George grinned and looked conscious; as he swallowed a gulp of whisky it crackled in his throat. The sound annoyed the old lady.

'Tha' might be scar'd at summat,' she said. 'Tha' niver 'ad six drops o' spunk in thee.'

She turned again with a sniff to her glass. He frowned with irritation, half filled his glass with liquor, and drank again.

'I dare bet as tha' niver kissed a wench in thy life – not proper' – and she tossed the last drops of her toddy down her skinny throat.

Here Meg came along the passage.

'Come, gran'ma,' she said. 'I'm sure it's time as you was in bed – come on.'

'Sit thee down an' drink a drop wi's – it's not ivry night as we 'a'e cumpny.'

'No, let me take you to bed – I'm sure you must be ready.'

'Sit thee down 'ere, I say, an' get thee a drop o' port. Come – no argy-bargyin'.'

Meg fetched more glasses and a decanter. I made a place for her between me and George. We all had port wine. Meg, naive and unconscious, waited on us deliciously. Her cheeks gleamed like satin when she laughed, save when the dimples held the shadow. Her suave, tawny neck was bare and bewitching, She turned suddenly to George as he asked her a question, and they found their faces close together. He kissed her, and when she started back, jumped and kissed her neck with warmth.

'Là – là – dy – da – là – dy – dà – dy – dà,' cried the old woman in delight, and she clutched her wineglass.

'Come on – chink!' she cried, 'all together – chink to him!'

We four chinked and drank. George poured wine in a tumbler, and drank it off. He was getting excited, and all the energy and passion that normally were bound down by his caution and self-instinct began to flame out.

'Here, aunt!' said he, lifting his tumbler, 'here's to what you want – you know!'

'I knowed tha' wor as spunky as ony on 'em,' she cried. 'Tha' nobbut wanted warmin' up. I'll see as you're all right. It's a bargain. Chink again, ivrybody.'

'A bargain,' said he before he put his lips to the glass.

'What bargain's that?' said Meg.

The old lady laughed loudly and winked at George, who, with his lips wet with wine, got up and kissed Meg soundly, saying:

'There it is – that seals it.'

Meg wiped her face with her big pinafore, and seemed uncomfortable.

'Aren't you comin,' gran'ma?' she pleaded.

'Eh, tha' wants ter 'orry me off – what's thai say, George – a deep un, isna 'er?'

'Dunna go, Aunt, dunna be hustled off.'

'Tush – Pish,' snorted the old lady. 'Yah, tha' 'rt a slow un, an' no mistakes! Get a candle, Meg, I'm ready.'

Meg brought a brass bedroom candlestick. Bill brought in the money in a tin box, and delivered it into the hands of the old lady.

'Go thy ways to bed, now lad,' said she to the ugly, wizened serving-man. He sat in a corner and pulled off his boots.

'Come an' kiss me good night, George,' said the old woman – and as he did so she whispered in his ear, whereat he laughed loudly. She poured whisky into her glass and called to the serving-man to drink it. Then, pulling herself up heavily, she leaned on Meg and went upstairs. She had been a big woman, one could see, but now her shapeless, broken figure looked pitiful beside Meg's luxuriant form. We heard them slowly, laboriously climb the stairs. George sat pulling his moustache and half-smiling; his eyes were alight with that peculiar childish look they had when he was experiencing new and doubtful sensations. Then he poured himself more whisky.

'I say, steady!' I admonished.

'What for!' he replied, indulging himself like a spoiled child and laughing.

Bill, who had sat for some time looking at the hole in his stocking, drained his glass, and with a sad 'Good night,' creaked off upstairs.

Presently Meg came down, and I rose and said we must be going.

'I'll just come an' lock the door after you,' said she, standing uneasily waiting.

George got up. He gripped the edge of the table to steady himself; then he got his balance, and, with his eyes on Meg, said:

''Ere!' he nodded his head to her. 'Come here, I want ter ax thee sumwhat.'

She looked at him, half smiling, half doubtful. He put his arm round her and looking down into her eyes, with his face very close to hers, said:

'Let's ha'e a kiss.'

Quite unresisting she yielded him her mouth, looking at him intently with her bright brown eyes. He kissed her, and pressed her closely to him.

'I'm going to marry thee,' he said.

'Go on!' she replied, softly, half glad, half doubtful.

'I am an' all,' he repeated, pressing her more tightly to him.

I went down the passage, and stood in the open doorway looking out into the night. It seemed a long time. Then I heard the thin voice of the old woman at the top of the stairs:

'Meg! Meg! Send 'im off now. Come on!'

In the silence that followed there was a murmur of voices, and then they came into the passage.

'Good night, my lad, good luck to thee!' cried the voice like a ghoul from upper regions.

He kissed his betrothed a rather hurried good night at the door.

'Good night,' she replied, softly, watching him retreat. Then we heard her shoot the heavy bolts.

'You know,' he began, and he tried to clear his throat. His throat was husky and strangulated with excitement. He tried again:

'You know – she – she's a clinker.'

I did not reply, but he took no notice.

'Damn!' he ejaculated. 'What did I let her go for!'

We walked along in silence – his excitement abated somewhat.

'It's the way she swings her body – an' the curves as she stands. It's when you look at her – you feel – you know.'

I suppose I knew, but it was unnecessary to say so.

'You know – if ever I dream in the night – of women – you know – it's always Meg; she seems to look so soft, and to curve her body –'

Gradually his feet began to drag. When we came to the place where the colliery railway crossed the road, he stumbled, and pitched forward, only just recovering himself. I took hold of his arm.

'Good Lord, Cyril, am I drunk?' he said.

'Not quite,' said I.

'No,' he muttered, 'couldn't be.'

But his feet dragged again, and he began to stagger from side to side. I took hold of his arm. He murmured angrily – then, subsiding again, muttered, with slovenly articulation:

'I – feel fit to drop with sleep.'

Along the dead, silent roadway, and through the uneven blackness of the wood, we lurched and stumbled. He was very heavy and difficult to direct. When at last we came to the brook we splashed straight through the water. I urged him to walk steadily and quietly across the yard. He did his best, and we made a fairly still entry into the farm. He dropped with all his weight on the sofa, and, leaning down, began to unfasten his leggings. In the midst of his fumblings he fell asleep, and I was afraid he would pitch forward on to his head. I took off his leggings and his wet boots and his collar. Then, as I was pushing and shaking him awake to get off his coat, I heard a creaking on the stairs, and my heart sank for I thought it was his mother. But it was Emily, in her long white nightgown. She looked at us with great dark eyes of terror, and whispered: 'What's the matter?'

I shook my head and looked at him. His head had dropped down on his chest again.

'Is he hurt?' she asked, her voice becoming audible, and dangerous. He lifted his head, and looked at her with heavy, angry eyes.

'George!' she said sharply, in bewilderment and fear. His eyes seemed to contract evilly.

'Is he drunk?' she whispered, shrinking away, and looking at me. 'Have you made him drunk – you?'

I nodded. I too was angry.

'Oh, if mother gets up! I must get him to bed! Oh, how could you!'

This sibilant whispering irritated him, and me. I tugged at his coat. He snarled incoherently, and swore. She caught her breath. He looked at her sharply, and I was afraid he would wake himself into a rage.

'Go upstairs!' I whispered to her. She shook her head. I could see him taking heavy breaths, and the veins of his neck were swelling. I was furious at her disobedience.

'Go at once,' I said fiercely, and she went, still hesitating and looking back.

I had hauled off his coat and waistcoat, so I let him sink again into stupidity while I took off my boots. Then I got him to his feet, and, walking behind him, impelled him slowly upstairs. I lit a candle in his bedroom. There was no sound from the other rooms. So I undressed him, and got him in bed at last, somehow. I covered him up and put over him the calf-skin rug, because the night was cold. Almost immediately he began to breathe heavily. I dragged him over to his side, and pillowed his head comfortably. He looked like a tired boy, asleep.

I stood still, now I felt myself alone, and looked round. Up to the low roof rose the carven pillars of dark mahogany; there was a chair by the bed, and a little yellow chest of drawers by the windows, that was all the furniture, save the calf-skin rug on the floor. In the drawers I noticed a book. It was a copy of *Omar Khayyam* that Lettie had given him in her *Khayyam* days, a little shilling book with coloured illustrations.

I blew out the candle, when I had looked at him again. As I crept on to the landing, Emily peeped from her room, whispering, 'Is he in bed?'

I nodded, and whispered good night. Then I went home, heavily.

After the evening at the farm, Lettie and Leslie drew closer together. They eddied unevenly down the little stream of courtship, jostling and drifting together and apart. He was unsatisfied and strove with every effort to bring her close to him, submissive. Gradually she yielded, and submitted to him. She folded round her and him the snug curtain of the present, and they sat like children playing a game behind the hangings of an old bed. She shut out all distant outlooks, as an Arab unfolds his tent and conquers the mystery and space of the desert. So she lived gleefully in a little tent of present pleasures and fancies.

Occasionally, only occasionally, she would peep from her tent into the out space. Then she sat poring over books, and nothing would be able to draw her away; or she sat in her room looking out of the window for hours together. She pleaded headaches; mother said liver; he, angry like a spoilt child denied his wish, declared it moodiness and perversity.

CHAPTER II

A Shadow in Spring

WITH spring came trouble. The Saxtons declared they were being bitten off the estate by rabbits. Suddenly, in a fit of despair, the father bought a gun. Although he knew that the Squire would not for one moment tolerate the shooting of that manna, the rabbits, yet he was out in the first cold morning twilight banging away. At first he but scared the brutes, and brought Annable on the scene; then, blooded by the use of the weapon, he played havoc among the furry beasts, bringing home some eight or nine couples.

George entirely approved of this measure; it rejoiced him even; yet he had never had the initiative to begin the like himself, or even to urge his father to it. He prophesied trouble, and possible loss of the farm. It disturbed him somewhat, to think they must look out for another place, but he postponed the thought of the evil day till the time should be upon him.

A vendetta was established between the Mill and the keeper, Annable. The latter cherished his rabbits:

'Call 'em vermin!' he said. 'I only know one sort of vermin – and that's the talkin' sort.' So he set himself to thwart and harass the rabbit slayers.

It was about this time I cultivated the acquaintance of the keeper. All the world hated him – to the people in the villages he was like a devil of the woods. Some miners had sworn vengeance on him for having caused their committal to gaol. But he had a great attraction for me; his magnificent physique, his great vigour and vitality, and his swarthy, gloomy face drew me.

He was a man of one idea: – that all civilization was the painted fungus of rottenness. He hated any sign of culture. I won his respect one afternoon when he found me trespassing in the woods because I was watching some maggots at work in a dead rabbit. They led us to a discussion of life. He was a thorough materialist – he scorned religion and all mysticism. He spent his days sleeping, making intricate traps for weasels and men, putting together a gun, or doing some amateur forestry, cutting down timber, splitting it in logs for use in the hall, and planting young trees. When he thought, he reflected on the decay of mankind – the decline of the human race into folly and weakness and rottenness. 'Be a good animal, true to your animal instinct,' was his motto. With all this, he was fundamentally very unhappy – and he made me also wretched. It was this power to communicate his unhappiness that made me somewhat dear to him, I think. He treated me as an affectionate father treats a delicate son; I noticed he liked to put his hand on my shoulder or my knee as we talked; yet withal, he asked me questions, and saved his thoughts to tell me, and believed in my knowledge like any acolyte.

I went up to the quarry woods one evening in early April, taking a look for Annable. I could not find him, however, in the wood. So I left the wild-lands, and went along by the old red wall of the kitchen garden, along the main road as far as the mouldering church which stands high on a bank by the roadside, just where the trees tunnel the darkness, and the gloom of the highway startles the travellers at noon. Great trees growing on the banks suddenly fold over everything at this point in the swinging road, and in the obscurity rots the Hall church, black and melancholy above the shrinking head of the traveller.

The grassy path to the churchyard was still clogged with decayed leaves. The church is abandoned. As I drew near an owl floated softly out of the black tower. Grass overgrew the threshold. I pushed open the door, grinding back a heap of fallen plaster and rubbish, and entered the place. In the twilight the pews were leaning in ghostly disorder, the prayer-books dragged from their ledges, and scattered on the floor in the dust and rubble, torn by mice and birds. Birds scuffled in the darkness of the roof. I looked up. In the upward well of the tower I could see a bell hanging. I stooped and picked up a piece of plaster from the ragged confusion of feathers, and broken nests, and remnants of dead birds. Up into the vault overhead I tossed pieces of plaster until one hit the bell, and it 'tonged' out its faint remonstrance. There was a rustle of many birds like spirits. I sounded the bell again, and dark forms moved with cries of alarm overhead, and something fell heavily. I shivered in the dark, evil-smelling place, and hurried to get out of doors. I clutched my hands with relief and pleasure when I saw the sky above me quivering with the last crystal lights, and the lowest red of sunset behind the yew-boles. I drank the fresh air, that sparkled with the sound of the blackbirds and thrushes whistling their strong bright notes.

I strayed round to where the headstones, from their eminence, leaned to look on the Hall below, where great windows shone yellow light on to the flagged court-yard, and the little fish pool. A stone staircase descended from the graveyard to the court, between stone balustrades whose pock-marked grey columns still swelled gracefully and with dignity, encrusted with lichens. The staircase was filled with ivy and rambling roses – impassable. Ferns were unrolling round the big square halting place, half way down where the stairs turned.

A peacock, startled from the back premises of the Hall, came flapping up the terraces to the churchyard. Then a heavy footstep crossed the flags. It was the keeper. I whistled the whistle he knew, and he broke his way through the vicious rose-boughs up the stairs. The peacock flapped beyond me, on to the neck of an old bowed angel, rough and dark, an angel which had long ceased sorrowing for the lost Lucy, and had died also. The bird bent its voluptuous neck and peered about. Then it lifted up its head and yelled. The sound tore the dark sanctuary of twilight. The old grey grass seemed to stir, and I could fancy the smothered primroses and violets beneath it waking and gasping for fear.

The keeper looked at me and smiled. He nodded his head towards the peacock, saying:

'Hark at that damned thing!'

Again the bird lifted its crested head and gave a cry, at the same time turning awkwardly on its ugly legs, so that it showed us the full wealth of its tail glimmering like a stream of coloured stars over the sunken face of the angel.

'The proud fool! – look at it! Perched on an angel, too, as

if it were a pedestal for vanity. That's the soul of a woman – or it's the devil.'

He was silent for a time, and we watched the great bird moving uneasily before us in the twilight.

'That's the very soul of a lady,' he said, 'the very, very soul. Damn the thing, to perch on that old angel. I should like to wring its neck.'

Again the bird screamed, and shifted awkwardly on its legs; it seemed to stretch its beak at us in derision. Annable picked up a piece of sod and flung it at the bird, saying:

'Get out, you screeching devil! God!' he laughed. 'There must be plenty of hearts twisting under here,' – and he stamped on a grave, 'when they hear that row.'

He kicked another sod from a grave and threw it at the big bird. The peacock flapped away, over the tombs, down the terraces.

'Just look!' he said, 'the miserable brute has dirtied that angel. A woman to the end, I tell you, all vanity and screech and defilement.'

He sat down on a vault and lit his pipe. But before he had smoked two minutes, it was out again. I had not seen him in a state of perturbation before.

'The church,' said I, 'is rotten. I suppose they'll stand all over the country like this, soon – with peacocks trailing the graveyards.'

'Ay,' he muttered, taking no notice of me.

'This stone is cold,' I said, rising.

He got up too, and stretched his arms as if he were tired. It was quite dark, save for the waxing moon which leaned over the east.

'It is a very fine night,' I said. 'Don't you notice a smell of violets?'

'Ay! The moon looks like a woman with child. I wonder what Time's got in her belly.'

'You?' I said. 'You don't expect anything exciting, do you?'

'Exciting! – No – about as exciting as this rotten old place – just rot off – Oh, my God! – I'm like a good house, built and finished, and left to tumble down again with nobody to live in it.'

'Why – what's up – really?'

He laughed bitterly, saying, 'Come and sit down.'

He led me off to a seat by the north door, between two pews, very black and silent. There we sat, he putting his gun carefully beside him. He remained perfectly still, thinking.

'What's up?' he said, at last, 'Why – I'll tell you. I went to Cambridge – my father was a big cattle dealer – he died bankrupt while I was in college, and I never took my degree. They persuaded me to be a parson, and a parson I was.

'I went a curate to a little place in Leicestershire – a bonnie place, with not many people, and a fine old church, and a great rich parsonage. I hadn't overmuch to do, and the rector – he was the son of an Earl – was generous. He lent me a horse and would have me hunt like the rest. I always think of that place with a smell of honeysuckle while the grass is wet in the morning. It was fine, and I enjoyed myself, and did the parish work all right. I believe I was pretty good.

'A cousin of the rector's used to come in the hunting season – a Lady Crystabel, lady in her own right. The second year I was there she came in June. There wasn't much company, so she used to talk to me – I used to read then – and she used to pretend to be so childish and unknowing, and would get me telling her things, and talking to her, and I was hot on things. We must play tennis together, and ride together, and I must row her down the river. She said we were in the wilderness and could do as we liked. She made me wear flannels and soft clothes. She was very fine and frank and unconventional – ripping, I thought her. All the summer she stopped on. I should meet her in the garden early in the morning when I came from a swim in the river – it was cleared and deepened on purpose – and she'd blush and make me walk with her. I can remember I used to stand and dry myself on the bank full where she might see me – I was mad on her – and she was madder on me.

'We went to some caves in Derbyshire once, and she would wander from the rest, and loiter, and, for a game, we played a sort of hide and seek with the party. They thought we'd gone, and they went and locked the door. Then she pretended to be frightened and clung to me, and said what would they think, and hid her face in my coat. I took her and kissed her, and we made it up properly. I found out afterwards – she actually told me – she'd got the idea from a sloppy French novel – the Romance of A Poor Young Man. I was the Poor Young Man.

'We got married. She gave me a living she had in her patronage, and we went to live at her Hall. She wouldn't let me out of her sight. Lord! – we were an infatuated couple – and she would choose to view me in an aesthetic light. I was Greek statues for her, bless you: Croton, Hercules, I don't know what! She had her own way too much – I let her do as she liked with me.

'Then gradually she got tired – it took her three years to be really glutted with me. I had a physique then – for that matter I have now.'

He held out his arm to me, and bade me try his muscle. I was startled. The hard flesh almost filled his sleeve.

'Ah,' he continued, 'You don't know what it is to have the pride of a body like mine. But she wouldn't have children – no, she wouldn't – said she daren't. That was the root of the difference at first. But she cooled down, and if you don't know the pride of my body you'd never know my humiliation. I tried to remonstrate – and she looked simply astounded at my cheek. I never got over that amazement.

'She began to get souly. A poet got hold of her, and she began to affect Burne-Jones – or Waterhouse – it was Waterhouse – she was a lot like one of his women – Lady of Shalott, I believe. At any rate, she got souly, and I was her animal – *son animal – son boeuf*. I put up with that for above a year. Then I got some servants' clothes and went.

'I was seen in France – then in Australia – though I never left England. I was supposed to have died in the bush. She married a young fellow. Then I was proved to have died, and I read a little obituary notice on myself in a woman's paper she subscribed to. She wrote it herself – as a warning to other young ladies of position not to be seduced by plausible "Poor Young Men".'

'Now she's dead. They've got the paper – her paper – in the kitchen down there, and it's full of photographs, even an old photo of me – "an unfortunate misalliance". I feel, somehow, as if I were at an end too. I thought I'd grown a solid, middle-aged-man, and here I feel sore as I did at twenty-six, and I talk as I used to.

'One thing – I have got some children, and they're of a breed as you'd not meet anywhere. I was a good animal before everything, and I've got some children.'

He sat looking up where the big moon swam through the black branches of the yew.

'So she's dead – your poor peacock!' I murmured.

He got up, looking always at the sky, and stretched himself again. He was an impressive figure massed in blackness against the moonlight, with his arms outspread.

'I suppose,' he said, 'it wasn't all her fault.'

'A white peacock, we will say,' I suggested.

He laughed.

'Go home by the top road, will you!' he said. 'I believe there's something on in the bottom wood.'

'All right,' I answered, with a quiver of apprehension.

'Yes, she was fair enough,' he muttered.

'Ay,' said I, rising. I held out my hand from the shadow. I was startled myself by the white sympathy it seemed to express, extended towards him in the moonlight. He gripped it, and cleaved to me for a moment, then he was gone.

*

I went out of the churchyard feeling a sullen resentment against the tousled graves that lay inanimate across the way. The air was heavy to breathe, and fearful in the shadow of the great trees. I was glad when I came out on the bare white road, and could see the copper lights from the reflectors of a pony-cart's lamps, and could hear the amiable chat-chat of the hoofs trotting towards me. I was lonely when they had passed.

Over the hill, the big flushed face of the moon poised just above the treetops, very majestic, and far off – yet imminent. I turned with swift sudden friendliness to the net of elm-boughs spread over my head, dotted with soft clusters winsomely. I jumped up and pulled the cool soft tufts against my face for company; and as I passed, still I reached upward for the touch of this budded gentleness of the trees. The wood breathed fragrantly, with a subtle sympathy. The firs softened their touch to me, and the larches woke from the barren winter-sleep, and put out velvet fingers to caress me as I passed. Only the clean, bare branches of the ash stood emblem of the discipline of life. I looked down on the blackness where trees filled the quarry, and the valley bottoms, and it seemed that the world, my own home-world, was strange again.

*

Some four or five days after Annable had talked to me in the churchyard, I went out to find him again. It was Sunday morning. The larch-wood was afloat with clear, lyric green, and some primroses scattered whitely on the edge under the fringing boughs. It was a clear morning, as when the latent life of the world begins to vibrate afresh in the air. The smoke from the cottage rose blue against the trees, and thick yellow against the sky. The fire, it seemed, was only just lighted, and the wood-smoke poured out.

Sam appeared outside the house, and looked round. Then he climbed the water-trough for a better survey. Evidently unsatisfied, paying slight attention to me, he jumped down and went running across the hillside to the wood. 'He is going for his father,' I said to myself, and I left the path to follow him down hill across the waste meadow, crackling the blanched stems of last year's thistles as I went, and stumbling in rabbit holes. He reached the wall that ran along the quarry's edge, and was over it in a twinkling.

When I came to the place, I was somewhat nonplussed, for, sheer from the stone fence, the quarryside dropped for some twenty or thirty feet, piled up with unmortared stones. I looked round – there was a plain dark thread down the hillside, which marked a path to this spot, and the wall was scored with the marks of heavy boots. Then I looked again down the quarry-side, and I saw – how could I have failed to see? – stones projecting to make an uneven staircase, such as is often seen in the Derbyshire fences. I saw this ladder was well used, so I trusted myself to it, and scrambled down, clinging to the face of the quarry wall. Once down, I felt pleased with myself for having

discovered and used the unknown access, and I admired the care
and ingenuity of the keeper, who had fitted and wedged the
long stones into the uncertain pile.

It was warm in the quarry: there the sunshine seemed to
thicken and sweeten; there the little mounds of overgrown waste
were aglow with very early dog-violets; there the sparks were
coming out on the bits of gorse, and among the stones the colts-
foot plumes were already silvery. Here was spring sitting just
awake, unloosening her glittering hair, and opening her purple
eyes.

I went across the quarry, down to where the brook ran murmuring a tale to the primroses and the budding trees. I was startled from my wandering among the fresh things by a faint
clatter of stones.

'What's that young rascal doing?' I said to myself, setting
forth to see. I came towards the other side of the quarry: on this,
the moister side, the bushes grew up against the wall, which was
higher than on the other side, though piled the same with old
dry stones. As I drew near I could hear the scrape and rattle of
stones, and the vigorous grunting of Sam as he laboured among
them. He was hidden by a great bush of sallow catkins, all
yellow, and murmuring with bees, warm with spice. When he
came in view I laughed to see him lugging and grunting among
the great pile of stones that had fallen in a mass from the quarry-
side; a pile of stones and earth and crushed vegetation. There
was a great bare gap in the quarry wall. Somehow, the lad's
labouring earnestness made me anxious, and I hurried up.

He heard me, and glancing round, his face red with exertion,
eyes big with terror, he called, commanding me:

'Pull 'em off 'im – pull 'em off!'

Suddenly my heart beating in my throat nearly suffocated me.
I saw the hand of the keeper lying among the stones. I set to
tearing away the stones, and we worked for some time without
a word. Then I seized the arm of the keeper and tried to drag
him out. But I could not.

'Pull it off him!' whined the lad, working in a frenzy.

When we got him out I saw at once he was dead, and I sat
down trembling with exertion. There was a great smashed
wound on the side of the head. Sam put his face against his

father's and snuffed round him like a dog, to feel the life in him. The child looked at me:

'He won't get up,' he said, and his little voice was hoarse with fear and anxiety.

I shook my head. Then the boy began to whimper. He tried to close the lips which were drawn with pain and death, leaving the teeth bare; then his fingers hovered round the eyes, which were wide open, glazed, and I could see he was trembling to touch them into life.

'He's not asleep,' he said, 'because his eyes is open – look !'

I could not bear the child's questioning terror. I took him up to carry him away, but he struggled and fought to be free.

'Ma'e 'im get up – ma'e 'im get up,' he cried in a frenzy, and I had to let the boy go.

He ran to the dead man, calling 'Feyther ! Feyther !' and pulling his shoulder; then he sat down, fascinated by the sight of the wound; he put out his finger to touch it, and shivered.

'Come away,' said I.

'Is it that ?' he asked, pointing to the wound. I covered the face with a big silk handkerchief.

'Now,' said I, 'he'll go to sleep if you don't touch him – so sit still while I go and fetch somebody. Will *you* run to the Hall ?'

He shook his head. I knew he would not. So I told him again not to touch his father, but to let him lie still till I came back. He watched me go, but did not move from his seat on the stones beside the dead man, though I know he was full of terror at being left alone.

I ran to the Hall – I dared not go to the Kennels. In a short time I was back with the squire and three men. As I led the way, I saw the child lifting a corner of the handkerchief to peep and see if the eyes were closed in sleep. Then he heard us, and started violently. When we removed the covering, and he saw the face unchanged in its horror, he looked at me with a look I have never forgotten.

'A bad business – an awful business !' repeated the squire. 'A bad business. I said to him from the first that the stones might come down when he was going up, and he said he had taken care to fix them. But you can't be sure, you can't be certain. And he'd be about half way up – ay – and the whole wall would come down on him. An awful business, it is really; a terrible piece of work!'

They decided at the inquest that the death came by misadventure. But there were vague rumours in the village that this was revenge which had overtaken the keeper.

*

They decided to bury him in our churchyard at Greymede under the beeches; the widow would have it so, and nothing might be denied her in her state.

It was a magnificent morning in early spring when I watched among the trees to see the procession come down the hillside. The upper air was woven with the music of the larks, and my whole world thrilled with the conception of summer. The young pale wind-flowers had arisen by the wood-gale, and under the hazels, when perchance the hot sun pushed his way, new little suns dawned, and blazed with real light. There was a certain thrill and quickening everywhere, as a woman must feel when she has conceived. A sallow tree in a favoured spot looked like a pale gold cloud of summer dawn; nearer it had poised a golden, fairy busby on every twig, and was voiced with a hum of bees, like any sacred golden bush, uttering its gladness in the thrilling murmur of bees, and in warm scent. Birds called and flashed on every hand; they made off exultant with streaming strands of grass, or wisps of fleece, plunging into the dark spaces of the wood, and out again into the blue.

A lad moved across the field from the farm below with a dog trotting behind him – a dog, no, a fussy, black-legged lamb trotting along on its toes, with its tail swinging behind. They were going to the mothers on the common, who moved like little grey clouds among the dark gorse.

I cannot help forgetting, and sharing the spink's triumph, when he flashes past with a fleece from a bramble bush. It will cover the bedded moss, it will weave among the soft red cowhair beautifully. It is a prize, it is an ecstasy to have captured it at the right moment, and the nest is nearly ready.

Ah, but the thrush is scornful, ringing out his voice from the hedge! He sets his breast against the mud, and models it warm for the turquoise eggs – blue, blue, bluest of eggs, which cluster so close and round against the breast, which round up beneath the breast, nestling content. You should see the bright ecstasy in the eyes of a nesting thrush, because of the rounded caress of the eggs against her breast!

What a hurry the jenny wren makes – hoping I shall not see her dart into the low bush. I have a delight in watching them against their shy little wills. But they have all risen with a rush of wings, and are gone, the birds. The air is brushed with agitation. There is no lark in the sky, not one; the heaven is clear of wings or twinkling dot –.

Till the heralds come – till the heralds wave like shadows in the bright air, crying, lamenting, fretting forever. Rising and falling and circling round and round, the slow-waving peewits cry and complain, and lift their broad wings in sorrow. They stoop suddenly to the ground, the lapwings, then in another throb of anguish and protest, they swing up again, offering a glistening white breast to the sunlight, to deny it in black shadow, then a glisten of green, and all the time crying and crying in despair.

The pheasants are frightened into cover, they run and dart through the hedge. The cold cock must fly in his haste, spread himself on his streaming plumes, and sail into the wood's security.

There is a cry in answer to the peewits, echoing louder and stronger the lamentation of the lapwings, a wail which hushes the birds. The men come over the brow of the hill, slowly, with the old squire walking tall and straight in front, six bowed men bearing the coffin on their shoulders, treading heavily and cautiously, under the great weight of the glistening white coffin; six men following behind, ill at ease, waiting their turn for the burden. You can see the red handkerchiefs knotted round their throats, and their shirt-fronts blue and white between the open waistcoats. The coffin is of new unpolished wood, gleaming and glistening in the sunlight; the men who carry it remember all their lives after the smell of new, warm elm-wood.

Again a loud cry from the hill-top. The woman has followed thus far, the big, shapeless woman, and she cries with loud cries after the white coffin as it descends the hill, and the children that cling to her skirts weep aloud, and are not to be hushed by the other woman, who bends over them, but does not form one of the group. How the crying frightens the birds, and the rabbits; and the lambs away there run to their mothers. But the peewits are not frightened, they add their notes to the sorrow; they circle after the white, retreating coffin, they circle round the woman; it is they who forever 'keen' the sorrows of this world. They are like priests in their robes, more black than white, more grief than hope, driving endlessly round and round, turning, lifting, falling and crying always in mournful desolation, repeating their last syllables like the broken accents of despair.

The bearers have at last sunk between the high banks, and turned out of sight. The big woman cannot see them, and yet she stands to look. She must go home, there is nothing left.

They have rested the coffin on the gate posts, and the bearers are wiping the sweat from their faces. They put their hands to their shoulders on the place where the weight has pressed.

The other six are placing the pads on their shoulders, when a girl comes up with a jug, and a blue pot. The squire drinks first, and fills for the rest. Meanwhile the girl stands back under the hedge, away from the coffin which smells of new elm-wood. In imagination she pictures the man shut up there in close darkness, while the sunlight flows all outside, and she catches her breast with terror. She must turn and rustle among the leaves of the violets for the flowers she does not see. Then, trembling, she comes to herself, and plucks a few flowers and breathes them hungrily into her soul, for comfort. The men put down the pots beside her, with thanks, and the squire gives the word. The bearers lift up the burden again, and the elm-boughs rattle along the hollow white wood, and the pitiful red clusters of elm-flowers sweep along it as if they whispered in sympathy – 'We are so sorry, so sorry –'; always the compassionate buds in their fullness of life bend down to comfort the dark man shut up there. 'Perhaps,' the girl thinks, 'he hears them, and goes softly to sleep.' She shakes the tears out of her eyes on to the ground, and, taking up her pots, goes slowly down, over the brooks.

In a while, I too got up and went down to the mill, which lay red and peaceful, with the blue smoke rising as winsomely and carelessly as ever. On the other side of the valley I could see a pair of horses nod slowly across the fallow. A man's voice called to them now and again with a resonance that filled me with longing to follow my horses over the fallow, in the still, lonely valley, full of sunshine and eternal forgetfulness. The day had already forgotten. The water was blue and white and dark-burnished with shadows; two swans sailed across the reflected trees with perfect blithe grace. The gloom that had passed across was gone. I watched the swan with his ruffled wings swell on-wards; I watched his slim consort go peeping into corners and under bushes; I saw him steer clear of the bushes, to keep full in view, turning his head to me imperiously, till I longed to pelt him with the empty husks of last year's flowers, knap-weed and scabious. I was too indolent, and I turned instead to the orchard.

There the daffodils were lifting their heads and throwing back their yellow curls. At the foot of each sloping, grey old tree stood a family of flowers, some bursten with golden fullness, some lift-ing their heads slightly, to show a modest, sweet countenance, others still hiding their faces, leaning forward pensively from the jaunty grey-green spears; I wished I had their language, to talk to them distinctly.

Overhead, the trees with lifted fingers shook out their hair to the sun, decking themselves with buds as white and cool as a water-nymph's breasts.

I began to be very glad. The colts-foot discs glowed and laughed in a merry company down the path; I stroked the velvet faces, and laughed also, and I smelled the scent of black-currant leaves, which is full of childish memories.

The house was quiet and complacent; it was peopled with ghosts again; but the ghosts had only come to enjoy the warm place once more, carrying sunshine in their arms and scattering it through the dusk of gloomy rooms.

CHAPTER III

The Irony of Inspired Moments

IT happened, the next day after the funeral, I came upon reproductions of Aubrey Beardsley's 'Atalanta', and of the tail-piece to 'Salome', and others. I sat and looked and my soul leaped out upon the new thing. I was bewildered, wondering, grudging, fascinated. I looked a long time, but my mind, or my soul, would come to no state of coherence. I was fascinated and overcome, but yet full of stubbornness and resistance.

Lettie was out, so, although it was dinner-time, even because it was dinner-time, I took the book and went down to the mill.

The dinner was over; there was the fragrance of cooked rhubarb in the room. I went straight to Emily, who was leaning back in her chair, and put the 'Salome' before her.

'Look,' said I, 'look here!'

She looked; she was short-sighted, and peered close. I was impatient for her to speak. She turned slowly at last and looked at me, shrinking, with questioning.

'Well?' I said.

'Isn't it – fearful!' she replied, softly.

'No! – why is it?'

'It makes you feel – Why have you brought it?'

'I wanted you to see it.'

Already I felt relieved, seeing that she too was caught in the spell.

George came and bent over my shoulder. I could feel the heavy warmth of him.

'Good Lord!' he drawled, half amused. The children came crowding to see, and Emily closed the book.

'I shall be late – Hurry up, Dave!' and she went to wash her hands before going to school.

'Give it me, will you?' George asked, putting out his hand

for the book. I gave it him, and he sat down to look at the drawings. When Mollie crept near to look, he angrily shouted to her to get away. She pulled a mouth, and got her hat over her wild brown curls. Emily came in ready for school.

'I'm going – good-bye,' she said, and she waited hesitatingly. I moved to get my cap. He looked up with a new expression in his eyes, and said:

'Are you going? – wait a bit – I'm coming.'

I waited.

'Oh, very well – good-bye,' said Emily bitterly, and she departed.

When he had looked long enough he got up and we went out. He kept his finger between the pages of the book as he carried it. We went towards the fallow land without speaking. There he sat down on a bank, leaning his back against a holly-tree, and saying, very calmly:

'There's no need to be in any hurry now –' whereupon he proceeded to study the illustrations.

'You know,' he said at last, 'I do want her.'

I started at the irrelevance of this remark, and said, 'Who?'

'Lettie. We've got notice, did you know?'

I started to my feet this time with amazement.

'Notice to leave? – what for?'

'Rabbits, I expect. I wish she'd have me, Cyril.'

'To leave Strelley Mill!' I repeated.

'That's it – and I'm rather glad. But do you think she might have me, Cyril?'

'What a shame! Where will you go? And you lie there joking –!'

'I don't. Never mind about the damned notice. I want her more than anything. – And the more I look at these naked lines, the more I want her. It's a sort of fine sharp feeling, like these curved lines. I don't know what I'm saying – but do you think she'd have me? Has she seen these pictures?'

'No.'

'If she did perhaps she'd want me – I mean she'd feel it clear and sharp coming through her.'

'I'll show her and see.'

'I'd been sort of thinking about it – since father had that

notice. It seemed as if the ground was pulled from under our feet. I never felt so lost. Then I began to think of her, if she'd have me – but not clear, till you showed me those pictures. I must have her if I can – and I must have something. It's rather ghostish to have the road suddenly smudged out, and all the world anywhere, nowhere for you to go. I must get something sure soon, or else I feel as if I should fall from somewhere and hurt myself. I'll ask her.'

I looked at him as he lay there under the holly-tree, his face all dreamy and boyish, very unusual.

'You'll ask Lettie?' said I, 'When – how?'

'I must ask her quick, while I feel as if everything had gone, and I was ghostish. I think I must sound rather a lunatic.'

He looked at me, and his eyelids hung heavy over his eyes as if he had been drinking, or as if he were tired.

'Is she at home?' he said.

'No, she's gone to Nottingham. She'll be home before dark.'

'I'll see her then. Can you smell violets?'

I replied that I could not. He was sure that he could, and he seemed uneasy till he had justified the sensation. So he arose, very leisurely, and went along the bank, looking closely for the flowers.

'I knew I could. White ones!'

He sat down and picked three flowers, and held them to his nostrils, and inhaled their fragrance. Then he put them to his mouth, and I saw his strong white teeth crush them. He chewed them for a while without speaking; then he spat them out, and gathered more.

'They remind me of her too,' he said, and he twisted a piece of honeysuckle stem round the bunch and handed it to me.

'A white violet, is she?' I smiled.

'Give them to her, and tell her to come and meet me just when it's getting dark in the wood.'

'But if she won't?'

'She will.'

'If she's not at home?'

'Come and tell me.'

He lay down again with his head among the green violet leaves, saying:

'I ought to work, because it all counts in the valuation. But I don't care.'

He lay looking at me for some time. Then he said:

'I don't suppose I shall have above twenty pounds left when we've sold up – but she's got plenty of money to start with – if she has me – in Canada. I could get well off – and she could have – what she wanted – I'm sure she'd have what she wanted.'

He took it all calmly as if it were realized. I was somewhat amused.

'What frock will she have on when she comes to meet me?' he asked.

'I don't know. The same as she's gone to Nottingham in, I suppose – a sort of gold-brown costume with a rather tight-fitting coat. Why?'

'I was thinking how she'd look.'

'What chickens are you counting now?' I asked.

'But what do you think I look best in?' he replied.

'You? Just as you are – no, put that old smooth cloth coat on – that's all.' I smiled as I told him, but he was very serious.

'Shan't I put my new clothes on?'

'No – you want to leave your neck showing.'

He put his hand to his throat, and said naively:

'Do I?' – and it amused him.

Then he lay looking dreamily up into the tree. I left him, and went wandering round the fields finding flowers and bird's nests.

When I came back, it was nearly four o'clock. He stood up and stretched himself. He pulled out his watch.

'Good Lord,' he drawled, 'I've lain there thinking all afternoon. I didn't know I could do such a thing. Where have you been? It's with being all upset, you see. You left the violets – here, take them, will you; and tell her: I'll come when it's getting dark. I feel like somebody else – or else really like myself. I hope I shan't wake up to the other things – you know, like I am always – before then.'

'Why not?'

'Oh, I don't know – only I feel as if I could talk straight off without arranging – like birds, without knowing what note is coming next.'

When I was going he said:

'Here, leave me that book – it'll keep me like this – I mean I'm not the same as I was yesterday, and that book'll keep me like it. Perhaps it's a bilious bout – I do sometimes have one, if something very extraordinary happens. When it's getting dark then!'

*

Lettie had not arrived when I went home. I put the violets in a little vase on the table. I remembered he had wanted her to see the drawings – it was perhaps as well he had kept them.

She came about six o'clock – in the motor-car with Marie. But the latter did not descend. I went out to assist with the parcels. Lettie had already begun to buy things; the wedding was fixed for July.

The room was soon over-covered with stuffs: table linen, underclothing, pieces of silken stuff and lace stuff, patterns for carpets and curtains, a whole gleaming glowing array. Lettie was very delighted. She could hardly wait to take off her hat, but went round cutting the string of her parcels, opening them, talking all the time to my mother.

'Look, Little Woman. I've got a ready-made underskirt – isn't it lovely! Listen!' and she ruffled it through her hands. 'Shan't I sound splendid! Frou-Frou! But it is a charming shade, isn't it, and not a bit bulky or clumsy anywhere.' She put the band of the skirt against her waist, and put forward her foot, and looked down, saying, 'It's just the right length, isn't it, Little Woman? – and they said I was tall – it was a wonder. Don't you wish it were yours, Little? – oh, you won't confess it. Yes you like to be as fine as anybody – that's why I bought you this piece of silk – isn't it sweet, though? – you needn't say there's too much lavender in it, there is not. Now!' She pleated it up and held it against my mother's chin. 'It suits you beautifully – doesn't it? Don't you like it, Sweet? You don't seem to like it a bit, and I'm sure it suits you – makes you look ever so young. I wish you wouldn't be so old-fashioned in your notions. You do like it, don't you?'

'Of course I do – I was only thinking what an extravagant mortal you are when you begin to buy. You know you mustn't keep on always –'

'Now – now, Sweet, don't be naughty and preachey. It's such a treat to go buying. You will come with me next time, won't you? Oh, I have enjoyed it – but I wished you were there – Marie takes anything, she's so easy to suit – I like to have a good buy – Oh, it was splendid! – and there's lots more yet. Oh, did you see this cushion cover – these are the colours I want for that room – gold and amber –'

This was a bad opening. I watched the shadows darken further and further along the brightness, hushing the glitter of the water. I watched the golden ripeness come upon the west, and thought the rencontre was never to take place. At last, however, Lettie flung herself down with a sigh, saying she was tired.

'Come into the dining-room and have a cup of tea,' said mother. 'I told Rebecca to mash when you came in.'

'All right. Leslie's coming up later on, I believe – about half-past eight, he said. Should I show him what I've bought?'

'There's nothing there for a man to see.'

'I shall have to change my dress, and I'm sure I don't want the fag. Rebecca, just go and look at the things I've bought – in the other room – and, Becky, fold them up for me, will you, and put them on my bed?'

As soon as she'd gone out, Lettie said:

'She'll enjoy doing it, won't she, mother, they're so nice! Do you think I need dress, mother?'

'Please yourself – do as you wish.'

'I suppose I shall have to; he doesn't like blouses and skirts of an evening he says; he hates the belt. I'll wear that old cream cashmere; it looks nice now I've put that new lace on it. Don't those violets smell nice? – who got them?'

'Cyril brought them in.'

'George sent them you,' said I.

'Well, I'll just run up and take my dress off. Why are we troubled with men!'

'It's a trouble you like well enough,' said mother.

'Oh, do I? such a bother!' and she ran upstairs.

The sun was red behind Highclose. I kneeled in the window seat and smiled at Fate and at people who imagine that strange states are near to the inner realities. The sun went straight down behind the cedar trees, deliberately and, it seemed as I watched, swiftly lowered itself behind the trees, behind the rim of the hill.

'I must go,' I said to myself, 'and tell him she will not come.'

Yet I fidgeted about the room, loath to depart. Lettie came down, dressed in white – or cream – cut low round the neck. She looked very delightful and fresh again, with a sparkle of the afternoon's excitement still.

'I'll put some of these violets on me,' she said, glancing at herself in the mirror, and then taking the flowers from their water, she dried them, and fastened them among her lace.

'Don't Lettie and I look nice tonight?' she said smiling, glancing from me to her reflexion which was like a light in the dusky room.

'That reminds me,' I said, 'George Saxton wanted to see you this evening.'

'Whatever for?'

'I don't know. They've got notice to leave their farm, and I think he feels a bit sentimental.'

'Oh, well – is he coming here?'

'He said would you go just a little way in the wood to meet him.'

'Did he! Oh, indeed! Well, of course I can't.'

'Of course not – if you won't. They're his violets you're wearing, by the way.'

'Are they – let them stay, it makes no difference. But whatever did he want to see me for?'

'I couldn't say, I assure you.'

She glanced at herself in the mirror, and then at the clock.

'Let's see,' she remarked, 'it's only a quarter to eight. Three quarters of an hour –! But what can he want me for? – I never knew anything like it.'

'Startling, isn't it!' I observed satirically.

'Yes,' she glanced at herself in the mirror:

'I can't go out like this.'

'All right, you can't then.'

'Besides – it's nearly dark, it will be too dark to see in the wood, won't it?'

'It will directly.'

'Well, I'll just go to the end of the garden, for one moment – run and fetch that silk shawl out of my wardrobe – be quick, while it's light.'

I ran and brought the wrap. She arranged it carefully over her head.

We went out, down the garden path. Lettie held her skirts carefully gathered from the ground. A nightingale began to sing in the twilight: we stepped along in silence as far as the rhododendron bushes, now in rosy bud.

'I cannot go into the wood,' she said.

'Come to the top of the riding' – and we went round the dark bushes.

George was waiting. I saw at once he was half distrustful of himself now. Lettie dropped her skirts and trailed towards him. He stood awkwardly awaiting her, conscious of the clownishness of his appearance. She held out her hand with something of a grand air:

'See,' she said, 'I have come.'

'Yes – I thought you wouldn't – perhaps' – he looked at her, and suddenly gained courage:

'You have been putting white on – you, you do look nice – though not like –'

'What? – Who else?'

'Nobody else – only I – well I'd – I'd thought about it different – like some pictures.'

She smiled with a gentle radiance, and asked indulgently, 'And how was I different?'

'Not all that soft stuff – plainer.'

'But don't I look very nice with all this soft stuff, as you call it?' – and she shook the silk away from her smiles.

'Oh, yes – better than those naked lines.'

'You are quaint tonight – what did you want me for – to say good-bye?'

'Good-bye?'

'Yes – you're going away, Cyril tells me. I'm very sorry – fancy horrid strangers at the Mill! But then I shall be gone away soon, too. We are all going you see, now we've grown up,' – she kept hold of my arm.

'Yes.'

'And where will you go – Canada? You'll settle there and be quite a patriarch, won't you?'

'I don't know.'

'You are not really sorry to go, are you?'

'No, I'm glad.'

'Glad to go away from us all.'

'I suppose so – since I must.'

'Ah, Fate – Fate! It separates you whether you want it or not.'

'What?'

'Why, you see, you have to leave. I mustn't stay out here – it is growing chilly. How soon are you going?'

'I don't know.'

'Not soon then?'

'I don't know.'

'Then I may see you again?'

'I don't know.'

'Oh, yes, I shall. Well, I must go. Shall I say good-bye now? – that was what you wanted, was it not?'

'To say good-bye?'

'Yes.'

'No – it wasn't – I wanted, I wanted to ask you –'

'What?' she cried.

'You don't know, Lettie, now the old life's gone, everything – how I want you – to set out with – it's like beginning life, and I want you.'

'But what could I do – I could only hinder – what help should I be?'

'I should feel as if my mind was made up – as if I could do something clearly. Now it's all hazy – not knowing what to do next.'

'And if – if you had – what then?'

'If I had you I could go straight on.'

'Where?'

'Oh – I should take a farm in Canada –'

'Well, wouldn't it be better to get it first and make sure –?'

'I have no money.'

'Oh! – so you wanted me –?'

'I only wanted you, I only wanted you. I would have given you –'

'What?'

'You'd have me – you'd have all me, and everything you wanted.'

'That I paid for – a good bargain! No, oh no, George, I beg your pardon. This is one of my flippant nights. I don't mean it like that. But you know it's impossible – look how I'm fixed – it *is* impossible, isn't it now?'

'I suppose it is.'

'You know it is – Look at me now, and say if it's not impossible – a farmer's wife – with you in Canada.'

'Yes – I didn't expect you like that. Yes, I see it is impossible. But I'd thought about it, and felt as if I must have you. Should have you ... Yes, it doesn't do to go on dreaming. I think it's the first time, and it'll be the last. Yes, it is impossible. Now I have made up my mind.'

'And what will you do?'

'I shall not go to Canada.'

'Oh, you must not – you must not do anything rash.'

'No – I shall get married.'

'You will? Oh, I am glad. I thought – you – you were too fond – . But you're not – of yourself I meant. I am so glad. Yes – do marry!'

'Well, I shall – since you are –'

'Yes,' said Lettie. 'It is best. But I thought that you –' she smiled at him in sad reproach.

'Did you think so?' he replied, smiling gravely.

'Yes,' she whispered. They stood looking at one another.

He made an impulsive movement towards her. She, however, drew back slightly, checking him.

'Well – I shall see you again sometime – so good-bye,' he said, putting out his hand.

We heard a foot crunching on the gravel. Leslie halted at the top of the riding. Lettie, hearing him, relaxed into a kind of feline graciousness, and said to George:

'I am so sorry you are going to leave – it breaks the old life up. You said I would see you again –' She left her hand in his a moment or two.

'Yes,' George replied. 'Good night' – and he turned away. She stood for a moment in the same drooping, graceful attitude watching him, then she turned round slowly. She seemed hardly to notice Leslie.

'Who was that you were talking to?' he asked.

'He has gone now,' she replied irrelevantly, as if even then she seemed hardly to realize it.

'It appears to upset you – his going – who is it?'

'He! – Oh, – why it's George Saxton.'

'Oh, him!'

'Yes.'

'What did he want?'

'Eh? What did he want? Oh, nothing.'

'A mere trysting – in the interim, eh!' – he said this laughing, generously passing off his annoyance in a jest.

'I feel so sorry,' she said.

'What for?'

'Oh – don't let us talk about him – talk about something else. I can't bear to talk about – him.'

'All right,' he replied – and after an awkward little pause. 'What sort of a time had you in Nottingham?'

'Oh, a fine time.'

'You'll enjoy yourself in the shops between now and – July. Some time I'll go with you and see them.'

'Very well.'

'That sounds as if you don't want me to go. Am I already in the way on a shopping expedition, like an old husband?'

'I should think you would be.'

'That's nice of you! Why?'

'Oh, I don't know.'

'Yes you do.'

'Oh, I suppose you'd hang about.'

'I'm much too well brought up.'

'Rebecca has lighted the hall lamp.'

'Yes, it's grown quite dark. I was here early. You never gave me a good word for it.'

'I didn't notice. There's a light in the dining-room, we'll go there.'

They went into the dining-room. She stood by the piano and

carefully took off the wrap. Then she wandered listlessly about the room for a minute.

'Aren't you coming to sit down?' he said, pointing to the seat on the couch beside him.

'Not just now,' she said, trailing aimlessly to the piano. She sat down and began to play at random, from memory. Then she did that most irritating thing – played accompaniments to songs, with snatches of the air where the voice should have predominated.

'I say, Lettie . . .' he interrupted after a time.

'Yes,' she replied, continuing to play.

'It's not very interesting . . .'

'No?' – she continued to play.

'Nor very amusing . . .'

She did not answer. He bore it for a little time longer, then he said:

'How much longer is it going to last, Lettie?'

'What?'

'That sort of business . . .'

'The piano? – I'll stop playing if you don't like it.'

She did not, however, cease.

'Yes – and all this dry business.'

'I don't understand.'

'Don't you? – you make *me*.'

Then she went on, tinkling away at: *If I built a world for you, dear.*

'I say, stop it, do I' he cried.

She tinkled to the end of the verse, and very slowly closed the piano.

'Come on – come and sit down,' he said.

'No, I don't want to. – I'd rather have gone on playing.'

'Go on with your damned playing then, and I'll go where there's more interest.'

'You ought to like it.'

He did not answer, so she turned slowly round on the stool, opened the piano, and laid her fingers on the keys. At the sound of the chord he started up, saying: 'Then I'm going.'

'It's very early – why?' she said, through the calm jingle of *Meine Ruh ist hin* –

He stood biting his lips. Then he made one more appeal.

'Lettie!'

'Yes?'

'Aren't you going to leave off – and be – amiable?'

'Amiable?'

'You are a jolly torment. What's upset you now?'

'Nay, it's not I who am upset.'

'I'm glad to hear it – what do you call yourself?'

'I? nothing.'

'Oh, well, I'm going then.'

'Must you? – so early tonight?'

He did not go, and she played more and more softly, languidly, aimlessly. Once she lifted her head to speak, but did not say anything.

'Look here!' he ejaculated all at once, so that she started and jarred the piano. 'What do you mean by it?'

She jingled leisurely a few seconds before answering, then she replied:

'What a worry you are!'

'I suppose you want me out of the way while you sentimentalize over that milkman. You needn't bother. You can do it while I'm here. Or I'll go and leave you in peace. I'll go and call him back for you, if you like – if that's what you want –'

She turned on the piano stool slowly and looked at him, smiling faintly.

'It is very good of you!' she said.

He clenched his fists and grinned with rage.

'You tantalizing little –' he began, lifting his fists expressively. She smiled. Then he swung round, knocked several hats off the stand in the hall, slammed the door, and was gone.

Lettie continued to play for some time, after which she went up to her own room.

*

Leslie did not return to us the next day, nor the day after. The first day Marie came and told us he had gone away to Yorkshire to see about the new mines that were being sunk there, and was likely to be absent for a week or so. These business visits to the north were rather frequent. The firm, of which Mr

Tempest was director and chief shareholder, were opening important new mines in the other county, as the seams at home were becoming exhausted or unprofitable. It was proposed that Leslie should live in Yorkshire when he was married, to superintend the new workings. He at first rejected the idea, but he seemed later to approve of it more.

During the time he was away Lettie was moody and cross-tempered. She did not mention George or the mill; indeed, she preserved her best, most haughty and ladylike manner.

On the evening of the fourth day of Leslie's absence we were out in the garden. The trees were 'uttering joyous leaves'. My mother was in the midst of her garden, lifting the dusky faces of the auriculas to look at the velvet lips, or tenderly taking a young weed from the black soil. The thrushes were calling and clamouring all round. The japonica flamed on the wall as the light grew thicker; the tassels of white cherry-blossom swung gently in the breeze.

'What shall I do, mother?' said Lettie, as she wandered across the grass to pick at the japonica flowers. 'What shall I do? – there's nothing to do.'

'Well, my girl – what do you want to do? You have been moping about all day – go and see somebody.'

'It's such a long way to Eberwich.'

'Is it? Then go somewhere nearer.'

Lettie fretted about with restless, petulant indecision.

'I don't know what to do,' she said. 'And I feel as if I might just as well never have lived at all as waste days like this. I wish we weren't buried in this dead little hole – I wish we were near the town – it's hateful having to depend on about two or three folk for your – your – your pleasure in life.'

'I can't help it, my dear – you must do something for yourself.'

'And what can I do? – I can do nothing.'

'Then I'd go to bed.'

'That I won't – with the dead weight of a wasted day on me. I feel as if I'd do something desperate.'

'Very well, then,' said mother, 'do it, and have done.'

'Oh, it's no good talking to you – I don't want –' She turned away, went to the laurestinus, and began pulling off it the long

red berries. I expected she would fret the evening wastefully
away. I noticed all at once that she stood still. It was the noise
of a motor-car running rapidly down the hill towards Nethermere – a light, quick-clicking sound. I listened also. I could
feel the swinging drop of the car as it came down the leaps of
the hill. We could see the dust trail up among the trees. Lettie
raised her head and listened expectantly. The car rushed along
the edge of Nethermere – then there was the jar of brakes, as the
machine slowed down and stopped. In a moment with a quick
flutter of sound, it was passing the lodge-gates and whirling up
the drive, through the wood, to us. Lettie stood with flushed
cheeks and brightened eyes. She went towards the bushes that
shut off the lawn from the gravelled space in front of the house,
watching. A car came racing through the trees. It was the small
car Leslie used on the firm's business – now it was white with
dust. Leslie suddenly put on the brakes, and tore to a standstill
in front of the house. He stepped to the ground. There he staggered a little, being giddy and cramped with the long drive. His
motor-jacket and cap were thick with dust.

Lettie called to him, 'Leslie!' – and flew down to him. He
took her into his arms, and clouds of dust rose round her. He
kissed her, and they stood perfectly still for a moment. She
looked up into his face – then she disengaged her arms to take off
his disfiguring motor-spectacles. After she had looked at him a
moment, tenderly, she kissed him again. He loosened his hold
of her, and she said, in a voice full of tenderness:

'You are trembling, dear.'

'It's the ride, I've never stopped.'

Without further words she took him into the house.

'How pale you are – see, lie on the couch – never mind the
dust. All right, I'll find you a coat of Cyril's. Oh, mother, he's
come all those miles in the car without stopping – make him lie
down.'

She ran and brought him a jacket, and put the cushions
round, and made him lie on the couch. Then she took off his
boots and put slippers on his feet. He lay watching her all the
time; he was white with fatigue and excitement.

'I wonder if I shall be had up for scorching – I can feel the
road coming at me yet,' he said.

'Why were you so headlong?'

'I felt as if I should go wild if I didn't come – if I didn't rush. I didn't know how you might have taken me, Lettie – when I said – what I did.'

She smiled gently at him, and he lay resting, recovering, looking at her.

'It's a wonder I haven't done something desperate – I've been half mad since I said – Oh, Lettie, I was a damned fool and a wretch – I could have torn myself in two. I've done nothing but curse and rage at myself ever since. I feel as if I'd just come up out of hell. You don't know how thankful I am, Lettie, that you've not – oh – turned against me for what I said.'

She went to him and sat down by him, smoothing his hair from his forehead, kissing him, her attitude tender, suggesting tears, her movements impulsive, as if with a self-reproach she would not acknowledge, but which she must silence with lavish tenderness. He drew her to him, and they remained quiet for some time, till it grew dark.

The noise of my mother stirring in the next room disturbed them. Lettie rose, and he also got up from the couch.

'I suppose,' he said, 'I shall have to go home and get bathed and dressed – though,' he added in tones which made it clear he did not want to go, 'I shall have to get back in the morning – I don't know what they'll say.'

'At any rate,' she said, 'You could wash here –'

'But I must get out of these clothes – and I want a bath.'

'You could – you might have some of Cyril's clothes – and the water's hot, I know. At all events, you can stay to supper –'

'If I'm going I shall have to go soon – or they'd not like it, if I go in late; – they have no idea I've come; – they don't expect me till next Monday or Tuesday –'

'Perhaps you could stay here – and they needn't know.'

They looked at each other with wide, smiling eyes – like children on the brink of a stolen pleasure.

'Oh, but what would your mother think! – no, I'll go.'

'She won't mind a bit.'

'Oh, but –'

'I'll ask her.'

He wanted to stay far more than she wished it, so it was she who put down his opposition and triumphed.

My mother lifted her eyebrows, and said very quietly:

'He'd better go home – and be straight.'

'But look how he'd feel – he'd have to tell them . . . and how would he feel! It's really my fault, in the end. Don't be piggling and mean and Grundyish, Matouchka.'

'It is neither meanness nor Grundyishness –'

'Oh, Ydgrun, Ydgrun –!' exclaimed Lettie ironically.

'He may certainly stay if he likes,' said mother, slightly nettled at Lettie's gibe.

'All right, Mütterchen – and be a sweetling, do!'

Lettie went out a little impatient at my mother's unwillingness, but Leslie stayed, nevertheless.

In a few moments Lettie was up in the spare bedroom, arranging and adorning, and Rebecca was running with hot-water bottles, and hurrying down with clean bed-clothes. Lettie hastily appropriated my best brushes – which she had given me – and took the suit of pyjamas of the thinnest, finest flannel – and discovered a new tooth-brush – and made selections from my shirts and handkerchiefs and underclothing – and directed me which suit to lend him. Altogether I was astonished, and perhaps a trifle annoyed, at her extraordinary thoughtfulness and solicitude.

He came down to supper, bathed, brushed, and radiant. He ate heartily and seemed to emanate a warmth of physical comfort and pleasure. The colour was flushed again into his face, and he carried his body with the old independent, assertive air. I have never known the time when he looked handsomer, when he was more attractive. There was a certain warmth about him, a certain glow that enhanced his words, his laughter, his movements; he was the predominant person and we felt a pleasure in his mere proximity. My mother, however, could not quite get rid of her stiffness, and soon after supper she rose, saying she would finish her letter in the next room, bidding him good night, as she would probably not see him again. The cloud of this little coolness was the thinnest and most transitory. He talked and laughed more gaily than ever, and was ostentatious in his movements, throwing back his head, taking little attitudes which displayed the broad firmness of his breast, the grace of his well-trained physique. I left them at the piano; he was sitting pretending to play, and looking up all the while at her, who stood with her hand on his shoulder.

*

In the morning he was up early, by six o'clock downstairs and attending to the car. When I got down I found him very busy, and very quiet.

'I know I'm a beastly nuisance,' he said, 'but I must get off early.'

Rebecca came and prepared breakfast, which we two ate alone. He was remarkably dull and wordless.

'It's a wonder Lettie hasn't got up to have breakfast with you – she's such a one for raving about the perfection of the early morning – its purity and promises and so forth,' I said.

He broke his bread nervously, and drank some coffee as if he were agitated, making noises in his throat as he swallowed.

'It's too early for her, I should think,' he replied, wiping his moustache hurriedly. Yet he seemed to listen for her. Lettie's bedroom was over the study, where Rebecca had laid breakfast, and he listened now and again, holding his knife and fork suspended in their action. Then he went on with his meal again.

When he was laying down his serviette, the door opened. He pulled himself together, and turned round sharply. It was mother. When she spoke to him, his face twitched with a little frown, half of relief, half of disappointment.

'I must be going now,' he said – 'thank you very much – Mother.'

'You are a harum-scarum boy. I wonder why Lettie doesn't come down. I know she is up.'

'Yes,' he replied. 'Yes, I've heard her. Perhaps she is dressing. I must get off.'

'I'll call her.'

'No – don't bother her – she'd come if she wanted –'

But mother had called from the foot of the stairs.

'Lettie, Lettie – he's going.'

'All right,' said Lettie, and in another minute she came

downstairs. She was dressed in dark, severe stuff, and she was somewhat pale. She did not look at any of us, but turned her eyes aside.

'Good-bye,' she said to him, offering him her cheek. He kissed her, murmuring: 'Good-bye – my love.'

He stood in the doorway a moment, looking at her with beseeching eyes. She kept her face half averted, and would not look at him, but stood pale and cold, biting her underlip. He turned sharply away with a motion of keen disappointment, set the engines of the car into action, mounted, and drove quickly away.

Lettie stood pale and inscrutable for some moments. Then she went in to breakfast and sat toying with her food, keeping her head bent down, her face hidden.

In less than an hour he was back again, saying he had left something behind. He ran upstairs, and then, hesitating, went into the room where Lettie was still sitting at table.

'I had to come back,' he said.

She lifted her face towards him, but kept her eyes averted, looking out of the window. She was flushed.

'What had you forgotten?' she asked.

'I'd left my cigarette case,' he replied.

There was an awkward silence.

'But I shall have to be getting off,' he added.

'Yes, I suppose you will,' she replied.

After another pause, he asked:

'Won't you just walk down the path with me?'

She rose without answering. He took a shawl and put it round her carefully. She merely allowed him. They walked in silence down the garden.

'You – are you – are you angry with me?' he faltered.

Tears suddenly came to her eyes.

'What did you come back for?' she said, averting her face from him. He looked at her.

'I knew you were angry – and –,' he hesitated.

'Why didn't you go away?' she said impulsively. He hung his head and was silent.

'I don't see why – why it should make trouble between us, Lettie,' he faltered. She made a swift gesture of repulsion, whereupon, catching sight of her hand, she hid it swiftly against her skirt again.

'You make my hands – my very hands disclaim me,' she struggled to say.

He looked at her clenched fist pressed against the folds of her dress.

'But –,' he began, much troubled.

'I tell you, I can't bear the sight of my own hands,' she said, in low, passionate tones.

'But surely, Lettie, there's no need – if you love me –'

She seemed to wince. He waited, puzzled and miserable.

'And we're going to be married, aren't we?' he resumed, looking pleadingly at her.

She stirred, and exclaimed:

'Oh, why don't you go away? What did you come back for?'

'You'll kiss me before I go?' he asked.

She stood with averted face, and did not reply. His forehead was twitching in a puzzled frown.

'Lettie!' he said.

She did not move or answer, but remained with her face turned full away, so that he could see only the contour of her cheek. After waiting awhile, he flushed, turned swiftly and set his machine rattling. In a moment he was racing between the trees.

CHAPTER IV

Kiss when She's Ripe for Tears

It was the Sunday after Leslie's visit. We had had a wretched week, with everybody mute and unhappy.

Though spring had come, none of us saw it. Afterwards it occurred to me that I had seen all the ranks of poplars suddenly bursten into a dark crimson glow, with a flutter of blood-red where the sun came through the leaves; that I had found high cradles where the swan's eggs lay by the waterside; that I had seen the daffodils leaning from the moss-grown wooden walls of the boat-house, and all, moss, daffodils, water, scattered with the pink scarves from the elm buds; that I had broken the half-spread fans of the sycamore, and had watched the white cloud of sloe-blossom go silver grey against the evening sky: but I had not perceived it, and I had not any vivid spring-pictures left from the neglected week.

It was Sunday evening, just after tea, when Lettie suddenly said to me:

'Come with me down to Strelley Mill.'

I was astonished, but I obeyed unquestioningly.

On the threshold we heard a chattering of girls, and immediately Alice's voice greeted us:

'Hello, Sybil, love! Hello, Lettie! Come on, here's a gathering of the goddesses. Come on, you just make us right. You're Juno, and here's Meg, she's Venus, and I'm – here, somebody, who am I, tell us quick – did you say Minerva, Sybil dear? Well you ought, then! Now Paris, hurry up. He's putting his Sunday clothes on to take us a walk – Laws, what a time it takes him! Get your blushes ready, Meg – now Lettie, look haughty, and I'll look wise. I wonder if he wants me to go and tie his tie. Oh, glory – where on earth did you get that antimacassar?'

'In Nottingham – don't you like it?' said George referring to his tie. 'Hello, Lettie – have you come?'

'Yes, it's a gathering of the goddesses. Have you that apple? If so, hand it over,' said Alice.

'What apple?'

'Oh, Lum, his education! Paris's apple – Can't you see we've come to be chosen?'

'Oh, well – I haven't got any apple – I've eaten mine.'

'Isn't he flat – he's like boiling magnesia that's done boiling for a week. Are you going to take us all to church then?'

'If you like.'

'Come on, then. Where's the Abode of Love? Look at Lettie looking shocked. Awfully sorry, old girl – thought love agreed with you.'

'Did you say *love*?' inquired George.

'Yes, I did; didn't I, Meg? And you say "Love" as well, don't you?'

'I don't know what it is,' laughed Meg, who was very red and rather bewildered.

'"*Amor est titillatio*" – "Love is a tickling," – there – that's it, isn't it, Sybil?'

'How should I know.'

'Of *course* not, old fellow. Leave it to the girls. See how knowing Lettie looks – and laws, Lettie, you are solemn.'

'It's love,' suggested George, over his new neck-tie.

'I'll bet it is "*degustasse sat est*" – ain't it, Lettie? "One lick's enough" – "and damned be he that first cries: Hold, enough!" – Which one do you like? But *are* you going to take us to church, Georgie darling – one by one, or all at once?'

'What do you want me to do, Meg?' he asked.

'Oh, I don't mind.'

'And do you mind, Lettie?'

'I'm not going to church.'

'Let's go a walk somewhere – and let us start now,' said Emily somewhat testily. She did not like this nonsense.

'There you are, Syb – you've got your orders – don't leave me behind,' wailed Alice.

Emily frowned and bit her finger.

'Come on, Georgie. You look like the finger of a pair scales – between two weights. Which'll draw?'

'The heavier,' he replied, smiling, and looking neither at Meg or Lettie.

'Then it's Meg,' cried Alice. 'Oh, I wish I was fleshy – I've no chance with Syb against Pem.'

Emily flashed looks of rage; Meg blushed and felt ashamed; Lettie began to recover from her first outraged indignation, and smiled.

Thus we went a walk, in two trios.

Unfortunately, as the evening was so fine, the roads were full of strollers: groups of three or four men dressed in pale trousers and shiny black cloth coats, following their suspicious little dogs: gangs of youths slouching along, occupied with nothing, often silent, talking now and then in raucous tones on some subject of brief interest: then the gallant husbands, in their tail coats very husbandly, pushing a jingling perambulator, admonished by a much dressed spouse round whom the small members of the family gyrated: occasionally, two lovers walking with a space between them, disowning each other; occasionally, a smartly dressed mother with two little girls in white silk frocks and much expanse of yellow hair, stepping mincingly, and, near by, a father awkwardly controlling his Sunday suit.

To endure all this it was necessary to chatter unconcernedly. George had to keep up the conversation behind, and he seemed to do it with ease, discoursing on the lambs, discussing the breed – when Meg exclaimed:

'Oh, aren't they black! They might ha' crept down th' chimney. I never saw any like them before.' He described how he had reared two on the bottle, exciting Meg's keen admiration by his mothering of the lambs. Then he went on to the peewits, harping on the same string: how they would cry and pretend to be wounded – 'Just fancy, though!' – and how he had moved the eggs of one pair while he was ploughing, and the mother had followed them, and had even sat watching as he drew near again with the plough, watching him come and go – 'Well, she knew you – but they *do* know those who are kind to them –'

'Yes,' he agreed, 'her little bright eyes seem to speak as you go by.'

'Oh, I do think they're nice little things – don't you, Lettie?' cried Meg in access of tenderness.

Lettie did – with brevity.

We walked over the hills and down into Greymede. Meg thought she ought to go home to her grandmother, and George bade her go, saying he would call and see her in an hour or so.

The dear girl was disappointed, but she went unmurmuring. We left Alice with a friend, and hurried home through Selsby to escape the after-church parade.

*

As you walk home past Selsby, the pit stands up against the west, with beautiful tapering chimneys marked in black against the swim of sunset, and the head-stocks etched with tall significance on the brightness. Then the houses are squat in rows of shadow at the foot of these high monuments.

'Do you know, Cyril,' said Emily, 'I *have* meant to go and see Mrs Annable – the keeper's wife – she's moved into Bonsart's Row, and the children come to school – Oh, it's awful ! – they've never been to school, and they are unspeakable.'

'What's she gone there for ?' I asked.

'I suppose the squire wanted the Kennels – and she chose it herself. But the way they live – it's fearful to think of !'

'And why haven't you been ?'

'I don't know – I've meant to – but –' Emily stumbled.

'You didn't want, and you daren't ?'

'Perhaps not – would you ?'

'Pah – let's go now ! – There, you hang back.'

'No, I don't,' she replied sharply.

'Come on then, we'll go through the twitchel. Let me tell Lettie.'

Lettie at once declared 'No !' – with some asperity.

'All right,' said George. 'I'll take you home.'

But this suited Lettie still less.

'I don't know what you want to go for, Cyril,' she said, 'and Sunday night, and, everybody everywhere. I want to go home.'

'Well – you go then – Emily will come with you.'

'Ha,' cried the latter, 'you think I won't go to see her.'

I shrugged my shoulders, and George pulled his moustache.

'Well, I don't care,' declared Lettie, and we marched down the twitchel, Indian file.

We came near to the ugly rows of houses that back up against the pit-hill. Everywhere is black and sooty: the houses are back to back, having only one entrance, which is from a square garden where black-speckled weeds grow sulkily, and which looks on to a row of evil little ash-pit huts. The road everywhere is trodden over with a crust of soot and coal-dust and cinders.

Between the rows, however, was a crowd of women and children, bare heads, bare arms, white aprons, and black Sunday frocks bristling with gimp. One or two men squatted on their heels with their backs against a wall, laughing. The women were waving their arms and screaming up at the roof of the end house.

Emily and Lettie drew back.

'Look there – it's that little beggar, Sam!' said George.

There, sure enough, perched on the ridge of the roof against the end chimney, was the young imp, coatless, his shirt-sleeves torn away from the cuffs. I knew his bright, reddish young head in a moment. He got up, his bare toes clinging to the tiles, and spread out his fingers fanwise from his nose, shouting something, which immediately caused the crowd to toss with indignation, and the women to shriek again. Sam sat down suddenly, having almost lost his balance.

The village constable hurried up, his thin neck stretching out of his tunic, and demanded to know the cause of the hub-bub.

Immediately a woman with bright brown squinting eyes, and a birthmark on her cheek, rushed forward and seized the police-man by the sleeve.

'Ta'e 'im up, ta'e 'im up, an' birch 'im till 'is bloody back's raw,' she screamed.

The thin policeman shook her off, and wanted to know what was the matter.

'I'll smosh 'im like a rotten tater,' cried the woman, 'if I can lay 'ands on 'im. 'E's not fit ter live nowhere where there's decent folks – the thievin', brazen little devil –' thus she went on.

'But what's up?' interrupted the thin constable, 'what's up wi' 'im?'

'Up – it's 'im as 'is up, an' let 'im wait till I get 'im down. A crafty little –'

Sam, seeing her look at him, distorted his honest features, and overheated her wrath, till Lettie and Emily trembled with dismay.

The mother's head appeared at the bedroom window. She slid the sash back, and craned out, vainly trying to look over the gutter below the slates. She was even more dishevelled than usual, and the tears had dried on her pale face. She stretched further out, clinging to the window frame and to the gutter overhead, till I was afraid she would come down with a crash.

The men, squatting on their heels against the wall of the ash-pit, laughed, saying:

'Nab 'im, Poll – can ter see 'm – clawk 'im!' and then the pitiful voice of the woman was heard crying: 'Come they ways down, my duckie, come on – on'y come ter thy mother – they shanna touch thee. Du thy mother's biddin', now – Sam – Sam – Sam!' her voice rose higher and higher.

'Sammy, Sammy, go to thy mammy,' jeered the wits below.

'Shonna ter come. Shonna ter come to they mother, my duckie – come on, come thy ways down.'

Sam looked at the crowd, and at the eaves from under which rose his mother's voice. He was going to cry. A big gaunt woman, with the family steel comb stuck in her back hair, shouted, 'Tha' mun well bend thy face, tha' needs ter scraight,' and aided by the woman with the birthmark and the squint, she reviled him. The little scoundrel, in a burst of defiance, picked a piece of mortar from between the slates, and in a second it flew into fragments against the family steel comb. The wearer thereof declared her head was laid open and there was general confusion. The policeman – I don't know how thin he must have been when he was taken out of his uniform – lost his head, and he too began brandishing his fists, spitting from under his sweep's-brush moustache as he commanded in tones of authority:

'Now then, no more on it – let's 'a'e thee down here, an' no more messin' about!'

The boy tried to creep over the ridge of the roof and escape down the other side. Immediately the brats rushed round yelling to the other side of the row, and pieces of red burnt gravel began to fly over the roof. Sam crouched against the chimney.

'Got 'im!' yelled one little devil. 'Got 'im! Hi – go again!'

A shower of stones came down, scattering the women and the policeman. The mother rushed from the house and made a wild onslaught on the throwers. She caught one, and flung him down. Immediately the rest turned and aimed their missiles at her. Then George and the policeman and I dashed after the young wretches, and the women ran to see what happened to their offspring. We caught two lads of fourteen or so, and made the policeman haul them after us. The rest fled.

When we returned to the field of battle, Sam had gone too.

'If 'e 'asna slived off!' cried the woman with a squint. 'But I'll see him locked up for this.'

At this moment a band of missioners from one of the chapels or churches arrived at the end of the row, and the little harmonium began to bray, and the place vibrated with the sound of a woman's powerful voice, propped round by several others, singing:

'At even ere the sun was set –'

Everybody hurried towards the new noise, save the policeman with his captives, the woman with the squint, and the woman with the family comb. I told the limb of the law he'd better get rid of the two boys and find out what mischief the others were after.

Then I inquired of the woman with the squint what was the matter.

'Thirty-seven young 'uns 'an we 'ad from that doe, an' there's no knowin' 'ow many more, if they 'adn't a-gone an' ate-n 'er,' she replied, lapsing, now her fury was spent, into sullen resentment.

'An' niver a word should we a' known,' added the family-comb-bearer, 'but for that blessed cat of ourn, as scrat it up.'

'Indeed,' said I, 'the rabbit?'

'No, there were nowt left but th' skin – they'd seen ter that, dirt-eatin' lot.'

'When was that?' said I.

'This mortal night – an' there was th' head an' th' back in

th' dirty stewpot – I can show you this instant – I've got 'em in our pantry for a proof, 'aven't I, Martha?'

'A fat lot o' good it is – but I'll rip th' neck out of 'im, if ever I lay 'ands on 'im.'

At last I made out that Samuel had stolen a large, lop-eared doe out of a hutch in the coal-house of the squint-eyed lady, had skinned it, buried the skin, and offered his booty to his mother as a wild rabbit, trapped. The doe had been the chief item of the Annable's Sunday dinner – albeit a portion was unluckily saved till Monday, providing undeniable proof of the theft. The owner of the rabbit had supposed the creature to have escaped. This peaceful supposition had been destroyed by the comb-bearer seeing her cat, scratching in the Annables' garden, unearth the white and brown doe-skin, after which the trouble had begun.

The squint-eyed woman was not so hard to manage. I talked to her as if she were some male friend of mine, only appealing to her womanliness with all the soft sadness I could press into the tones of my voice. In the end she was mollified, and even tender and motherly in her feelings towards the unfortunate family. I left on her dresser the half-crown I shrank from offering her, and having reduced the comb-wearer also, I marched off, carrying the stew-pot and the fragments of the ill-fated doe to the cottage of the widow, where George and the girls awaited me.

The house was in a woeful state. In the rocking chair, beside the high guard that surrounded the hearth, sat the mother, rocking, looking sadly shaken now her excitement was over. Lettie was nursing the little baby, and Emily the next child. George was smoking his pipe and trying to look natural. The little kitchen was crowded – there was no room – there was not even a place on the table for the stew-jar, so I gathered together cups and mugs containing tea sops, and set down the vessel of ignominy on the much slopped teacloth. The four little children were striped and patched with tears – at my entrance one under the table recommenced to weep, so I gave him my pencil which pushed in and out, but which pushes in and out no more.

The sight of the stew pot affected the mother afresh. She wept again, crying:

'An I niver thought as 'ow it were aught but a snared un;

as if I should set 'im on ter thieve their old doe; an' tough it
was an' all; an' 'im a thief, an me called all the names they
could lay their tongues to: an' then in my bit of a pantry,
takin' the very pots out: that stewpot as I brought all the
way from Nottingham, an' I've 'ad it afore our Minnie wor
born –'

The baby, the little baby, then began to cry. The mother got
up suddenly, and took it.

'Oh, come then, come then my pet. Why, why cos they
shanna, no they shanna. Yes, he's his mother's least little lad,
he is, a little un. Hush then, there, there – what's a matter, my
little?'

She hushed the baby, and herself. At length she asked:

''As th' p'liceman gone as well?'

'Yes – it's all right,' I said.

She sighed deeply, and her look of weariness was painful to
see.

'How old is your eldest?' I asked.

'Fanny – she's fourteen. She's out service at Websters. Then
Jim, as is thirteen next month – let's see, yes, it is next month
– he's gone to Flints – farming. They can't do much – an' I
shan't let 'em go into th' pit, if I can help it. My husband always
used to say they should never go in th' pit.'

'They can't do much for you.'

'They dun what they can. But it's a hard job, it is, ter keep
'em all goin'. Wi' weshin, an' th' parish pay, an' five shillin'
from th' squire – it's 'ard. It was diff'rent when my husband
was alive. It ought ter 'a been me as should 'a died – I don't
seem as if I can manage 'em – they get beyond me. I wish I
was dead this minnit, an' 'im 'ere. I can't understand it: 'im as
wor so capable, to be took, an' me left. 'E wor a man in a
thousand, 'e wor – full o' management like a gentleman. I
wisht it was me as 'ad a been took. 'An 'e's restless, 'cos 'e
knows I find it 'ard. I stood at th' door last night, when they
was all asleep, looking out over th' pit pond – an' I saw a
light, an' I knowed it was 'im – cos it wor our weddin' day
yesterday – by the day an' th' date. An' I said to 'im "Frank,
is it thee, Frank? I'm all right, I'm gettin' on all right," – an'
then 'e went; seemed to go ower the whimsey an' back towards

th' wood. I know it wor 'im, an' 'e couldna rest, thinking I couldna manage –'

After a while we left, promising to go again, and to see after the safety of Sam.

It was quite dark, and the lamps were lighted in the houses. We could hear the throb of the fan-house engines, and the soft whirr of the fan.

'Isn't it cruel?' said Emily, plaintively.

'Wasn't the man a wretch to marry the woman like that,' added Lettie with decision.

'Speak of Lady Crystabel,' said I, and then there was silence. 'I suppose he did not know what he was doing, any more than the rest of us.'

'I thought you were going to your aunt's – to the Ram Inn,' said Lettie to George when they came to the cross-roads.

'Not now – it's too late,' he answered quietly. 'You will come round our way, won't you?'

'Yes,' she said.

*

We were eating bread and milk at the farm, and the father was talking with vague sadness and reminiscence, lingering over the thought of their departure from the old house. He was a pure romanticist, forever seeking the colour of the past in the present's monotony. He seemed settling down to an easy contended middle-age, when the unrest on the farm and development of his children quickened him with fresh activity. He read books on the land question, and modern novels. In the end he became an advanced radical, almost a socialist. Occasionally his letters appeared in the newspapers. He had taken a new hold on life.

Over supper he became enthusiastic about Canada, and to watch him, his ruddy face lighted up, his burly form straight and nerved with excitement, was to admire him; to hear him, his words of thoughtful common-sense all warm with a young man's hopes, was to love him. At forty-six he was more spontaneous and enthusiastic than George, and far more happy and hopeful.

Emily would not agree to go away with them – what should

she do in Canada, she said – and she did not want the little ones 'to be drudges on a farm – in the end to be nothing but cattle'.

'Nay,' said her father gently, 'Mollie shall learn the dairying, and David will just be right to take to the place when I give up. It'll perhaps be a bit rough and hard at first, but when we've got over it we shall think it was one of the best times – like you do.'

'And you, George?' asked Lettie.

'I'm not going. What should I go for? There's nothing at the end of it only a long life. It's like a day here in June – a long work day, pleasant enough, and when it's done you sleep well – but it's work and sleep and comfort – half a life. It's not enough. What's the odds? – I might as well be Flower, the mare.'

His father looked at him gravely and thoughtfully.

'Now it seems to me so different,' he said sadly, 'It seems to me you can live your own life, and be independent, and think as you like without being choked with harassments. I feel as if I could keep on – like that –'

'I'm going to get more out of my life, I hope,' laughed George. 'No. Do you know?' and here he turned straight to Lettie. 'Do you know, I'm going to get pretty rich, so that I can do what I want for a bit. I want to see what it's like, to taste all sides – to taste the towns. I want to know what I've got in me. I'll get rich – or at least I'll have a good try.'

'And pray how will you manage it?' asked Emily.

'I'll begin by marrying – and then you'll see.'

Emily laughed with scorn – 'Let us see you begin.'

'Ah, you're not wise!' said the father sadly – then, laughing, he said to Lettie in coaxing, confidential tones, 'but he'll come out there to me in a year to two – you see if he doesn't.'

'I wish I could come now,' said I.

'If you would,' said George, 'I'd go with you. But not by myself, to become a fat stupid fool, like my own cattle.'

While he was speaking Gyp burst into a rage of barking. The father got up to see what it was, and George followed. Trip, the great bull-terrier, rushed out of the house shaking the buildings with his roars. We saw the white dog flash down the yard, we heard a rattle from the hen-house ladder, and in a moment a scream from the orchard side.

We rushed forward, and there on the sharp bank-side lay a little figure, face down, and Trip standing over it, looking rather puzzled.

I picked up the child – it was Sam. He struggled as soon as he felt my hands, but I bore him off to the house. He wriggled like a wild hare, and kicked, but at last he was still. I set him on the hearthrug to examine him. He was a quaint little figure, dressed in a man's trousers that had been botched small for him, and a coat hanging in rags.

'Did he get hold of you?' asked the father. 'Where was it he got hold of you?'

But the child stood unanswering, his little pale lips pinched together, his eyes staring out at nothing. Emily went on her knees before him, and put her face close to his, saying, with a voice that made one shrink from its unbridled emotion of caress:

'Did he hurt you, eh? – tell us where he hurt you.' She would have put her arms around him, but he shrank away.

'Look here,' said Lettie, 'it's here – and it's bleeding. Go and get some water, Emily, and some rags. Come on, Sam, let me look and I'll put some rags round it. Come along.'

She took the child and stripped him of his grotesque garments. Trip had given him a sharp grab on the thigh before he had realized that he was dealing with a little boy. It was not much, however, and Lettie soon had it bathed, and anointed with elderflower ointment. On the boy's body were several scars and bruises – evidently he had rough times. Lettie tended to him and dressed him again. He endured these attentions like a trapped, wild rabbit – never looking at us, never opening his lips – only shrinking slightly. When Lettie had put on him his torn little shirt, and had gathered the great breeches about him, Emily went to him to coax him and make him at home. She kissed him, and talked to him with her full vibration of emotional caress. It seemed almost to suffocate him. Then she tried to feed him with bread and milk from a spoon, but he would not open his mouth, and he turned his head away.

'Leave him alone – take no notice of him,' said Lettie, lifting him into the chimney seat, with the basin of bread and milk beside him. Emily fetched the two kittens out of their basket, and put them too beside him.

'I wonder how many eggs he'd got,' said the father laughing softly.

'Hush!' said Lettie. 'When do you think you will go to Canada, Mr Saxton?'

'Next spring – it's no good going before.'

'And then you'll marry?' asked Lettie of George.

'Before then – oh, before then,' he said.

'Why – how is it you are suddenly in such a hurry? – when will it be?'

'When are you marrying?' he asked in reply.

'I don't know,' she said, coming to a full stop.

'Then I don't know,' he said, taking a large wedge of cheese and biting a piece from it.

'It was fixed for June,' she said, recovering herself at his suggestion of hope.

'July!' said Emily.

'Father?' said he, holding the piece of cheese up before him as he spoke – he was evidently nervous: 'Would you advise me to marry Meg?'

His father started, and said:

'Why, was you thinking of doing?'

'Yes – all things considered.'

'Well – if she suits you –'

'We're cousins –'

'If you want her, I suppose you won't let that hinder you. She'll have a nice bit of money, and if you like her –'

'I like her all right – I shan't go out to Canada with her though. I shall stay at the Ram – for the sake of the life.'

'It's a poor life, that!' said the father, ruminating.

George laughed. 'A bit mucky!' he said – 'But it'll do. It would need Cyril or Lettie to keep me alive in Canada.'

It was a bold stroke – everybody was embarrassed.

'Well,' said the father, 'I suppose we can't have everything we want – we generally have to put up with the next best thing – don't we, Lettie?' – he laughed. Lettie flushed furiously.

'I don't know,' she said. 'You can generally get what you

want if you want it badly enough. Of course – if you *don't mind* –'

She rose, and went across to Sam.

He was playing with the kittens. One was patting and cuffing his bare toe, which had poked through his stocking. He pushed and teased the little scamp with his toe till it rushed at him, clinging, tickling, biting till he gave little bubbles of laughter, quite forgetful of us. Then the kitten was tired, and ran off. Lettie shook her skirts, and directly the two playful mites rushed upon it, darting round her, rolling head over heels, and swinging from the soft cloth. Suddenly becoming aware that they felt tired the young things trotted away and cuddled together by the fender, where in an instant they were asleep. Almost as suddenly, Sam sank into drowsiness.

'He'd better go to bed,' said the father.

'Put him in my bed,' said George. 'David would wonder what had happened.'

'Will you go to bed, Sam?' asked Emily, holding out her arms to him, and immediately startling him by the terrible gentleness of her persuasion. He retreated behind Lettie.

'Come along,' said the latter, and she quickly took him and undressed him. Then she picked him up, and his bare legs hung down in front of her. His head drooped drowsily on to her shoulder, against her neck.

She put down her face to touch the loose riot of his ruddy hair. She stood so, quiet, still and wistful, for a few moments; perhaps she was vaguely aware that the attitude was beautiful for her, and irresistibly appealing to George, who loved, above all in her, her delicate dignity of tenderness. Emily waited with the lighted candle for her some moments.

When she came down there was a softness about her.

'Now,' said I to myself. 'If George asks her again he is wise.'

'He is asleep,' she said, quietly.

'I'm thinking we might as well let him stop while we're here, should we, George?' said the father.

'Eh?'

'We'll keep him here, while we *are* here –'

'Oh – the lad! I should. Yes – he'd be better here than up yonder.'

'Ah yes – ever so much. It is good of you,' said Lettie.

'Oh, he'll make no difference,' said the father.

'Not a bit,' added George.

'What about his mother?' asked Lettie.

'I'll call and tell her in the morning,' said George.

'Yes,' she said, 'call and tell her.'

Then she put on her things to go. He also put on his cap.

'Are you coming a little way, Emily?' I asked.

She ran, laughing, with bright eyes as we went out into the darkness.

We waited for them at the wood gate. We all lingered, not knowing what to say. Lettie said finally:

'Well – it's no good – the grass is wet – Good night – Good night, Emily.'

'Good night,' he said, with regret, and hesitation, and a trifle of impatience in his voice and his manner. He lingered still a moment; she hesitated – then she struck off sharply.

'He has not asked her, the idiot!' I said to myself.

'Really,' she said bitterly, when we were going up the garden path, 'You think rather quiet folks have a lot in them, but it's only stupidity – they are mostly fools.'

CHAPTER V

An Arrow from the Impatient God

On an afternoon three or four days after the recovery of Sam, matters became complicated. George, as usual, discovered that he had been dawdling in the portals of his desires, when the doors came to with a bang. Then he hastened to knock.

'Tell her,' he said, 'I will come up tomorrow after milking – tell her I'm coming to see her.'

On the evening of that morrow, the first person to put in an appearance was a garrulous spinster who had called ostensibly to inquire into the absence of the family from church: 'I said to Elizabeth, "Now what a *thing* if anything happens to them just now, and the wedding is put off." I felt I *must* come and make myself sure – that nothing had happened. We all feel *so* interested in Lettie just now. I'm sure everybody is talking of her, she seems in the air. – I really think we shall have thunder: I *hope* we shan't. – Yes, we are all so glad that Mr Tempest is content with a wife from at home – the others, his father and Mr Robert and the rest – they were none of them to be suited at home, though to be sure the wives they brought were nothing – indeed they were not – as many a one said – Mrs Robert was a paltry choice – neither in looks nor manner had she anything to boast of – if her family was older than mine. Family wasn't much to make up for what she lacked in other things, that I could easily have supplied her with; and, oh, dear, what an object she is now, with her wisp of hair and her spectacles! She for one hasn't kept much of her youth. But when *is* the exact date, dear? – Some say this and some that, but as I always say, I never trust a "they say". It is so nice that you have that cousin a canon to come down for the service, Mrs Beardsall, and Sir Walter Houghton for the groom's man! What? – You don't think so – oh, but I know, dear, I know; you do like to treasure up these secrets, don't you; you are greedy for all the good things just now.'

She shook her head at Lettie, and the jet ornaments on her bonnet twittered like a thousand wagging little tongues. Then she sighed, and was about to recommence her song when she happened to turn her head and to espy a telegraph boy coming up the path.

'Oh, I hope nothing is wrong, dear – I hope nothing is wrong! I always feel so terrified of a telegram. You'd better not open it yourself, dear – don't now – let your brother go.'

Lettie, who had turned pale, hurried to the door. The sky was very dark – there was a mutter of thunder.

'It's all right,' said Lettie, trembling, 'it's only to say he's coming tonight.'

'I'm very thankful, very thankful,' cried the spinster. 'It might have been so much worse. I'm sure I never open a telegram without feeling as if I was opening a death-blow. I'm so glad, dear; it must have upset you. What news to take back to the village, supposing something had happened!' she sighed again, and the jet drops twinkled ominously in the thunder light, as if declaring they would make something of it yet.

It was six o'clock. The air relaxed a little, and the thunder was silent. George would be coming about seven; and the spinster showed no signs of departure; and Leslie might arrive at any moment. Lettie fretted and fidgeted, and the old woman gabbled on. I looked out of the window at the water and the sky.

The day had been uncertain. In the morning it was warm, and the sunshine had played and raced among the cloud-shadows on the hills. Later, great cloud masses had stalked up from the north-west and crowded thick across the sky; in this little night, sleet and wind, and rain whirled furiously. Then the sky had laughed at us again. In the sunshine came the spinster. But as she talked, over the hill-top rose the wide forehead of the cloud, rearing slowly, ominously higher. A first messenger of storm passed darkly over the sky, leaving the way clear again.

'I will go round to Highclose,' said Lettie. 'I am sure it will be stormy again. Are you coming down the road, Miss Slaighter, or do you mind if I leave you?'

'I will go, dear, if you think there is going to be another storm – I dread it so. Perhaps I had better wait –'

'Oh, it will not come over for an hour, I am sure. We read the weather well out here, don't we, Cyril? You'll come with me, won't you?'

We three set off, the gossip leaning on her toes, tripping between us. She was much gratified by Lettie's information concerning the proposals for the new home. We left her in a glow of congratulatory smiles on the highway. But the clouds had upreared, and stretched in two great arms, reaching overhead. The little spinster hurried along, but the black hands of the clouds kept pace and clutched her. A sudden gust of wind shuddered in the trees, and rushed upon her cloak, blowing its bugles.

An icy raindrop smote into her cheek. She hurried on, praying fervently for her bonnet's sake that she might reach Widow Harriman's cottage before the burst came. But the thunder crashed in her ear, and a host of hailstones flew at her. In despair and anguish she fled from under the ash trees; she reached the widow's garden gate, when out leapt the lightning full at her. 'Put me in the stair-hole!' she cried. 'Where is the stair-hole?'

Glancing wildly round, she saw a ghost. It was the reflexion of the sainted spinster, Hilda Slaighter, in the widow's mirror; a reflexion with a bonnet fallen backwards, and to it attached a thick rope of grey-brown hair. The author of the ghost instinctively twisted to look at the back of her head. She saw some ends of grey hair, and fled into the open stair-hole as into a grave.

We had gone back home till the storm was over, and then, restless, afraid of the arrival of George, we set out again into the wet evening. It was fine and chilly, and already a mist was rising from Nethermere, veiling the farther shore, where the trees rose loftily, suggesting groves beyond the Nile. The birds were singing riotously. The fresh green hedge glistened vividly and glowed again with intense green. Looking at the water, I perceived a delicate flush from the west hiding along it. The mist licked and wreathed up the shores; from the hidden white distance came the mournful cry of water fowl. We went slowly

along behind a heavy cart, which clanked and rattled under
the dripping trees, with the hoofs of the horse moving with
broad thuds in front. We passed over black patches where the
ash flowers were beaten down, and under great massed clouds
of green sycamore. At the sudden curve of the road, near the
foot of the hill, I stopped to break off a spray of larch, where
the soft cones were heavy as raspberries, and gay like flowers
with petals. The shaken bough spattered a heavy shower on my
face, of drops so cold that they seemed to sink into my blood
and chill it.

'Hark!' said Lettie, as I was drying my face. There was the
quick patter of a motor-car coming downhill. The heavy cart
was drawn across the road to rest, and the driver hurried to
turn the horse back. It moved with painful slowness, and we
stood in the road in suspense. Suddenly, before we knew it,
the car was dropping down on us, coming at us in a curve,
having rounded the horse and cart. Lettie stood faced with
terror. Leslie saw her, and swung round the wheels on the
sharp, curving hillside; looking only to see that he should miss
her. The car slid sideways; the mud crackled under the wheels,
and the machine went crashing into Nethermere. It caught the
edge of the old stone wall with a smash. Then for a few moments I think I was blind. When I saw again, Leslie was lying
across the broken hedge, his head hanging down the bank,
his face covered with blood; the car rested strangely on the
brink of the water, crumpled as if it had sunk down to rest.

Lettie, with hands shuddering, was wiping the blood from
his eyes with a piece of her underskirt. In a moment she said:

'He is not dead – let us take him home – let us take him
quickly.'

I ran and took the wicket gate off its hinges, and laid him
on that. His legs trailed down, but we carried him thus, she
at the feet, I at the head. She made me stop and put him down.
I thought the weight was too much for her, but it was not that.

'I can't bear to see his hand hanging, knocking against the
bushes and things.'

It was not many yards to the house. A maid-servant saw us,
came running out, and went running back, like the frightened
lapwing from the wounded cat.

We waited until the doctor came. There was a deep graze down the side of the head – serious, but not dangerous; there was a cut across the cheek-bone that would leave a scar; and the collar-bone was broken. I stayed until he had recovered consciousness. 'Lettie,' he wanted Lettie, so she had to remain at Highclose all night. I went home to tell my mother.

When I went to bed I looked across at the lighted windows of Highclose, and the lights trailed mistily towards me across the water. The cedar stood dark guard against the house; bright the windows were, like the stars, and, like the stars, covering their torment in brightness. The sky was glittering with sharp lights – they are too far off to take trouble for us, so little, little almost to nothingness. All the great hollow vastness roars overhead, and the stairs are only sparks that whirl and spin in the restless space. The earth must listen to us; she covers her face with a thin veil of mist, and is sad; she soaks up our blood tenderly, in the darkness, grieving and in the light she soothes and reassures us. Here on our earth is sympathy and hope, and the heavens have nothing but distances.

A corn-crake talked to me across the valley, talked and talked endlessly, asking and answering in hoarse tones from the sleeping, mist-hidden meadows. The monotonous voice, that on past summer evenings had had pleasant notes of romance, now was intolerable to me. Its inflexible harshness and cacophony seemed like the voice of fate speaking out its tuneless perseverance in the night.

In the morning Lettie came home wan, sad-eyed, and self-reproachful. After a short time they came for her, as he wanted her again.

When in the evening I went to see George, he too was very despondent.

'It's no good now,' said I. 'You should have insisted and made your own destiny.'

'Yes – perhaps so,' he drawled, in his best reflective manner.

'I would have had her – she'd have been glad if you'd done as you wanted with her. She won't leave him till he's strong, and he'll marry her before then. You should have had the courage to risk yourself – you're always too careful

of yourself and your own poor feelings – you never could
brace yourself up to a shower-bath of contempt and hard usage,
so you've saved your feelings and lost – not much, I suppose –
you couldn't.'

'But –' he began, not looking up; and I laughed at him.

'Go on,' I said.

'Well – she was engaged to him –'

'Pah – you thought you were too good to be rejected.'

He was very pale, and when he was pale, the tan on his
skin looked sickly. He regarded me with his dark eyes, which
were now full of misery and a child's big despair.

'And nothing else,' I completed, with which the little,
exhausted gunboat of my anger wrecked and sank utterly.
Yet no thoughts would spread sail on the sea of my pity:
I was like water that heaves with yearning, and is still.

Leslie was very ill for some time. He had a slight brain fever,
and was delirious, insisting that Lettie was leaving him. She
stayed most of her days at Highclose.

One day in June he lay resting on a deck chair in the shade
of the cedar, and she was sitting by him. It was a yellow,
sultry day, when all the atmosphere seemed inert, and all things
were languid.

'Don't you think, dear,' she said, 'it would be better for us
not to marry?'

He lifted his head nervously from the cushions; his face was
emblazoned with a livid red bar on a field of white, and he
looked worn, wistful.

'Do you mean not yet?' he asked.

'Yes – and, perhaps – perhaps never.'

'Ha,' he laughed, sinking down again. 'I must be getting like
myself again, if you begin to tease me.'

'But,' she said, struggling valiantly, 'I'm not sure I ought
to marry you.'

He laughed again, though a little apprehensively.

'Are you afraid I shall always be weak in my noddle?' he
asked. 'But you wait a month.'

'No, that doesn't bother me –'

'Oh, doesn't it!'

'Silly boy – no, it's myself.'

'I'm sure I've made no complaint about you.'

'Not likely – but I wish you'd let me go.'

'I'm a strong man to hold you, aren't I? Look at my muscular paw!' – he held out his hands, frail and white with sickness.

'You know you hold me – and I want you to let me go. I don't want to –'

'To what?'

'To get married at all – let me be, let me go.'

'What for?'

'Oh – for my sake.'

'You mean you don't love me?'

'Love – love – I don't know anything about it. But I can't – we can't be – don't you see – oh, what do they say – flesh of one flesh.'

'Why?' he whispered, like a child that is told some tale of mystery.

She looked at him, as he lay propped upon his elbow, turning towards hers his white face of fear and perplexity, like a child that cannot understand, and is afraid, and wants to cry. Then slowly tears gathered full in her eyes, and she wept from pity and despair.

This excited him terribly. He got up from his chair, and the cushions fell on to the grass:

'What's the matter, what's the matter! – Oh, Lettie – is it me? – don't you want me now? – is that it? – tell me, tell me now, tell me,' – he grasped her wrists, and tried to pull her hands from her face. The tears were running down his cheeks. She felt him trembling, and the sound of his voice alarmed her from herself. She hastily smeared the tears from her eyes, got up, and put her arms round him. He hid his head on her shoulder and sobbed, while she bent over him, and so they cried out their cries, till they were ashamed looking round to see if anyone were near. Then she hurried about, picking up the cushions, making him lie down, and arranging him comfortably, so that she might be busy. He was querulous, like a sick, indulged child. He would have her arm under his shoulders, and her face near his.

'Well,' he said, smiling faintly again after a time. 'You are naughty to give us such rough times – is it for the pleasure of making up, bad little Schnucke – aren't you?'

She kept close to him, and he did not see the wince and quiver of her lips.

'I wish I was strong again – couldn't we go boating – or ride on horseback – and you'd have to behave then. Do you think I shall be strong in a month? Stronger than you?'

'I hope so,' she said.

'Why, I don't believe you do, I believe you like me like this – so that you can lay me down and smooth me – don't you, quiet girl?'

'When you're good.'

'Ah, well, in a month I shall be strong, and we'll be married and go to Switzerland – do you hear, Schnucke – you won't be able to be naughty any more then. Oh – do you want to go away from me again?'

'No – only my arm is dead,' she drew it from beneath him, standing up, swinging it, smiling because it hurt her.

'Oh, my darling – what a shame! oh, I am a brute, a kiddish brute. I wish I was strong again, Lettie, and didn't do these things.'

'You boy – it's nothing.' She smiled at him again.

CHAPTER VI

The Courting

DURING Leslie's illness I strolled down to the mill one Saturday evening. I met George tramping across the yard with a couple of buckets of swill, and eleven young pigs rushing squealing about his legs, shrieking in an agony of suspense. He poured the stuff into a trough with luscious gurgle, and instantly ten noses were dipped in, and ten little mouths began to slobber. Though there was plenty of room for ten, yet they shouldered and shoved and struggled to capture a larger space, and many little trotters dabbled and spilled the stuff, and the ten sucking, clapping snouts twitched fiercely, and twenty little eyes glared askance, like so many points of wrath. They gave uneasy, gasping grunts in their haste. The unhappy eleventh rushed from point to point trying to push in his snout, but for his pains he got rough squeezing, and sharp grabs on his ears. Then he lifted up his face and screamed screams of grief and wrath unto the evening sky.

But the ten little gluttons only twitched their ears to make sure there was no danger in the noise, and they sucked harder, with much spilling and slobbing. George laughed like a sardonic Jove, but at last he gave ear, and kicked the ten gluttons from the trough, and allowed the residue to the eleventh. This one, poor wretch, almost wept with relief as he sucked and swallowed in sobs, casting his little eyes apprehensively upwards, though he did not lift his nose from the trough, as he heard the vindictive shrieks of ten little fiends kept at bay by George. The solitary feeder, shivering with apprehension, rubbed the wood bare with his snout, then, turning up to heaven his eyes of gratitude, he reluctantly left the trough. I expected to see the ten fall upon him and devour him, but they did not; they rushed upon the empty trough, and rubbed the wood still drier, shrieking with misery.

'How like life,' I laughed.

'Fine litter,' said George; 'there were fourteen, only that damned she-devil, Circe, went and ate three of 'em before we got at her.'

The great ugly sow came leering as he spoke.

'Why don't you fatten her up, and devour her, the old gargoyle? She's an offence to the universe.'

'Nay – she's a fine sow.'

I snorted, and he laughed, and the old sow grunted with contempt, and her little eyes twisted towards us with a demoniac leer as she rolled past.

'What are you going to do tonight?' I asked. 'Going out?'

'I'm going courting,' he replied grinning.

'Oh! – wish *I* were!'

'You can come if you like – and tell me where I make mistakes, since you're an expert on such matters.'

'Don't you get on very well then?' I asked.

'Oh, all right – it's easy enough when you don't care a damn. Besides, you can always have a Johnny Walker. That's the best of courting at the Ram Inn. I'll go and get ready.'

In the kitchen Emily sat grinding out some stitching from a big old hand-machine that stood on the table before her: she was making shirts, for Sam, I presumed. That little fellow, who was installed at the farm, was seated by her side firing off words from a reading book. The machine rumbled and rattled on, like a whole factory at work, for an inch or two, during which time Sam shouted in shrill explosions like irregular pistol shots: 'Do – not – pot –' 'Put!' cried Emily from the machine; 'put –' shrilled the child, 'the soot – on – my – boot,' – there the machine broke down, and, frightened by the sound of his own voice, the boy stopped in bewilderment and looked round.

'Go on!' said Emily, as she poked in the teeth of the old machine with the scissors, then pulled and prodded again. He began '– boot, – but – you –' here he died off again, made nervous by the sound of his voice in the stillness. Emily sucked a piece of cotton and pushed it through the needle.

'Now go on,' she said, '– "but you may".'

'But – you – may – shoot': – he shouted away, reassured by

the rumble of the machine: 'Shoot – the – fox. I – I – It – is
– at – the – rot –'

'Root,' shrieked Emily, as she guided the stuff through the
doddering jaws of the machine.

'Root,' echoed the boy, and he went off with these crackers:
'Root – of – the – tree.'

'Next one!' cried Emily.

'Put – the – ol –' began the boy.

'What?' cried Emily.

'Ole – on –'

'Wait a bit!' cried Emily, and then the machine broke down.

'Hang!' she ejaculated.

'Hang!' shouted the child.

She laughed, and leaned over to him:

'"Put the oil in the pan to boil, while I toil in the soil" –
Oh, Cyril, I never knew you were there! Go along now, Sam:
David'll be at the back somewhere.'

'He's in the bottom garden,' said I, and the child ran out.

Directly George came in from the scullery, drying himself.
He stood on the hearthrug as he rubbed himself, and surveyed
his reflexion in the mirror above the high mantelpiece; he
looked at himself and smiled. I wondered that he found such
satisfaction in his image, seeing that there was a gap in his
chin, and an uncertain moth-eaten appearance in one cheek.
Mrs Saxton still held this mirror an object of dignity; it was
fairly large, and had a well-carven frame; but it left gaps and
spots and scratches in one's countenance, and even where it
was brightest, it gave one's reflexion a far-away dim aspect.
Notwithstanding, George smiled at himself as he combed his
hair, and twisted his moustache.

'You seem to make a good impression on yourself,' said I.

'I was thinking I looked all right – sort of face to go courting
with,' he replied, laughing: 'You just arrange a patch of black
to come and hide your faults – and you're all right.'

'I always used to think,' said Emily, 'that the black spots
had swallowed so many faces they were full up, and couldn't
take any more – and the rest was misty because there were so
many faces lapped one over the other – reflected.'

'You do see yourself a bit ghostish –' said he, 'on a back-

ground of your ancestors. I always think when you stop in
an old place like this you sort of keep company with your ancestors too much; I sometimes feel like a bit of the old building
walking about; the old feelings of the old folks stick to you like
the lichens on the walls; you sort of get hoary.'

'That's it – it's true,' asserted the father, 'people whose
families have shifted about much don't know how it feels.
That's why I'm going to Canada.'

'And I'm going in a pub,' said George, 'where it's quite
different – plenty of life.'

'Life!' echoed Emily with contempt.

'That's the word, my wench,' replied her brother, lapsing
into the dialect. 'That's what I'm after. We know such a
lot, an' we know nowt.'

'You do –' said the father, turning to me, 'you stay in one
place, generation after generation, and you seem to get proud,
an' look on things outside as foolishness. There's many a thing
as any common man knows, as we haven't a glimpse of. We
keep on thinking and feeling the same, year after year, till we've
only got one side; an' I suppose they've done it before us.'

'It's "Good-night an' God bless you," to th' owd place,
granfeythers an' grammothers,' laughed George as he ran upstairs – 'an' off we go on the gallivant,' he shouted from the
landing.

His father shook his head, saying:

'I can't make out how it is, he's so different. I suppose it's
being in love –'

*

We went into the barn to get the bicycles to cycle over to
Greymede. George struck a match to look for his pump, and
he noticed a great spider scuttle off into the corner of the wall,
and sit peeping out at him like a hoary little ghoul.

'How are you, old chap?' said George, nodding to him –
'Thought he looked like an old grandfather of mine,' he said to
me, laughing, as he pumped up the tyres of the old bicycle for
me.

It was Saturday night, so the bar parlour of the Ram Inn was
fairly full.

'Hello, George – come co'tin'?' was the cry, followed by a nod and a 'Good evenin',' to me, who was a stranger in the parlour.

'It's a raïght for thaïgh,' said a fat young fellow with an unwilling white moustache, ' – tha can co'te as much as ter likes ter 'ae, as well as th' lass, an't it costs thee nowt –' at which the room laughed, taking pipes from mouths to do so. George sat down, looking round.

' 'Owd on a bit,' said a black-whiskered man, 'tha mun 'a 'e patience when tu 't co'tin' a lass. Ow's puttin' th' öwd lady ter bed – 'ark thee – can t' ear – that wor th' bed latts goin' bang. Ow'll be dern in a minnit now, gie 'er time ter tuck th' öwd lady up. Can' ter 'ear say 'er prayers.'

'Strike!' cried the fat young man, exploding:

'Fancy th' öwd lady sayin' 'er prayers! – it 'ud be enough ter ma'e 'er false teeth drop out.'

The room laughed.

They began to tell tales about the old landlady. She had practised bone-setting, in which she was very skilful. People came to her from long distances that she might divine their trouble and make right their limbs. She would accept no fee.

Once she had gone up to Dr Fullwood to give him a piece of her mind, inasmuch as he had let a child go for three weeks with a broken collar-bone, whilst treating him for dislocation. The doctor had tried the high hand with her, since when, wherever he went, the miners placed their hands on their shoulders, and groaned: 'Oh my collar-bone!'

Here Meg came in. She give a bright, quick, bird-like look at George, and flushed a brighter red.

'I thought you wasn't commin',' she said.

'Dunna thee bother – 'e'd none stop away,' said the black-whiskered man.

She brought us glasses of whisky, and moved about supplying the men, who chaffed with her honestly and good-naturedly. Then she went out, but we remained in our corner. The men talked on the most peculiar subjects: there was a bitter discussion as to whether London is or is not a seaport – the matter was thrashed out with heat; then an embryo artist set the room ablaze by declaring there were only three colours, red, yellow, and blue, and the rest were not colours, they were mixtures: this amounted almost to atheism, and one man asked the artist to dare to declare that his brown breeches were not a colour, which the artist did, and almost had to fight for it; next they came to strength, and George won a bet of five shillings, by lifting a piano; then they settled down, and talked sex, *sotto voce,* one man giving startling accounts of Japanese and Chinese prostitutes in Liverpool. After this the talk split up: a farmer began to counsel George how to manage the farm attached to the Inn, another bargained with him about horses, and argued about cattle, a tailor advised him thickly to speculate, and unfolded a fine secret by which a man might make money, if he had the go to do it – and so, till eleven o'clock. Then Bill came and called 'time!' and the place was empty, and the room shivered as a little fresh air came in between the foul tobacco smoke, and smell of drink, and foul breath.

We were both affected by the whisky we had drunk. I was ashamed to find that when I put out my hand to take my glass, or to strike a match, I missed my mark, and fumbled; my hands seemed hardly to belong to me, and my feet were not much more sure. Yet I was acutely conscious of every change in myself and in him; it seemed as if I could make my body drunk, but could never intoxicate my mind, which roused itself and kept the sharpest guard. George was frankly half drunk: his eyelids sloped over his eyes and his speech was thick; when he put out his hand he knocked over his glass, and the stuff was spilled all over the table; he only laughed. I, too, felt a great prompting to giggle on every occasion, and I marvelled at myself.

Meg came into the room when all the men had gone.

'Come on, my duck,' he said, waving his arm with the generous flourish of a tipsy man. 'Come an' sit 'ere.'

'Shan't you come in th' kitchen?' she asked, looking round on the tables where pots and glasses stood in little pools of liquor, and where spent matches and tobacco-ash littered the white wood.

'No – what for? – come an' sit 'ere!' – he was reluctant to get on his feet; I knew it and laughed inwardly; I also laughed to hear his thick speech, and his words which seemed to slur against his cheeks.

She went and sat by him, having moved the little table with its spilled liquor.

'They've been tellin' me how to get rich,' he said, nodding his head, and laughing, showing his teeth, 'An' I'm goin' ter show 'em. You see, Meg, you see – I'm goin' ter show 'em I can be as good as them, you see.'

'Why,' said she, indulgent, 'what are you going to do?'

'You wait a bit an' see – they don't know yet what I can do – they don't know – *you* don't know – none of you know.'

'An' what shall you do when we're rich, George?'

'Do? – I shall do what I like. I can make as good a show as anybody else, can't I?' – he put his face very near to hers, and nodded at her, but she did not turn away. – 'Yes – I'll see what it's like to have my fling. We've been too cautious, our family has – an' I have; we're frightened of ourselves, to do anything. I'm goin' to do what I like, my duck, now – I don't care – I don't care – that!' – he brought his hand down heavily on the table nearest him, and broke a glass. Bill looked in to see what was happening.

'But you won't do anything that's not right, George!'

'No – I don't want to hurt nobody – but I don't care – that!'

'You're too good-hearted to do anybody any harm.'

'I believe I am. You know me a bit, you do, Meg – you don't think I'm a fool now, do you?'

'I'm sure I don't – who does?'

'No – you don't – I know you don't. Gi'e me a kiss – thou'rt a little beauty, thou art – like a ripe plum! I could set my teeth in thee, thou'rt that nice – full o' red juice' – he playfully pretended to bite her. She laughed, and gently pushed him away.

'Tha likest me, doesna ta?' he asked softly.

'What do you want to know for?' she replied, with a tender archness.

'But tha does – say now, tha does.'

'I should a' thought you'd a' known, without telling.'

'Nay, but, I want to hear thee.'

'Go on,' she said, and she kissed him.

'But what should you do if I went to Canada and left you?'

'Ah – you wouldn't do that.'

'But I might – and what then?'

'Oh, I don't know what I should do. But you wouldn't do it, I know you wouldn't – you couldn't.' He quickly put his arms round her and kissed her, moved by the trembling surety of her tone:

'No, I wouldna – I'd niver leave thee – tha'd be as miserable as sin, shouldna ta, my duck?'

'Yes,' she murmured.

'Ah,' he said, 'tha'rt a warm little thing – tha loves me, eh?'

'Yes,' she murmured, and he pressed her to him, and kissed her, and held her close.

'We'll be married soon, my bird – are ter glad? – in a bit – tha'rt glad, aren't ta?'

She looked up at him as if he were noble. Her love for him was so generous that it beautified him.

He had to walk his bicycle home, being unable to ride; his shins, I know, were a good deal barked by the pedals.

CHAPTER VII

The Fascination of the Forbidden Apple

On the first Sunday in June, when Lettie knew she would keep her engagement with Leslie, and when she was having a day at home from Highclose, she got ready to go down to the mill. We were in mourning for an aunt, so she wore a dress of fine black voile, and a black hat with long feathers. Then, when I looked at her fair hands, and her arms closely covered in the long black cuffs of her sleeves, I felt keenly my old brother-love shielding, indulgent.

It was a windy, sunny day. In shelter the heat was passionate, but in the open the wind scattered its fire. Every now and then a white cloud broad-based, blue-shadowed, travelled slowly along the sky-road after the forerunner small in the distance, and trailing over us a chill shade, a gloom which we watched creep on over the water, over the wood and the hill. These royal, rounded clouds had sailed all day along the same route, from the harbour of the south to the wastes in the northern sky, following the swift wild geese. The brook hurried along singing, only here and there lingering to whisper to the secret bushes, then setting off fresh with a new snatch of song.

The fowls pecked staidly in the farmyard, with Sabbath decorum. Occasionally a lost, sportive wind-puff would wander across the yard and ruffle them, and they resented it. The pigs were asleep in the sun, giving faint grunts now and then from sheer luxury. I saw a squirrel go darting down the mossy garden wall, up into the laburnum tree, where he lay flat along the bough, and listened. Suddenly away he went, chuckling to himself. Gyp all at once set off barking, but I soothed her down; it was the unusual sight of Lettie's dark dress that startled her, I suppose.

We went quietly into the kitchen. Mrs Saxton was just putting a chicken, wrapped in a piece of flannel, on the warm hob to coax it into life; it looked very feeble. George was asleep, with his head in his arms on the table; the father was asleep on the sofa, very comfortable and admirable; I heard Emily fleeing upstairs, presumably to dress.

'He stays out so late – up at the Ram Inn,' whispered the mother in a high whisper, looking at George, 'and then he's up at five – he doesn't get his proper rest.' She turned to the chicks, and continued in her whisper – 'the mother left them just before they hatched out, so we've been bringing them on here. This one's a bit weak – I thought I'd hot him up a bit,' she laughed with a quaint little frown of deprecation. Eight or nine yellow, fluffy little mites were cheeping and scuffling in the fender. Lettie bent over them to touch them; they were tame, and ran among her fingers.

Suddenly George's mother gave a loud cry, and rushed to the fire. There was a smell of singed down. The chicken had toddled into the fire, and gasped its faint gasp among the red-hot cokes. The father jumped from the sofa; George sat up with wide eyes; Lettie gave a little cry and a shudder; Trip rushed round and began to bark. There was a smell of cooked meat.

'There goes number one!' said the mother, with her queer little laugh. It made me laugh too.

'What's a matter – what's a matter?' asked the father excitedly.

'It's a chicken been and walked into the fire – I put it on the hob to warm,' explained his wife.

'Goodness – I couldn't think what was up!' he said, and dropped his head to trace gradually the border between sleeping and waking.

George sat and smiled at us faintly, he was too dazed to speak. His chest still leaned against the table, and his arms were spread out thereon, but he lifted his face, and looked at Lettie with his dazed, dark eyes, and smiled faintly at her. His hair was all ruffled, and his shirt collar unbuttoned. Then he got up slowly, pushing his chair back with a loud noise, and stretched himself, pressing his arms upwards with a long, heavy stretch.

'Oh – h – h!' he said, bending his arms and then letting

them drop to his sides. 'I never thought you'd come today.'

'I wanted to come and see you – I shan't have many more chances,' said Lettie, turning from him and yet looking at him again.

'No, I suppose not,' he said, subsiding into quiet. Then there was silence for some time. The mother began to inquire after Leslie, and kept the conversation up till Emily came down, blushing and smiling and glad.

'Are you coming out?' said she, 'there are two or three robins' nests, and a spinkie's –'

'I think I'll leave my hat,' said Lettie, unpinning it as she spoke, and shaking her hair when she was free. Mrs Saxton insisted on her taking a long white silk scarf; Emily also wrapped her hair in a gauze scarf, and looked beautiful.

George came out with us, coatless, hatless, his waistcoat all unbuttoned, as he was. We crossed the orchard, over the old bridge, and went to where the slopes ran down to the lower pond, a bank all covered with nettles, and scattered with a hazel bush or two. Among the nettles old pans were rusting, and old coarse pottery cropped up.

We came upon a kettle heavily coated with lime. Emily bent down and looked, and then we peeped in. There were the robin birds with their yellow beaks stretched so wide apart I feared they would never close them again. Among the naked little mites, that begged from us so blindly and confidently, were huddled three eggs.

'They are like Irish children peeping out of a cottage,' said Emily, with the family fondness for romantic similes.

We went on to where a tin lay with the lid pressed back, and inside it, snug and neat, was another nest, with six eggs, cheek to cheek.

'How warm they are,' said Lettie, touching them, 'you can fairly feel the mother's breast.'

He tried to put his hand into the tin, but the space was too small, and they looked into each other's eyes and smiled. 'You'd think the father's breast had marked them with red,' said Emily.

As we went up the orchard side we saw three wide displays of coloured pieces of pots arranged at the foot of three trees.

'Look,' said Emily, 'those are the children's houses. You

don't know how our Mollie gets all Sam's pretty bits – she is a cajoling hussy!'

The two looked at each other again, smiling. Up on the pond-side, in the full glitter of light, we looked round where the blades of clustering corn were softly healing the red bosom of the hill. The larks were overhead among the sun-beams. We straggled away across the grass. The field was all afroth with cowslips, a yellow, glittering, shaking froth on the still green of the grass. We trailed our shadows across the fields, extinguishing the sunshine on the flowers as we went. The air was tingling with the scent of blossoms.

'Look at the cowslips, all shaking with laughter,' said Emily, and she tossed back her head, and her dark eyes sparkled among the flow of gauze. Lettie was on in front, flitting darkly across the field, bending over the flowers, stooping to the earth like a sable Persephone come into freedom. George had left her at a little distance, hunting for something in the grass. He stopped, and remained standing in one place.

Gradually, as if unconsciously, she drew near to him, and when she lifted her head, after stooping to pick some chimney-sweeps, little grass flowers, she laughed with a slight surprise to see him so near.

'Ah!' she said. 'I thought I was all alone in the world – such a splendid world – it was so nice.'

'Like Eve in a meadow in Eden – and Adam's shadow somewhere on the grass,' said I.

'No – no Adam,' she asserted, frowning slightly, and laughing.

'Who ever would want streets of gold,' Emily was saying to me, 'when you can have a field of cowslips! Look at that hedgebottom that gets the south sun – one stream and glitter of buttercups.'

'Those Jews always had an eye to the filthy lucre – they even made Heaven out of it,' laughed Lettie, and, turning to him, she said, 'Don't you wish we were wild – hark, like wood-pigeons – or larks – or, look, like peewits? Shouldn't you love flying and wheeling and sparkling and – courting in the wind?' She lifted her eyelids, and vibrated the question. He flushed, bending over the ground.

'Look,' he said, 'here's a larkie's.'

Once a horse had left a hoofprint in the soft meadow; now the larks had rounded, softened the cup, and had laid there three dark-brown eggs. Lettie sat down and leaned over the nest; he leaned above her. The wind, running over the flower heads, peeped in at the little brown buds, and bounded off again gladly. The big clouds sent messages to them down the shadows, and ran in raindrops to touch them.

'I wish,' she said, 'I wish we were free like that. If we could put everything safely in a little place in the earth – couldn't we have a good time as well as the larks?'

'I don't see,' said he, 'why we can't.'

'Oh – but *I* can't – you know we can't' – and she looked at him fiercely.

'Why can't you?' he asked.

'You know we can't – you know as well as I do,' she replied, and her whole soul challenged him. 'We have to consider things,' she added. He dropped his head. He was afraid to make the struggle, to rouse himself to decide the question for her. She turned away, and went kicking through the flowers. He picked up the blossoms she had left by the nest – they were still warm from her hands – and followed her. She walked on towards the end of the field, the long strands of her white scarf running before her. Then she leaned back to the wind, while he caught her up.

'Don't you want your flowers?' he asked humbly.

'No, thanks – they'd be dead before I got home – throw them away, you look absurd with a posy.'

He did as he was bidden. They came near the hedge. A crab-apple tree blossomed up among the blue.

'You may get me a bit of that blossom,' said she, and suddenly added – 'no, I can reach it myself,' whereupon she stretched upward and pulled several sprigs of the pink and white, and put it in her dress.

'Isn't it pretty?' she said, and she began to laugh ironically, pointing to the flowers – 'pretty, pink-cheeked petals, and stamens like yellow hair, and buds like lips promising something nice' – she stopped, and looked at him, flickering with a smile. Then she pointed to the ovary beneath the flower, and said: 'Result: Crab-apples!'

She continued to look at him, and to smile. He said nothing. So they went on to where they could climb the fence into the spinney. She climbed to the top rail, holding by an oak bough. Then she let him lift her down bodily.

'Ah!' she said, 'you like to show me how strong you are – a veritable Samson!' – she mocked, although she had invited him with her eyes to take her in his arms.

We were entering the spinney of black poplar. In the hedge was an elm tree, with myriads of dark dots pointed against the bright sky, myriads of clusters of flaky green fruit.

'Look at that elm,' she said, 'you'd think it was in full leaf, wouldn't you? Do you know why it's so prolific?'

'No,' he said, with a curious questioning drawl of the monosyllable.

'It's casting its bread upon the winds – no, it is dying, so it puts out all its strength and loads its bough with the last fruit. It'll be dead next year. If you're here then, come and see. Look at the ivy, the suave smooth ivy, with its fingers in the tree's throat. Trees know how to die, you see – we don't.'

With her whimsical moods she tormented him. She was at the bottom a seething confusion of emotion, and she wanted to make him likewise.

'If we were trees with ivy – instead of being fine humans with free active life – we should hug our thinning lives, shouldn't we?'

'I suppose we should.'

'You, for instance – fancy *your* sacrificing yourself – for the next generation – that reminds you of Schopenhauer, doesn't it? – for the next generation, or love, or anything!'

He did not answer her; she was too swift for him. They passed on under the poplars, which were hanging strings of green beads above them. There was a little open space, with tufts of bluebells. Lettie stooped over a wood-pigeon that lay on the ground on its breast, its wings half spread. She took it up – it's eyes were bursten and bloody; she felt its breast, ruffling the dimming iris on its throat.

'It's been fighting,' he said.

'What for – a mate?' she asked, looking at him.

'I don't know,' he answered.

'Cold – he's quite cold, under the feathers! I think a wood-pigeon must enjoy being fought for – and being won; especially if the right one won. It would be a fine pleasure, to see them fighting – don't you think?' she said, torturing him.

'The claws are spread – it fell dead off the perch,' he replied.

'Ah, poor thing – it was wounded – and sat and waited for death – when the other had won. Don't you think life is very cruel, George – and love the cruellest of all?'

He laughed bitterly under the pain of her soft, sad tones.

'Let me bury him – and have done with the beaten lover. But we'll make him a pretty grave.'

She scooped a hole in the dark soil, and snatching a handful of bluebells, threw them in on top of the dead bird. Then she smoothed the soil over all, and pressed her white hands on the black loam.

'There,' she said, knocking her hands one against the other to shake off the soil, 'he's done with. Come on.'

He followed her, speechless with emotion.

The spinney opened out; the ferns were serenely uncoiling, the bluebells stood grouped with blue curls mingled. In the freer spaces forget-me-nots flowered in nebulae, and dog-violets gave an undertone of dark purple, with primroses for planets in the night. There was a slight drift of woodruff, sweet new-mown hay, scenting the air under boughs. On a wet bank was the design of golden saxifrage, glistening unholily as if varnished by its minister, the snail. George and Lettie crushed the veined bells of wood-sorrel and broke the silken mosses. What did it matter to them what they broke or crushed?

Over the fence of the spinney was the hillside, scattered with old thorn trees. There the little grey lichens held up ruby balls to us unnoticed. What did it matter, when all the great red apples were being shaken from the Tree to be left to rot?

'If I were a man,' said Lettie, 'I would go out west and be free. I should love it.'

She took the scarf from her head and let it wave out on the wind; the colour was warm in her face with climbing, and her curls were freed by the wind, sparkling and rippling.

'Well – you're not a man,' he said, looking at her, and speaking with timid bitterness.

'No,' she laughed, 'if I were, I would shape things – oh, wouldn't I have my own way!'

'And don't you now?'

'Oh – I don't want it particularly – when I've got it. When I've had my way, I *do want* somebody to take it back from me.'

She put her head back, and looked at him sideways, laughing through the glitter of her hair.

They came to the Kennels. She sat down on the edge of the great stone water-trough, and put her hands in the water, moving them gently like submerged flowers through the clear pool.

'I love to see myself in the water,' she said, 'I don't mean *on* the water, Narcissus – but that's how I should like to be out west, to have a little lake of my own, and swim with my limbs quite free in the water.

'Do you swim well?' he asked.

'Fairly.'

'I would race you – in your little lake.'

She laughed, took her hands out of the water, and watched the clear drops trickle off. Then she lifted her head suddenly, at some thought or other. She looked across the valley, and saw the red roofs of the Mill.

> '– *Ilion, Ilion*
> *Fatalis incestusque judex*
> *Et mulier peregrina vertit*
> *In pulverem –*'

'What's that?' he said.

'Nothing.'

'That's a private trough,' exclaimed a thin voice, high like a peewit's cry. We started in surprise to see a tall, black-bearded man looking at us and away from us nervously, fidgeting uneasily some ten yards off.

'Is it?' said Lettie, looking at her wet hands, which she proceeded to dry on a fragment of a handkerchief.

'You mustn't meddle with it,' said the man, in the same reedy, oboe voice. Then he turned his head away, and his pale grey eyes roved the countryside – when he had courage, he turned his back to us, shading his eyes to continue his scrutiny. He walked hurriedly, a few steps, then craned his neck, peering into the valley, and hastened a dozen yards in another direction, again stretching and peering about. Then he went indoors.

'He is pretending to look for somebody,' said Lettie, 'but it's only because he's afraid we shall think he came out just to look at us' – and they laughed.

Suddenly a woman appeared at the gate; she had pale eyes like the mouse-voiced man.

'You'll get Bright's disease sitting on that there damp stone,' she said to Lettie, who at once rose apologetically.

'I ought to know,' continued the mouse-voiced woman, 'my own mother died of it.'

'Indeed,' murmured Lettie, 'I'm sorry.'

'Yes,' continued the woman, 'it behooves you to be careful. Do you come from Strelley Mill Farm?' she asked suddenly of George, surveying his shameful *déshabille* with bitter reproof.

He admitted the imputation.

'And you're going to leave, aren't you?'

Which also he admitted.

'Humph! – we s'll 'appen get some neighbours. It's a dog's life for loneliness. I suppose you knew the last lot that was here.'

Another brief admission.

'A dirty lot – a dirty beagle she must have been. You should just ha' seen these grates.'

'Yes,' said Lettie, 'I have seen them.'

'Faugh – the state! But come in – come in, you'll see a difference.'

They entered, out of curiosity.

The kitchen was indeed different. It was clean and sparkling warm with bright red chintzes on the sofa and on every chair cushion. Unfortunately the effect was spoiled by green and yellow antimacassars, and by a profusion of paper and woollen flowers. There were three cases of woollen flowers, and on the wall, four fans stitched over with ruffled green and yellow papers, adorned with yellow paper roses, carnations, arum lilies, and poppies; there were also wall pockets full of paper flowers; while the wood outside was loaded with blossom.

'Yes,' said Lettie, 'there is a difference.'

The woman swelled, and looked round. The black-bearded man peeped from behind the *Christian Herald* – those long blaring trumpets! – and shrank again. The woman darted at his pipe, which he had put on a piece of newspaper on the hob, and blew some imaginary ash from it. Then she caught sight of something – perhaps some dust – on the fireplace.

'There!' she cried, 'I knew it; I couldn't leave him one second! I haven't work enough burning wood, but he must be poke – poke –'

'I only pushed a piece in between the bars,' complained the mouse-voice from behind the paper.

'Pushed a piece in!' she re-echoed, with awful scorn, seizing the poker and thrusting it over his paper. 'What do you call that, sitting there telling your stories before folks –'

They crept out and hurried away. Glancing round, Lettie saw the woman mopping the doorstep after them, and she laughed. He pulled his watch out of his breeches' pocket; it was half-past three.

'What are you looking at the time for?' she asked.

'Meg's coming to tea,' he replied.

She said no more, and they walked slowly on.

When they came on to the shoulder of the hill, and looked down on to the mill, and the mill-pond, she said:

'I will not come down with you – I will go home.'

'Not come down to tea!' he exclaimed, full of reproach and amazement, 'Why, what will they say?'

'No, I won't come down – let me say farewell – *jamque Vale!* Do you remember how Eurydice sank back into Hell?'

'But' – he stammered, 'you must come down to tea – how can I tell them? Why won't you come?'

She answered him in Latin, with two lines from Virgil. As she watched him, she pitied his helplessness, and gave him a last cut as she said, very softly and tenderly:

'It wouldn't be fair to Meg.'

He stood looking at her; his face was coloured only by the grey-brown tan; his eyes, the dark, self-mistrustful eyes of the family, were darker than ever, dilated with misery of helplessness; and she was infinitely pitiful. She wanted to cry in her yearning.

'Shall we go into the wood for a few minutes?' she said, in a low, tremulous voice, as they turned aside.

The wood was high and warm. Along the ridings the forget-me-nots were knee deep, stretching, glimmering into the distance like the Milky Way through the night. They left the tall, flower-tangled paths to go in among the bluebells, breaking through the close-pressed flowers and ferns till they came to an oak which had fallen across the hazels, where they sat half screened. The hyacinths drooped magnificently with an overweight of purple, or they stood pale and erect, like unripe ears of purple corn. Heavy bees swung down in a blunder of extravagance among the purple flowers. They were intoxicated even with the sight of so much blue. The sound of their hearty, wanton humming came clear upon the solemn boom of the wind overhead. The sight of their clinging, clambering riot gave satisfaction to the soul. A rosy campion flower caught the sun and shone out. An elm sent down a shower of flesh-tinted sheaths upon them.

'If there were fauns and hamadryads!' she said softly, turning to him to soothe his misery. She took his cap from his head, ruffled his hair, saying:

'If you were a faun, I would put guelder roses round your hair, and make you look Bacchanalian.' She left her hand lying on his knee, and looked up at the sky. Its blue looked pale and green in comparison with the purple tide ebbing about the wood. The clouds rose up like towers, and something had touched them into beauty, and poised them up among the winds. The clouds passed on, and the pool of sky was clear.

'Look,' she said, 'now we are netted down – boughs with knots of green buds. If we were free on the winds! – But I'm glad we're not.' She turned suddenly to him, and with the same movement, she gave him her hand, and he clasped it in both his. 'I'm glad we're netted down here; if we were free in the winds – Ah!'

She laughed a peculiar little laugh, catching her breath.

'Look!' she said, 'it's a palace, with the ash-trunks smooth like a girl's arm, and the elm-columns, ribbed and bossed and fretted, with the great steel shafts of beech, all rising up to hold an embroidered care-cloth over us; and every thread of the care-cloth vibrates with music for us, and the little broidered birds sing; and the hazel-bushes fling green spray round us, and the honeysuckle leans down to pour out scent over us. Look at the harvest of bluebells – ripened for us! Listen to the bee, sounding among all the organ-play – if he sounded exultant for us!' She looked at him, with tears coming up into her eyes, and a little, winsome, wistful smile hovering round her mouth. He was very pale, and dared not look at her. She put her hand in his, leaning softly against him. He watched, as if fascinated, a young thrush with full pale breast who hopped near to look at them – glancing with quick, shining eyes.

'The clouds are going on again,' said Lettie.

'Look at that cloud face – see – gazing right up into the sky. The lips are opening – he is telling us something – now the form is slipping away – it's gone – come, we must go too.'

'No,' he cried, 'don't go – don't go away.'

Her tenderness made her calm. She replied in a voice perfect in restrained sadness and resignation.

'No, my dear, no. The threads of my life were untwined; they drifted about like floating threads of gossamer; and you didn't put out your hand to take them and twist them up into the chord with yours. Now another has caught them up, and the chord of my life is being twisted, and I cannot wrench it free and untwine it again – I can't. I am not strong enough. Besides, you have twisted another thread far and tight into your chord; could you get free?'

'Tell me what to do – yes, if you tell me.'

'I can't tell you – so let me go.'

'No, Lettie,' he pleaded, with terror and humility. 'No, Lettie; don't go. What should I do with my life? Nobody would love you like I do – and what should I do with my love for you? – hate it and fear it, because it's too much for me?'

She turned and kissed him gratefully. He then took her in a long, passionate embrace, mouth to mouth. In the end it had so wearied her, that she could only wait in his arms till he was too tired to hold her. He was trembling already.

'Poor Meg!' she murmured to herself dully, her sensations having become vague.

He winced, and the pressure of his arms slackened. She loosened his hands, and rose half dazed from her seat by him. She left him, while he sat dejected, raising no protest.

*

When I went out to look for them, when tea had already been waiting on the table half an hour or more, I found him leaning against the gatepost at the bottom of the hill. There was no blood in his face, and his tan showed livid; he was haggard as if he had been ill for some weeks.

'Whatever's the matter?' I said, 'Where's Lettie?'

'She's gone home,' he answered, and the sound of his own voice, and the meaning of his own words made him heave.

'Why?' I asked in alarm.

He looked at me as if to say 'What are you talking about? I cannot listen!'

'Why?' I insisted.

'I don't know,' he replied.

'They are waiting tea for you,' I said.

He heard me, but took no notice.

'Come on,' I repeated, 'there's Meg and everybody waiting tea for you.'

'I don't want any,' he said.

I waited a minute or two. He was violently sick.

> *'Vae meum*
> *Fervens difficile bile tumet jecur,'*

I thought to myself.

When the sickness passed over, he stood up away from the post, trembling, and lugubrious. His eyelids drooped heavily over his eyes, and he looked at me, and smiled a faint, sick smile.

'Come and lie down in the loft,' I said, 'and I'll tell them you've got a bilious bout.'

He obeyed me, not having energy to question; his strength had gone, and his splendid physique seemed shrunken; he

walked weakly. I looked away from him, for in his feebleness
he was already beginning to feel ludicrous.

We got into the barn unperceived, and I watched him
climb the ladder to the loft. Then I went indoors to tell them.

I told them Lettie had promised to be at Highclose for tea,
that George had a bilious attack, and was mooning about the
barn till it was over; he had been badly sick. We ate tea without
zest or enjoyment. Meg was wistful and ill at ease; the father
talked to her and made much of her; the mother did not care
for her much.

'I can't understand it,' said the mother, 'he so rarely has
anything the matter with him – why, I've hardly known the
day! Are you sure it's nothing serious, Cyril? It seemed such
a thing – and just when Meg happened to be down – just when
Meg was coming – !'

About half-past six I had again to go and look for him,
to satisfy the anxiety of his mother and his sweetheart. I went
whistling to let him know I was coming. He lay on a pile of
hay in a corner, asleep. He had put his cap under his head to
stop the tickling of the hay, and he lay half curled up, sleeping
soundly. He was still very pale, and there was on his face the
repose and pathos that a sorrow always leaves. As he wore
no coat I was afraid he might be chilly, so I covered him up
with a couple of sacks, and I left him. I would not have him
disturbed – I helped the father about the cowsheds, and with
the pigs.

Meg had to go at half-past seven. She was so disappointed
that I said:

'Come and have a look at him – I'll tell him you did.'

He had thrown off the sacks, and spread out his limbs.
As he lay on his back, flung out on the hay, he looked big
again, and manly. His mouth had relaxed, and taken its old,
easy lines. One felt for him now the warmth one feels for
anyone who sleeps in an attitude of abandon. She leaned over
him, and looked at him with a little rapture of love and tenderness; she longed to caress him. Then he stretched himself, and
his eyes opened. Their sudden unclosing gave her a thrill. He
smiled sleepily, and murmured, 'Allo, Meg!' Then I saw him

awake. As he remembered, he turned with a great sighing yawn, hid his face again, and lay still.

'Come along, Meg,' I whispered, 'he'll be best asleep.'

'I'd better cover him up,' she said, taking the sack and laying it very gently over his shoulders. He kept perfectly still, while I drew her away.

CHAPTER VIII

A Poem of Friendship

THE magnificent promise of spring was broken before the May-blossom was fully out. All through the beloved month the wind rushed in upon us from the north and north-east, bringing the rain fierce and heavy. The tender-budded trees shuddered and moaned; when the wind was dry, the young leaves flapped limp. The grass and corn grew lush, but the light of the dandelions was quite extinguished, and it seemed that only a long time back had we made merry before the broad glare of these flowers. The bluebells lingered and lingered; they fringed the fields for weeks like purple fringe of mourning. The pink campions came out only to hang heavy with rain; hawthorn buds remained tight and hard as pearls, shrinking into the brilliant green foliage; the forget-me-nots, the poor pleiades of the wood, were ragged weeds. Often at the end of the day, the sky opened, and stately clouds hung over the horizon infinitely far away, glowing, through the yellow distance, with an amber lustre. They never came any nearer, always they remained far off, looking calmly and majestically over the shivering earth, then saddened, fearing their radiance might be dimmed, they drew away, and sank out of sight. Sometimes, towards sunset, a great shield stretched dark from the west to the zenith, tangling the light along its edges. As the canopy rose higher, it broke, dispersed, and the sky was primrose-coloured, high and pale above the crystal moon. Then the cattle crouched among the gorse, distressed by the cold, while the long-billed snipe flickered round high overhead, round and round in great circles, seeming to carry a serpent from its throat, and crying a tragedy, more painful than the poignant lamentations and protests of the peewits. Following these evenings came mornings cold and grey.

Such a morning I went up to George, on the top fallow. His father was out with the milk – he was alone; as I came up the hill I could see him standing in the cart, scattering manure over the bare red fields; I could hear his voice calling now and then to the mare, and the creak and clank of the cart as it moved on. Starlings and smart wagtails were running briskly over the clods, and many little birds flashed, fluttered, hopped here and there. The lapwings wheeled and cried as ever between the low clouds and the earth, and some ran beautifully among the furrows, too graceful and glistening for the rough field.

I took a fork and scattered the manure along the hollows, and thus we worked, with a wide field between us, yet very near in the sense of intimacy. I watched him through the wheeling peewits, as the low clouds went stealthily overhead. Beneath us, the spires of the poplars in the spinney were warm gold, as if the blood shone through. Further gleamed the grey water, and below it the red roofs. Nethermere was half hidden, and far away. There was nothing in this grey, lonely world but the peewits swinging and crying, and George swinging silently at his work. The movement of active life held all my attention, and when I looked up, it was to see the motion of his limbs and his head, the rise and fall of his rhythmic body, and the rise and fall of the slow waving peewits. After a while, when the cart was empty, he took a fork and came towards me, working at my task.

It began to rain, so he brought a sack from the cart, and we crushed ourselves under the thick hedge. We sat close together and watched the rain fall like a grey striped curtain before us, hiding the valley; we watched it trickle in dark streams off the mare's back, as she stood dejectedly; we listened to the swish of the drops falling all about; we felt the chill of the rain, and drew ourselves together in silence. He smoked his pipe, and I lit a cigarette. The rain continued; all the little pebbles and the red earth glistened in the grey gloom. We sat together, speaking occasionally. It was at these times we formed the almost passionate attachment which later years slowly wore away.

When the rain was over, we filled our buckets with potatoes, and went along the wet furrows, sticking the spritted tubers in the cold ground. Being sandy, the field dried quickly. About twelve o'clock, when nearly all the potatoes were set, he left me, and fetching up Bob from the far hedge-side, harnessed the mare and him to the ridger, to cover the potatoes. The sharp light plough turned the soil in a fine furrow over the potatoes; host of little birds fluttered, settled, bounded off again after the plough. He called to the horses, and they came down-hill, the white stars on the two brown noses nodding up and down, George striding firm and heavy behind. They came down upon me; at a call the horses turned, shifting awkwardly side-ways; he flung himself against the plough, and leaning well in, brought it round with a sweep; a click, and they are off uphill again. There is a great rustle as the birds sweep round after him and follow up the new turned furrow. Untackling the horses when the rows were all covered, we tramped behind them down the wet hillside to dinner.

I kicked through the drenched grass, crushing the withered cowslips under my clogs, avoiding the purple orchids that were stunted with harsh upbringing, but magnificent in their powerful colouring, crushing the pallid ladysmocks, the washed-out wild gillivers. I became conscious of something near my feet, something little and dark, moving indefinitely. I had found again the larkie's nest. I perceived the yellow beaks, the bulging eyelids of two tiny larks, and the blue lines of their wing quills. The indefinite movement was the swift rise and fall of the brown fledged backs, over which waved long strands fine down. The two little specks of birds lay side by side, beak to beak, their tiny bodies rising and falling in quick unison. I gently put down my fingers to touch them; they were warm; gratifying to find them warm, in the midst of so much cold and wet. I became curiously absorbed in them, as an eddy of wind stirred the strands of down. When one fledgling moved uneasily, shifting his soft ball, I was quite excited; but he nestled down again, with his head close to his brother's. In my heart of hearts, I longed for someone to nestle against, some-one who would come between me and the coldness and wetness of the surroundings. I envied the two little miracles exposed to any tread, yet so serene. It seemed as if I were always wandering, looking for something which they had found even before the light broke into their shell. I was cold; the lilacs in the Mill garden looked blue and perished. I ran with my heavy clogs and my heart heavy with vague longing, down to the Mill, while the wind blanched the sycamores, and pushed the sullen pines rudely, for the pines were sulking because their million creamy sprites could not fly wet-winged. The horse-chestnuts bravely kept their white candles erect in the socket of every bough, though no sun came to light them. Drearily a cold swan swept up the water, trailing its black feet, clacking its great hollow wings, rocking the frightened water hens, and insulting the staid black-necked geese. What did I want that I turned thus from one thing to another?

*

At the end of June the weather became fine again. Hay harvest was to begin as soon as it settled. There were only two fields to be mown this year, to provide just enough stuff to last until the spring. As my vacation had begun I decided I would help, and that we three, the father, George and I, would get in the hay without hired assistance.

I rose the first morning very early, before the sun was well up. The clear sound of challenging cocks could be heard along the valley. In the bottoms, over the water and over the lush wet grass, the night mist still stood white and substantial. As I passed along the edge of the meadow the cow-parsnip was as tall as I, frothing up to the top of the hedge, putting the faded hawthorn to a wan blush. Little, early birds – I had not heard the lark – fluttered in and out of the foamy meadow-sea, plunging under the surf of flowers washed high in one corner, swinging out again, dashing past the crimson sorrel cresset. Under the froth of flowers were the purple vetch-clumps, yellow milk vetches, and the scattered pink of the wood-betony, and the floating stars of marguerites. There was a weight of honeysuckle on the hedges, where pink roses were waking up for their broadspread flight through the day.

Morning silvered the swaths of the far meadow, and swept in smooth, brilliant curves round the stones of the brook;

morning ran in my veins, morning chased the silver, darting fish out of the depth, and I, who saw them, snapped my fingers at them, driving them back.

I heard Trip barking, so I ran towards the pond. The punt was at the island, where from behind the bushes I could hear George whistling. I called to him, and he came to the water's edge half dressed.

'Fetch a towel,' he called, 'and come on.'

I was back in a few moments, and there stood my Charon fluttering in the cool air. One good push sent us to the islet. I made haste to undress, for he was ready for the water, Trip dancing round, barking with excitement at his new appearance.

'He wonders what's happened to me,' he said, laughing, pushing the dog playfully away with his bare foot. Trip bounded back, and came leaping up, licking him with little caressing licks. He began to play with the dog, and directly they were rolling on the fine turf, the laughing, expostulating, naked man, and the excited dog, who thrust his great head on to the man's face, licking, and, when flung away, rushed forward again, snapping playfully at the naked arms and breasts. At last George lay back, laughing and panting, holding Trip by the two fore feet which were planted on his breast, while the dog, also panting, reached forward his head for a flickering lick at the throat pressed back on the grass, and the mouth thrown back out of reach. When the man had thus lain still for a few moments, and the dog was just laying his head against his master's neck to rest too, I called, and George jumped up, and plunged into the pond with me, Trip after us.

The water was icily cold, and for a moment deprived me of my senses. When I began to swim, soon the water was buoyant, and I was sensible of nothing but the vigorous poetry of action. I saw George swimming on his back laughing at me, and in an instant I had flung myself like an impulse after him. The laughing face vanished as he swung over and fled, and I pursued the dark head and the ruddy neck. Trip, the wretch, came paddling towards me, interrupting me; then, all bewildered with excitement, he scudded to the back. I chuckled to myself as I saw him run along, then plunge in and go plodding to George. I was gaining. He tried to drive off the dog, and I gained rapidly. As I came up to him and caught him, with my hand on his shoulder, there came a laughter from the bank. It was Emily.

I trod the water, and threw handfuls of spray at her. She laughed and blushed. Then Trip waded out to her and she fled swiftly from his shower-bath. George was floating just beside me, looking up and laughing.

We stood and looked at each other as we rubbed ourselves dry. He was well proportioned, and naturally of handsome physique, heavily limbed. He laughed at me, telling me I was like one of Aubrey Beardsley's long, lean ugly fellows. I referred him to many classic examples of slenderness, declaring myself more exquisite than his grossness, which amused him.

But I had to give in, and bow to him, and he took on an indulgent, gentle manner. I laughed and submitted. For he knew not I admired the noble, white fruitfulness of his form. As I watched him, he stood in white relief against the mass of green. He polished his arm, holding it out straight and solid; he rubbed his hair into curls, while I watched the deep muscles of his shoulders, and the bands stand out in his neck as he held it firm; I remembered the story of Annable.

He saw I had forgotten to continue my rubbing, and laughing he took hold of me and began to rub me briskly, as if I were a child, or rather, a woman he loved and did not fear. I left myself quite limply in his hands, and, to get a better grip of me, he put his arm round me and pressed me against him, and the sweetness of the touch of our naked bodies one against the other was superb. It satisfied in some measure the vague, indecipherable yearning of my soul; and it was the same with him. When he had rubbed me all warm, he let me go, and we looked at each other with eyes of still laughter, and our love was perfect for a moment, more perfect than any love I have known since, either for man or woman.

We went together down to the fields, he to mow the island of grass he had left standing the previous evening, I to sharpen the machine knife, to mow out the hedge-bottoms with the scythe, and to rake the swaths from the way of the machine when the unmown grass was reduced to a triangle. The cool, moist fragrance of the morning, the intentional stillness of everything, of the tall bluish trees, of the wet, frank flowers, of the trustful moths folded and unfolded in the fallen swaths, was a perfect medium of sympathy. The horses moved with a still dignity, obeying his commands. When they were harnessed, and the machine oiled, still he was loath to mar the perfect morning, but stood looking down the valley.

'I shan't mow these fields any more,' he said, and the fallen, silvered swaths flickered back his regret, and the faint scent of the limes was wistful. So much of the field was cut, so much remained to cut; then it was ended. This year the elder flowers were widespread over the corner bushes, and the pink roses fluttered high above the hedge. There were the same flowers in the grass as we had known many years; we should not know them any more.

'But merely to have mown them is worth having lived for,' he said, looking at me.

We felt the warmth of the sun trickling through the morning's mist of coolness.

'You see that sycamore,' he said, 'that bushy one beyond the big willow? I remember when father broke off the leading shoot because he wanted a fine straight stick, I can remember I felt sorry. It was running up so straight, with such a fine balance of leaves – you know how a young strong sycamore looks about nine feet high – it seemed a cruelty. When you are gone, and we are left from here. I shall feel like that, as if my leading shoot were broken off. You see, the tree is spoiled. Yet how it went on growing. I believe I shall grow faster. I can remember the bright red stalks of the leaves as he broke them off from the bough.'

He smiled at me, half proud of his speech. Then he swung into the seat of the machine, having attended to the horses' heads. He lifted the knife.

'Good-bye,' he said, smiling whimsically back at me. The machine started. The bed of the knife fell, and the grass shivered and dropped over. I watched the heads of the daisies and the splendid lines of the cocksfoot grass quiver, shake against the crimson burnet, and drop over. The machine went singing down the field, leaving a track of smooth, velvet green in the way of the swath-broad. The flowers in the wall of uncut grass waited

unmoved, as the days wait for us. The sun caught in the uplick-
ing scarlet sorrel flames, the butterflies woke, and I could hear
the fine ring of his 'Whoa!' from the far corner. Then he
turned, and I could see only the tossing ears of the horses, and
the white of his shoulder as they moved along the wall of high
grass on the hill slope. I sat down under the elm, to file the
sections of the knife. Always as he rode he watched the falling
swath, only occasionally calling the horses into line. It was his
voice which rang the morning awake. When we were at work
we hardly noticed one another. Yet his mother had said:

'George is so glad when you're in the field – he doesn't care
how long the day is.'

Later, when the morning was hot, and the honeysuckle had
ceased to breathe, and all the other scents were moving in the
air about us, when all the field was down, when I had seen the
last trembling ecstasy of the harebells, trembling to fall; when
the thick clump of purple vetch had sunk; when the green
swaths were settling, and the silver swaths were glistening and
glittering as the sun came along them, in the hot ripe morning
we worked together turning the hay, tipping over the yesterday's
swaths with our forks, and bringing yesterday's fresh, hidden
flowers into the death of sunlight.

It was then that we talked of the past, and speculated on
the future. As the day grew older, and less wistful, we forgot
everything, and worked on, singing, and sometimes I would
recite him verses as we went, and sometimes I would tell him
about books. Life was full of glamour for us both.

CHAPTER IX

Pastorals and Peonies

AT dinner-time the father announced to us the exciting fact that Leslie had asked if a few of his guests might picnic that afternoon in the Strelley hayfields. The closes were so beautiful, with the brook under all its sheltering trees, running into the pond that was set with two green islets. Moreover, the squire's lady had written a book filling these meadows and the mill precincts with pot-pourri romance. The wedding guests at Highclose were anxious to picnic in so choice a spot.

The father, who delighted in a gay throng, beamed at us from over the table. George asked who were coming.

'Oh, not many – about half a dozen – mostly ladies down for the wedding.'

George at first swore warmly; then he began to appreciate the affair as a joke.

Mrs Saxton hoped they wouldn't want her to provide them pots, for she hadn't two cups that matched, nor had any of her spoons the least pretence to silver. The children were hugely excited, and wanted a holiday from school, which Emily at once vetoed firmly, thereby causing family dissension.

As we went round the field in the afternoon turning the hay, we were thinking apart, and did not talk. Every now and then – and at every corner – we stopped to look down towards the wood, to see if they were coming.

'Here they are!' George exclaimed suddenly, having spied the movement of white in the dark wood. We stood still and watched. Two girls, heliotrope and white, a man with two girls, pale green and white, and a man with a girl last.

'Can you tell who they are?' I asked.

'That's Marie Tempest, that first girl in white, and that's him and Lettie at the back, I don't know any more.'

He stood perfectly still until they had gone out of sight behind the banks down by the brooks, then he stuck his fork in the ground, saying:

'You can easily finish – if you like. I'll go and mow out that bottom corner.'

He glanced at me to see what I was thinking of him. I was thinking that he was afraid to meet her, and I was smiling to myself. Perhaps he felt ashamed, for he went silently away to the machine, where he belted his riding breeches tightly round his waist, and slung the scythe strap on his hip. I heard the clanging slur of the scythe stone as he whetted the blade. Then he strode off to mow the far bottom corner, where the ground was marshy, and the machine might not go, to bring down the lush green grass, and the tall meadow-sweet.

I went to the pond to meet the newcomers. I bowed to Louie Denys, a tall, graceful girl of the drooping type, elaborately gowned in heliotrope linen; I bowed to Agnes D'Arcy, an erect, intelligent girl with magnificent auburn hair – she wore no hat, and carried a sunshade; I bowed to Hilda Seconde, a svelte, petite girl, exquisitely and delicately pretty; I bowed to Marie and to Lettie, and I shook hands with Leslie and with his friend, Freddy Cresswell. The latter was to be best man, a broad-shouldered, pale-faced fellow, with beautiful soft hair like red wheat, and laughing eyes and a whimsical, drawling manner of speech, like a man who has suffered enough to bring him to manhood and maturity, but who in spite of all remains a boy, irresponsible, loveable – a trifle pathetic. As the day was very hot, both men were in flannels, and wore flannel collars, yet it was evident that they had dressed with scrupulous care. Instinctively I tried to pull my trousers into shape within my belt, and I felt the inferiority cast upon the father, big and fine as he was in his way, for his shoulders were rounded with work, and his trousers were much distorted.

'What can we do?' said Marie; 'you know we don't want to hinder, we want to help you. It was so good of you to let us come.'

The father laughed his fine indulgence, saying to them – they loved him for the mellow, laughing modulation of his voice:

'Come on, then – I see there's a bit of turning-over to do, as Cyril's left. Come and pick your forks.'

From among a sheaf of hayforks he chose the lightest for them, and they began anywhere, just tipping at the swaths. He showed them carefully – Marie and the charming little Hilda – just how to do it, but they found the right way the hardest way, so they worked in their own fashion, and laughed heartily with him when he made playful jokes at them. He was a great lover of girls, and they blossomed from timidity under his hearty influence.

'Ain't it flippin 'ot?' drawled Cresswell, who had just taken his M.A. degree in classics: 'This bloomin' stuff's dry enough – come an' flop on it.'

He gathered a cushion of hay, which Louie Denys carefully appropriated, arranging first her beautiful dress, that fitted close to her shape, without any belt or interruption, and then laying her arms, that were netted to the shoulder in open lace, gracefully at rest. Lettie, who was also in a closefitting white dress which showed her shape down to the hips, sat where Leslie had prepared for her, and Miss D'Arcy reluctantly accepted my pile.

Cresswell twisted his clean-cut mouth in a little smile, saying:

'Lord, a giddy little pastoral – fit for old Theocritus, ain't it, Miss Denys?'

'Why do you talk to me about those classic people – I daren't even say their names. What would he say about us?'

He laughed, winking his blue eyes:

'He'd make old Daphnis there,' – pointing to Leslie–'sing a match with me, Damoetas – contesting the merits of our various shepherdesses – begin Daphnis, sing up for Amaryllis, I mean Nais, damn 'em, they were for ever getting mixed up with their nymphs.'

'I say, Mr Cresswell, your language! Consider whom you're damning,' said Miss Denys, leaning over and tapping his head with her silk glove.

'You say any giddy thing in a pastoral,' he replied, taking the edge of her skirt and lying back on it, looking up at her as she leaned over him. 'Strike up, Daphnis, something about honey or white cheese – or else the early apples that'll be ripe in a week's time.'

'I'm sure the apples you showed me are ever so little and

green,' interrupted Miss Denys; 'they will never be ripe in a week – ugh, sour!'

He smiled up at her in his whimsical way:

'Hear that, Tempest – "Ugh, sour!" – not much! Oh, love us, haven't you got a start yet? – isn't there aught to sing about, you blunt-faced kid?'

'I'll hear you first – I'm no judge of honey and cheese.'

'An' darn little apples – takes a woman to judge them; don't it, Miss Denys?'

'I don't know,' she said, stroking his soft hair from his forehead, with her hand whereon rings were sparkling.

'"My love is not white, my hair is not yellow, like honey dropping through the sunlight – my love is brown, and sweet, and ready for the lips of love." Go on, Tempest – strike up, old cowherd. Who's that tuning his pipe? – oh, that fellow sharpening his scythe! It's enough to make your back ache to look at him working – go an' stop him, somebody.'

'Yes, let us go and fetch him,' said Miss D'Arcy. 'I'm sure he doesn't know what a happy pastoral state he's in – let us go and fetch him.'

'They don't like hindering at their work, Agnes – besides, where ignorance is bliss – ,' said Lettie, afraid lest she might bring him. The other hesitated, then with her eyes she invited me to go with her.

'Oh, dear,' she laughed, with a little *moue*, 'Freddy is such an ass, and Louie Denys is like a wasp at treacle. I wanted to laugh, yet I felt just a tiny bit cross. Don't you feel great when you go mowing like that? Father Time sort of feeling? Shall we go and look! We'll say we want those foxgloves he'll be cutting down directly – and those bell flowers. I suppose you needn't go on with your labours –'

He did not know we were approaching till I called him, then he started slightly as he saw the tall, proud girl.

'Mr Saxton – Miss D'Arcy,' I said, and he shook hands with her. Immediately his manner became ironic, for he had seen his hand big and coarse and inflamed with the snaith clasping the lady's hand.

'We thought you looked so fine,' she said to him, 'and men are so embarrassing when they make love to somebody else –

aren't they? Save us those foxgloves, will you – they are splendid
– like savage soldiers drawn up against the hedge – don't cut
them down – and those campanulas – bell-flowers, ah, yes! They
are spinning idylls up there. I don't care for idylls, do you? Oh,
you don't know what a classical pastoral person you are – but
there, I don't suppose you suffer from idyllic love –' she laughed,
' – one doesn't see the silly little god fluttering about in our
hayfields, does one? Do you find much time to sport with
Amaryllis in the shade? – I'm sure it's a shame they banished
Phyllis from the fields –'

He laughed and went on with his work. She smiled a little,
too, thinking she had made a great impression. She put out
her hand with a dramatic gesture, and looked at me, when the
scythe crunched through the meadow-sweet.

'Crunch! – isn't it fine!' she exclaimed, 'a kind of inevitable
fate – I think it's fine!'

We wandered about picking flowers and talking until tea-
time. A man-servant came with the tea-basket, and the girls
spread the cloth under a great willow tree. Lettie took the little
silver kettle, and went to fill it at the small spring which trickled
into a stone trough all pretty with cranesbill and stellaria hanging
over, while long blades of grass waved in the water. George,
who had finished his work, and wanted to go home to tea,
walked across to the spring where Lettie sat playing with the
water, getting little cupfuls to put into the kettle, watching the
quick skating of the water beetles, and the large faint spots of
their shadows darting on the silted mud at the bottom of the
trough.

She glanced round on hearing him coming, and smiled nervously: they were mutually afraid of meeting each other again.

'It is about tea-time,' he said.

'Yes – it will be ready in a moment – this is not to make the
tea with – it's only to keep a little supply of hot water.'

'Oh,' he said, 'I'll go on home – I'd rather.'

'No,' she replied, 'you can't, because we are all having tea
together: I had some fruits put up, because I know you don't
trifle with tea – and your father's coming.'

'But,' he replied pettishly, 'I can't have my tea with all those
folks – I don't want to – look at me!'

He held out his inflamed, barbaric hands.

She winced and said:

'It won't matter – you'll give the realistic touch.'

He laughed ironically.

'No – you must come,' she insisted.

'I'll have a drink then, if you'll let me,' he said, yielding.

She got up quickly blushing, offering him the tiny, pretty cup.

'I'm awfully sorry,' she said.

'Never mind,' he muttered, and turning from the proffered cup he lay down flat, put his mouth to the water, and drank deeply. She stood and watched the motion of his drinking, and of his heavy breathing afterwards. He got up, wiping his mouth, not looking at her. Then he washed his hands in the water, and stirred up the mud. He put his hand to the bottom of the trough, bringing out a handful of silt, with the grey shrimps twisting in it. He flung the mud on the floor where the poor grey creatures writhed.

'It wants cleaning out,' he said.

'Yes,' she replied, shuddering. 'You won't be long,' she added, taking up the silver kettle.

In a few moments he got up and followed her reluctantly down. He was nervous and irritable.

The girls were seated on tufts of hay, with the men leaning in attendance on them, and the man-servant waiting on all. George was placed between Lettie and Hilda. The former handed him his little egg-shell of tea, which, as he was not very thirsty, he put down on the ground beside him. Then she passed him the bread and butter, cut for five-o'clock tea, and fruits, grapes and peaches, and strawberries, in a beautifully carved oak tray. She watched for a moment his thick, half-washed fingers fumbling over the fruits, then she turned her head away. All the gay tea-time, when the talk bubbled and frothed over all the cups, she avoided him with her eyes. Yet again and again, as someone said: 'I'm sorry, Mr Saxton – will you have some cake?' – or 'See Mr Saxton – try this peach, I'm sure it will be mellow right to the stone,' – speaking very naturally, but making the distinction between him and the other men by their indulgence towards him, Lettie was forced to glance at him as he sat eating, answering in monosyllables, laughing with constraint and awkwardness, and her irritation flickered between her brows. Although she kept up the gay frivolity of the conversation, still the discord was felt by everybody, and we did not linger as we should have done over the cups. 'George,' they said afterwards, 'was a wet blanket on the party.' Lettie was intensely annoyed with him. His presence was unbearable to her. She wished him a thousand miles away. He sat listening to Cresswell's whimsical affection of vulgarity which flickered with fantasy and he laughed in a strained fashion.

He was the first to rise, saying he must get the cows up for milking.

'Oh, let us go – let us go. May we come and see the cows milked?' said Hilda, her delicate, exquisite features flushing, for she was very shy.

'No,' drawled Freddy, 'the stink o' live beef ain't salubrious. You be warned and stop here.'

'I never could bear cows, except those lovely little highland cattle, all woolly, in pictures,' said Louie Denys, smiling archly, with a little irony.

'No,' laughed Agnes D'Arcy, 'they – they're smelly,' – and she pursed up her mouth, and ended in a little trill of deprecatory laughter, as she often did. Hilda looked from one to the other, blushing.

'Come, Lettie,' said Leslie good-naturedly, 'I know you have a farm-yard fondness – come on,' and they followed George down.

As they passed along the pond bank a swan and her tawny, fluffy brood sailed with them the length of the water, 'tipping on their little toes, the darlings – pitter-patter through the water, tiny little things,' as Maria said.

We heard George below calling 'Bully – Bully – Bully – Bully!' – and then, a moment or two after, in the bottom garden: 'Come out, you little fool – are you coming out of it?' in manifestly angry tones.

'Has it run away?' laughed Hilda, delighted, and we hastened out of the lower garden to see.

There in the green shade, between the tall gooseberry bushes the heavy crimson peonies stood gorgeously along the path. The full red globes, poised and leaning voluptuously, sank their crimson weight on to the seeding grass of the path, borne down by secret rain, and by their own splendour. The path was poured over with red rich silk of strewn petals. The great flowers swung their crimson grandly about the walk, like crowds of cardinals in pomp among the green bushes. We burst into the new world of delight. As Lettie stooped, taking between both hands the gorgeous silken fulness of one blossom that was sunk to the earth, George came down the path, with the brown bull-calf straddling behind him, its neck stuck out, sucking zealously at his middle finger.

The unconscious attitudes of the girls, all bent enraptured over the peonies, touched him with sudden pain. As he came up, with the calf stalking grudgingly behind, he said:

'There's a fine show of pyeenocks this year, isn't there?'

'What do you call them?' cried Hilda, turning to him her sweet, charming face full of interest.

'Pyeenocks,' he replied.

Lettie remained crouching with a red flower between her hands, glancing sideways unseen to look at the calf, which with its shiny nose uplifted was mumbling in its sticky gums the seductive finger. It sucked eagerly, but unprofitably, and it appeared to cast a troubled eye inwards to see if it were really receiving any satisfaction – doubting, but not despairing. Marie, and Hilda, and Leslie laughed, while he, after looking at Lettie as she crouched, wistfully, as he thought, over the flower, led the little brute out of the garden, and sent it running into the yard with a smack on the haunch.

Then he returned, rubbing his sticky finger dry against his breeches. He stood near to Lettie, and she felt rather than saw the extraordinary pale cleanness of the one finger among the others. She rubbed her finger against her dress in painful sympathy.

'But aren't the flowers lovely!' exclaimed Marie again. 'I want to hug them.

'Oh, yes!' assented Hilda.

'They are like a romance – D'Annunzio – a romance in passionate sadness, said Lettie, in an ironical voice, speaking half out of conventional necessity of saying something, half out of desire to shield herself, and yet in a measure express herself.

'There is a tale about them,' I said.

The girls clamoured for the legend.

'Pray, do tell us,' pleaded Hilda, the irresistible.

'It was Emily told me – she says it's a legend, but I believe
it's only a tale. She says the peonies were brought from the
Hall long since by a fellow of this place – when it was a mill.
He was brown and strong, and the daughter of the Hall, who
was pale and fragile and young, loved him. When he went up to
the Hall gardens to cut the yew hedges, she would hover round
him in her white frock, and tell him tales of old days, in little
snatches like a wren singing, till he thought she was a fairy
who had bewitched him. He would stand and watch her, and
one day, when she came near to him telling him a tale that set
the tears swimming in her eyes, he took hold of her and kissed
her and kept her. They used to tryst in the poplar spinney. She
would come with her arms full of flowers, for she always kept
to her fairy part. One morning she came early through the mists.
He was out shooting. She wanted to take him unawares, like a
fairy. Her arms were full of peonies. When she was moving
beyond the trees he shot her, not knowing. She stumbled on,
and sank down in their tryst place. He found her lying there
among the red pyeenocks, white and fallen. He thought she was
just lying talking to the red flowers, so he stood waiting. Then
he went up, and bent over her, and found the flowers full of
blood. It was he set the garden here with these pyeenocks.'

The eyes of the girls were round with the pity of the tale and
Hilda turned away to hide her tears.

'It is a beautiful ending,' said Lettie, in a low tone, looking
at the floor.

'It's all a tale,' said Leslie, soothing the girls.

George waited till Lettie looked at him. She lifted her eyes
to him at last. Then each turned aside, trembling.

Marie asked for some of the peonies.

'Give me just a few – and I can tell the others the story – it
is so sad – I feel so sorry for him, it was so cruel for him –
And Lettie says it ends beautifully – !'

George cut the flowers with his great clasp knife, and Marie
took them, carefully, treating their romance with great tender-

ness. Then all went out of the garden and he turned to the cowshed.

'Good-bye for the present,' said Lettie, afraid to stay near him.

'Good-bye,' he laughed.

'Thank you *so* much for the flowers – and the story – it was splendid,' said Marie, '– but so sad!'

Then they went, and we did not see them again.

Later, when all had gone to bed at the mill, George and I sat together on opposite sides of the fire, smoking, saying little. He was casting up the total of discrepancies, and now and again he ejaculated one of his thoughts.

'And all day,' he said, 'Blench has been ploughing his wheat in, because it was that bitten off by the rabbits it was no manner of use, so he's ploughed it in: an' they say with idylls, eating peaches in our close.'

Then there was silence, while the clock throbbed heavily, and outside a wild bird called, and was still; softly the ashes rustled lower in the grate.

'She said it ended well – but what's the good of death – what's the good of that?' He turned his face to the ashes in the grate, and sat brooding.

Outside, among the trees, some wild animal set up a thin wailing cry.

'Damn that row!' said I, stirring, looking also into the grey fire.

'It's some stoat or weasel, or something. It's been going on like that for nearly a week. I've shot in the trees ever so many times. There were two – one's gone.'

Continuously, through the heavy, chilling silence, came the miserable crying from the darkness among the trees.

'You know,' he said, 'she hated me this afternoon, and I hated her –'

It was midnight, full of sick thoughts.

'It is no good,' said I. 'Go to bed – it will be morning in a few hours.'

PART THREE

CHAPTER I

A New Start in Life

LETTIE was wedded, as I had said, before Leslie lost all the wistful traces of his illness. They had been gone away to France five days before we recovered anything like the normal tone in the house. Then, though the routine was the same, everywhere was a sense of loss, and of change. The long voyage in the quiet home was over; we had crossed the bright sea of our youth, and already Lettie had landed and was travelling to a strange destination in a foreign land. It was time for us all to go, to leave the valley of Nethermere whose waters and whose woods were distilled in the essence of our veins. We were the children of the valley of Nethermere, a small nation with language and blood of our own, and to cast ourselves each one into separate exile was painful to us.

'I shall have to go now,' said George. 'It is my nature to linger an unconscionable time, yet I dread above all things this slow crumbling away from my foundations by which I free myself at last. I must wrench myself away now –'

It was the slack time between the hay and the corn harvest, and we sat together in the grey, still morning of August, pulling the stack. My hands were sore with tugging the loose wisps from the lower part of the stack, so I waited for the touch of rain to send us indoors. It came at last, and we hurried into the barn. We climbed the ladder into the loft that was strewn with farming implements and with carpenters' tools. We sat together on the shavings that littered the bench before the high gable window, and looked out over the brooks and the woods and the ponds. The tree-tops were very near to us, and we felt ourselves the centre of the waters and the woods that spread down the rainy valley.

'In a few years,' I said, 'we shall be almost strangers.'

He looked at me with fond, dark eyes and smiled incredulously.

'It is as far,' said I, 'to the Ram as it is for me to London – farther.'

'Don't you want me to go there?' he asked, smiling quietly.

'It's all as one where you go; you will travel north, and I east, and Lettie south. Lettie has departed. In seven weeks I go. – And you?'

'I must be gone before you,' he said decisively.

'Do you know –' and he smiled timidly in confession, 'I feel alarmed at the idea of being left alone on a loose end. I must not be the last to leave –' he added almost appealingly.

'And you will go to Meg?' I asked.

He sat tearing the silken shavings into shreds, and telling me in clumsy fragments all he could of his feelings:

'You see it's not so much what you call love. I don't know. You see I built on Lettie,' – he looked up at me shamefacedly, then continued tearing the shavings – 'you must found your castles on something, and I founded mine on Lettie. You see I'm like plenty of folks, I have nothing definite to shape my life to. I put brick upon brick, as they come, and if the whole topples down in the end, it does. But you see, you and Lettie have made me conscious, and now I'm at a dead loss. I have looked to marriage to set me busy on my house of life, something whole and complete, of which it will supply the design. I must marry or be in a lost lane. There are two people I could marry – and Lettie's gone. I love Meg just as well, as far as love goes. I'm not sure I don't feel better pleased at the idea of marrying her. You know I should always have been second to Lettie, and the best part of love is being made much of, being first and foremost in the whole world for somebody. And Meg's easy and lovely. I can have her without trembling, she's full of soothing and comfort. I can stroke her hair and pet her, and she looks up at me, full of trust and lovingness, and there is no flaw, all restfulness in one another –'

*

Three weeks later, as I lay in the August sunshine in a deck-chair on the lawn, I heard the sound of wheels along the gravel path. It was George calling for me to accompany him to his marriage. He pulled up the dog-cart near the door, and came up the steps to me on the lawn. He was dressed as if for the cattle market, in jacket and breeches and gaiters.

'Well, are you ready?' he said standing smiling down on me. His eyes were dark with excitement, and had that vulnerable look which was so peculiar to the Saxtons in their emotional moments.

'You are in good time,' said I, 'it is but half-past nine.'

'It wouldn't do to be late on a day like this,' he said gaily, 'see how the sun shines. Come, you don't look as brisk as a best man should. I thought you would have been on tenter-hooks of excitement. Get up, get up! Look here, a bird has given me luck' – he showed me a white smear on his shoulder.

I drew myself up lazily.

'All right,' I said, 'but we must drink a whisky to establish it.'

He followed me out of the fragrant sunshine into the dark house. The rooms were very still and empty, but the cool silence responded at once to the gaiety of our sunwarm entrance. The sweetness of the summer morning hung invisible like glad ghosts of romance through the shadowy room. We seemed to feel the sunlight dancing golden in our veins as we filled again the pale liqueur.

'Joy to you – I envy you today.'

His teeth were white, and his eyes stirred like dark liquor as he smiled.

'Here is my wedding present!'

I stood the four large water-colours along the wall before him. They were drawings among the waters and the fields of the mill, grey rain and twilight, morning with the sun pouring gold into the mist, and the suspense of a midsummer noon upon the pond. All the glamour of our yesterdays came over him like an intoxicant, and he quivered with wonderful beauty of life that was weaving him into the large magic of the years. He realized the splendour of the pageant of days which had him in train.

'It's been wonderful, Cyril, all the time,' he said, with sur-prised joy.

We drove away through the freshness of the wood, and among the flowing of the sunshine along the road. The cottages of Greymede filled the shadows with colour of roses, and the sunlight with odour of pinks and the blue of cornflowers and larkspur. We drove briskly up the long, sleeping hill, and bowled down the hollow past the farms where the hens were walking with the red gold cocks in the orchard, and the ducks like white cloudlets under the aspen trees revelled on the pond.

'I told her to be ready any time,' said George – 'but she doesn't know it's today. I didn't want the public-house full of the business.'

The mare walked up the sharp little rise on top of which stood the Ram Inn. In the quiet, as the horse slowed to a standstill, we heard the crooning of a song in the garden. We sat still in the cart, and looked across the flagged yard to where the tall madonna lilies rose in clusters out of the alyssum. Beyond the border of flowers was Meg, bending over the gooseberry bushes. She saw us and came swinging down the path, with a bowl of gooseberries poised on her hip. She was dressed in a plain, fresh holland frock, with a white apron. Her black, heavy hair reflected the sunlight, and her ripe face was luxuriant with laughter.

'Well, I never!' she exclaimed, trying not to show that she guessed his errand. 'Fancy you here at this time o' morning!'

Her eyes, delightful black eyes like polished jet, untroubled and frank, looked at us as a robin might, with bright questioning. Her eyes were so different from the Saxton's: dark, but never still and full, never hesitating, dreading a wound, never dilating with hurt or with timid ecstasy.

'Are you ready then?' he asked, smiling down on her.

'What?' she asked in confusion.

'To come to the registrar with me – I've got the licence.'

'But I'm just going to make the pudding,' she cried, in full expostulation.

'Let them make it themselves – put your hat on.'

'But look at me! I've just been getting the gooseberries. Look!' she showed us the berries, and the scratches on her arms and hands.

'What a shame!' he said, bending to stroke her hand and

her arm. She drew back smiling, flushing with joy. I could smell the white lilies where I sat.

'But you don't mean it, do you?' she said, lifting to him her face that was round and glossy like a blackheart cherry. For answer, he unfolded the marriage licence. She read it, and turned aside her face in confusion, saying:

'Well, I've got to get ready. Shall you come an' tell Gran'-ma?'

'Is there any need?' he answered reluctantly.

'Yes, you come an' tell 'er,' persuaded Meg.

He got down from the trap. I preferred to stay out of doors. Presently Meg ran out with a glass of beer for me.

'We shan't be many minutes,' she apologized, 'I've on'y to slip another frock on.'

I heard George go heavily up the stairs and enter the room over the bar-parlour, where the grandmother lay bed-ridden.

'What, is it thaïgh, ma lad? What are thaïgh doin' 'ere this mornin'?' she asked.

'Well A'nt, how does ta feel by now?' he said.

'Eh, sadly, lad, sadly! It'll not be long afore they carry me downstairs head first –'

'Nay, dunna thee say so! – I'm just off to Nottingham – I want Meg ter come.'

'What for?' cried the old woman sharply.

'I wanted 'er to get married,' he replied.

'What! What does't say? An' what about th' licence, an' th' ring, an ivrything?'

'I've seen to that all right,' he answered.

'Well, tha 'rt a nice'st un, I must say! What's want goin' in this pig-in-a-poke fashion for? This is a nice shabby trick to serve on a body! What does ta mean by it?'

'You knowed as I wor goin' ter marry 'er directly, so I can't see as it matters o' th' day. I non wanted a' th' pub talking –'

'Tha'rt mighty partiklar, an' all, an' all! An' why shouldn't the pub talk? Tha 'rt non marryin' a nigger, as ta should be so frightened – I niver thought it on thee! – An' what's thy 'orry, all of a sudden?'

'No hurry as I know of.'

'No 'orry –!' replied the old lady, with withering sarcasm.

'Tha wor niver i na 'orry a' thy life! She's non commin' wi' thee this day, though.'

He laughed, also sarcastic. The old lady was angry. She poured on him her abuse, declaring she would not have Meg in the house again, nor leave her a penny, if she married him that day.

'Tha can please thysen,' answered George, also angry.

Meg came hurriedly into the room.

'Ta'e that 'at off – ta'e it off! Tha non goos wi' 'im this day, not if I know it! Does 'e think tha 'rt a cow, or a pig, to be fetched wheniver 'e thinks fit. Ta'e that 'at off, I say!'

The old woman was fierce and peremptory.

'But gran'ma –!' began Meg.

The bed creaked as the old lady tried to rise.

'Ta'e that 'at off, afore I pull it off!' she cried.

'Oh, be still Gran'ma – you'll be hurtin' yourself, you know you will –'

'Are you coming, Meg?' said George suddenly.

'She is not!' cried the old woman.

'Are you coming, Meg?' repeated George, in a passion.

Meg began to cry. I suppose she looked at him through her tears. The next thing I heard was a cry from the old woman, and the sound of staggering feet.

'Would ta drag 'er from me! – if tha goos, ma wench, tha enters this 'ouse no more, tha' 'eers that! Tha does thysen my lady! Dunna venture anigh me after this, my gel!' – the old woman called louder and louder. George appeared in the doorway, holding Meg by the arm. She was crying in a little distress. Her hat with its large silk roses was slanting over her eyes. She was dressed in white linen. They mounted the trap. I gave him the reins and scrambled up behind. The old woman heard us through the open window, and we listened to her calling as we drove away:

'Dunna let me clap eyes on thee again, tha ungrateful 'ussy. Tha'll rue it, my wench, tha'll rue it, an' then dunna come ter me –'

We drove out of hearing. George sat with a shut mouth scowling. Meg wept awhile to herself, woefully. We were swinging at a good pace under the beeches of the churchyard

which stood above the level of the road. Meg, having settled
her hat, bent her head to the wind, too much occupied with
her attire to weep. We swung round the hollow by the bog
end, and rattled a short distance up the steep hill to Watnall.
Then the mare walked slowly. Meg, at leisure to collect herself, exclaimed plaintively:

'Oh, I've only got one glove!'

She looked at the odd silk glove that lay in her lap, then
peered about among her skirts.

'I must 'a left it in th' bedroom,' she said piteously.

He laughed, and his anger suddenly vanished.

'What does it matter? You'll do without all right.'

At the sound of his voice, she recollected, and her tears and
her weeping returned.

'Nay,' he said, 'don't fret about the old woman. She'll come
round tomorrow – an' if she doesn't, it's her lookout. She's
got Polly to attend to her.'

'But she'll be that miserable –!' wept Meg.

'It's her own fault. At any rate, don't let it make you miserable' – he glanced to see if anyone were in sight, then he put
his arm round her waist and kissed her, saying softly, coaxingly:
'She'll be all right tomorrow. We'll go an' see her then, an'
she'll be glad enough to have us. We'll give in to her then, poor
old Gran'ma. She can boss you about, an' me as well, tomorrow
as much as she likes. She feels it hard, being tied to her bed.
But today is ours, surely – isn't it? Today is ours, an' you're
not sorry, are you?'

'But I've got no gloves, an' I'm sure my hair's a sight. I
never thought she could 'a reached up like that.'

George laughed, tickled.

'No,' he said, 'she was in a temper. But we can get you some
gloves directly we get to Nottingham.'

'I haven't a farthing of money,' she said.

'I've plenty!' he laughed. 'Oh, an' let's try this on.'

They were merry together as he tried on her wedding ring,
and they talked softly, he gentle and coaxing, she rather plaintive. The mare took her own way, and Meg's hat was dis-
arranged once more by the sweeping elm-boughs. The yellow
corn was dipping and flowing in the fields, like a cloth of gold

pegged down at the corners under which the wind was heaving. Sometimes we passed cottages where the scarlet lilies rose like bonfires, and the tall larkspur like bright blue leaping smoke. Sometimes we smelled the sunshine on the browning corn, sometimes the fragrance of the shadow of leaves. Occasionally it was the dizzy scent of new haystacks. Then we rocked and jolted over the rough cobblestones of Cinderhill, and bounded forward again at the foot of the enormous pit hill, smelling of sulphur, inflamed with slow red fires in the daylight, and crusted with ashes. We reached the top of the rise and saw the city before us, heaped high and dim upon the broad range of the hill. I looked for the square tower of my old school, and the sharp proud spire of St Andrews. Over the city hung a dullness, a thin dirty canopy against the blue sky.

We turned and swung down the slope between the last sullied cornfields towards Basford, where the swollen gasometers stood like toadstools. As we neared the mouth of the street, Meg rose excitedly, pulling George's arm, crying:

'Oh, look, the poor little thing!'

On the causeway stood two small boys lifting their faces and weeping to the heedless heavens, while before them, upside down, lay a baby strapped to a shut-up baby-chair. The gim-crack carpet-seated thing had collapsed as the boys were dismounting the curb-stone with it. It had fallen backwards, and they were unable to right it. There lay the infant strapped head downwards to its silly cart, in imminent danger of suffocation. Meg leaped out, and dragged the child from the wretched chair. The boys, drenched with tears, howled on. Meg crouched on the road, the baby on her knee, its tiny feet dangling against her skirt. She soothed the pitiful tear-wet mite. She hugged it to her, and kissed it, and hugged it, and rocked it in an abandonment of pity. When at last the childish trio were silent, the boys shaken only by the last ebbing sobs, Meg calmed also from her frenzy of pity for the little thing. She murmured to it tenderly, and wiped its wet little cheeks with her handkerchief, soothing, kissing, fondling the bewildered mite, smoothing the wet strands of brown hair under the scrap of cotton bonnet, twitching the inevitable baby cape into order.

It was a pretty baby, with wisps of brown-gold silken hair, and large blue eyes.

'Is it a girl?' I asked one of the boys – 'How old is she?'

'I don't know,' he answered awkwardly, 'We've 'ad 'er about a three week.'

'Why, isn't she your sister?'

'No – my mother keeps 'er,' – they were very reluctant to tell us anything.

'Poor little lamb!' cried Meg, in another access of pity, clasping the baby to her bosom with one hand, holding its winsome slippered feet in the other. She remained thus, stung through with acute pity, crouching, folding herself over the mite. At last she raised her head, and said, in a voice difficult with emotion:

'But you love her – don't you?'

'Yes – she's – she's all right. But we 'ave to mind 'er,' replied the boy in great confusion.

'Surely,' said Meg, 'Surely you don't begrudge that. Poor little thing – so little, she is – surely you don't grumble at minding her a bit – ?'

The boys would not answer.

'Oh, poor little lamb, poor little lamb!' murmured Meg over the child, condemning with bitterness the boys and the whole world of men.

I taught one of the lads how to fold and unfold the wretched chair. Meg very reluctantly seated the unfortunate baby therein, gently fastening her with the strap.

'Wheer's 'er dummy?' asked one of the boys in muffled, self-conscious tones. The infant began to cry thinly. Meg crouched over it. The 'dummy' was found in the gutter and wiped on the boy's coat, then plugged into the baby's mouth. Meg released the tiny clasping hand from over her finger, and mounted the dog cart, saying sternly to the boys:

'Mind you looked after her well, poor little baby with no mother. God's watching to see what you do to her – so you be careful, mind.'

They stood very shamefaced. George clicked to the mare, and as we started threw coppers to the boys. While we drove away I watched the little group diminish down the road.

'It's such a shame,' she said, and the tears were in her voice, '– A sweet little thing like that –'

'Ay,' said George, softly, 'there's all sorts of things in towns.'

Meg paid no attention to him, but sat woman-like thinking of the forlorn baby, and condemning the hard world. He, full of tenderness and protectiveness towards her, having watched her with softening eyes, felt a little bit rebuffed that she ignored him, and sat alone in her fierce womanhood. So he busied himself with the reins, and the two sat each alone until Meg was roused by the bustle of the town. The mare sidled past the electric cars nervously, and jumped when a traction engine came upon us. Meg, rather frightened, clung to George again. She was very glad when we had passed the cemetery with its white population of tombstones, and drew up in a quiet street.

But when we had dismounted, and given the horse's head to a loafer, she became confused and bashful and timid to the last degree. He took her on his arm; he took the whole charge of her, and laughing, bore her away towards the steps of the office. She left herself entirely in his hands; she was all confusion, so he took the charge of her.

When, after a short time, they came out, she began to chatter with blushful animation. He was very quiet, and seemed to be taking his breath.

'Wasn't he a funny little man? Did I do it all proper? – I didn't know what I was doing. I'm sure they were laughing at me – do you think they were? Oh, just look at my frock – what a sight! What would they think –!' The baby had slightly soiled the front of her dress.

George drove up the long hill into the town. As we came down between the shops on Mansfield Road he recovered his spirits.

'Where are we going – where are you taking us?' asked Meg.

'We may as well make a day of it while we are here,' he answered, smiling and flicking the mare. They both felt that they were launched forth on an adventure. He put up at the Spread Eagle, and we walked towards the market-place for Meg's gloves. When he had bought her these and a large lace scarf to give her a more clothed appearance, he wanted dinner.

'We'll go,' he said, 'to an hotel.'

His eyes dilated as he said it, and she shrank away with delighted fear. Neither of them had ever been to an hotel. She was really afraid. She begged him to go to an eating house, to a café. He was obdurate. His one idea was to do the thing that he was half-afraid to do. His passion – and it was almost intoxication – was to dare to play with life. He was afraid of the town. He was afraid to venture into the foreign places of life, and all was foreign to save the valley of Nethermere. So he crossed the borders flauntingly, and marched towards the heart of the unknown. We went to the Victoria Hotel – the most imposing he could think of – and we had luncheon according to the menu. They were like two children, very much afraid, yet delighting in the adventure. He dared not, however, give the orders. He dared not address anybody, waiters or otherwise. I did that for him, and he watched me, absorbing, learning, wondering that things were so easy and so delightful. I murmured them injunctions across the table and they blushed and laughed with each other nervously. It would be hard to say whether they enjoyed that luncheon. I think Meg did not – even though she was with him. But of George I am doubtful. He suffered exquisitely from self-consciousness and nervous embarrassment, but he felt also the intoxication of the adventure, he felt as a man who has lived in a small island when he first sets foot on a vast continent. This was the first step into a new life, and he mused delightedly upon it over his brandy. Yet he was nervous. He could not get over the feeling that he was trespassing.

'Where shall we go this afternoon?' he asked.

Several things were proposed, but Meg pleaded warmly for Colwick.

'Let's go on a steamer to Colwick Park. There'll be entertainments there this afternoon. It'll be lovely.'

In a few moments we were on the top of the car swinging down to the Trent Bridges. It was dinner-time, and crowds of people from shops and warehouses were hurrying in the sunshine along the pavements. Sunblinds cast their shadows on the shop-fronts, and in the shade streamed the people dressed brightly for summer. As our car stood in the great space of the market place we could smell the mingled scent of fruit, oranges, and small apricots, and pears piled in their vividly coloured sections on the stalls. Then away we sailed through the shadows of the dark streets, and the open pools of sunshine. The castle on its high rock stood in the dazzling dry sunlight; the fountain stood shadowy in the green glimmer of the lime trees that surrounded the almshouses.

There were many people at the Trent. We stood awhile on the bridge to watch the bright river swirling in a silent dance to the sea, while the light pleasure-boats lay asleep along the banks. We went on board the little paddle steamer and paid our 'sixpence return'. After much waiting we set off, with great excitement, for our mile-long voyage. Two banjos were tumming somewhere below, and the passengers hummed and sang to their tunes. A few boats dabbled on the water. Soon the river meadows with their high thorn hedges lay green on our right, while the scarp of red rock rose on our left, covered with the dark trees of summer.

We landed at Colwick Park. It was early, and few people were there. Dead glass fairy-lamps were slung about the trees. The grass in places was worn threadbare. We walked through the avenues and small glades of the park till we came to the boundary where the race-course stretched its level green, its winding white barriers running low into the distance. They sat in the shade for some time while I wandered about. Then many people began to arrive. It became noisy, even rowdy. We listened for some time to an open-air concert, given by the pierrots. It was rather vulgar, and very tiresome. It took me back to Cowes, to Yarmouth. There were the same foolish over-eyebrowed faces, the same perpetual jingle from an out-of-tune piano, the restless jigging to the songs, the same choruses, the same escapading. Meg was well pleased. The vulgarity passed by her. She laughed, and sang the choruses half audibly, daring, but not bold. She was immensely pleased. 'Oh, it's Ben's turn now. I like him, he's got such a wicked twinkle in his eye. Look at Joey trying to be funny! – he can't to save his life. Doesn't he look soft –!' She began to giggle in George's shoulder. He saw the funny side of things for the time and laughed with her.

During tea, which we took on the green verandah of the degraded hall, she was constantly breaking forth into some chorus, and he would light up as she looked at him and sing with her, *sotto voce*. He was not embarrassed at Colwick. There he had on his best careless, superior air. He moved about with a certain scornfulness, and ordered lobster for tea offhandedly. This also was a new walk of life. Here he was not hesitating or tremulously strung; he was patronizing. Both Meg and he thoroughly enjoyed themselves.

When we got back into Nottingham she entreated him not to go to the hotel as he had proposed, and he readily yielded. Instead they went to the Castle. We stood on the high rock in the cool of the day, and watched the sun sloping over the great river-flats where the menial town spread out, and ended, while the river and the meadows continued into the distance. In the picture galleries, there was a fine collection of Arthur Melville's paintings. Meg thought them very ridiculous. I began to expound them, but she was manifestly bored, and he was half-hearted. Outside in the grounds was a military band playing. Meg longed to be there. The townspeople were dancing on the grass. She longed to join them, but she could not dance. So they sat awhile looking on.

We were to go to the theatre in the evening. The Carl Rosa Company was giving 'Carmen' at the Royal. We went into the dress circle 'like giddy dukes', as I said to him, so that I could see his eyes dilate with adventure again as he laughed. In the theatre, among the people in evening dress, he became once more childish and timorous. He had always the air of one who does something forbidden, and is charmed, yet fearful, like a trespassing child. He had begun to trespass that day outside his own estates of Nethermere.

'Carmen' fascinated them both. The gaudy, careless Southern life amazed them. The bold free way in which 'Carmen' played with life startled them with hints of freedom. They stared on the stage fascinated. Between the acts they held each other's hands, and looked full into each other's wide bright eyes, and, laughing with excitement, talked about the opera. The theatre surged and roared dimly like a hoarse shell. Then the music rose like a storm, and swept and rattled at their feet. On the stage the strange storm of life clashed in music towards tragedy and futile death. The two were shaken with a tumult of wild feeling. When it was all over they rose bewildered, stunned, she with tears in her eyes, he with a strange wild beating of his heart.

They were both in a tumult of confused emotion. Their ears were full of the roaring passion of life, and their eyes were blinded by a spray of tears and that strange quivering laughter which burns with real pain. They hurried along the pavement to the Spread Eagle, Meg clinging to him, running, clasping her lace scarf over her white frock, like a scared white butterfly shaken through the night. We hardly spoke as the horse was being harnessed and the lamps lighted. In the little smoke-room he drank several whiskies, she sipping out of his glass, standing all the time ready to go. He pushed into his pocket great pieces of bread and cheese, to eat on the way home. He seemed now to be thinking with much acuteness. His few orders were given sharp and terse. He hired an extra light rug in which to wrap Meg, and then we were ready.

'Who drives?' said I.

He looked at me and smiled faintly.

'You,' he answered.

Meg, like an impatient white flame stood waiting in the light of the lamps. He covered her, extinguished her in the dark rug.

CHAPTER II

Puffs of Wind in the Sail

THE year burst into glory to usher us forth out of the valley of Nethermere. The cherry trees had been gorgeous with heavy out-reaching boughs of red and gold. Immense vegetable marrows lay prostrate in the bottom garden, their great tentacles clutching the pond bank. Against the wall the globed crimson plums hung close together, and dropped occasionally with a satisfied plunge into the rhubarb leaves. The crop of oats was very heavy. The stalks of corn were like strong reeds of bamboo; the heads of grain swept heavily over like tresses weighted with drops of gold.

George spent his time between the Mill and the Ram. The grandmother had received them with much grumbling but with real gladness. Meg was re-installed, and George slept at the Ram. He was extraordinary bright, almost gay. The fact was that his new life interested and pleased him keenly. He often talked to me about Meg, how quaint and naive she was, how she amused him and delighted him. He rejoiced in having a place of his own, a home, and a beautiful wife who adored him. Then the public-house was full of strangeness and interest. No hour was ever dull. If he wanted company he could go into the smoke-room, if he wanted quiet he could sit with Meg, and she was such a treat, so soft and warm, and so amusing. He was always laughing at her quaint crude notions, and at her queer little turns of speech. She talked to him with a little language, she sat on his knee and twisted his moustache, finding small unreal fault with his features for the delight of dwelling upon them. He was, he said, incredibly happy. Really he could not believe it. Meg was, ah! she was a treat. Then he would laugh, thinking how indifferent he had been about taking her. A little shadow might cross his eyes, but he would laugh again, and tell me one of his wife's funny little notions. She was quite uneducated, and such fun, he said. I looked at him as he sounded this note. I remembered his crude superiority of early days, which had angered Emily so deeply. There was in him something of the prig. I did not like his amused indulgence of his wife.

At threshing day, when I worked for the last time at the Mill, I noticed the new tendency in him. The Saxtons had always kept up a certain proud reserve. In former years, the family had moved into the parlour on threshing day, and an extra woman had been hired to wait on the men who came with the machine. This time George suggested: 'Let us have dinner with the men in the kitchen, Cyril. They are a rum gang. It's rather good sport mixing with them. They've seen a bit of life, and I like to hear them, they're so blunt. They're good studies though.'

The farmer sat at the head of the table. The seven men trooped in, very sheepish, and took their places. They had not much to say at first. They were a mixed set, some rather small, young, and furtive-looking, some unshapely and coarse, with unpleasant eyes, the eyelids slack. There was one man whom we called the Parrot, because he had a hooked nose, and put forward his head as he talked. He had been a very large man, but he was grey, and bending at the shoulders. His face was pale and fleshy, and his eyes seemed dull-sighted.

George patronized the men, and they did not object. He chaffed them, making a good deal of demonstration in giving them more beer. He invited them to pass up their plates, called the woman to bring more bread and altogether played mine host of a feast of beggars. The Parrot ate very slowly.

'Come, Dad,' said George, 'you're not getting on. Not got many grinders –'

'What I've got's in th' road. Is'll 'ae ter get em out. I can manage wi' bare gums, like a baby again.'

'Second childhood, eh? Ah well, we must all come to it,' George laughed.

The old man lifted his head and looked at him, and said slowly:

'You'n got ter get ower th' first afore that.'

George laughed, unperturbed. Evidently he was well used to the thrusts of the public-house.

'I suppose you soon got over yours,' he said.

The old man raised himself and his eyes flickered into life. He chewed slowly, then said:

'I'd married, an' paid for it; I'd broke a constable's jaw an' paid for it; I'd deserted from the army, an' paid for that: I'd had a bullet through my cheek in India atop of it all, by I was your age.'

'Oh!' said George, with condescending interest, 'you've seen a bit of life then?'

They drew the old man out, and he told them, in his slow, laconic fashion, a few brutal stories. They laughed and chaffed him. George seemed to have a thirst for tales of brutal experience, the raw gin of life. He drank it all in with relish, enjoying the sensation. The dinner was over. It was time to go out again to work.

'And how old are you, Dad?' George asked. The Parrot looked at him again with his heavy, tired, ironic eyes, and answered:

'If you'll be any better for knowing – sixty-four.'

'It's a bit rough on you, isn't it,' continued the young man, 'going round with the threshing machine and sleeping outdoors at that time of life, I should 'a thought you'd a wanted a bit o' comfort –'

'How do you mean, "rough on me"?' the Parrot replied slowly.

'Oh, I think you know what I mean,' answered George easily.

'Don't know as I do,' said the slow old Parrot.

'Well, you haven't made exactly a good thing out of life, have you?'

'What d'you mean by a good thing? I've had my life, an' I'm satisfied wi' it. Is'll die with a full belly.'

'Oh, so you have saved a bit?'

'No,' said the old man deliberately, 'I've spent as I've gone on. An' I've had all I wish for. But I pity the angels, when the Lord sets me before them like a book to read. Heaven won't be heaven just then.'

'You're a philosopher in your way,' laughed George.

'And you,' replied the old man, 'toddling about your back-yard, think yourself mighty wise. But your wisdom 'll go with your teeth. You'll learn in time to say nothing.'

The old man went out and began his work, carrying the sacks of corn from the machine to the chamber.

'There's a lot in the old Parrot,' said George, 'as he'll never tell.'

I laughed.

'He makes you feel, as well, as if you'd a lot to discover in life,' he continued, looking thoughtfully over the dusty straw-stack at the chuffing machine.

*

After the harvest was ended the father began to deplete his farm. Most of the stock was transferred to the Ram. George was going to take over his father's milk business, and was going to farm enough of the land attaching to the Inn to support nine or ten cows. Until the spring, however, Mr Saxton retained his own milk round, and worked at improving the condition of the land ready for the valuation. George, with three cows, started a little milk supply in the neighbourhood of the Inn, prepared his land for the summer, and helped in the public-house.

Emily was the first to depart finally from the Mill. She went to a school in Nottingham, and shortly afterwards Mollie, her younger sister, went to her. In October I moved to London. Lettie and Leslie were settled in their home in Brentwood, Yorkshire. We all felt very keenly our exile from Nethermere. But as yet the bonds were not broken; only use could sever them. Christmas brought us all home again, hastening to greet each other. There was a slight change in everybody. Lettie was brighter, more imperious, and very gay; Emily was quiet, self-restrained, and looked happier; Leslie was jollier and at the same time more subdued and earnest; George looked very healthy and happy, and sounded well pleased with himself; my mother with her gaiety at our return brought tears to our eyes.

We dined one evening at Highclose with the Tempests. It

was dull as usual, and we left before ten o'clock. Lettie had changed her shoes and put on a fine cloak of greenish blue. We walked over the frost-bound road. The ice on Nethermere gleamed mysteriously in the moonlight, and uttered strange half-audible whoops and yelps. The moon was very high in the sky, small and brilliant like a vial full of the pure white liquid of light. There was no sound in the night save the haunting movement of the ice, and the clear tinkle of Lettie's laughter.

On the drive leading to the wood we saw someone approaching. The wild grass was grey on either side, the thorn trees stood with shaggy black beards sweeping down, the pine trees were erect like dark soldiers. The black shape of the man drew near, with a shadow running at its feet. I recognised George, obscured as he was in his cap and his upturned collar. Lettie was in front with her husband. As George was passing, she said, in bright clear tones:

'A Happy New Year to you.'

He stopped, swung round, and laughed.

'I thought you wouldn't have known me,' he said.

'What, is it you, George?' cried Lettie in great surprise – 'Now, what a joke! How are you?' – she put out her white hand from her draperies. He took it, and answered, 'I am very well – and you –?' However meaningless the words were, the tone was curiously friendly, intimate, informal.

'As you see,' she replied laughing, interested in his attitude – 'but where are you going?'

'I am going home,' he answered, in a voice that meant 'have you forgotten that I too am married?'

'Oh, of course!' cried Lettie. 'You are now mine host of the Ram. You must tell me about it. May I ask him to come home with us for an hour, mother? – It is New Year's Eve, you know.'

'You have asked him already,' laughed mother.

'Will Mrs Saxton spare you for so long?' asked Lettie of George.

'Meg? Oh, she does not order my comings and goings.'

'Does she not?' laughed Lettie. 'She is very unwise. Train

up a husband in the way he should go, and in after life – . I
never could quote a text from end to end. I am full of begin-
nings, but as for a finish –! Leslie, my shoe-lace is untied –
shall I wait till I can put my foot on the fence ? '

Leslie knelt down at her feet. She shook the hood back
from her head, and her ornaments sparkled in the moonlight.
Her face with its whiteness and its shadows was full of
fascination, and in their dark recesses her eyes thrilled George
with hidden magic. She smiled at him along her cheeks while
her husband crouched before her. Then, as the three walked
along towards the wood she flung her draperies into loose
eloquence and there was a glimpse of her bosom white with
the moon. She laughed and chattered, and shook her silken
stuff, sending out a perfume exquisite on the frosted air.
When we reached the house Lettie dropped her draperies and
rustled into the drawing-room. There the lamp was low-lit,
shedding a yellow twilight from the window space. Lettie
stood between the firelight and the dusky lamp glow, tall and
warm between the lights. As she turned laughing to the two
men, she let her cloak slide over her white shoulder and fall
with silk splendour of a peacock's gorgeous blue over the
arm of the large settee. There she stood, with her white hand
upon the peacock of her cloak, where it tumbled against her
dull orange dress. She knew her own splendour, and she drew
up her throat laughing and brilliant with triumph. Then she
raised both her arms to her head and remained for a moment
delicately touching her hair into order, still fronting the two
men. Then with a final little laugh she moved slowly and
turned up the lamp, dispelling some of the witchcraft from the
room. She had developed strangely in six months. She seemed
to have discovered the wonderful charm of her womanhood.
As she leaned forward with her arm outstretched to the lamp,
as she delicately adjusted the wicks with mysterious fingers,
she seemed to be moving in some alluring figure of a dance,
her hair like a nimbus clouding the light, her bosom lit with
wonder. The soft outstretching of her hand was like the whispering of strange words into the blood, and as she fingered a
book the heart watched silently for the meaning.

'Won't you take off my shoes, darling ? ' she said, sinking

among the cushions of the settee. Leslie kneeled again before her, and she bent her head and watched him.

'My feet are a tiny bit cold,' she said, plaintively, giving him her foot, that seemed like gold in the yellow silk stocking. He took it between his hands, stroking it:

'It is quite cold,' he said, and he held both her feet in his hands.

'Ah, you dear boy!' she cried with sudden gentleness, bending forward and touching his cheek.

'Is it great fun being mine host of "Ye Ramme Inne"?' she said, playfully to George. There seemed a long distance between them now as she sat, with the man in evening dress crouching before her putting golden shoes on her feet.

'It is rather,' he replied, 'the men in the smoke-room say such rum things. My word, you hear some tales there.'

'Tell us, do!' she pleaded.

'Oh! I couldn't. I never could tell a tale, and even if I could – well –.'

'But I do long to hear,' she said, 'what the men say in the smoke-room of "Ye Ramme Inne". Is it quite untellable?'

'Quite!' he laughed.

'What a pity! See what a cruel thing it is to be a woman, Leslie: we never know what men say in smoke-rooms, while you read in your novels everything a woman ever uttered. It is a shame! George, you are a wretch, you should tell me. I do envy you –.'

'What do you envy me, exactly?' he asked laughing always at her whimsical way.

'Your smoke-room. The way you see life – or the way you hear it, rather.'

'But I should have thought you saw life ten times more than me,' he replied.

'I! I only see manners – good manners and bad manners. You know "manners maketh a man". That's when a woman's there. But you wait awhile, you'll see.'

'When shall I see?' asked George flattered and interested.

'When you have made the fortune you talked about,' she replied.

He was uplifted by her remembering the things he had said.

'But when I have made it – when!' – he said sceptically, –
'even then – well, I shall only be, or have been, landlord of "Ye
Ramme Inne".' He looked at her, waiting for her to lift up his
hopes with her gay balloons.

'Oh, that doesn't matter! Leslie might be landlord of some
Ram Inn when he's at home, for all anybody would know –
mightn't you, hubby, dear?'

'Thanks!' replied Leslie, with good-humoured sarcasm.

'You can't tell a publican from a peer, if he's a rich publican,'
she continued. 'Money maketh the man, you know.'

'Plus manners,' added George, laughing.

'Oh they are always there – where I am. I give you ten years.
At the end of that time you must invite us to your swell place
– say the Hall at Eberwich – and we will come – "with all our
numerous array".'

She sat among her cushions smiling upon him. She was half
ironical, half sincere. He smiled back at her, his dark eyes full
of trembling hope, and pleasure, and pride.

'How is Meg?' she asked. 'Is she as charming as ever – or
have you spoiled her?'

'Oh, she is as charming as ever,' he replied. 'And we are
tremendously fond of one another.'

'That is right! – I do think men are delightful,' she added,
smiling.

'I am glad you think so,' he laughed.

They talked on brightly about a thousand things. She touched
on Paris, and pictures, and new music, with her quick chatter,
sounding to George wonderful in her culture and facility. And
at last he said he must go.

'Not until you have eaten a biscuit, and drunk good luck with
me,' she cried, catching her dress about her like a dim flame
and running out of the room. We all drank to the New Year in
the cold champagne.

'To the *Vita Nuova!*' said Lettie, and we drank smiling.

'Hark!' said George, 'the hooters.'

We stood still and listened. There was a faint booing noise far
away outside. It was midnight. Lettie caught up a wrap and we
went to the door. The wood, the ice, the grey dim hills lay frozen
in the light of the moon. But outside the valley, far away in

Derbyshire, away towards Nottingham, on every hand the distant hooters and buzzers of mines and ironworks crowed small on the borders of the night, like so many strange, low voices of cockerels bursting forth at different pitch, with different tone, warning us of the dawn of the New Year.

CHAPTER III

The First Pages of Several Romances

I FOUND a good deal of difference in Leslie since his marriage. He had lost his assertive self-confidence. He no longer pronounced emphatically and ultimately on every subject, nor did he seek to dominate, as he had always done, the company in which he found himself. I was surprised to see him so courteous and attentive to George. He moved unobtrusively about the room while Lettie was chattering, and in his demeanour there was a new reserve, a gentleness and grace. It was charming to see him offering the cigarettes to George, or, with beautiful tact, asking with his eyes only whether he should refill the glass of his guest, and afterwards replacing it softly close to the other's hand.

To Lettie he was unfailingly attentive, courteous, and undemonstrative.

Towards the end of my holiday he had to go to London on business, and we agreed to take the journey together. We must leave Woodside soon after eight o'clock in the morning. Lettie and he had separate rooms. I thought she would not have risen to take breakfast with us, but at a quarter past seven, just as Rebecca was bringing in the coffee, she came downstairs. She wore a blue morning gown, and her hair was as beautifully dressed as usual.

'Why, my darling, you shouldn't have troubled to come down so early,' said Leslie, as he kissed her.

'Of course, I should come down,' she replied, lifting back the heavy curtains and looking out on the snow where the darkness was wilting into daylight. 'I should not let you go away into the cold without having seen you take a good breakfast. I think it is thawing. The snow on the rhododendrons looks sodden and drooping. Ah, well, we can keep out the dismal of the morning for another hour.' She glanced at the clock – 'just an hour!' she added. He turned to her with a swift tenderness. She smiled at him, and sat down at the coffee-maker. We took our places at table.

'I think I shall come back tonight,' he said quietly, almost appealingly.

She watched the flow of the coffee before she answered. Then the brass urn swung back, and she lifted her face to hand him the cup.

'You will not do anything so foolish, Leslie,' she said calmly.

He took his cup, thanking her, and bent his face over the fragrant steam.

'I can easily catch the 7-15 from St Pancras,' he replied, without looking up.

'Have I sweetened to your liking, Cyril?' she asked, and then, as she stirred her coffee, she added, 'It is ridiculous Leslie! You catch the 7-15 and very probably miss the connexion at Nottingham. You can't have the motor-car there, because of the roads. Besides, it is absurd to come toiling home in the cold slushy night when you may just as well stay in London and be comfortable.'

'At any rate I should get the 10-30 down to Lawton Hill,' he urged.

'But there is no need,' she replied, 'there is not the faintest need for you to come home tonight. It is really absurd of you. Think of all the discomfort! Indeed I should not want to come trailing dismally home at midnight, I should not indeed. You would be simply wretched. Stay and have a jolly evening with Cyril.'

He kept his head bent over his plate and did not reply. His persistence irritated her slightly.

'That is what you can do!' she said. 'Go to the pantomime. Or wait – go to Maeterlinck's "Blue Bird". I am sure that is on somewhere. I wonder if Rebecca has destroyed yesterday's paper. Do you mind touching the bell, Cyril?' Rebecca came, and the paper was discovered. Lettie carefully read the notices, and planned for us with zest a delightful programme for the evening. Leslie listened to it all in silence.

When the time had come for our departure Lettie came with us into the hall to see that we were well wrapped up. Leslie had spoken very few words. She was conscious that he was deeply offended, but her manner was quite calm, and she petted us both brightly.

'Good-bye, dear!' she said to him, when he came mutely to

kiss her. 'You know it would have been miserable for you to sit
all those hours in the train at night. You will have ever such a
jolly time. I know you will. I shall look for you tomorrow. Good-
bye, then, good-bye!'

He went down the steps and into the car without looking at
her. She waited in the doorway as we moved round. In the black-
grey morning she seemed to harbour the glittering blue sky and
the sunshine of March in her dress and her luxuriant hair. He did
not look at her till we were curving to the great, snow-cumbered
rhodendrons, when, at the last moment he stood up in a sudden
panic to wave to her. Almost as he saw her the bushes came between them and he dropped dejectedly into his seat.

'Good-bye!' we heard her call cheerfully and tenderly like a
blackbird.

'Good-bye!' I answered, and: 'Good-bye darling, good-bye!'
he cried, suddenly staring up in a passion of forgiveness and tenderness.

The car went cautiously down the soddened white path, under
the trees.

I suffered acutely the sickness of exile in Norwood. For weeks
I wandered the streets of the suburb, haunted by the spirit of
some part of Nethermere. As I went along the quiet roads
where the lamps in yellow loneliness stood among the leafless
trees of the night I would feel the feeling of the dark, wet bit
of path between the wood meadow and the brooks. The spirit
of that wild little slope to the Mill would come upon me, and
there in the suburb of London I would walk wrapt in the
sense of a small wet place in the valley of Nethermere. A
strange voice within me rose and called for the hill path; again
I could feel the wood waiting for me, calling and calling, and
I crying for the wood, yet the space of many miles was between
us. Since I left the valley of home I have not much feared any
other loss. The hills of Nethermere had been my walls, and the
sky of Nethermere my roof overhead. It seemed almost as if,
at home, I might lift my hand to the ceiling of the valley, and
touch my own beloved sky, whose familiar clouds came again
and again to visit me, whose stars were constant to me, born
when I was born, whose sun had been all my father to me. But
now the skies were strange over my head, and Orion walked

past me unnoticing, he who night after night had stood over the woods to spend with me a wonderful hour. When does day now lift up the confines of my dwelling place, when does the night throw open her vastness for me, and send me the stars for company? There is no night in a city. How can I lose myself in the magnificent forest of darkness when night is only a thin scattering of the trees of shadow with barrenness of lights between!

I could never lift my eyes save to the Crystal Palace, crouching, cowering wretchedly among the yellow-grey clouds, pricking up its two round towers like pillars of anxious misery. No landmark could have been more foreign to me, more depressing, than the great dilapidated palace which lay forever prostrate above us, fretting because of its own degradation and ruin.

I watched the buds coming on the brown almond trees; I heard the blackbirds, and I saw the restless starlings; in the streets were many heaps of violets, and men held forward to me snowdrops whose white mute lips were pushed upwards in a bunch: but these things had no meaning for me, and little interest.

Most eagerly I waited for my letters. Emily wrote to me very constantly:

Don't you find it quite exhilarating, almost intoxicating, to be so free? I think it is quite wonderful. At home you cannot live your own life. You have to struggle to keep even a little part for yourself. It is so hard to stand aloof from our mothers, and yet they are only hurt and insulted if you tell them what is in your heart. It is such a relief not to have to be anything to anybody, but just to please yourself. I am sure mother and I have suffered a great deal from trying to keep up our old relations. Yet she would not let me go. When I come home in the evening and think that I needn't say anything to anybody, nor do anything for anybody, but just have the evening for myself, I am overjoyed.

I have begun to write a story —

Again, a little later, she wrote:

As I go to school by Old Brayford village in the morning the birds are trilling wonderfully and everything seems stirring. Very likely there will be a set-back, and after that spring will come in truth.

When shall you come and see me? I cannot think of a spring with-out you. The railways are the only fine exciting things here – one is only a few yards away from school. All day long I am watching the great Midland trains go south. They are very lucky to be able to rush southward through the sunshine.

The crows are very interesting. They flap past all the time we're out in the yard. The railways and the crows make the charm of my life in Brayford. The other day I saw no end of pairs of crows. Do you remember what they say at home? – 'One for sorrow.' Very often one solitary creature sits on the telegraph wires. I almost hate him when I look at him. I think my badge for life ought to be – one crow –

Again, a little later:

I have been home for the week-end. Isn't it nice to be made much of, to be an important cherished person for a little time? It is quite a new experience for me.

The snowdrops are full out among the grass in the front garden – and such a lot. I imagined you must come in the sunshine of the Sunday afternoon to see them. It did not seem possible you should not. The winter aconites are out along the hedge. I knelt and kissed them. I have been so glad to go away, to breathe the free air of life, but I felt as if I could not come away from the aconites. I have sent you some – are they much withered?

Now I am in my lodgings, I have the quite unusual feeling of being contented to stay here a little while – not long – not above a year, I am sure. But even to be contented for a little while is enough for me –

In the beginning of March I had a letter from the father:

You'll not see us again in the old place. We shall be gone in a fort-night. The things are most of them gone already. George has got Bob and Flower. I have sold three of the cows, Stafford, and Julia and Hannah. The place looks very empty. I don't like going past the cow-sheds, and we miss hearing the horses stamp at night. But I shall not be sorry when we have really gone. I begin to feel as if we'd stagnated here. I begin to feel as if I was settling and getting narrow and dull. It will be a new lease of life to get away.

But I'm wondering how we shall be over there. Mrs Saxton feels very nervous about going. But at the worst we can but come back. I feel as if I must go somewhere, it's stagnation and starvation for us here. I wish George would come with me. I never thought he would have taken to public-house keeping, but he seems to like it all right.

He was down with Meg on Sunday. Mrs Saxton says he's getting a public-house tone. He is certainly much livelier, more full of talk than he was. Meg and he seem very comfortable, I'm glad to say. He's got a good milk-round, and I've no doubt but what he'll do well. He is very cautious at the bottom; he'll never lose much if he never makes much.

Sam and David are very great friends. I'm glad I've got the boy. We often talk of you. It would be very lonely if it wasn't for the excitement of selling things and so on. Mrs Saxton hopes you will stick by George. She worries a bit about him, thinking he may go wrong. I don't think he will ever go far. But I should be glad to know you were keeping friends. Mrs Saxton says she will write to you about it –

George was a very poor correspondent. I soon ceased to expect a letter from him. I received one directly after the Father's.

MY DEAR CYRIL,

Forgive me for not having written you before, but you see, I cannot sit down and write to you any time. If I cannot do it just when I am in the mood, I cannot do it at all. And so it so often happens that the mood comes upon me when I am in the fields at work, when it is impossible to write. Last night I sat by myself in the kitchen on purpose to write to you, and then I could not. All day, at Greymede, when I was drilling in the fallow at the back of the church, I had been thinking of you, and I could have written there if I had had materials, but I had not, and at night I could not.

I am sorry to say that in my last letter I did not thank you for the books. I have not read them both, but I have nearly finished Evelyn Innes. I get a bit tired of it towards the end. I do not do much reading now. There seems to be hardly any chance for me, either somebody is crying for me in the smoke-room, or there is some business, or else Meg won't let me. She doesn't like me to read at night, she says I ought to talk to her, so I have to.

It is half-past seven, and I am sitting ready dressed to go and talk to Harry Jackson about a young horse he wants to sell me. He is in pretty low water, and it will make a pretty good horse. But I don't care much whether I have it or not. The mood seized me to write to you. Somehow at the bottom I feel miserable and heavy, yet there is no need. I am making pretty good money, and I've got all I want. But when I've been ploughing and getting the oats in those fields on the hillside at the back of Greymede church, I've felt as if I didn't care whether I got on or not. It's very funny. Last week I made over five pounds clear, one way and another, and yet now I'm as restless, and discontented as I can be, and I seem eager for something, but I don't know what it is. Sometimes I wonder where I am going. Yesterday I watched broken white masses of cloud sailing across the sky in a fresh strong wind. They all seemed to be going somewhere. I wondered where the wind was blowing them. I don't seem to have hold on anything, do I? Can you tell me what I want at the bottom of my heart? I wish you were here, then I think I should not feel like this. But generally I don't, generally I am quite jolly, and busy.

By jove, here's Harry Jackson come for me. I will finish this letter when I get back.

— I have got back, we have turned out, but I cannot finish. I cannot tell you all about it. I've had a little row with Meg. Oh, I've had a rotten time. But I cannot tell you about it tonight, it is late, and I'am tired, and have a headache. Some other time perhaps —

GEORGE SAXTON

The spring came bravely, even in south London, and the town was filled with magic. I never knew the sumptuous purple of evening till I saw the round arc-lamps fill with light, and roll like golden bubbles along the purple dusk of the high road. Everywhere at night the city is filled with the magic of lamps : over the river they pour in golden patches their floating luminous oil on the restless darkness; the bright lamps float in and out of the cavern of London Bridge Station like round shining bees in and out of a black hive; in the suburbs the street lamps glimmer with the brightness of lemons among the trees. I began to love the town.

In the mornings I loved to move in the aimless street's procession, watching the faces come near to me, with the sudden glance of dark eyes, watching the mouths of the women blossom with talk as they passed, watching the subtle movements of the shoulders of men beneath their coats, and the naked warmth of their necks that went glowing along the street. I loved the city intensely for its movement of men and women, the soft, fascinating flow of the limbs of men and women, and the sudden flash of eyes and lips as they pass. Among all the faces of the street my attention roved like a bee which clambers drunkenly among blue flowers. I became intoxicated with the strange nectar which I sipped out of the eyes of the passers-by.

I did not know how time was hastening by on still bright

wings, till I saw the scarlet hawthorn flaunting over the road, and the lime-buds lit up like wine drops in the sun, and the pink scarves of the lime-buds pretty as louse-wort a-blossom in the gutters, and a silver-pink tangle of almond boughs against the blue sky. The lilacs came out, and in the pensive stillness of the suburb, at night, came the delicious tarry scent of lilac flowers, wakening a silent laughter of romance.

Across all this, strangely, came the bleak sounds of home. Alice wrote to me at the end of May:

Cyril dear, prepare yourself. Meg has got twins yesterday. I went up to see how she was this afternoon, not knowing anything, and there I found a pair of bubs in the nest, and old ma Stainwright bossing the show. I nearly fainted. Sybil dear, I hardly knew whether to laugh or to cry when I saw those two rummy little round heads, like two larch cones cheek by cheek on a twig. One is a darkie, with lots of black hair, and the other is red, would you believe it, just lit up with thin red hair like a flicker of firelight. I gasped. I believe I did shed a few tears, though what for, I don't know.

The old grandma is a perfect old wretch over it. She lies chuckling and passing audible remarks in the next room, as pleased as punch really, but so mad because ma Stainwright wouldn't have them taken in to her. You should have heard her when we took them in at last. They are both boys. She did make a fuss, poor old woman. I think she's going a bit funny in the head. She seemed sometimes to think they were hers, and you should have heard her, the way she talked to them, it made me feel quite funny. She wanted them lying against her on the pillow, so that she could feel them with her face. I shed a few more tears, Sybil. I think I must be going dotty also. But she came round when we took them away, and began to chuckle to herself, and talk about the things she'd say to George when he came – awful shocking things, Sybil, made me blush dreadfully.

George didn't know about it then. He was down at Bingham, buying some horses. I believe. He seems to have got a craze for buying horses. He got in with Harry Jackson and Mayhew's sons – you know, they were horse dealers – at least their father was. You remember he died bankrupt about three years ago. There are Fred and Duncan left, and they pretend to keep on the old business. They are always up at the Ram, and Georgie is always driving about with them. I don't like it – they are a loose lot, rather common, and poor enough now.

Well, I thought I'd wait and see Georgie. He came about half-past five. Meg had been fidgeting about him, wondering where he was, and how he was, and so on. Bless me if I'd worry and whittle about a man. The old grandma heard the cart, and before he could get down she shouted – you know her room is in the front – 'Hi', George, ma lad, sharpen thy shins an' com' an' a'e a look at 'em – thee'r's two on 'em two on 'em!' and she laughed something awful.

''Ello, Granma, what art ter shoutin' about?' he said, and at the sound of his voice Meg turned to me so pitiful, and said:

'He's been wi' them Mayhews.'

'Tha's gotten twins, a couple at a go ma lad!' shouted the old woman, and you know how she gives a squeal before she laughs! She made the horse shy, and he swore at it something awful. Then Bill took it, and Georgie came upstairs. I saw Meg seem to shrink when she heard him kick at the stairs as he came up, and she went white. When he got to the top he came in. He fairly reeked of whisky and horses. Bah, a man is hateful when he reeks of drink! He stood by the side of the bed grinning like a fool, and saying, quite thick:

'You've bin in a bit of a 'urry, 'aven't you, Meg. An' how are ter feeling' then?'

'Oh, I'm a' right,' said Meg.

'Is it twins, straight?' he said, 'wheer is 'em?'

Meg looked over at the cradle, and he went round the bed to it, holding to the bed-rail. He had never kissed her, nor anything. When he saw the twins, asleep with their fists shut tight as wax, he gave a laugh as if he was amused, and said:

'Two right enough – an' one on 'em red! Which is the girl, Meg, the black un?'

'They're both boys,' said Meg, quite timidly.

He turned round, and his eyes went little.

'Blast 'em then!' he said. He stood there looking like a devil. Sybil dear, I did not know our George could look like that. I thought he could only look like a faithful dog or a wounded stag. But he looked fiendish. He stood watching the poor little twins, scowling at them, till at last the little red one began to whine a bit. Ma Stainwright came pushing her fat carcass in front of him and bent over the baby, saying:

'Why, my pretty, what are they doin' to thee, what are they? – what are they doin' to thee?'

Georgie scowled blacker than ever, and went out, lurching against the wash-stand and making the pots rattle till my heart jumped in my throat.

'Well, if you don't call that scandylos – !' said old Ma Stainwright, and Meg began to cry. You don't know, Cyril! She sobbed fit to break her heart. I felt as if I could have killed him.

That old gran'ma began talking to him, and he laughed at her. I do hate to hear a man laugh when he's half drunk. It makes my blood boil all of a sudden. That old grandmother backs him up in everything, she's a regular nuisance. Meg has cried to me before over the pair of them. The wicked, vulgar old thing that she is –

I went home to Woodside early in September. Emily was staying at the Ram. It was strange that everything was so different. Nethermere even had changed. Nethermere was no longer a complete, wonderful little world that held us charmed inhabitants. It was a small, insignificant valley lost in the spaces of the earth. The tree that had drooped over the brook with such delightful, romantic grace was a ridiculous thing when I came home after a year of absence in the south. The old symbols were trite and foolish.

Emily and I went down one morning to Strelley Mill. The house was occupied by a labourer and his wife, strangers from the north. He was tall, very thin, and silent, strangely suggesting kinship with the rats of the place. She was small and very active, like some ragged domestic fowl run wild. Already Emily had visited her, so she invited us into the kitchen of the mill, and set forward the chairs for us. The large room had the barren air of a cell. There was a small table stranded towards the fireplace, and a few chairs by the walls; for the rest, desert spaces of flagged floor retreating into shadow. On the walls by the windows were five cages of canaries, and the small sharp movements of the birds made the room more strange in its desolation. When we began to talk the birds began to sing, till we were quite bewildered, for the little woman spoke Glasgow Scotch, and she had a hare lip. She rose and ran towards the cages, crying herself like some wild fowl, and flapping a duster at the warbling canaries.

'Stop it, stop it!' she cried, shaking her thin weird body at them. 'Silly little devils, fool, fools, fools!!' and she flapped the duster till the birds were subdued. Then she brought us delicious scones and apple jelly, urging us, almost nudging us with her thin elbows to make us eat.

'Don't you like 'em, don't you? Well eat 'em, eat 'em then. Go on Emily, go on, eat some more. Only don't tell Tom — don't tell Tom when 'e comes in,' — she shook her head and laughed her shrilling, weird laughter.

As we were going she came out with us, and went running on in front. We could not help noting how ragged and unkempt was her short black skirt. But she hastened around us, hither and thither like an excited fowl, talking in her high-pitched, unintelligible manner. I could not believe the brooding mill was in her charge. I could not think this was the Strelley Mill of a year ago. She fluttered up the steep orchard bank in front of us. Happening to turn round and see Emily and me smiling at each other she began to laugh her strident, weird laughter saying, with a leer:

'Emily, he's your sweetheart, your sweetheart Emily! You never told me!' and she laughed aloud.

We blushed furiously. She came away from the edge of the sluice gully, nearer to us, crying:

'You've been here o' nights, haven't you Emily — haven't you?' and she laughed again. Then she sat down suddenly, and pointing above our heads, shrieked:

'Ah, look there!' — we looked and saw the mistletoe. 'Look at her, look at her! How many kisses a night, Emily? — Ha! Ha! kisses all the year! Kisses o' nights in a lonely place.'

She went on wildly for a short time, then she dropped her voice and talked in low, pathetic tones. She pressed on us scones and jelly and oat-cakes, and we left her.

When we were out on the road by the brook Emily looked at me with shamefaced, laughing eyes. I noticed a small movement of her lips, and in an instant I found myself kissing her, laughing with some of the little woman's wildness.

CHAPTER IV

Domestic Life at the Ram

GEORGE was very anxious to receive me at his home. The Ram had as yet only a six days licence, so on Sunday afternoon I walked over to tea. It was very warm and still and sunny as I came through Greymede. A few sweethearts were sauntering under the horse-chestnut trees, or crossing the road to go into the fields that lay smoothly carpeted after the hay-harvest.

As I came round the flagged track to the kitchen door of the Inn I heard the slur of a baking tin and the bang of the oven door, and Meg, saying crossly:

'No, don't you take him, Emily – naughty little thing! Let his father hold him!'

One of the babies was crying.

I entered, and found Meg all flushed and untidy, wearing a large white apron, just rising from the oven. Emily, in a cream dress, was taking a red-haired, crying baby from out of the cradle. George sat in the small arm-chair, smoking and looking cross.

'I can't shake hands,' said Meg, rather flurried. 'I am all floury. Sit down, will you –' and she hurried out of the room. Emily looked up from the complaining baby to me, and smiled a woman's rare, intimate smile, which says: 'See, I am engaged thus for a moment, but I keep my heart for you all the time.'

George rose and offered me the round arm-chair. It was the highest honour he could do me. He asked me what I would drink. When I refused everything, he sat down heavily on the sofa, frowning, and angrily cudgelling his wits for something to say – in vain.

The room was large and comfortably furnished with rush-chairs, a glass-knobbed dresser, a cupboard with glass doors, perched on a shelf in the corner, and the usual large sofa whose cosy loose-bed and pillows were covered with red cotton stuff. There was a peculiar reminiscence of victuals and drink in the room; beer, and a touch of spirits, and bacon. Teenie, the sullen, black-browed servant girl, came in carrying the other baby, and Meg called from the scullery to ask her if the child were asleep. Meg was evidently in a bustle and a flurry, a most uncomfortable state.

'No,' replied Teenie, 'he's not for sleep this day.'

'Mend the fire and see to the oven, and then put him his frock on,' replied Meg, testily. Teenie set the black-haired baby in the second cradle. Immediately he began to cry, or rather to shout his remonstrance. George went across to him and picked up a white furry rabbit, which he held before the child:

'Here, look at bun-bun! Have your nice rabbit! Hark at it squeaking!'

The baby listened for a moment, then, deciding that this was only a put-off, began to cry again. George threw down the rabbit and took the baby, swearing inwardly. He dangled the child on his knee.

'What's up then? – What's up wi' thee? Have a ride then – dee-de-dee-de-dee!'

But the baby knew quite well what was the father's feeling towards him, and he continued to cry.

'Hurry up, Teenie!' said George as the maid rattled the coal on the fire. Emily was walking about hushing her charge, and smiling at me, so that I had a peculiar pleasure in gathering for myself the honey of endearment which she shed on the lips of the baby. George handed over his child to the maid, and said to me with patient sarcasm:

'Will you come in the garden?'

I rose and followed him, across the sunny flagged yard, along the path between the bushes. He lit his pipe and sauntered along as a man on his own estate does, feeling as if he were untrammeled by laws or conventions.

'You know,' he said, 'she's a dam rotten manager.'

I laughed, and remarked how full of plums the trees were.

'Yes!' he replied heedlessly – 'you know she ought to have sent the girl out with the kids this afternoon, and have got dressed directly. But no, she must sit gossiping with Emily all the time they were asleep, and then as soon as they wake up she begins to make cake –'

'I suppose she felt she'd enjoy a pleasant chat, all quiet,' I answered.

'But she knew quite well you were coming, and what it would be. But a woman's no dam foresight.'

'Nay, what does it matter!' said I.

'Sunday's the only day we can have a bit of peace, so she might keep 'em quiet then.'

'I suppose it was the only time, too, that she could have a quiet gossip,' I replied.

'But you don't know,' he said, 'there seems to be never a minute of freedom. Teenie sleeps in now, and lives with us in the kitchen – Oswald as well – so I never know what it is to have a moment private. There doesn't seem a single spot anywhere where I can sit quiet. It's the kids all day, and the kids all night, and the servants, and then all the men in the house – I sometimes feel as if I should like to get away. I shall leave the pub as soon as I can – only Meg doesn't want to.'

'But if you leave the public-house – what then?'

'I should like to get back on a farm. This is no sort of a place, really, for farming. I've always got some business on hand. There's a traveller to see, or I've got to go to the brewers, or I've somebody to look at a horse, or something. Your life's all messed up. If I had a place of my own, and farmed it in peace –'

'You'd be as miserable as you could be,' I said.

'Perhaps so,' he assented, in his old reflective manner. 'Perhaps so! Anyhow, I needn't bother, for I feel as if I never shall go back – to the land.'

'Which means at the bottom of your heart you don't intend to,' I said laughing.

'Perhaps so!' he again yielded. 'You see I'm doing pretty well here – apart from the public-house: I always think that's Meg's. Come and look in the stable. I've got a shire mare, and two nags: pretty good. I went down to Melton Mowbray with Tom Mayhew, to a chap they've had dealings with. Tom's all right, and he knows how to buy, but he is such a lazy careless devil, too lazy to be bothered to sell –'

George was evidently interested. As we went round to the stables, Emily came out with the baby, which was dressed in a new silk frock. She advanced, smiling to me with dark eyes:

'See, now he is good! Doesn't he look pretty?'

She held the baby for me to look at. I glanced at it, but I was only conscious of the near warmth of her cheek, and of the scent of her hair.

'Who is he like?' I asked, looking up and finding myself full in her eyes. The question was quite irrelevant: her eyes spoke a whole clear message that made my heart throb; yet she answered.

'Who is he? Why, nobody, of course! But he *will* be like father, don't you think?'

The question drew my eyes to hers again, and again we looked each other the strange intelligence that made her flush and me breathe in as I smiled.

'Ay! Blue eyes like your father's – not like yours –'

Again the wild messages in her looks.

'No!' she answered very softly. 'And I think he'll be jolly, like father – they have neither of them our eyes, have they?'

'No,' I answered, overcome by a sudden hot flush of tenderness. 'No – not vulnerable. To have such soft, vulnerable eyes as you used makes one feel nervous and irascible. But you have clothed over the sensitiveness of yours, haven't you? – like naked life, naked defenceless protoplasm they were, is it not so?'

She laughed, and at the old painful memories she dilated in the old way, and I felt the old tremor at seeing her soul flung quivering on my pity.

'And were mine like that?' asked George, who had come up.

He must have perceived the bewilderment of my look as I tried to adjust myself to him. A light shadow, a slight chagrin appeared on his face.

'Yes,' I answered, 'yes – but not so bad. You never gave yourself away so much – you were most cautious: but just as defenceless.'

'And am I altered?' he asked, with quiet irony, as if he knew I was not interested in him.

'Yes, more cautious. You keep in the shadow. But Emily has clothed herself, and can now walk among the crowd at her own gait.'

It was with an effort I refrained from putting my lips to kiss her at that moment as she looked at me with womanly dignity and tenderness. Then I remembered, and said:

'But you are taking me to the stable, George! Come and see the horses too, Emily.'

'I will. I admire them so much,' she replied, and thus we both indulged him.

He talked to his horses and of them, laying his hand upon them, running over their limbs. The glossy, restless animals interested him more than anything. He broke into a little flush of enthusiasm over them. They were his new interest. They were quiet and yet responsive; he was their master and owner. This gave him real pleasure.

But the baby became displeased again. Emily looked at me for sympathy with him.

'He is a little wanderer,' she said, 'he likes to be always moving. Perhaps he objects to the ammonia or stables too,' she added, frowning and laughing slightly, 'it is not very agreeable, is it?'

'Not particularly,' I agreed, and as she moved off I went with her, leaving him in the stables. When Emily and I were alone we sauntered aimlessly back to the garden. She persisted in talking to the baby, and in talking to me about the baby, till I wished the child in Jericho. This made her laugh, and she continued to tantalize me. The hollyhock flowers of the second whorl were flushing to the top of the spires. The bees, covered with pale crumbs of pollen, were swaying a moment outside the wide gates of the florets, then they swung in with excited hum, and clung madly to the furry white capitols, and worked riotously round the waxy bases. Emily held out the baby to watch, talking all the time in low, fond tones. The child stretched towards the bright flowers. The sun glistened on his smooth hair as on bronze dust, and the wondering blue eyes of the baby followed the bees. Then he made small sounds, and suddenly waved his hands, like rumpled pink hollyhock buds.

'Look!' said Emily, 'look at the little bees! Ah, but you

mustn't touch them, they bite. They're coming!' she cried, with sudden laughing apprehension, drawing the child away. He made noises of remonstrance. She put him near to the flowers again till he knocked the spire with his hand and two indignant bees came sailing out. Emily drew back quickly crying in alarm, then laughing with excited eyes at me, as if she had just escaped a peril in my presence. Thus she teased me by flinging me all kinds of bright gages of love while she kept me aloof because of the child. She laughed with pure pleasure at this state of affairs, and delighted the more when I frowned, till at last I swallowed my resentment and laughed too, playing with the hands of the baby, and watching his blue eyes change slowly like a softly sailing sky.

Presently Meg called us in to tea. She wore a dress of fine blue stuff with cream silk embroidery, and she looked handsome, for her hair was very hastily dressed.

'What, have you had that child all this time?' she exclaimed, on seeing Emily. 'Where is his father?'

'I don't know – we left him in the stable, didn't we, Cyril? But I like nursing him, Meg. I like it ever so much,' replied Emily.

'Oh, yes, you may be sure George would get off it if he could. He's always in the stable. As I tell him, he fair stinks of horses. He's not that fond of the children, I can tell you. Come on, my pet – why, come to its mammy.'

She took the baby and kissed it passionately, and made extravagant love to it. A clean-shaven young man with thick bare arms went across the yard.

'Here, just look and tell George as tea is ready,' said Meg.

'Where is he?' asked Oswald, the sturdy youth who attended to the farm business.

'You know where to find him,' replied Meg, with that careless freedom which was so subtly derogatory to her husband.

George came hurrying from the out-building. 'What, is it tea already?' he said.

'It's a wonder you haven't been crying out for it this last hour,' said Meg.

'It's a marvel you've got dressed so quick,' he replied.

'Oh, is it?' she answered – 'well, it's not with any of your help that I've done it, that is a fact. Where's Teenie?'

The maid, short, stiffly built, very dark and sullen-looking, came forward from the gate.

'Can you take Alfy as well, just while we have tea?' she asked. Teenie replied that she should think she could, whereupon she was given the ruddy-haired baby, as well as the dark one. She sat with them on a seat at the end of the yard. We proceeded to tea.

It was a very great spread. There were hot cakes, three or four kinds of cold cakes, tinned apricots, jellies, tinned lobster, and trifles in the way of jam, cream, and rum.

'I don't know what those cakes are like,' said Meg. 'I made them in such a fluster. Really, you have to do things as best you can when you've got children – especially when there's two. I never seem to have time to do my hair up even – look at it now.'

She put up her hands to her head, and I could not help noticing how grimy and rough were her nails.

The tea was going on pleasantly, when one of the babies began to cry. Teenie bent over it crooning gruffly. I leaned back and looked out of the door to watch her. I thought of the girl in Chekhov's story, who smothered her charge, and I hoped the grim Teenie would not be driven to such desperation. The other child joined in this chorus. Teenie rose from her seat and walked about the yard, gruffly trying to soothe the twins.

'It's a funny thing, but whenever anybody comes they're sure to be cross,' said Meg, beginning to simmer.

'They're no different from ordinary,' said George, 'it's only that you're forced to notice it then.'

'No, it is not!' cried Meg in a sudden passion:

'Is it now, Emily? Of course, *he* has to say something! Weren't they as good as gold this morning, Emily? – and yesterday! why they never murmured, as good as gold they were. But he wants them to be as dumb as fishes: he'd like them shutting up in a box as soon as they make a bit of noise.'

'I was not saying anything about it,' he replied.

'Yes, you were,' she retorted. 'I don't know what you call it then –'

The babies outside continued to cry.

'Bring Alfy to me,' called Meg, yielding to the mother feeling.

'Oh, no, damn it!' said George, 'let Oswald take him.'

'Yes,' replied Meg bitterly, 'let anybody take him so long as he's out of your sight. You never ought to have children, you didn't –'

George murmured something about 'today'.

'Come then!' said Meg with a whole passion of tenderness, as she took the red-haired baby and held it to her bosom, 'Why, what is it then, what is it, my precious? Hush then pet, hush then!'

The baby did not hush. Meg rose from her chair and stood rocking the baby in her arms, swaying from one foot to the other.

'He's got a bit of wind,' she said.

We tried to continue the meal, but everything was awkward and difficult.

'I wonder if he's hungry,' said Meg, 'let's try him.'

She turned away and gave him her breast. Then he was still, so she covered herself as much as she could, and sat down again to tea. We had finished, so we sat and waited while she ate. This disjointing of the meal, by reflex action, made Emily and me more accurate. We were exquisitely attentive, and polite to a nicety. Our very speech was clipped with precision, as we drifted to a discussion of Strauss and Debussy. This of course put a breach between us two and our hosts, but we could not help it; it was our only way of covering over the awkwardness of the occasion. George sat looking glum and listening to us. Meg was quite indifferent. She listened occasionally, but her position as mother made her impregnable. She sat eating calmly, looking down now and again at her baby, holding us in slight scorn, babblers that we were. She was secure in her high maternity; she was mistress and sole authority. George, as father, was first servant; as an indifferent father, she humiliated him and was hostile to his wishes. Emily and I were mere intruders, feeling ourselves such. After tea we went upstairs to wash our hands. The grandmother had had a second stroke of paralysis, and lay inert, almost stupefied. Her large bulk upon the bed was horrible to me, and her face, with the muscles all slack and awry, seemed like some cruel cartoon. She spoke a few thick words to me. George asked her if she felt all right, or should he rub her. She turned her old eyes slowly to him.

'My leg – my leg a bit,' she said in her strange guttural.

He took off his coat, and pushing his hand under the bedclothes, sat rubbing the poor old woman's limb patiently, slowly for some time. She watched him for a moment, then without her turning her eyes from him, he passed out of her vision and she lay staring at nothing, in his direction.

'There,' he said at last, 'is that any better then, mother?'

'Ay, that's a bit better,' she said slowly.

'Should I gi'e thee a drink?' he asked, lingering, wishing to minister all he could to her before he went.

She looked at him, and he brought the cup. She swallowed a few drops with difficulty.

'Doesn't it make you miserable to have her always there?' I asked him, when we were in the next room. He sat down on the large white bed and laughed shortly.

'We're used to it – we never notice her, poor old gran'ma.'

'But she must have made a difference to you – she must make a big difference at the bottom, even if you don't know it,' I said.

'She's got such a strong character,' he said musing, '– she seemed to understand me. She was a real friend to me, before she was so bad. Sometimes I happen to look at her – generally I never see her, you know how I mean – but sometimes I do – and then – it seems a bit rotten –'

He smiled at me peculiarly, '– it seems to take the shine off things,' he added, and then, smiling again with ugly irony – 'She's our skeleton in the closet.' He indicated her large bulk.

The church bells began to ring. The grey church stood on a rise among the fields not far away, like a handsome old stag looking over towards the inn. The five bells began to play, and the sound came beating upon the window.

'I hate Sunday night,' he said, restlessly.

'Because you've nothing to do?' I asked.

'I don't know,' he said. 'It seems like a gag, and you feel helpless. I don't want to go to church, and hark at the bells, they make you feel uncomfortable.'

'What do you generally do?' I asked.

'Feel miserable – I've been down to Mayhew's these last two Sundays, and Meg's been pretty mad. She says it's the only night I could stop with her, or go out with her. But if I stop with her, what can I do? – and if we go out, it's only for half an hour. I hate Sunday night – it's a dead end.'

When we went downstairs, the table was cleared, and Meg was bathing the dark baby. Thus she was perfect. She handled the bonny, naked child with beauty of gentleness. She kneeled over him nobly. Her arms and her bosom and her throat had a nobility of roundness and softness. She drooped her head with the grace of a Madonna, and her movements were lovely, accurate and exquisite, like an old song perfectly sung. Her voice, playing and soothing round the curved limbs of the baby, was like water, soft as wine in the sun, running with delight.

We watched humbly, sharing the wonder from afar.

Emily was very envious of Meg's felicity. She begged to be allowed to bathe the second baby. Meg granted her bounteous permission:

'Yes, you can wash him if you like, but what about your frock?'

Emily, delighted, began to undress the baby, whose hair was like crocus petals. Her fingers trembled with pleasure as she loosed the little tapes. I always remember the inarticulate delight with which she took the child in her hands, when at last his little shirt was removed, and felt his soft white limbs and body. A distinct, glowing atmosphere seemed suddenly to burst out around her and the child, leaving me outside. The moment before she had been very near to me, her eyes searching mine, her spirit clinging timidly about me. Now I was put away, quite alone, neglected, forgotten, outside the glow which surrounded the woman and the baby.

'Ha! – Ha-a-a!' she said with a deep-throated vowel, as she put her face against the child's small breasts, so round, almost like a girl's, silken and warm and wonderful. She kissed him, and touched him, and hovered over him, drinking in his baby sweetnesses, the sweetness of the laughing little mouth's wide, wet kisses, of the round, waving limbs, of the little shoulders so winsomely curving to the arms and the breasts, of the tiny soft neck hidden very warm beneath the chin, tasting deliciously with her lips and her cheeks all the exquisite softness, silkiness, warmth, and tender life of the baby's body.

A woman is so ready to disclaim the body of a man's love; she yields him her own soft beauty with so much gentle patience and regret; she clings to his neck, to his head and his cheeks, fondling them for the soul's meaning that is there, and shrinking from his passionate limbs and his body. It was with some perplexity, some anger and bitterness that I watched Emily moved almost to ecstasy by the baby's small, innocuous person.

'Meg never found any pleasure in me as she does in the kids,' said George bitterly, for himself.

The child, laughing and crowing, caught his hands in Emily's hair and pulled dark tresses down, while she cried out in remonstrance, and tried to loosen the small fists that were shut so fast. She took him from the water and rubbed him dry, with marvellous gentle little rubs, he kicking and expostulating. She brought his fine hair into one silken up-springing of ruddy gold like an aureole. She played with his tiny balls of toes, like wee pink mushrooms, till at last she dare detain him no longer, when she put on his flannel and his night-gown and gave him to Meg.

Before carrying him to bed Meg took him to feed him. His mouth was stretched round the nipple as he sucked, his face was pressed close and closer to the breast, his fingers wandered over the fine white globe, blue-veined and heavy, trying to hold it. Meg looked down upon him with a consuming passion of tenderness, and Emily clasped her hands and leaned forward to him. Even thus they thought him exquisite.

When the twins were both asleep, I must tip-toe upstairs to see them. They lay cheek by cheek in the crib next the large white bed, breathing little, ruffling breaths, out of unison, so small and pathetic with their tiny shut fingers. I remembered the two larks.

From the next room came a heavy sound of the old woman's breathing. Meg went in to her. As in passing I caught sight of the large, prone figure in the bed, I thought of Guy de Maupassant's 'Toine', who acted as an incubator.

CHAPTER V

The Dominant Motif of Suffering

THE old woman lay still another year, then she suddenly sank out of life. George ceased to write to me, but I learned his news elsewhere. He became more and more intimate with the Mayhews. After old Mayhew's bankruptcy, the two sons had remained on in the large dark house that stood off the Nottingham Road in Eberwich. This house had been bequeathed to the oldest daughter by the mother. Maud Mayhew, who was married and separated from her husband, kept house for her brothers. She was a tall, large woman with high cheekbones and oily black hair looped over her ears. Tom Mayhew was also a handsome man, very dark and ruddy, with insolent bright eyes.

The Mayhews' house was called the Hollies. It was a solid building, of old red brick, standing fifty yards back from the Eberwich highroad. Between it and the road was an unkempt lawn, surrounded by very high black holly trees. The house seemed to be imprisoned among the bristling hollies. Passing through the large gate, one came immediately upon the bare side of the house and upon the great range of stables. Old Mayhew had in his day stabled thirty or more horses there. Now grass was between the red bricks, and all the bleaching doors were shut, save perhaps two or three which were open for George's horses.

The Hollies became a kind of club for the disconsolate, 'better-off' men of the district. The large dining-room was gloomily and sparsely furnished, the drawing-room was a desert, but the small morning-room was comfortable enough, with wicker arm-chairs, heavy curtains, and a large side-board. In this room George and the Mayhews met with several men two or three times week. There they discussed horses and made mock of the authority of women. George provided the whisky, and they all gambled timidly at cards. These bachelor parties were the source of great annoyance to the wives of the married men who attended them.

'He's quite unbearable when he's been at those Mayhews',' said Meg. 'I'm sure they do nothing but cry us down.'

Maud Mayhew kept apart from these meetings, watching over her two children. She had been very unhappily married, and now was reserved, silent. The women of Eberwich watched her as she went swiftly along the street in the morning with her basket, and they gloried a little in her overthrow, because she was too proud to accept consolation, yet they were sorry in their hearts for her, and she was never touched with calumny. George saw her frequently, but she treated him coldly as she treated the other men, so he was afraid of her.

He had more facilities now for his horse-dealing. When the grandmother died, in the October two years after the marriage of George, she left him seven hundred pounds. To Meg she left the Inn, and the two houses she had built in Newerton, together with brewery shares to the value of nearly a thousand pounds. George and Meg felt themselves to be people of property. The result, however, was only a little further coldness between them. He was very careful that she had all that was hers. She said to him once when they were quarrelling, that he needn't go feeding the Mayhews on the money that came out of her business. Thenceforward he kept strict accounts of all his affairs, and she must audit them, receiving her exact dues. This was a mortification to her woman's capricious soul of generosity and cruelty.

The Christmas after the grandmother's death another son was born to them. For the time George and Meg became very good friends again.

When in the following March I heard he was coming down to London with Tom Mayhew on business, I wrote and asked him to stay with me. Meg replied, saying she was so glad I had asked him: she did not want him going off with that fellow again; he had been such a lot better lately, and she was sure it was only those men at Mayhew's made him what he was.

He consented to stay with me. I wrote and told him Lettie

and Leslie were in London, and that we should dine with them one evening. I met him at King's Cross and we all three drove west. Mayhew was a remarkably handsome, well-built man; he and George made a notable couple. They were both in breeches and gaiters, but George still looked like a yeoman, while Mayhew had all the braggadocio of the stable. We made an impossible trio. Mayhew laughed and jested broadly for a short time, then he grew restless and fidgety. He felt restrained and awkward in my presence. Later, he told George I was a damned parson. On the other hand, I was content to look at his rather vulgar beauty – his teeth were blackened with smoking – and to listen to his ineffectual talk, but I could find absolutely no response. George was go-between. To me he was cautious and rather deferential, to Mayhew he was careless, and his attitude was tinged with contempt.

When the son of the horse-dealer at last left us to go to some of his father's old cronies, we were glad. Very uncertain, very sensitive and wavering, our old intimacy burned again like the fragile burning of alcohol. Closed together in the same blue flames, we discovered and watched the pageant of life in the town revealed wonderfully to us. We laughed at the tyranny of old romance. We scorned the faded procession of old years, and made mock of the vast pilgrimage of by-gone romances travelling farther into the dim distance. Were we not in the midst of the bewildering pageant of modern life, with all its confusion of bannerets and colours, with its infinite inter-weaving of sounds, the screech of the modern toys of haste striking like keen spray, the heavy boom of busy mankind gathering its bread, earnestly, forming the bed of all other sounds; and between these two the swiftness of songs, the trium-phant tilt of the joy of life, the hoarse oboes of privation, the shuddering drums of tragedy, and the eternal scraping of the two deep-toned strings of despair?

We watched the taxicabs coursing with their noses down to the street, we watched the rocking hansoms, and the lumber-ing stateliness of buses. In the silent green cavern of the park we stood and listened to the surging of the ocean of life. We watched a girl with streaming hair go galloping down the Row, a dark man, laughing and showing his white teeth, galloping more heavily at her elbow. We saw a squad of Life Guards enter the gates of the park, erect and glittering with silver and white and red. They came near to us, and we thrilled a little as we watched the muscles of their white smooth thighs answering the movement of the horses, and their cheeks and their chins bending with proud manliness to the rhythm of the march. We watched the exquisite rhythm of the body of men moving in scarlet and silver further down the leafless avenue, like a slightly wavering spark of red life blown along. At the Marble Arch Corner we listened to a little socialist who was flaring fiercely under a plane tree. The hot stream of his words flowed over the old wounds that the knowledge of the unending miseries of the poor had given me, and I winced. For him the world was all East-end, and all the East-end was as a pool from which the waters are drained off, leaving the water-things to wrestle in the wet mud under the sun, till the whole of the city seems a heaving, shuddering struggle of black-mudded objects deprived of the elements of life. I felt a great terror of the little man, lest he should make me see all mud, as I had seen before. Then I felt a breathless pity for him, that his eyes should be always filled with mud, and never brightened. George listened intently to the speaker, very much moved by him.

At night, after the theatre, we saw the outcasts sleep in a rank under the Waterloo bridge, their heads to the wall, their feet lying out on the pavement: a long, black, ruffled heap at the foot of the wall. All the faces were covered but two, that of a peaked, pale little man, and that of a brutal woman. Over these two faces, floating like uneasy pale dreams on their obscurity, swept now and again the trailing light of the tram cars. We picked our way past the line of abandoned feet, shrinking from the sight of the thin bare ankles of a young man, from the draggled edge of the skirts of a bunched-up woman, from the pitiable sight of the men who had wrapped their legs in newspaper for a little warmth, and lay like worthless parcels. It was raining. Some men stood at the edge of the causeway fixed in dreary misery, finding no room to sleep. Outside, on a seat in the blackness and the rain, a woman sat sleeping, while the water trickled and hung heavily at the ends of her loosened strands of hair. Her hands were pushed in the bosom of her jacket. She lurched forward in her sleep, started, and one of her hands fell out of her bosom. She sank again to sleep. George gripped my arm.

'Give her something,' he whispered in panic. I was afraid. Then suddenly getting a florin from my pocket, I stiffened my nerves and slid it into her palm. Her hand was soft, and warm, and curled in sleep. She started violently, looking up at me, then down at her hand. I turned my face aside, terrified lest she should look in my eyes, and full of shame and grief I ran down the embankment to him. We hurried along under the plane trees in silence. The shining cars were drawing tall in the distance over Westminster Bridge, a fainter, yellow light running with them on the water below. The wet streets were spilled with golden liquor of light, and on the deep blackness of the river were the restless yellow slashes of the lamps.

*

Lettie and Leslie were staying up at Hampstead with a friend of the Tempests, one of the largest shareholders in the firm of Tempest, Wharton & Co. The Raphaels had a substantial house, and Lettie preferred to go to them rather than to an' hotel, especially as she had brought with her her infant son, now ten months old, with his nurse. They invited George and me to dinner on the Friday evening. The party included Lettie's host and hostess, and also a Scottish poetess, and an Irish musician, composer of songs and pianoforte rhapsodies.

Lettie wore a black lace dress in mourning for one of Leslie's maternal aunts. This made her look older, otherwise there seemed to be no change in her. A subtle observer might have noticed a little hardness about her mouth, and disillusion hanging slightly on her eyes. She was, however, excited by the company in which she found herself, therefore she overflowed with clever speeches and rapid, brilliant observations. Certainly on such occasions she was admirable. The rest of the company formed, as it were, the orchestra which accompanied her.

George was exceedingly quiet. He spoke a few words now and then to Mrs Raphael, but on the whole he was altogether silent, listening.

'Really!' Lettie was saying, 'I don't see that one thing is worth doing any more than another. It's like dessert: you are equally indifferent whether you have grapes, or pears, or pineapple.'

'Have you already dined so far?' sang the Scottish poetess in her musical, plaintive manner.

'The only thing worth doing is producing,' said Lettie.

'Alas, that is what all the young folk are saying nowadays!' sighed the Irish musician.

'That is the only thing one finds any pleasure in – that is to say, any satisfaction,' continued Lettie, smiling, and turning to the two artists.

'Do you not think so?' she added.

'You do come to a point at last,' said the Scottish poetess, 'when your work is a real source of satisfaction.'

'Do you write poetry then?' asked George of Lettie.

'I? Oh, dear no! I have tried strenuously to make up a limerick for a competition, but in vain. So you see, I am a failure there. Did you know I have a son, though? – a marvellous little fellow, is he not, Leslie? – he is my work. I am a wonderful mother, am I not, Leslie?'

'Too devoted,' he replied.

'There!' she exclaimed in triumph – 'When I have to sign my name and occupation in a visitor's book, it will be "Mother". I hope my business will flourish,' she concluded, smiling.

There was a touch of ironical brutality in her now. She was, at the bottom, quite sincere. Having reached that point in a woman's career when most, perhaps all of the things in life seem worthless and insipid, she had determined to put up with it, to ignore her own self, to empty her own potentialities into the vessel of another or others, and to live her life at second hand. This peculiar abnegation of self is the resource of a woman for the escaping of the responsibilities of her own development. Like a nun, she puts over her living face a veil, as a sign that the woman no longer exists for herself: she is the servant of God, of some man, of her children, or may be of some cause. As a servant, she is no longer responsible for herself, which would make her terrified and lonely. Service is light and easy.

To be responsible for the good progress of one's life is terrifying. It is the most insufferable form of loneliness, and the heaviest of responsibilities. So Lettie indulged her husband, but did not yield her independence to him; rather it was she who took much of the responsibility of him into her hands, and therefore he was so devoted to her. She had, however, now determined to abandon the charge of herself to serve her children. When the children grew up, either they would unconsciously fling her away, back upon herself again in bitterness and loneliness, or they would tenderly cherish her, chafing at her love-bonds occasionally.

George looked and listened to all the flutter of conversation, and said nothing. It seemed to him like so much unreasonable rustling of pieces of paper, of leaves of books, and so on. Later in the evening Lettie sang, no longer Italian folk songs, but the fragmentary utterances of Debussy and Strauss. These also to George were quite meaningless, and rather wearisome. It made him impatient to see her wasting herself upon them.

'Do you like those songs?' she asked in the frank, careless manner she affected.

'Not much,' he replied, ungraciously.

'Don't you?' she exclaimed, adding with a smile, 'Those are the most wonderful things in the world, those little things' – she began to hum a Debussy idiom. He could not answer her on the point, so he sat with the arrow sticking in him, and did not speak.

She inquired of him concerning Meg and his children and the affairs of Eberwich, but the interest was flimsy, as she preserved a wide distance between them, although apparently she was so unaffected and friendly. We left before eleven.

When we were seated in the cab and rushing down hill, he said:

'You know, she makes me mad.'

He was frowning, looking out of the window away from me.

'Who, Lettie? Why, what riles you?' I asked.

He was some time in replying.

'Why, she's so affected.'

I sat still in the small, close space and waited.

'Do you know –?' he laughed, keeping his face averted from me. 'She makes my blood boil. I could hate her.'

'Why?' I said gently.

'I don't know. I feel as if she'd insulted me. She does lie, doesn't she?'

'I didn't notice it,' I said, but I knew he meant her shirking, her shuffling of her life.

'And you think of those poor devils under the bridge – and then of her and them frittering away themselves and money in that idiocy –'

He spoke with passion.

'You are quoting Longfellow,' I said.

'What?' he asked, looking at me suddenly.

'"Life is real, life is earnest –"'

He flushed slightly at my good-natured gibe.

'I don't know what it is,' he replied. 'But it's a pretty rotten business, when you think of her fooling about wasting herself, and all the waste that goes on up there, and the poor devils rotting on the embankment – and –'

'And you – and Mayhew – and me –' I continued.

He looked at me very intently to see if I were mocking. He laughed. I could see he was very much moved.

'Is the time quite out of joint?' I asked.

'Why!' – he laughed. 'No. But she makes me feel so angry – as if I should burst – I don't know when I felt in such a rage. I wonder why. I'm sorry for him, poor devil. "Lettie and Leslie" – they seemed christened for one another, didn't they?'

'What if you'd had her?' I asked.

'We should have been like a cat and dog; I'd rather be with Meg a thousand times – now!' he added significantly. He sat watching the lamps and the people and the dark buildings slipping past us.

'Shall we go and have a drink?' I asked him, thinking we would call in Frascati's to see the come-and-go.

'I could do with a brandy,' he replied, looking at me slowly.

We sat in the restaurant listening to the jigging of the music, watching the changing flow of the people. I like to sit a long time by the hollyhocks watching the throng of varied bees which poise and hesitate outside the wild flowers, then swing in with a hum which sets everything aquiver. But still more fascinating it is to watch the come and go of people weaving and intermingling in the complex mesh of their intentions, with all the subtle grace and mystery of their moving, shapely bodies.

I sat still, looking out across the amphitheatre. George looked also, but he drank glass after glass of brandy.

'I like to watch the people,' said I.

'Ay – and doesn't it seem an aimless, idiotic business – look at them!' he replied in tones of contempt. I looked instead at him, in some surprise and resentment. His face was gloomy, stupid and unrelieved. The amount of brandy he had drunk had increased his ill-humour.

'Shall we be going?' I said. I did not want him to get drunk in his present state of mind.

'Ay – in half a minute,' he finished the brandy, and rose. Although he had drunk a good deal, he was quite steady, only there was a disagreeable look always on his face, and his eyes seemed smaller and more glittering than I had seen them. We took a bus to Victoria. He sat swaying on his seat in the dim, clumsy vehicle, saying not a word. In the vast cavern of the station the theatre-goers were hastening, crossing the pale grey strand, small creatures scurrying hither and thither in the space beneath the lonely lamps. As the train crawled over the river we watched the far-flung hoop of diamond lights curving slowly round and striping with bright threads the black water. He sat looking with heavy eyes, seeming to shrink from the enormous unintelligible lettering of the poem of London.

The town was too large for him, he could not take in its immense, its stupendous poetry. What did come home to him was its flagrant discords. The unintelligibility of the vast city made him apprehensive, and the crudity of its big, coarse contrasts wounded him unutterably.

'What is the matter?' I asked him as we went along the silent pavement at Norwood.

'Nothing,' he replied. 'Nothing!' and I did not trouble him further.

We occupied a large, two-bedded room – that looked down the hill and over to the far woods of Kent. He was morose and untalkative. I brought up a soda-syphon and whisky, and we proceeded to undress. When he stood in his pyjamas he waited as if uncertain.

'Do you want a drink?' he asked.

I did not. He crossed to the table, and as I got into my bed I heard the brief fizzing of the syphon. He drank his glass at one draught, then switched off the light. In the sudden darkness I saw his pale shadow go across to the sofa in the window-space. The blinds were undrawn, and the stars looked in. He gazed out on the great bay of darkness wherein, far away and below, floated a few sparks of lamps like herring boats at sea.

'Aren't you coming to bed?' I asked.

'I'm not sleepy – you go to sleep,' he answered, resenting having to speak at all.

'Then put on a dressing gown – there's one in that corner – turn the light on.'

He did not answer, but fumbled for the garment in the darkness. When he had found it, he said:

'Do you mind if I smoke?'

I did not. He fumbled again in his pockets for cigarettes, always refusing to switch on the light. I watched his face bowed to the match as he lighted his cigarette. He was still handsome in the ruddy light, but his features were coarser. I felt very sorry for him, but I saw that I could get no nearer to him, to relieve him. For some time I lay in the darkness watching the end of his cigarette like a ruddy, malignant insect hovering near his lips, putting the timid stars immensely far away. He sat quite still, leaning on the sofa arm. Occasionally there was a little glow on his cheeks as the cigarette burned brighter, then again I could see nothing but the dull red bee.

I suppose I must have dropped asleep. Suddenly I started as something fell to the floor. I heard him cursing under his breath.

'What's the matter?' I asked.

'I've only knocked something down – cigarette case or something,' he replied, apologetically.

'Aren't you coming to bed?' I asked.

'Yes, I'm coming,' he answered quite docile.

He seemed to wander about and knock against things as he came. He dropped heavily into bed.

'Are you sleepy now?' I asked.

'I dunno – I shall be directly,' he replied.

'What's up with you?' I asked.

'I dunno,' he answered. 'I am like this sometimes, when there's nothing I want to do, and nowhere I want to go, and nobody I want to be near. Then you feel so rottenly lonely, Cyril. You feel awful, like a vacuum, with a pressure on you, a sort of pressure of darkness, and you yourself – just nothing, a vacuum – that's what it's like – a little vacuum that's not dark, all loose in the middle of a space of darkness, that's pressing on you.'

'Good gracious!' I exclaimed, rousing myself in bed. 'That sounds bad!'

He laughed slightly.

'It's all right,' he said, 'it's only the excitement of London, and that little man in the park, and that woman on the seat – I wonder where she is tonight, poor devil – and then Lettie. I seem thrown off my balance. – I think, really, I ought to have made something of myself –'

'What?' I asked, as he hesitated.

'I don't know,' he replied slowly, '– a poet or something, like Burns – I don't know. I shall laugh at myself for thinking so, tomorrow. But I am born a generation too soon – I wasn't ripe enough when I came. I wanted something I hadn't got. I'm something short. I'm like corn in a wet harvest – full, but pappy, no good. Is'll rot. I came too soon; or I wanted something that would ha' made me grow fierce. That's why I wanted Lettie – I think. But am I talking damn rot? What am I saying? What are you making me talk for? What are you listening for?'

I rose and went across to him, saying:

'I don't want you to talk! If you sleep till morning things will look different.'

I sat on his bed and took his hand. He lay quite still.

'I'm only a kid after all, Cyril,' he said, a few moments later.

'We all are,' I answered, still holding his hand. Presently he fell asleep.

When I awoke the sunlight was laughing with the young morning in the room. The large blue sky shone against the window, and the birds were calling in the garden below, shouting to one another and making fun of life. I felt glad to have opened my eyes. I lay for a moment looking out on the morning as on a blue bright sea in which I was going to plunge.

Then my eyes wandered to the little table near the couch. I noticed the glitter of George's cigarette case, and then, with a start, the whisky decanter. It was nearly empty. He must have drunk three-quarters of a pint of liquor while I was dozing. I could not believe it. I thought I must have been mistaken as to the quantity the bottle contained. I leaned out to see what it was that had startled me by its fall the night before. It was the large, heavy drinking glass which he had knocked down but not broken. I could see no stain on the carpet.

George was still asleep. He lay half uncovered, and was breathing quietly. His face looked inert like a mask. The pallid, uninspired clay of his features seemed to have sunk a little out of shape, so that he appeared rather haggard, rather ugly, with grooves of ineffectual misery along his cheeks. I wanted him to wake, so that his inert, flaccid features might be inspired with life again. I could not believe his charm and his beauty could have forsaken him so, and left his features dreary, sunken clay.

As I looked he woke. His eyes opened slowly. He looked at me and turned away, unable to meet my eyes. He pulled the bedclothes up over his shoulders, as though to cover himself from me, and he lay with his back to me, quite still, as if he were asleep, although I knew he was quite awake; he was suffering the humiliation of lying waiting for his life to crawl back and inhabit his body. As it was, his vitality was not yet sufficient to inform the muscles of his face and give him an expression, much less to answer my challenge.

CHAPTER VI

Pisgah

WHEN her eldest boy was three years old Lettie returned to live at Eberwich. Old Mr Tempest died suddenly, so Leslie came down to inhabit Highclose. He was a very much occupied man. Very often he was in Germany or in the south of England engaged on business. At home he was unfailingly attentive to his wife and his two children. He had cultivated a taste for public life. In spite of his pressure of business he had become a County Councillor, and one of the prominent members of the Conservative Association. He was very fond of answering or proposing toasts at some public dinner, of entertaining political men at Highclose, of taking the chair at political meetings, and finally, of speaking on this or that platform. His name was fairly often seen in the newspapers. As a mine owner, he spoke as an authority on the employment of labour, on royalties, landowning, and so on.

At home he was quite tame. He treated his wife with respect, romped in the nursery, and domineered the servants royally. They liked him for it – her they did not like. He was noisy, but unobservant, she was quiet and exacting. He would swear and bluster furiously, but when he was round the corner they smiled. She gave her orders and passed very moderate censure, but they went away cursing to themselves. As Lettie was always a very good wife, Leslie adored her when he had the time, and when he had not, forgot her comfortably.

She was very contradictory. At times she would write to me in terms of passionate dissatisfaction: she had nothing at all in her life, it was a barren futility.

'I hope I shall have another child next spring,' she would write, 'there is only that to take away the misery of this torpor. I seem full of passion and energy, and it all fizzles out in day-to-day domestics –'

When I replied to her urging her to take some work that she could throw her soul into, she would reply indifferently. Then later:

'You charge me with contradiction. Well, naturally. You see I wrote that screeching letter in a mood which won't come again for some time. Generally I am quite content to take the rain and the calm days just as they come, then something flings me out of myself – and I am a trifle demented : – very, very blue, as I tell Leslie.'

Like so many women, she seemed to live, for the most part contentedly, a small indoor existence with artificial light and padded upholstery. Only occasionally, hearing the winds of life outside, she clamoured to be out in the black, keen storm. She was driven to the door, she looked out and called into the tumult wildly, but feminine caution kept her from stepping over the threshold.

George was flourishing in his horse-dealing.

In the morning, processions of splendid shire horses, tied tail and head, would tramp grandly along the quiet lanes of Eberwich, led by George's man, or by Tom Mayhew, while in the fresh clean sunlight George would go riding by, two restless nags dancing beside him.

When I came home from France five years after our meeting in London I found him installed in the Hollies. He had rented the house from the Mayhews, and had moved there with his family, leaving Oswald in charge of the Ram. I called at the large house one afternoon, but George was out. His family surprised me. The twins were tall lads of six. There were two more boys, and Meg was nursing a beautiful baby girl about a year old. This child was evidently mistress of the household. Meg, who was growing stouter, indulged the little creature in every way.

'How is George?' I asked her.

'Oh, he's very well,' she replied. 'He's always got something on hand. He hardly seems to have a spare moment; what with his socialism, and one thing and another.'

It was true, the outcome of his visit to London had been a wild devotion to the cause of the down-trodden. I saw a picture of Watts' 'Mammon', on the walls of the morning-room, and

the works of Blatchford, Masterman, and Chiozza Money on
the side table. The socialists of the district used to meet every
other Thursday evening at the Hollies to discuss reform. Meg
did not care for these earnest souls.

'They're not my sort,' she said, 'too jerky and bumptious.
They think everybody's slow-witted but them. There's one thing
about them, though, they don't drink, so that's a blessing.'

'Why!' I said, 'Have you had much trouble that way?'

She lowered her voice to a pitch which was sufficiently mysterious to attract the attention of the boys.

'I shouldn't say anything if it wasn't that you were like
brothers,' she said. 'But he did begin to have dreadful drinking
bouts. You know it was always spirits, and generally brandy: –
and that makes such work with them. You've no idea what he's
like when he's evil-drunk. Sometimes he's all for talk, sometimes he's laughing at everything, and sometimes he's just
snappy. And then –' here her tones grew ominous, '– he'll come
home evil-drunk.'

At the memory she grew serious.

'You couldn't imagine what it's like, Cyril,' she said. 'It's
like having Satan in the house with you, or a black tiger glow-
ering at you. I'm sure nobody knows what I've suffered with
him –'

The children stood with large, awful eyes and paling lips,
listening.

'But he's better now?' I said.

'Oh, yes – since Gertie came,' – she looked fondly at the baby
in her arms – 'He's a lot better now. You see he always wanted
a girl, and he's very fond of her – isn't he, pet? – are you your
Dadda's girlie? – and Mamma's too, aren't you?'

The baby turned with sudden coy shyness, and clung to her
mother's neck. Meg kissed her fondly, then the child laid her
cheek against her mother's. The mother's dark eyes, and the
baby's large, hazel eyes looked at me serenely. The two were
very calm, very complete and triumphant together. In their com-
pleteness was a security which made me feel alone and ineffectual. A woman who has her child in her arms is a tower of
strength, a beautiful, unassailable tower of strength that may in
its turn stand quietly dealing death.

I told Meg I would call again to see George. Two evenings later I asked Lettie to lend me a dog-cart to drive over to the Hollies. Leslie was away on one of his political jaunts, and she was restless. She proposed to go with me. She had called on Meg twice before in the new large home.

We started about six o'clock. The night was dark and muddy. Lettie wanted to call in Eberwich village, so she drove the long way round Selsby. The horse was walking through the gate of the Hollies at about seven o'clock. Meg was upstairs in the nursery, the maid told me, and George was in the dining-room getting baby to sleep.

'All right!' I said, 'we will go in to him. Don't bother to tell him.'

As we stood in the gloomy, square hall we heard the rumble of a rocking-chair, the stroke coming slow and heavy to the tune of 'Henry Martin', one of our Strelley Mill folk songs. Then, through the man's heavily-accented singing floated the long, light crooning of the baby as she sang, in her quaint little fashion, a mischievous second to her father's lullaby. He waxed a little louder; and without knowing why, we found ourselves smiling with piquant amusement. The baby grew louder too, till there was a shrill ring of laughter and mockery in her music. He sang louder and louder, the baby shrilled higher and higher, the chair swung in long, heavy beats. Then suddenly he began to laugh. The rocking stopped, and he said, still with laughter and enjoyment in his tones:

'Now that is very wicked! Ah, naughty Girlie – go to boh, go to bohey! – at once.'

The baby chuckled her small, insolent mockery.

'Come, Mamma!' he said, 'come and take Girlie to bohey!'

The baby laughed again, but with an uncertain touch of appeal in her tone. We opened the door and entered. He looked up very much startled to see us. He was sitting in a tall rocking-chair by the fire, coatless, with white shirtsleeves. The baby, in her high-waisted, tight little night-gown, stood on his knee, her wide eyes fixed on us, wild wisps of her brown hair brushed across her forehead and glinting like puffs of bronze dust over her ears. Quickly she put her arms round his neck and tucked her face under his chin, her small feet poised on his thigh, the night-gown dropping upon them. He shook his head as the puff of soft brown hair tickled him. He smiled at us, saying:

'You see I'm busy!'

Then he turned again to the little brown head tucked under his chin, blew away the luminous cloud of hair, and rubbed his lips and his moustache on the small white neck, so warm and secret. The baby put up her shoulders, and shrank a little, bubbling in his neck with hidden laughter. She did not lift her face or loosen her arms.

'She thinks she is shy,' he said. 'Look up, young hussy, and see the lady and gentleman. She is a positive owl, she won't go to bed – will you, young brown-owl?'

He tickled her neck again with his moustache, and the child bubbled over with naughty, merry laughter.

The room was very warm, with a red bank of fire up the chimney mouth. It was half lighted from a heavy bronze chandelier, black and gloomy, in the middle of the room. There was the same sombre, sparse furniture that the Mayhews had had. George looked large and handsome, the glossy black silk of his waistcoat fitting close to his sides, the roundness of the shoulder muscle filling the white linen of his sleeves.

Suddenly the baby lifted her head and stared at us, thrusting into her mouth the dummy that was pinned to the breast of her night-gown. The faded pink sleeves of the night-gown were tight on her fat little wrists. She stood thus sucking her dummy, one arm round her father's neck, watching us with hazel solemn eyes. Then she pushed her fat little fist up among the bush of small curls, and began to twist her fingers about her ear that was white like a camellia flower.

'She is really sleepy,' said Lettie.

'Come then!' said he, folding her for sleep against his breast. 'Come and go to boh.'

But the young rascal immediately began to cry her remonstrance. She stiffened herself, freed herself, and stood again on his knee, watching us solemnly, vibrating the dummy in her mouth as she suddenly sucked at it, twisting her father's ear in her small fingers till he winced.

'Her nails *are* sharp,' he said, smiling.

He began asking and giving the small informations that pass between friends who have not met for a long time. The baby laid her head on his shoulder, keeping her tired, owl-like eyes fixed darkly on us. Then gradually the lids fluttered and sank, and she dropped on to his arm.

'She is asleep,' whispered Lettie.

Immediately the dark eyes opened again. We looked significantly at one another, continuing our subdued talk. After a while the baby slept soundly.

Presently Meg came downstairs. She greeted us in breathless whispers of surprise, and then turned to her husband.

'Has she gone?' she whispered, bending over the sleeping child in astonishment. 'My, this is wonderful, isn't it!'

She took the sleeping, drooping baby from his arms, putting her mouth close to its forehead, murmuring with soothing, inarticulate sounds.

We stayed talking for some time when Meg had put the baby to bed. George had a new tone of assurance and authority. In the first place he was an established man, living in a large house, having altogether three men working for him. In the second place he had ceased to value the conventional treasures of social position and ostentatious refinement. Very, very many things he condemned as flummery and sickly waste of time. The life of an ordinary well-to-do person he set down as adorned futility, almost idiocy. He spoke passionately of the monstrous denial of life to the many by the fortunate few. He talked at Lettie most flagrantly.

'Of course,' she said, 'I have read Mr Wells and Mr Shaw, and even Neil Lyons and a Dutchman – what is his name, Querido? But what can I do? I think the rich have as much misery as the poor, and of quite as deadly a sort. What can I do? It is a question of life and the development of the human race. Society and its regulations is not a sort of drill that endless Napoleons have forced on us : it is the only way we have yet found of living together.'

'Pah!' said he, 'that is rank cowardice. It is feeble and futile to the last degree.'

'We can't grow consumption-proof in a generation, nor can we grow poverty-proof.'

'We can begin to take active measures,' he replied contemptuously.

'We can all go into a sanatorium and live miserably and dejectedly warding off death,' she said, 'but life is full of goodliness for all that.'

'It is fuller of misery,' he said.

Nevertheless, she had shaken him. She still kept her astonishing power of influencing his opinions. All his passion, and heat, and rude speech, analysed out, was only his terror at her threatening of his life-interest.

She was rather piqued by his rough treatment of her, and by his contemptuous tone. Moreover, she could never quite let him be. She felt a driving force which impelled her almost against her will to interfere in his life. She invited him to dine with them at Highclose. He was now quite possible. He had, in the course of his business, been sufficiently in the company of gentlemen to be altogether *comme il faut* at a private dinner, and after dinner.

She wrote me concerning him occasionally :

George Saxton was here to dinner yesterday. He and Leslie had frightful battles over the nationalization of industries. George is rather more than a match for Leslie, which, in his secret heart, makes our friend gloriously proud. It is very amusing. I, of course, have to preserve the balance of power, and, of course, to bolster my husband's dignity. At a crucial, dangerous moment, when George is just going to wave his bloody sword and Leslie lies bleeding with rage, I step in and prick the victor under the heart with some little satire or some esoteric question, I raise Leslie and say his blood is luminous for the truth, and vous voilà! Then I abate for the thousandth time Leslie's conservative crow, and I appeal once more to George – it is no use my arguing with him, he gets so angry – I make an abstruse appeal for all the wonderful, sad, and beautiful expressions on the countenance of life, expressions which he does not see or which he distorts by his oblique vision of socialism into grimaces – and there I am! I think I am something of a Machiavelli, but it is quite true, what I say –

Again she wrote:

We happened to be motoring from Derby on Sunday morning, and as we came to the top of the hill, we had to thread our way through quite a large crowd. I looked up, and whom should I see but our friend George, holding forth about the state endowment of mothers. I made Leslie stop while we listened. The market-place was quite full of people. George saw us, and became fiery. Leslie then grew excited, and although I clung to the skirts of his coat with all my strength, he jumped up and began to question. I must say it with shame and humility – he made an ass of himself. The men all round were jeering and muttering under their breath. I think Leslie is not very popular among them, he is such an advocate of machinery which will do the work of men. So they cheered our friend George when he thundered forth his replies and his demonstrations. He pointed his finger at us, and flung his hand at us, and shouted till I quailed in my seat. I cannot understand why he should become so frenzied as soon as I am within range. George had a triumph that morning, but when I saw him a few days later he seemed very uneasy, rather self-mistrustful –

Almost a year later I heard from her again on the same subject.

I have had such a lark. Two or three times I have been to the Hollies; to socialist meetings. Leslie does not know. They are great fun. Of course, I am in sympathy with the socialists, but I cannot narrow my eyes till I see one thing only. Life is like a large, rather beautiful man who is young and full of vigour, but hairy, barbaric, with hands hard and dirty, the dirt ingrained. I know his hands are very ugly, I know his mouth is not firmly shapen, I know his limbs are hairy and brutal: but his eyes are deep and very beautiful. That is what I tell George.

The people are so earnest, they make me sad. But then, they are so didactic, they hold forth so much, they are so cock-sure and so narrow-eyed, they make me laugh. George laughs too. I am sure we made such fun of a straight-haired goggle of a girl who had suffered in prison for the cause of women, that I am ashamed when I see my 'Women's League' badge. At the bottom, you know, Cyril, I don't care for anything very much, except myself. Things seem so frivolous. I am the only real thing, I and the children –

Gradually George fell out of the socialist movement. It wearied him. It did not feed him altogether. He began by mocking his friends of the confraternity. Then he spoke in bitter dislike of Hudson, the wordy, humorous, shallow leader of the movement in Eberwich; it was Hudson with his wriggling and his clap-trap who disgusted George with the cause.

Finally the meetings at the Hollies ceased, and my friend dropped all connexion with his former associates.

He began to speculate in land. A hosiery factory moved to Eberwich, giving the place a new stimulus to growth. George happened to buy a piece of land at the end of the street of the village. When he got it, it was laid out in allotment gardens. These were becoming valueless owing to the encroachment of houses. He took it, divided it up, and offered it as sites for a new row of shops. He sold at a good profit.

Altogether he was becoming very well off. I heard from Meg that he was flourishing, that he did not drink 'anything to speak of', but that he was always out, she hardly saw anything of him. If getting-on was to keep him so much away from home, she would be content with a little less fortune. He complained that she was narrow, and that she would not entertain any sympathy with any of his ideas.

'Nobody comes here to see me twice,' he said. 'Because Meg receives them in such an off-hand fashion. I asked Jim Curtiss and his wife from Everley Hall one evening. We were uncomfortable all the time. Meg had hardly a word for anybody – "Yes" and "No" and "Hm Hm!" – They'll never come again.'

Meg herself said:

'Oh, I can't stand stuck-up folks. They make me feel uncomfortable. As soon as they begin mincing their words I'm done for – I can no more talk than a lobster –'

Thus their natures contradicted each other. He tried hard to gain a footing in Eberwich. As it was he belonged to no class of society whatsoever. Meg visited and entertained the wives of small shopkeepers and publicans: this was her set.

George voted the women loud-mouthed, vulgar, and narrow – not without some cause. Meg, however, persisted. She visited when she thought fit, and entertained when he was out. He made acquaintance after acquaintance: Dr Francis; Mr Cartridge, the veterinary surgeon; Toby Heswall, the brewer's son; the Curtisses, farmers of good standing from Everley Hall. But it was no good. George was by nature a family man. He wanted to be private and secure in his own rooms, then he was at ease. As Meg never went out with him, and as every attempt to entertain at the Hollies filled him with shame and mortification, he began to give up trying to place himself, and remained suspended in social isolation at the Hollies.

*

The friendship between Lettie and himself had been kept up, in spite of all things. Leslie was sometimes jealous, but he dared not show it openly, for fear of his wife's scathing contempt. George went to Highclose perhaps once in a fortnight, perhaps not so often. Lettie never went to the Hollies, as Meg's attitude was too antagonistic.

Meg complained bitterly of her husband. He often made a beast of himself drinking, he thought more of himself than he ought, home was not good enough for him, he was selfish to the back-bone, he cared neither for her nor the children, only for himself.

*

I happened to be at home for Lettie's thirty-first birthday. George was then thirty-five. Lettie had allowed her husband to forget her birthday. He was now very much immersed in politics, foreseeing a general election in the following year, and intending to contest the seat in parliament. The division was an impregnable Liberal stronghold, but Leslie had hopes that he might capture the situation. Therefore he spent a great deal of time at the Conversative club, and among the men of influence in the southern division. Lettie encouraged him in these affairs. It relieved her of him. It was thus that she let him forget her birthday, while, for some unknown reason, she let the intelligence slip to George. He was invited to dinner, as I was at home.

George came at seven o'clock. There was a strange feeling of festivity in the house, although there were no evident signs. Lettie had dressed with some magnificence in a blackish purple gauze over soft satin of lighter tone, nearly the colour of double violets. She wore vivid green azurite ornaments on the fairness of her bosom, and her bright hair was bound by a band of the same colour. It was rather startling. She was conscious of her effect, and was very excited. Immediately George saw her his eyes wakened with a dark glow. She stood up as he entered, her hand stretched straight out to him, her body very erect, her eyes bright and rousing, like two blue pennants.

'Thank you so much,' she said softly, giving his hand a last pressure before she let it go. He could not answer, so he sat down, bowing his head, then looking up at her in suspense. She smiled at him.

Presently the children came in. They looked very quaint, like acolytes, in their long straight dressing-gowns of quilted blue silk. The boy, particularly, looked as if he were going to light the candles in some childish church in paradise. He was very tall and slender, and fair, with a round fine head, and serene features. Both children looked remarkably, almost transparently, clean: it is impossible to consider anything more fresh and fair. The girl was a merry, curly-headed puss of six. She played with her mother's green jewels and prattled prettily, while the boy stood at his mother's side, a slender and silent acolyte in his pale blue gown. I was impressed by his patience and his purity. When the girl had bounded away into George's arms, the lad laid his hand timidly on Lettie's knee and looked with a little wonder at her dress.

'How pretty those green stones are, mother!' he said.

'Yes,' replied Lettie brightly, lifting them and letting their strange pattern fall again on her bosom. 'I like them.'

'Are you going to sing, mother?' he asked.

'Perhaps. But why?' said Lettie, smiling.

'Because you generally sing when Mr Saxton comes.'

He bent his head and stroked Lettie's dress shyly.

'Do I,' she said, laughing. 'Can you hear?'

'Just a little,' he replied. 'Quite small, as if it were nearly lost in the dark.'

He was hesitating, shy as boys are. Lettie laid her hand on his head and stroked his smooth fair hair.

'Sing a song for us before we go, mother –' he asked, almost shamefully. She kissed him.

'You shall sing with me,' she said. 'What shall it be?'

She played without a copy of the music. He stood at her side, while Lucy, the little mouse, sat on her mother's skirts, pressing Lettie's silk slippers in turn upon the pedals. The mother and the boy sang their song.

> Gaily the troubadour touched his guitar
> As he was hastening from the war.

The boy had a pure treble, clear as the flight of swallows in the morning. The light shone on his lips. Under the piano the girl child sat laughing, pressing her mother's feet with all her strength, and laughing again. Lettie smiled as she sang.

At last they kissed us a gentle 'good night', and flitted out of the room. The girl popped her curly head round the door again. We saw the white cuff on the nurse's wrist as she held the youngster's arm.

'You'll come and kiss us when we're in bed, Mum?' asked the rogue. Her mother laughed and agreed.

Lucy was withdrawn for a moment; then we heard her, 'Just a tick, nurse, just half-a-tick!'

The curly head appeared round the door again.

'And *one* teenie sweetie,' she suggested, 'only *one*!'

'Go, you – !' Lettie clapped her hands in mock wrath. The child vanished, but immediately there appeared again round the door two blue laughing eyes and the snub tip of a nose.

'A nice one, Mum – not a jelly-one!'

Lettie rose with a rustle to sweep upon her. The child vanished with a glitter of laughter. We heard her calling breathlessly on the stairs – 'Wait a bit, Freddie – wait for me!'

George and Lettie smiled at each other when the children had gone. As the smile died from their faces they looked down sadly, and until dinner was announced they were very still and heavy with melancholy. After dinner Lettie debated pleasantly which bon-bon she should take for the children. When she came down again she smoked a cigarette with us over coffee. George did not like to see her smoking, yet he brightened a little when he sat down after giving her a light, pleased with the mark of recklessness in her.

'It is ten years today since my party at Woodside,' she said, reaching for the small Roman salt-cellar of green jade that she used as an ash-tray.

'My lord – ten years!' he exclaimed bitterly. 'It seems a hundred.'

'It does and it doesn't,' she answered, smiling.

'If I look straight back, and think of my excitement, it seems only yesterday. If I look between then and now, at all the days that lie between, it is an age.'

'If I look at myself,' he said, 'I think I am another person altogether.'

'You have changed,' she agreed, looking at him sadly. 'There is a great change – but you are not another person. I often think – there is one of his old looks, he is just the same at the bottom!'

They embarked on a barge of bloomy recollections and drifted along the soiled canal of their past.

'The worst of it is,' he said. 'I have got a miserable carelessness, a contempt for things. You know I had such a faculty for reverence. I always believed in things.'

'I know you did,' she smiled. 'You were so humbly-minded – too humbly-minded, I always considered. You always thought things had a deep religious meaning, somewhere hidden, and you reverenced them. Is it different now?'

'You know me very well,' he laughed. 'What is there left for me to believe in, if not in myself?'

'You have to live for your wife and children,' she said with firmness.

'Meg has plenty to secure her and the children as long as they live,' he said, smiling. 'So I don't know that I'm essential.'

'But you are,' she replied. 'You are necessary as a father and a husband, if not as a provider.'

'I think,' said he, 'marriage is more of a duel than a duet. One party wins and takes the other captive, slave, servant – what you like. It is so, more or less.'

'Well?' said Lettie.

'Well!' he answered. 'Meg is not like you. She wants me, part of me, so she'd kill me rather than let me go loose.'

'Oh, no!' said Lettie, emphatically.

'You know nothing about it,' he said quietly. 'In the marital duel Meg is winning. The woman generally does; she has the children on her side. I can't give her any of the real part of me, the vital part that she wants – I can't, any more than you could give kisses to a stranger. And I feel that I'm losing – and don't care.'

'No,' she said, 'you are getting morbid.'

He put the cigarette between his lips, drew a deep breath, then slowly sent the smoke down his nostrils.

'No,' he said.

'Look here!' she said. 'Let me sing to you, shall I, and make you cheerful again?'

She sang from Wagner. It was the music of resignation and despair. She had not thought of it. All the time he listened he was thinking. The music stimulated his thoughts and illuminated the trend of his brooding. All the time he sat looking at her his eyes were dark with his thoughts. She finished the 'Star of Eve' from Tannhäuser and came over to him.

'Why are you so sad tonight, when it is my birthday?' she asked plaintively.

'Am I slow?' he replied. 'I am sorry.'

'What is the matter?' she said, sinking on to the small sofa near to him.

'Nothing!' he replied – 'You are looking very beautiful.'

'There, I wanted you to say that! You ought to be quite gay, you know, when I am so smart tonight.'

'Nay,' he said, 'I know I ought. But the tomorrow seems to have fallen in love with me. I can't get out of its lean arms.'

'Why!' she said. 'Tomorrow's arms are not lean. They are white, like mine.' She lifted her arms and looked at them, smiling.

'How do you know?' he asked, pertinently.

'Oh, of course they are,' was her light answer.

He laughed, brief and sceptical.

'No!' he said. 'It came when the children kissed us.'

'What?' she asked.

'These lean arms of tomorrow's round me, and the white round you,' he replied, smiling whimsically. She reached out and clasped his hand.

'You foolish boy,' she said.

He laughed painfully, not able to look at her.

'You know,' he said, and his voice was low and difficult,

'I have needed you for a light. You will soon be the only light again.'

'Who is the other?' she asked.

'My little girl!' he answered. Then he continued. 'And you know, I couldn't endure complete darkness, I couldn't. It's the solitariness.'

'You mustn't talk like this,' she said. 'You know you mustn't.' She put her hand on his head and ran her fingers through the hair he had so ruffled.

'It is as thick as ever, your hair,' she said.

He did not answer, but kept his face bent out of sight. She rose from her seat and stood at the back of his low armchair. Taking an amber comb from her hair, she bent over him, and with the translucent comb and her white fingers she busied herself with his hair.

'I believe you *would* have a parting,' she said softly.

He laughed shortly at her playfulness. She continued combing, just touching, pressing the strands in place with the tips of her fingers.

'I was only a warmth to you,' he said, pursuing the same train of thought. 'So you could do without me. But you were like the light to me, and otherwise it was dark and aimless. Aimlessness is horrible.'

She had finally smoothed his hair, so she lifted her hands and put back her head.

'There!' she said. 'It looks fair fine, as Alice would say. Raven's wings are raggy in comparison.'

He did not pay any attention to her.

'Aren't you going to look at yourself?' she said, playfully reproachful. She put her finger-tips under his chin. He lifted his head and they looked at each other, she smiling, trying to make him play, he smiling with his lips, but not with eyes, dark with pain.

'We can't go on like this, Lettie, can we?' he said softly.

'Yes,' she answered him, 'Yes; why not?'

'It can't!' he said. 'It can't, I couldn't keep it up, Lettie.'

'But don't think about it,' she answered. 'Don't think of it.'

'Lettie,' he said. 'I have to set my teeth with loneliness.'

'Hush!' she said. 'No! There are the children. Don't say anything – do not be serious, will you?'

'No, there are the children,' he replied, smiling dimly.

'Yes! Hush now! Stand up and look what a fine parting I have made in your hair. Stand up, and see if my style becomes you.'

'It is no good, Lettie,' he said, 'we can't go on.'

'Oh, but come, come, come!' she exclaimed. 'We are not talking about going on; we are considering what a fine parting I have made you down the middle, like two wings of a spread bird –' she looked down, smiling playfully on him, just closing her eyes slightly in petition.

He rose and took a deep breath, and set his shoulders.

'No,' he said, and at the sound of his voice, Lettie went pale and also stiffened herself.

'No!' he repeated. 'It is impossible. I felt as soon as Fred came into the room – it must be one way or another.'

'Very well then,' said Lettie, coldly. Her voice was 'muted' like a violin.

'Yes,' he replied, submissive. 'The children.' He looked at her, contracting his lips in a smile of misery.

'Are you sure it must be so final?' she asked, rebellious, even resentful. She was twisting the azurite jewels on her bosom, and pressing the blunt points into her flesh. He looked up from the fascination of her action when he heard the tone of her last question. He was angry.

'Quite sure!' he said at last, simply, ironically.

She bowed her head in assent. His face twitched sharply as he restrained himself from speaking again. Then he turned and quietly left the room. She did not watch him go, but stood as he had left her. When, after some time, she heard the grating of his dog-cart on the gravel, and then the sharp trot of hoofs down the frozen road, she dropped herself on the settee, and lay with her bosom against the cushions, looking fixedly at the wall.

CHAPTER VII

The Scarp Slope

LESLIE won the Conservative victory in the general election which took place a year or so after my last visit to Highclose.

In the interim the Tempests had entertained a continuous stream of people. I heard occasionally from Lettie how she was busy, amused, or bored. She told me that George had thrown himself into the struggle on behalf of the candidate of the Labour Party; that she had not seen him, except in the streets, for a very long time.

When I went down to Eberwich in the March succeeding the election, I found several people staying with my sister. She had under her wing a young literary fellow who affected the 'Doady' style – Dora Copperfield's 'Doady'. He had bunches of half-curly hair, and a romantic black cravat; he played the impulsive part, but was really as calculating as any man of the Stock Exchange. It delighted Lettie to 'mother' him. He was so shrewd as to be less than harmless. His fellow guests, a woman much experienced in music and an elderly man who was in the artistic world without being of it, were interesting for a time. Bubble after bubble of floating fancy and wit we blew with our breath in the evenings. I rose in the morning loathing the idea of more bubble-blowing.

I wandered around Nethermere, which had now forgotten me. The daffodils under the boat-house continued their golden laughter, and nodded to one another in gossip, as I watched them, never for a moment pausing to notice me. The yellow reflexion of daffodils among the shadows of grey willow in the water trembled faintly as they told haunted tales in the gloom. I felt like a child left out of the group of my playmates. There was a wind running across Nethermere, and on the eager water blue and glistening grey shadows changed places swiftly. Along the shore the wild birds rose, flapping in expostulation as I passed, peewits mewing fiercely round my head, while two white swans lifted their glistening feathers till they looked like grand double water-lilies, laying back their orange beaks among the petals, and fronting me with haughty resentment, charging towards me insolently.

I wanted to be recognized by something. I said to myself that the dryads were looking out for me from the wood's edge. But as I advanced they shrank, and glancing wistfully, turned back like pale flowers falling in the shadow of the forest. I was a stranger, an intruder. Among the bushes a twitter of lively birds exclaimed upon me. Finches went leaping past in bright flashes, and a robin sat and asked rudely: 'Hello! Who are you?'

The bracken lay sere under the trees, broken and chavelled by the restless wild winds of the long winter.

The trees caught the wind in their tall netted twigs, and the young morning wind moaned at its captivity. As I trod the discarded oak-leaves and the bracken they uttered their last sharp gasps, pressed into oblivion. The wood was roofed with a wide young sobbing sound, and floored with a faint hiss like the intaking of the last breath. Between, was all the glad out-peeping of buds and anemone flowers and the rush of birds. I wandering alone, felt them all, the anguish of the bracken fallen face-down in defeat, the careless dash of the birds, the sobbing of the young wind arrested in its haste, the trembling, expanding delight of the buds. I alone among them could hear the whole succession of chords.

The brooks talked on just the same, just as gladly, just as boisterously as they had done when I had netted small, glittering fish in the rest-pools. At Strelley Mill a servant girl in a white cap, and white apron-bands, came running out of the house with purple prayer-books, which she gave to the elder of two finicking girls who sat disconsolately with their black-silked mother in the governess cart at the gate, ready to go to church. Near Woodside there was barbed-wire along the path, and at the end of every riding it was tarred on the tree-trunks, 'Private'.

*

I had done with the valley of Nethermere. The valley of

Nethermere had cast me out many years before, while I had fondly believed it cherished me in memory.

I went along the road to Eberwich. The church bells were ringing boisterously, with the careless boisterousness of the brooks and the birds and the rollicking coltsfoots and celandines.

A few people were hastening blithely to service. Miners and other labouring men were passing in aimless gangs, walking nowhere in particular, so long as they reached a sufficiently distant public house.

I reached the Hollies. It was much more spruce than it had been. The yard, however, and the stables, had again a somewhat abandoned air. I asked the maid for George.

'Oh, master's not up yet,' she said, giving a little significant toss of her head, and smiling. I waited a moment.

'But he rung for a bottle of beer about ten minutes since, so I should think –' she emphasized the word with some ironical contempt, ' – he won't be very long,' she added, in tones which conveyed that she was not by any means sure. I asked for Meg.

'Oh, Missis is gone to church – and the children – But Miss Saxton is in, she might –'

'Emily!' I exclaimed.

The maid smiled.

'She's in the drawing-room. She's engaged, but perhaps if I tell her –'

'Yes, do,' said I, sure that Emily would receive me.

I found my old sweetheart sitting in a low chair by the fire, a man standing on the hearthrug pulling his moustache. Emily and I both felt a thrill of old delight at meeting.

'I can hardly believe it is really you,' she said, laughing me one of the old intimate looks. She had changed a great deal. She was very handsome, but she had now a new self-confidence, a fine, free indifference.

'Let me introduce you. Mr Renshaw, Cyril. Tom, you know who it is, you have heard me speak often enough of Cyril. I am going to marry Tom in three weeks' time,' she said, laughing.

'The devil you are!' I exclaimed involuntarily.

'If he will have me,' she added, quite as a playful afterthought.

Tom was a well-built fair man, smoothly, almost delicately tanned. There was something soldierly in his bearing, something self-conscious in the way he bent his head and pulled his moustache, something charming and fresh in the way he laughed at Emily's last preposterous speech.

'Why didn't you tell me?' I asked.

'Why didn't you ask me?' she retorted, arching her brows.

'Mr Renshaw,' I said. 'You have out-manoeuvred me all unawares, quite indecently.'

'I am very sorry,' he said, giving one more twist to his moustache, then breaking into a loud, short laugh at his joke.

'Do you really feel cross?' said Emily to me, knitting her brows and smiling quaintly.

'I do!' I replied, with truthful emphasis.

She laughed, and laughed again, very much amused.

'It is such a joke,' she said. 'To think you should feel cross, now, when it is – how long is it ago –?'

'I will not count up,' said I.

'Are you not sorry for me?' I asked of Tom Renshaw.

He looked at me with his young blue eyes, eyes so bright, so naively inquisitive, so winsomely meditative. He did not know quite what to say, or how to take it.

'Very!' he replied in another short burst of laughter, quickly twisting his moustache again and looking down at his feet.

He was twenty-nine years old; had been a soldier in China for five years, was now farming his father's farm at Papplewick, where Emily was schoolmistress. He had been at home eighteen months. His father was an old man of seventy who had had his right hand chopped to bits in the chopping machine. So they told me. I liked Tom for his handsome bearing, and his fresh, winsome way. He was exceedingly manly: that is to say he did not dream of questioning or analysing anything. All that came his way was ready labelled nice or nasty, good or bad. He did not imagine that anything could be other than just what it appeared to be: – and with this appearance, he was quite content. He looked up to Emily as one wiser, nobler, nearer to God than himself.

'I am a thousand years older than he,' she said to me, laughing. 'Just as you are centuries older than I.'

'And you love him for his youth?' I asked.

'Yes,' she replied. 'For that and – he is wonderfully sagacious – and so gentle.'

'And I was never gentle, was I?' I said.

'No! As restless and as urgent as the wind,' she said, and I saw a last flicker of the old terror.

'Where is George?' I asked.

'In bed,' she replied briefly. 'He's recovering from one of his orgies. If I were Meg I would not live with him.'

'Is he so bad?' I asked.

'Bad!' she replied. 'He's disgusting, and I'm sure he's dangerous. I'd have him removed to an inebriates' home.'

'You'd have to persuade him to go,' said Tom, who had come into the room again. 'He does have dreadful bouts, though! He's killing himself, sure enough. I feel awfully sorry for the fellow.'

'It seems so contemptible to me,' said Emily, 'to become enslaved to one of your likings till it makes a beast of you. Look what a spectacle he is for his children, and what a disgusting disgrace for his wife.'

'Well, if he can't help it, he can't, poor chap,' said Tom. 'Though I do think a man should have more backbone.'

We heard heavy noises from the room above.

'He is getting up,' said Emily. 'I suppose I'd better see if he'll have any breakfast.' She waited, however. Presently the door opened, and there stood George with his hand on the knob, leaning, looking in.

'I thought I heard three voices,' he said, as if it freed him from a certain apprehension. He smiled. His waistcoat hung open over his woollen shirt, he wore no coat and was slipperless. His hair and his moustache were dishevelled, his face pale and stupid with sleep, his eyes small. He turned aside from our looks as from a bright light. His hand as I shook it was flaccid and chill.

'How do you come to be here, Cyril?' he said subduedly, faintly smiling.

'Will you have any breakfast?' Emily asked him coldly.

'I'll have a bit if there's any for me,' he replied.

'It has been waiting for you, long enough,' she answered.

He turned and went with a dull thud of his stockinged feet across to the dining-room. Emily rang for the maid, I followed George, leaving the betrothed together. I found my host moving about the dining-room, looking behind the chairs and in the corners.

'I wonder where the devil my slippers are!' he muttered explanatorily. Meanwhile he continued his search. I noticed he did not ring the bell to have them found for him. Presently he came to the fire, spreading his hands over it. As he was smashing the slowly burning coal the maid came in with the tray. He desisted, and put the poker carefully down. While the maid spread his meal on one corner of the table, he looked in the fire, paying her no heed. When she had finished:

'It's fried whitebait,' she said. 'Shall you have that?'

He lifted his head and looked at the plate.

'Ay,' he said. 'Have you brought the vinegar?'

Without answering, she took the cruet from the sideboard and set it on the table. As she was closing the door, she looked back to say:

'You'd better eat it now, while it's hot.'

He took no notice, but sat looking in the fire.

'And how are you going on?' he asked me.

'I? Oh, very well! And you –?'

'As you see,' he replied, turning his head on one side with a little gesture of irony.

'As I am very sorry to see,' I rejoined.

He sat forward with his elbows on his knees, tapping the back of his hand with one finger, in monotonous two-pulse like heart-beats.

'Aren't you going to have breakfast?' I urged. The clock at that moment began to ring a sonorous twelve. He looked up at it with subdued irritation.

'Ay, I suppose so,' he answered me, when the clock had finished striking. He rose heavily and went to the table. As he poured out a cup of tea he spilled it on the cloth, and stood looking at the stain. It was still some time before he began to eat. He poured vinegar freely over the hot fish, and ate with an indifference that made eating ugly, pausing now and again to wipe the tea off his moustache, or to pick a bit of fish from off his knee.

'You are not married, I suppose?' he said in one of his pauses.

'No,' I replied. 'I expect I shall have to be looking round.'

'You're wiser not,' he replied, quiet and bitter.

A moment or two later the maid came in with a letter.

'This came this morning,' she said, as she laid it on the table beside him. He looked at it, then he said :

'You didn't give me a knife for the marmalade.'

'Didn't I?' she replied. 'I thought you wouldn't want it. You don't as a rule.'

'And do you know where my slippers are?' he asked.

'They ought to be in their usual place.' She went and looked in the corner. 'I suppose Miss Gertie's put them somewhere. I'll get you another pair.'

As he waited for her he read the letter. He read it twice, then he put it back in the envelope, quietly, without any change of expression. But he ate no more breakfast, even after the maid had brought the knife and his slippers, and though he had had but a few mouthfuls.

At half-past twelve there was an imperious woman's voice in the house. Meg came to the door. As she entered the room, and saw me, she stood still. She sniffed, glanced at the table, and exclaimed, coming forward effusively :

'Well I never, Cyril! Who'd a thought of seeing you here this morning! How are you?'

She waited for the last of my words, then immediately she turned to George, and said:

'I must say you're in a nice state for Cyril to see you! Have you finished? – if you have, Kate can take that tray out. It smells quite sickly. Have you finished?'

He did not answer, but drained his cup of tea and pushed it away with the back of his hand. Meg rang the bell, and having taken off her gloves, began to put the things on the tray, tipping the fragments of fish and bones from the edge of his plate to the middle with short, disgusted jerks of the fork. Her attitude and expression were of resentment and disgust. The maid came in.

'Clear the table, Kate, and open the window. Have you opened the bedroom windows?'

'No'm – not yet,' – she glanced at George as if to say he had only been down a few minutes.

'Then do it when you have taken the tray,' said Meg.

'You don't open this window,' said George churlishly. 'It's cold enough as it is.'

'You should put a coat on then if you're starved,' replied Meg contemptuously. 'It's warm enough for those that have got any life in their blood. You do not find it cold, do you, Cyril?'

'It is fresh this morning,' I replied.

'Of course it is, not cold at all. And I'm sure this room needs airing.'

The maid, however, folded the cloth and went out without approaching the windows.

Meg had grown stouter, and there was a certain immovable confidence in her. She was authoritative, amiable, calm. She wore a handsome dress of dark green, and a toque with opulent ostrich feathers. As she moved about the room she seemed to dominate everything, particularly her husband, who sat ruffled and dejected, his waistcoat hanging loose over his shirt.

A girl entered. She was proud and mincing in her deportment. Her face was handsome, but too haughty for a child. She wore a white coat, with ermine tippet, muff, and hat. Her long brown hair hung twining down her back.

'Has dad only just had his breakfast?' she exclaimed in high censorious tones as she came in.

'He has!' replied Meg.

The girl looked at her father in calm, childish censure.

'And we have been to church, and come home to dinner,' she said, as she drew off her little white gloves. George watched her with ironical amusement.

'Hello!' said Meg, glancing at the opened letter which lay near his elbow. 'Who is that from?'

He glanced round, having forgotten it. He took the envelope, doubled it and pushed it in his waistcoat pocket.

'It's from William Housley,' he replied.

'Oh! And what has he to say?' she asked.

George turned his dark eyes at her.

'Nothing!' he said.

'Hm-Hm!' sneered Meg. 'Funny letter, about nothing!'

'I suppose,' said the child, with her insolent, high-pitched superiority, 'It's some money that he doesn't want us to know about.'

'That's about it!' said Meg, giving a small laugh at the child's perspicuity.

'So's he can keep it for himself, that's what it is,' continued the child, nodding her head in rebuke at him.

'I've no right to any money, have I?' asked the father sarcastically.

'No, you haven't,' the child nodded her head at him dictatorially, 'you haven't, because you only put it in the fire.'

'You've got it wrong,' he sneered. 'You mean it's like giving a child fire to play with.'

'Um! - and it is, isn't it, Mam?' - the small woman turned to her mother for corroboration. Meg had flushed at his sneer, when he quoted for the child its mother's dictum.

'And you're very naughty!' preached Gertie, turning her back disdainfully on her father.

'Is that what the parson's been telling you?' he asked, a grain of amusement still in his bitterness.

'No, it isn't!' retorted the youngster. 'If you want to know you should go and listen for yourself. Everybody that goes to church looks nice -' she glanced at her mother and at herself, pruning herself proudly, ' - and God loves them,' she added. She assumed a sanctified expression, and continued after a little thought: 'Because they look nice and are meek.'

'What!' exclaimed Meg, laughing, glancing with secret pride at me.

'Because they're meek!' repeated Gertie, with a superior little smile of knowledge.

'You're off the mark this time,' said George.

'No, I'm not, am I, Mam? Isn't it right, Mam? "The meek shall inevit the erf"?'

Meg was too much amused to answer.

'The meek shall have herrings on earth,' mocked the father, also amused. His daughter looked dubiously at him. She smelled impropriety.

'It's not, Mam, is it?' she asked, turning to her mother. Meg laughed.

'The meek shall have herrings on earth,' repeated George with soft banter.

'No it's not, Mam, is it?' cried the child in real distress.

'Tell your father he's always teaching you something wrong,' answered Meg.

Then I said I must go. They pressed me to stay.

'Oh, yes – do stop to dinner,' suddenly pleaded the child, smoothing her wild ravels of curls after having drawn off her hat. She asked me again and again, with much earnestness.

'But why?' I asked.

'So's you can talk to us this afternoon – an' so's Dad won't be so dis'greeable,' she replied plaintively, poking the black spots of her muff.

Meg moved nearer to her daughter with a little gesture of compassion.

'But,' said I, 'I promised a lady I would be back for lunch, so I must. You have some more visitors, you know.'

'Oh, well!' she complained. 'They go in another room and Dad doesn't care about them.'

'But come!' said I.

'Well, he's just as dis'greeable when Auntie Emily's here – he is with her an' all.'

'You *are* having your character given away,' said Meg brutally, turning to him.

I bade them good-bye. He did me the honour of coming with me to the door. We could neither of us find a word to say, though we were both moved. When at last I held his hand and was looking at him as I said 'Good-bye', he looked back at me for the first time during our meeting. His eyes were heavy and as he lifted them to me, seemed to recoil in an agony of shame.

CHAPTER VIII

A Prospect Among the Marshes of Lethe

GEORGE steadily declined from this time. I went to see him two years later. He was not at home. Meg wept to me as she told me of him, how he let the business slip, how he drank, what a brute he was in drink, and how unbearable afterwards. He was ruining his constitution, he was ruining her life and the children's. I felt very sorry for her as she sat, large and ruddy, brimming over with bitter tears. She asked me if I did not think I might influence him. He was, she said, at the Ram. When he had an extra bad bout on he went up there, and stayed sometimes for a week at a time, with Oswald, coming back to the Hollies when he had recovered – 'though,' said Meg, 'he's sick every morning and almost after every meal.'

All the time Meg was telling me this, sat curled up in a large chair their youngest boy, a pale, sensitive, rather spoiled lad of seven or eight years, with a petulant mouth, and nervous dark eyes. He sat watching his mother as she told her tale, heaving his shoulders and settling himself in a new position when his feelings were nearly too much for him. He was full of wild, childish pity for his mother, and furious, childish hate of his father, the author of all their trouble. I called at the Ram and saw George. He was half drunk.

I went up to Highclose with a heavy heart. Lettie's last child had been born, much to the surprise of everybody, some few months before I came down. There was a space of seven years between her youngest girl and this baby. Lettie was much absorbed in motherhood.

When I went up to talk to her about George I found her in the bedroom nursing the baby, who was very good and quiet on her knee. She listened to me sadly, but her attention was caught away by each movement made by the child. As I was telling her of the attitude of George's children towards their father and mother, she glanced from the baby to me, and exclaimed:

'See how he watches the light flash across your spectacles when you turn suddenly – Look !'

But I was weary of babies. My friends had all grown up and married and inflicted them on me. There were storms of babies. I longed for a place where they would be obsolete, and young, arrogant, impervious mothers might be a forgotten tradition. Lettie's heart would quicken in answer to only one pulse, the easy, light ticking of the baby's blood.

I remembered, one day as I sat in the train hastening to Charing Cross on my way from France, that that was George's birthday. I had the feeling of him upon me, heavily, and I could not rid myself of the depression. I put it down to travel fatigue, and tried to dismiss it. As I watched the evening sun glitter along the new corn-stubble in the fields we passed, trying to describe the effect to myself, I found myself asking: 'But – what's the matter? I've not had bad news, have I, to make my chest feel so weighted?'

I was surprised when I reached my lodging in New Malden to find no letters for me, save one fat budget from Alice. I knew her squat, saturnine handwriting on the envelope, and I thought I knew what contents to expect from the letter.

She had married an old acquaintance who had been her particular aversion. This young man had got himself into trouble, so that the condemnations of the righteous pursued him like clouds of gnats on a summer evening. Alice immediately rose to sting back his vulgar enemies, and having rendered him a service, felt she could only wipe out the score by marrying him. They were fairly comfortable. Occasionally, as she said, there were displays of small fireworks in the back yard. He worked in the offices of some iron foundries just over the Erewash in Derbyshire. Alice lived in a dirty little place in the valley a mile and a half from Eberwich, not far from his work. She had no children, and practically no friends; a few young matrons for acquaintances. As wife of a superior clerk, she had to preserve her dignity among the work people. So all her little crackling fires were sodded down with the sods of British respectability. Occasionally she smouldered a fierce smoke that made one's eyes water. Occasionally, perhaps once a year, she wrote me a whole venomous budget, much to my amusement.

I was not in any haste to open this fat letter, until, after supper, I turned to it as a resource from my depression.

Oh dear Cyril, I'm in a bubbling state, I want to yell, not write. Oh, Cyril, why didn't *you* marry me, or why didn't our Georgie Saxton, or somebody. I'm deadly sick. Percival Charles is enough to stop a clock. Oh, Cyril, he lives in an eternal Sunday suit, holy broadcloth and righteous three inches of cuffs! He goes to bed in it. Nay, he wallows in bibles when he goes to bed. I can feel the brass covers of all his family bibles sticking in my ribs as I lie by his side. I could weep with wrath, yet I put on my black hat and trot to chapel with him like a lamb.

Oh, Cyril, nothing's happened. Nothing has happened to me all these years. I shall die of it. When I see Percival Charles at dinner after having asked a blessing, I feel as if I should never touch a bit at his table again. In about an hour I shall hear him hurrying up the entry – prayers always make him hungry – and his first look will be on the table. But I'm not fair to him – he's really a good fellow – I only wish he wasn't.

It's George Saxton who's put this seidlitz powder in my marital cup of cocoa. Cyril, I must a tale unfold. It is fifteen years since our George married Meg. When I count up, and think of the future, it nearly makes me scream. But my tale, my tale!

Can you remember his faithful-dog, wounded-stag, gentle-gazelle eyes? Cyril, you can see the whisky, or the brandy combusting in them. He's got d.t.s, blue-devils – and I've seen him, and I'm swarming myself with little red devils after it. I went up to Eberwich on Wednesday afternoon for a pound of fry for Percival Charles' Thursday dinner. I walked by that little path which you know goes round the back of the Hollies – it's as near as any way for me. I thought I heard a row in the paddock at the back of the stables, so I said I might as well see the fun. I went to the gate, basket in one hand, ninepence in coppers in the other, a demure deacon's wife. I didn't take in the scene at first.

There was our Georgie, in leggings and breeches as of yore, and a whip. He was flourishing, and striding, and yelling. 'Go it old boy,' I said, 'you'll want your stocking round your throat tonight.' But Cyril, I had spoken too soon. Oh, lum! There came raking up the croft that long, wire-springy racehorse of his, ears flat, and, clinging to its neck, the pale-faced lad, Wilfred. The kid was white as death, and squealing 'Mam! mam!' I thought it was a bit rotten of George trying to teach the kid to jockey. The racehorse, Bonny-Boy – Boney Boy I call him – came bouncing round like a spiral egg-whisk. Then I saw our Georgie rush up screaming, nearly spitting the moustache off his face, and fetch the horse a cut with the whip. It went off like a flame along hot paraffin. The kid shrieked and clung. Georgie went rushing after him, running staggery, and swearing, fairly screaming – awful – 'a lily-livered little swine!' The high lanky racehorse went larroping round as if it was going mad. I was dazed. Then Meg came rushing, and the other two lads all screaming. She went for George, but he lifted his whip like the devil. She daren't go near him – she rushed at him, and stopped, rushed at him, and stopped, striking at him with her two fists. He waved his whip and kept her off, and the racehorse kept tearing along. Meg flew to stop it, he ran with his drunken totter-step, brandishing his whip. I flew as well. I hit him with my basket. The kid fell off, and Meg rushed to him. Some men came running. George stood fairly shuddering. You would never have known his face, Cyril. He was mad, demoniacal. I feel sometimes as if I should burst and shatter to bits like a sky-rocket when I think of it. I've got such a weal on my arm.

I lost Percival Charles' ninepence, and my nice white cloth out of the basket, and everything, beside having black looks on Thursday because it was mutton chops, which he hates. Oh, Cyril, 'I wish I was a cassowary, on the banks of the Timbuctoo.' When I saw Meg sobbing over that lad – thank goodness he wasn't hurt – ! I wished our Georgie was dead; I do now, also; I wish we only had to remember him. I haven't been to see them lately – can't stand Meg's ikeyness. I wonder how it all will end.

There's P. C. bidding 'Good-night and God Bless You' to Brother Jakes, and no supper ready –

As soon as I could, after reading Alice's letter, I went down to Eberwich to see how things were. Memories of the old days came over me again till my heart hungered for its old people.

They told me at the Hollies that, after a bad attack of delirium tremens, George had been sent to Papplewick in the lonely country to stay with Emily. I borrowed a bicycle to ride the nine miles. The summer had been wet, and everything was late. At the end of September the foliage was heavy green, and the wheat stood dejectedly in stook. I rode through the still sweetness of an autumn morning. The mist was folded blue along the hedges; the elm trees loomed up along the dim walls of the morning, the horse-chestnut trees at hand flickered with a few yellow leaves like bright blossoms. As I rode through the tree tunnel by the church where, on his last night, the keeper had told me his story, I smelled the cold rotting of the leaves of the cloudy summer.

I passed silently through the lanes, where the chill grass was weighed down with grey-blue seed-pearls of dew in the shadow, where the wet woollen spidercloths of autumn were spread as on a loom. Brown birds rustled in flocks like driven leaves before me. I heard the far-off hooting of the 'loose-all' at the pits, telling me it was half-past eleven, that the men and boys would be sitting in the narrow darkness of the mines eating their 'snap', while shadowy mice darted for the crumbs, and the boys laughed with red mouths rimmed with grime, as the bold little creatures peeped at them in the dim light of the lamps. The dog-wood berries stood jauntily scarlet on the hedge-tops, the bunched scarlet and green berries of the con-volvulus and bryony hung amid golden trails, and blackberries dropped ungathered. I rode slowly on, the plants dying around me, the berries leaning their heavy ruddy mouths, and lan-guishing for the birds, the men imprisoned underground below me, the brown birds dashing in haste along the hedges.

Swineshed Farm, where the Renshaws lived, stood quite alone among its fields, hidden from the highway and from everything. The lane leading up to it was deep and unsunned. On my right, I caught glimpses through the hedge of the corn-fields, where the shocks of wheat stood like small yellow-sailed ships in a wide-spread flotilla. The upper part of the field was cleared. I heard the clank of a wagon and the voices of men, and I saw the high load of sheaves go lurching, rock-ing up the incline to the stackyard.

The lane debouched into a close-bitten field, and out of this empty land the farm rose up with its buildings like a huddle of old, painted vessels floating in still water. White fowls went stepping discreetly through the mild sunshine and the shadow. I leaned my bicycle against the grey, silken doors of the old coach-house. The place was breathing with silence. I hesitated to knock at the open door. Emily came. She was rich as always with her large beauty, and stately now with the stateliness of a strong woman six months gone with child.

She exclaimed with surprise, and I followed her into the kitchen, catching a glimpse of the glistening pans and the white wood baths as I passed through the scullery. The kitchen was a good-sized, low room that through long course of years had become absolutely a home. The great beams of the ceiling bowed easily, the chimney-seat had a bit of dark-green curtain, and under the high mantelpiece was another low shelf that the men could reach with their hands as they sat in the ingle-nook. There the pipes lay. Many generations of peaceful men and fruitful women had passed through the room, and not one but had added a new small comfort; a chair in the right place, a hook, a stool, a cushion, a certain pleasing cloth for the sofa covers, a shelf of books. The room, that looked so quiet and crude, was a home evolved through generations to fit the large bodies of the men who dwelled in it, and the placid fancy of the women. At last, it had an individuality. It was the home of the Renshaws, warm, lovable, serene. Emily was in perfect accord with its brownness, its shadows, its ease. I, as I sat on the sofa under the window, felt rejected by the kind room. I was distressed with a sense of ephemerality, of pale, erratic fragility.

Emily, in her full-blooded beauty, was at home. It is rare now to feel a kinship between a room and the one who inhabits it, a close bond of blood relation. Emily had at last found her place, and had escaped from the torture of strange, complex modern life. She was making a pie, and the flour was white on her brown arms. She pushed the tickling hair from her face with her arm, and looked at me with tranquil pleasure, as she worked the paste in the yellow bowl. I was quiet, subdued before her.

'You are very happy?' I said.

'Ah, very!' she replied. 'And you? – you are not, you look worn.'

'Yes,' I replied. 'I am happy enough. I am living my life.'

'Don't you find it wearisome?' she asked pityingly.

She made me tell her all my doings, and she marvelled, but all the time her eyes were dubious and pitiful.

'You have George here,' I said.

'Yes. He's in a poor state, but he's not as sick as he was.'

'What about the delirium tremens?'

'Oh, he was better of that – very nearly – before he came here. He sometimes fancies they're coming on again, and he's terrified. Isn't it awful! And he's brought it all on himself. Tom's very good to him.'

'There's nothing the matter with him – physically, is there?' I asked.

'I don't know,' she replied, as she went to the oven to turn a pie that was baking. She put her arm to her forehead and brushed aside her hair, leaving a mark of flour on her nose. For a moment or two she remained kneeling on the fender, looking into the fire and thinking. 'He was in a poor way when he came here, could eat nothing, sick every morning. I suppose it's his liver. They all end like that.' She continued to wipe the large black plums and put them in the dish.

'Hardening of the liver?' I asked. She nodded.

'And is he in bed?' I asked again.

'Yes,' she replied. 'It's as I say, if he'd get up and potter about a bit, he'd get over it. But he lies there skulking.'

'And what time will he get up?' I insisted.

'I don't know. He may crawl down somewhere towards tea-time. Do you want to see him? That's what you came for, isn't it?'

She smiled at me with a little sarcasm, and added: 'You always thought more of him than anybody, didn't you? Ah, well, come up and see him.'

I followed her up the back stairs, which led out of the kitchen, and which emerged straight in a bedroom. We crossed the hollow-sounding plaster-floor of this naked room and opened a door at the opposite side. George lay in bed watching us with apprehensive eyes.

'Here is Cyril come to see you,' said Emily, 'so I've brought him up, for I didn't know when you'd be downstairs.'

A small smile of relief came on his face, and he put out his hand from the bed. He lay with the disorderly clothes pulled up to his chin. His face was discoloured, and rather bloated, his nose swollen.

'Don't you feel so well this morning?' asked Emily, softening with pity when she came into contact with his sickness.

'Oh, all right,' he replied, wishing only to get rid of us.

'You should try to get up a bit, it's a beautiful morning, warm and soft –' she said gently. He did not reply, and she went downstairs.

I looked round to the cold, whitewashed room, with its ceiling curving and sloping down the walls. It was sparsely furnished, and bare of even the slightest ornament. The only things of warm colour were the cow and horse skins on the floor. All the rest was white or grey or drab. On one side, the roof sloped down so that the window was below my knees, and nearly touching the floor, on the other side was a larger window, breast high. Through it one could see the jumbled, ruddy roofs of the sheds and the skies. The tiles were shining with patches of vivid orange lichen. Beyond was the cornfield, and the men, small in the distance, lifting the sheaves on the cart.

'You will come back to farming again, won't you?' I asked him, turning to the bed. He smiled.

'I don't know,' he answered dully.

'Would you rather I went downstairs?' I asked.

'No, I'm glad to see you,' he replied, in the same uneasy fashion.

'I've only just come back from France,' I said.

'Ah!' he replied, indifferent.

'I am sorry you're ill,' I said.

He stared unmovedly at the opposite wall. I went to the window, and looked out. After some time, I compelled myself to say, in a casual manner:

'Won't you get up and come out a bit?'

'I suppose Is'll have to,' he said, gathering himself slowly together for the effort. He pushed himself up in bed.

When he took off the jacket of his pyjamas to wash himself I turned away. His arms seemed thin, and he had bellied, and was bowed and unsightly. I remembered the morning we swam in the mill-pond. I remembered that he was now in the prime of his life. I looked at his bluish feeble hands as he laboriously washed himself. The soap once slipped from his fingers as he was picking it up, and fell, rattling the pot loudly. It startled us, and he seemed to grip the sides of the washstand to steady himself. Then he went on with his slow, painful toilet. As he combed his hair he looked at himself with dull eyes of shame.

The men were coming in from the scullery when we got downstairs. Dinner was smoking on the table. I shook hands with Tom Renshaw, and with the old man's hard, fierce left hand. Then I was introduced to Arthur Renshaw, a clean-faced, large, bashful lad of twenty. I nodded to the man, Jim, and to Jim's wife, Annie. We all sat down to table.

'Well, an' 'ow are ter feelin' by now, like?' asked the old man heartily of George. Receiving no answer, he continued, 'Tha should 'a gor up an' com' an' gen us a 'and wi' th' wheat, it 'ud 'a done thee good.'

'You will have a bit of this mutton, won't you?' Tom asked him, tapping the joint with the carving knife. George shook his head.

'It's quite lean, and tender,' he said gently.

'No, thanks,' said George.

'Gi'e 'im a bit, gi'e 'im a bit!' cried the old man. 'It'll do 'im good – it's what 'e wants, a bit o' strengthenin' nourishment.'

'It's no good if his stomach won't have it,' said Tom, in mild reproof, as if he were speaking of a child. Arthur filled George's glass with beer without speaking. The two young men were full of kind, gentle attention.

'Let 'im 'a'e a spoonful o' tonnup then,' persisted the old man. 'I canna eat while 'is plate stands there emp'y.'

So they put turnip and onion sauce on George's plate, and he took up his fork and tasted a few mouthfuls. The men ate largely, and with zest. The sight of their grand satisfaction, amounting almost to gusto, sickened him.

When at last the old man laid down the dessert spoon which he used in place of a knife and fork, he looked again at George's plate, and said:

'Why tha 'asna aten a smite, not a smite! Tha non goos th' raight road to be better.'

George maintained a stupid silence.

'Don't bother him, father,' said Emily.

'Tha art an owd whittle, feyther,' added Tom, smiling good-naturedly. He spoke to his father in dialect, but to Emily in good English. Whatever she said had Tom's immediate support. Before serving us with pie, Emily gave her brother junket and damsons, setting the plate and the spoon before him as if he were a child. For this act of grace Tom looked at her lovingly, and stroked her hand as she passed.

After dinner, George said, with a miserable struggle for an indifferent tone:

'Aren't you going to give Cyril a glass of whisky?'

He looked up furtively, in a conflict of shame and hope. A silence fell on the room.

'Ay!' said the old man softly. 'Let 'im 'ave a drop.'

'Yes!' added Tom, in submissive pleading.

All the men in the room shrank a little, awaiting the verdict of the woman.

'I don't know,' she said clearly, 'that Cyril wants a glass.'

'I don't mind.' I answered, feeling myself blush. I had not the courage to counteract her will directly. Not even the old man had that courage. We waited in suspense. After keeping us so for a few minutes, while we smouldered with mortification, she went into another room, and we heard her unlocking a door. She returned with a decanter containing rather less than half a pint of liquor. She put out five tumblers.

'Tha nedna gi'e me none,' said the old man. 'Ah'm non a proud chap. Ah'm not.'

'Nor me neither,' said Arthur.

'You will, Tom?' she asked.

'Do you want me to?' he replied, smiling.

'I don't,' she answered sharply. 'I want nobody to have it, when you look at the results of it. But if Cyril is having a glass, you may as well have one with him.'

Tom was pleased with her. She gave her husband and me fairly stiff glasses.

'Steady, steady!' he said. 'Give that George, and give me not so much. Two fingers, two of your fingers, you know.'

But she passed him the glass. When George had had his share, there remained but a drop in the decanter.

Emily watched the drunkard coldly as he took this remainder.

George and I talked for a time while the men smoked. He, from his glum stupidity, broke into a harsh, almost imbecile loquacity.

'Have you seen my family lately?' he asked, continuing. 'Yes! Not badly set up, are they, the children? But the little devils are soft, mard-soft, every one of 'em. It's their mother's bringin' up – she marded 'em till they were soft, an' would never let me have a say in it. I should 'a brought 'em up different, you know I should.'

Tom looked at Emily, and, remarking her angry contempt, suggested that she should go out with him to look at the stacks. I watched the tall, square-shouldered man leaning with deference and tenderness towards his wife as she walked calmly at his side. She was the mistress, quiet and self-assured, he her rejoiced husband and servant.

George was talking about himself. If I had not seen him, I should hardly have recognized the words as his. He was lamentably decayed. He talked stupidly, with vulgar contumely of others, and in weak praise of himself.

The old man rose, with a:

'Well, I suppose we mun ma'e another dag at it,' and the men left the house.

George continued his foolish, harsh monologue, making gestures of emphasis with his head and his hands. He continued when we were walking round the buildings into the fields, the same babble of bragging and abuse. I was wearied and disgusted. He looked, and he sounded, so worthless.

Across the empty cornfield the partridges were running. We walked through the September haze slowly, because he was feeble on his legs. As he became tired he ceased to talk. We leaned for some time on a gate, in the brief glow of the transient afternoon, and he was stupid again. He did not notice the brown haste of the partridges, he did not care to share with me the handful of ripe blackberries, and when I pulled the bryony ropes off the hedges, and held the great knots of red and green berries in my hand, he glanced at them without interest or appreciation.

'Poison-berries, aren't they?' he said dully.

Like a tree that is falling, going soft and pale and rotten, clammy with small fungi, he stood leaning against the gate, while the dim afternoon drifted with a flow of thick sweet sunshine past him, not touching him.

In the stackyard, the summer's splendid monuments of wheat and grass were reared in gold and grey. The wheat was littered brightly round the rising stack. The loaded wagon clanked slowly up the incline, drew near, and rode like a ship at anchor against the scotches, brushing the stack with a crisp, sharp sound. Tom climbed the ladder and stood a moment there against the sky, amid the brightness and fragrance of the gold corn, and waved his arm to his wife who was passing in the shadow of the building. Then Arthur began to lift the sheaves to the stack, and the two men worked in an exquisite, subtle rhythm, their white sleeves and their dark heads gleaming, moving against the mild sky and the corn. The silence was broken only by the occasional lurch of the body of the wagon, as the teamer stepped to the front, or again to the rear of the load. Occasionally I could catch the blue glitter of the prongs of the forks. Tom, now lifted high above the small wagon load, called to his brother some question about the stack. The sound of his voice was strong and mellow.

I turned to George, who also was watching, and said:

'You ought to be like that.'

We heard Tom calling, 'All right!' and saw him standing high up on the tallest corner of the stack, as on the prow of a ship.

George watched, and his face slowly gathered expression. He turned to me, his dark eyes alive with horror and despair.

'I shall soon – be out of everybody's way!' he said. His moment of fear and despair was cruel. I cursed myself for having roused him from his stupor.

'You will be better,' I said.

He watched again the handsome movement of the men at the stack.

'I couldn't team ten sheaves,' he said.

'You will in a month or two,' I urged.

He continued to watch, while Tom got on the ladder and came down the front of the stack.

'Nay, the sooner I clear out, the better,' he repeated to himself.

When we went into tea, he was, as Tom said, 'downcast'. The men talked uneasily with abated voices. Emily attended to him with a little, palpitating solicitude. We were all uncomfortably impressed with the sense of our alienation from him. He sat apart and obscure among us, like a condemned man.